THE LOSS BETWEEN US

BROOKE MCBRIDE

Publisher: Brooke McBride Books, LLC
brooke@brookemcbride.com

Editing: Jessica Nelson at Rare Bird Editing
Cover Design: Perfect Pear Creative Covers
Cover Models: Jori Iser and Thomas Ware
Cover Image: Perrywinkle Photography

VISIT ME AT MY WEBSITE
www.brookemcbide.com

DEDICATION

To my husband for helping me find my passion.
To God for giving me the talent and courage to pursue it.

CHAPTER 1

I grip the steering wheel until my knuckles turn white. Glancing around the parking lot, I ask for a sign, any sign. Do I stay or do I go? My phone rings, and I already know who it is. Not exactly the sign I was hoping for.

"Hi, Mom."

"Jensen dear, I'm glad I caught you."

She knows where I am. She should, since she's the reason I'm here. But, she's checking up on me as usual. "I'm going, Mom. No need to call." I sip my coffee and wish it were something stronger.

She releases a breath. "Oh, good."

"Anything for you." I try not to be sarcastic, but my mouth has different plans.

"Jensen, we've been through this. It's not for me, it's for you. I truly believe it will help."

I check the clock. Ten minutes before I decide if I am getting out of the car. "That's easy for you to say. You're not the one who has to sit there and listen to the sob stories."

She clears her throat. My mother is a throat clearer. It's a horrible habit. Yet, as I've gotten older, I realize it's her way of stalling, getting up the confidence to say what she wants to say.

I've never had this problem. I'm more like my dad in that I typically have strong opinions. And a big mouth, or so I've been told. Add that to the fact that I don't care what anyone thinks about me anymore, and you've got a ticking time bomb on your hands. She clears her throat again.

"Well honey, I wouldn't expect the mood to be light at a bereavement support group."

I sigh and shift in my seat. "Mom, you checked on me. I'm going, okay?"

"Well…" Throat clears. "You know the offer still stands."

"I'm aware." I rub my eye. "But this isn't someplace you take mommy and daddy."

She sighs and I know she's given up for today. I've won. "Okay, I'll check in with you tomorrow, dear."

"Of course you will. I'll pencil you in." I wait for her to say something, but she doesn't. "It's a joke."

"Well, I would welcome your sense of humor. You used to have one."

"I'm aware, Mom." Weariness overtakes me as I lay my head back and sigh. It's not her fault I'm no longer the vibrant, strong and fun daughter she raised. I don't like it any more than she does. But it's my reality. So I do what has become normal. Deflect. "I didn't mean to upset you. Thank you for checking up on me and for pushing me to go to group." There. The façade is back, and everyone, including me, can go back to pretending that it's all going to be fine.

"I know it's hard dear, but I think it's what's best for you."

"Okay, Mom. Bye." Beep. I drop my phone into the cupholder. It's been five months since a friend recommended this group to my mother, and she has been like a dog with a bone ever since.

Killing the ignition, I glance at the clock. Five minutes before I decide to get out of the car or not. I pull out a cigarette and roll it between my fingers. I don't smoke—well, not anymore. It's something I started after Jeff died. A distraction. An escape. An opportunity to excuse myself when people walked up with downcast eyes oozing sympathy. But they always took the hint when I blew smoke in their direction and didn't respond to their remarks. Once people got tired of asking how I was and left me alone, I stopped smoking. Now it's a security blanket I use when I'm uneasy.

I've done this exact ritual in this parking lot several times, only to turn around and go back home. These people meet every Tuesday, so in theory, I should have participated in this group over twenty times. But this would only be my fourth time attending. It's not for me. I don't see the point. Therapy can't change what happened, but I go to appease my mother.

I glance at the clock again. Three minutes. I'm not going, not today. I'm reaching for the keys when a motorcycle rumbles into the church parking lot. A man rides in like it's his personal driveway. He slows, glances around, and pulls away to park closer to the entrance. I never park close to the entrance. I sit back off to the side while I weigh going versus not going. If I don't go, my mother will hear about it, somehow. She seems to have eyes and ears everywhere in this city. And Kansas City is not small, so I'm not sure how she does it. If I do go, the pain of sitting in that room usually outweighs the pain of my mother's guilt trip.

Clenching the steering wheel, I check the clock one final time and realize it's time to go. As I reach for my keys, there's a tapping on my window. I glance to my left and see a chest covered in a tight, plain white T-shirt embraced by a leather jacket. Before my cheeks have a chance to warm, the rider leans down and smiles. "You comin'?"

I glance behind him. He's backed his bike in right next to me, essentially blocking me in. "Excuse me?"

I peer up at him as he removes his aviator sunglasses. "I asked if you were coming. Saw you sitting here. Assumed you're here for group?" He says it as a question, and I feel the need to slap that smirk right off his face. Why does he care if I'm going?

He's speaking loudly so I can hear him through the closed window. I'm not deaf, idiot. But if he's going in, I'm not. I'm not used to sharing the circle with men I find attractive. I never find men attractive anymore. But especially not Harley-riding epitomes of bad-boy man meat. I would tell my ovaries to calm down, but they haven't had a pulse for what seems like years. Yet it's only been nine months.

He tucks his sunglasses into his shirt. "Come on, we're going to be late."

"I don't know why it's any concern of yours, but no, I'm not here for group."

"Are you sure? I, uh...thought I've seen you here before."

There is something familiar about him, but I don't recognize him. His voice is familiar. Was he at group when I was in one of my grief comas? Maybe, but I don't think so. Fidgeting with my brown hair, I glance in the rearview mirror realizing it's a lost cause. I'm not the most attractive person, but certainly not the worst. As with anything in life, you should put some effort into it, but I haven't since Jeff died. I don't care what I look like, or at least I'm not supposed to as the grieving widow.

He's still staring at me. I grow more nervous. Not in that potential serial killer, let-me-grab-my-mace way, but like a schoolgirl crush where your hands start to sweat and you want to avert your eyes. "Um, don't think so. You, I would have remembered."

He weaves his hand through hair that matches the color and sheen of his black leather jacket, and sections of it stand on end. It gives a new definition of helmet hair. It suits him. His mouth twitches up on one side, like a little boy's mischievous grin. "You would have remembered me, huh?"

Huffing, I swing open my door and step into his space. "Look, I'm sure you get off on this in some weird way, but whatever you're selling, I'm not buying."

His grin only broadens. He walks backward, his hands in the air. "I get it. Just trying to be nice."

My glare follows him through the church doors. What a smug asshole. My pulse is pounding, and I feel tingly and anxious. My breathing becomes shallow, and I take a few deep breaths to calm myself down. I've let my anger take over. Again. It's a lovely side effect of my situation that I've grown quite used to. People rub me the wrong way on a pretty consistent basis. I remind myself it's me, not him. I'm already out of the car, so I might as well follow him. I sigh, reach for my phone, and hit the key lock. As I cross the parking lot, I try and calm myself down by focusing on the cool March breeze. I push a few stray hair tendrils that are blowing around my face and tuck them behind my ear.

Inside the double doors, my eyes adjust from the outside sun to the blinding overhead fluorescent lights. Smells of glue, play dough and peanut butter waft through the room. The church preschool classroom has been transformed into a support group with chairs in a circle. I feel sorry for these walls. They spend their days getting boogers wiped on them and crayons dug into them. Then they spend their nights listening to sad and pathetic people bare their souls about how hard it is to move forward. How unfair life is.

I scan the room and see three open seats. One is next to Harley man with another empty seat next to it. The other is sandwiched between Mrs. Olsen, who smells like mothballs, and Larry Riley, a mechanic who smells like oil. I break through the circle and move toward Mrs. Olsen and Larry.

Larry's eyes light up as I move in his direction. "Well, hi there."

Forcing a smile, I wedge myself between them. Mrs. Olsen pats my thigh. "Good to see you."

I try to ignore Larry but I feel him eyeing me. He seems to think since we're the only ones here under the age of fifty that we're somehow meant to be friends—or more. His eyes roam down my body, and I scoot my chair more toward Mrs. Olsen.

Pastor Paul greets the group. "Okay folks, we're a few minutes late, so we need to get started. It looks like we have a new face in the crowd."

The pastor's welcome is for Harley man. That jerk said he had been here before. He smirks at me and then says, "Hi, I'm Nash."

The rooms says "Hi, Nash" in unison, except for me. I roll my eyes. I've always thought that welcome was inconsequential.

CHAPTER 2

*P*astor Paul's pearly whites shine as he welcomes Nash. It's standard operating procedure for any grief-stricken person who comes to group. Even though he's doing his job, I still want to punch him in the face. I won't, of course. As a former lawyer, I'm aware that the ramifications of third-degree assault aren't worth it, but damn is he annoying. Maybe next time I'll spike his coffee with a laxative. I sigh, realizing once again it's me, not him.

"We're glad you're here. Please let me go over some ground rules. What happens in this room stays in this room. This is a safe space, one of respect, understanding and confidentiality. We assume good intent, and we listen when other people are talking. Simple, right?"

"Sounds simple enough." Nash stares at me as he answers. I force my eyes downward so that I don't have to look at him. Why is he focusing only on me?

"Okay, great." Pastor Paul regards the circle and rubs his hands together. "Who would like to start?"

Mrs. Olsen starts. As always. "Forty-six wonderful years we had together, and then poof." I grab her hand as she wipes her eyes with her ever-present hankie. I can't imagine spending forty-six years with anyone. Jeff and I married at twenty-six, right after law school. I said till death do us part, and though I never imagined forty-six years, I certainly imagined more than four.

I sneak a peek at Nash and he is still gawking at me. He grins and I dart my eyes away. I run my hands through my hair and realize it's a little greasy. When did I last shower? Three—no, four days ago. Ugh.

Mrs. Olsen finally shuts up and lets go of my hand, and a couple more people chime in. I don't talk. I never have, and I don't plan to. That doesn't mean Pastor Paul hasn't tried *every* time I've been here.

"Jensen, you've been quiet tonight."

Refusing to look up, I pick at my jagged nails. "Same as every other night."

"Right. Well...would you like to talk about anything?"

I cross my arms and slide down my chair. "Nope."

"Are you sure?" His pleading eyes remind me of every other counselor I've come in contact with since Jeff died. They all want you to talk. In nine months, I have yet to see how talking helps.

"No." My voice is firmer now. "Thank you."

Resigned, he sighs and drifts his attention to Nash. "I know you're new, but would you like to share anything with the group?"

Nash studies the group and mirrors my stance by crossing his arms. "Not tonight."

Pastor Paul makes one more circle around the group. "Anyone else care to contribute?" I notice no hands shooting up in the air saying "Pick me, pick me." Big surprise. "Okay, then I guess we're done early. Thank you and we'll see you next week."

I shoot up from my chair and try to make my escape. But Pastor Paul isn't finished. "Jensen, can I have a word?"

Stepping back, I pivot as Pastor Paul stands. But he's the one with the crossed arms now. I take a peek at Nash. He's still sitting, ankle resting on his knee, one arm on the back of the chair beside him, studying his phone. In his own world. I face Pastor Paul, dread in my stomach as if I'm being sent to the principal's office. Then Larry is approaching me, and I waffle between the lesser of two evils.

Mrs. Olsen begins speaking with Larry, so I don't have a choice but to move toward Pastor Paul. "Yes?"

"Let's take a walk, shall we?"

I'm not falling for that again. He's going to try to get me to open up to him one-on-one. "I don't have time."

"I talked to your mom recently."

Great. "Oh?"

"Yes, she wanted to know how you were doing."

She already knows how I'm doing. She just wishes for something different. "And?"

"I told her that I couldn't share what happens in our group."

My fist clenches. "But you can share when I'm here and when I'm not, right?" That would explain the phone calls and lectures from my mother on the nights I don't get out of the car.

"That's not the point."

I'm glaring at him, but he started it. "Really? What is the point then?"

He shakes his head and glares at me. "The point is that I don't see you making much progress."

"How would you know? I haven't shared anything about myself." I remind myself to control my breathing and to not get upset, especially with a pastor.

"Exactly. How do you expect this to help if you won't share anything?"

I don't talk about Jeff, not out loud. When I talk about him, it's in the past tense, and I can't stand to hear his name in a world where he no longer exists. Isn't it enough that everywhere I look, every scent I encounter, and every song I hear somehow reminds me of him and the life we had together? Do I need to talk about him, too? Deep breath. "I don't think talking about the situation will help. What good would it possibly do?"

"Have you tried?"

"No, and I don't plan to. Talking about it won't change anything." My frustration mounts as I square my chin and look directly into his eyes. "Is bullying a type of treatment you frequently use, *pastor?*"

"You know Jensen, you can't be angry forever. At some point, you're going to have to take steps to move forward, or you won't be able to recover."

That does it. I move into his space and he takes a small step back. "I doubt you could ever understand this, but you *don't* recover from losing your soul mate. You don't recover from losing the one person who meant everything to you. The person you were supposed to grow old with. Share everything with." My mouth clamps shut as heat rises through my chest. He can't understand.

He doesn't know it's my fault. All of it. But no one knows that. Eyes burning, I whip around and try to flee before I break down in front of him.

A chair squeaks against the floor and heavy footsteps follow me. My shins burn as I scamper toward the door. Someone calls my name, but I keep moving. I beg myself to hold it together. I don't break down in public, not anymore, and I'm so close. I walk faster, wanting the solace of my car. Just as I cross the threshold of the church door, someone tugs on my left arm. "Jensen!"

Whirling around, I see Larry. "Please don't touch me."

"Sorry." He looks down and releases me. I try to focus on his face. His beady black eyes and crooked nose. "I wanted to make sure you were okay."

Stop staring at his nose hairs, Jensen. "I'm fine." I turn to walk away when he grabs my arm again. My body tenses as my voice becomes steel. "I said don't. Touch. Me."

"I can tell you're upset, and I know how that feels. I'm just trying to help."

"I didn't ask for your help. I didn't ask for anyone to help me." The dam is breaking, and I no longer have control. Heat fills my face as the volume of my voice rises. "Don't you people understand? Why can't you just leave me the hell alone? Why is it so har— Owww!"

"Excuse us, Larry."

Nash steps between me and Larry. Grabbing my arm, he pulls me down the stairs, but it doesn't bother me like when Larry touched me. My brain finally registers that he's dragging me across the parking lot, and I plant my feet. "What the hell do you think you're doing?"

"Saving you from yourself. You really want to take out that guy with all those blue hairs staring?"

Straightening my shirt, I glance over my shoulder. Mrs. Olsen and Mrs. Arney are whispering to each other. I raise my chin to Nash. "Do you think I care what people think of me?"

He crosses his arms and emotions chase across his face. For a moment, I feel as if he's looking into my soul. "Yes," he whispers.

"You don't even know me." I push past him and rush toward my car. Twenty feet, just twenty more feet. His footsteps echo behind me.

"I know how grief turns people into someone they don't recognize."

I stop. I *have* lost myself. I no longer know who I am, and that's the only thing I'm sure of at this point. But I don't want to give him the satisfaction of being right. So I don't acknowledge it. I keep walking. I press the button on my key ring, and the headlights flicker on and off. They call me home to a sanctuary where nothing makes sense, but that at least provides some normalcy in a world that no longer feels normal.

"Jensen, stop. Just give me a minute!"

Shaking my head, I spin around. "I don't know you from Adam. Why would I give you even a *second*?"

"Because you're desperate."

I laugh. "Desperate? Really?"

He steps closer. On instinct, I back up. The door handle grazes my lower back, and I realize I have nowhere to retreat. He moves closer. All of his focus is on my face. I watch as his eyes make their way around. My forehead, down to my nose and my chin and finally back up to my eyes. And I stare back. Square chin, and white, almost perfect teeth except for the top middle one that has a slight slant to it. He's harsh with soft edges. Small wrinkles at the corner of his eyes that wouldn't be noticeable unless you were standing as close as we are. Hair dark as my heart, with sun-kissed skin. Does he work outside, landscaping, construction? He has the build for construction. Rugged and lean, defined muscles but not overly large. I feel his breath on my face, and I realize neither of us has spoken a word. My gaze drifts back to his blue eyes, the color of ice, yet warm and caring. My voice finally squeaks out, but the anger is gone, replaced with confusion.

"Why do you say that?" I ask.

"Because you're grieving. I see it in those big, beautiful green eyes of yours. You're looking for a way out, any way out." He licks his lips and grabs the bottom one with his teeth. Half of his bottom lip disappears, yet even with half of it gone, it's still larger than his upper lip. *Focus on his eyes, Jensen.* "But I'm going to let you in on a secret. A secret I had to learn the hard way." Another pause and he glances along the edges of my face.

Desire pools in my belly, and the feeling is so foreign to me that I want to push him away while also wanting to pull him closer.

"No matter what people tell you, grief can't be summed up in five neat stages. Not the grief you've experienced. It's messy and confusing and makes you think all sorts of things you wish you didn't have to think about. Yet you don't have a choice but to survive it," he says. "The sooner you accept that, the easier it will be."

The world begins to spin around me as my chest aches with pain. My eyes close and the need to cry overwhelms me. Cool air replaces his body heat, and I open my eyes to the sound of his bike peeling out of the parking lot.

CHAPTER 3

*H*iding in my car, I sit for a few minutes wiping the tears away and trying to catch my breath. The parking lot empties and I head home. I feel raw, as if I have been sliced down the middle and all of my pain has been exposed. Only someone who has experienced grief would have seen through me. But not just any grief. Grief that changes your life so completely that you wonder if you will ever be whole again.

I pull into my garage and walk through the door to an empty house. It's so fitting it makes me nauseous. I drop into a chair and stare at nothing. One of the many grief books I've read said to rationalize why you feel as you do. And that if you're more in touch with the feelings and the reasons behind them, you're more likely to recognize if they're valid or not. I try for about two minutes. Then I move to the bar and pour myself a drink.

I try not to use alcohol as a crutch. In the beginning, it was easier to be numb. Grief left my brain foggy, and the alcohol amplified that. Days would drift by as well as full bottles. I used alcohol just like I did the cigarettes. It felt better to be in a different place, out of my norm. To be someone else, to think a different way and to forget the battle that was raging inside. But the only thing I learned from alcohol is that grief and guilt are formidable opponents.

My chair cradles me and a half glass of vodka as I force myself to focus and gaze into the backyard. A manicured lawn surrounded by overgrown trees with buds starting to peek out again for spring. It's a little early, but Missouri has seen extra rain this year. I remember Jeff getting four bids from different landscape services to find the right one who would make it look like a checker board. That was important to a man who grew up with a single mom. There was never enough money to go around for him and his sister. He worked hard to become a lawyer, and although he didn't spend our money frivolously, he knew what it took to become a partner. Image was half the battle. That was one of the reasons we bought this huge house, 3,700 square feet for the two of us. But in his defense, the plan was to fill it with children. Was. Everything I think and feel is about what was *supposed* to happen.

What would my normal be if he hadn't died? What would I be doing right now? Certainly not sitting in the dark, with a drink in my hand, dwelling on the fact that a complete stranger saw through me. No, not through me. That implies no compassion or care. Nash didn't see through me, he saw *into* me. The me that exists without Jeff. Why do I feel as though he knows that person better than me?

Taking a gulp, I focus on the burn that trickles down my throat. I lean back and stare up at the chandelier I had to have for this room. Jeff didn't see any difference between this one and the one the builder picked out. Just the difference in price. I drag myself to the dining room switch and flip it on. The second I do, I regret it. My eyes drift above the fireplace to a picture above the mantel. It's Jeff and me on our wedding day. He holds me in his arms, my legs flailing, flanked by our best friends. I stare at the expression on our faces, and I see nothing but pure, blissful happiness. And ignorance. So ignorant that we didn't know it could be taken away in one swift second.

This isn't working. I grab my phone and pray my best friend isn't on duty. The phone rings once, twice, three times, and I prepare to leave a message. The question is, which Jensen do I want to be right now? The strong best friend who leaves a casual message, just checking in? Or the depressed widow who needs someone to lean on? When she answers, I already know who I'm going to be: myself, all depressed, weak, and angry. The anger never leaves my side.

"Hey, Parker. It must be group night."

Olivia, my best friend for over twenty years, still calls me by my maiden name. She and I met in second grade when her family moved to Springfield, Missouri. I still remember that day. She walked into our classroom and the teacher introduced her. The faces of all the boys in the room lit up. I knew at that moment she was one of those girls every boy would want to date and every girl would hate. Feeling threatened, even at age seven, I raised my hand and in a snotty voice asked the teacher, "Is she going to be in *our* class?" Most girls would have hated me for it, but not Olivia. She smiled at me while the teacher informed us that she *would* be in our class and it was now my responsibility to show her around. We became instant friends, and even after all this time, she knows me better than anyone. Jeff was the only person on this earth who gave her competition in that department. And she's the only person I haven't shut out since he died. It may have something to do with the fact that she lives 1,200 miles away.

"Hey, not on rounds tonight?" I ask.

"Not tonight, so I'm living it up. What's up?"

"I guess that means it's pizza and wine night?" I hear a cork pop in the background.

"You're good, but let's face it, I'm pretty predictable. Just as you are. You're not calling to shoot the shit. What happened?"

I appreciate having a friend that knows when to call me out. "Weird day, that's all."

"Would this have anything to do with group? Did you actually get out of the car tonight?"

There's also something about a friend knowing you so well that you don't want to tell them anything because they can use it as a weapon against you. "I did, after being coerced."

"Coerced? Who coerced you?" I hear the gulps on the other end and know that the bottle will be done before our conversation is. People used to call Olivia "Elbow" when she was in college. She's wicked smart, as a doctor at Yale should be. But she knows how to play hard too. I've always had trouble keeping up with her.

"Just some guy."

"Oh!" I hear her perk up on the other end. "Details please and spare none. What guy?"

"This guy came rolling in on his Harley thinking he owned the joint."

"Well now, this sounds promising. Is he hot?"

I roll my eyes as I remember the face I seemed to memorize tonight when he was just a few short feet from me. "Who cares?"

"I do, and so should you."

"Liv, please don't start the 'move along' speech. I'm not in the mood, not tonight."

"All right." She sighs. "How did he coerce you?"

"I was sitting in the car debating on going in when he tapped on my window. Asked me if I was going. One thing led to another, and the night ended with him giving me some psycho-babble bull about grief and not having a choice but to survive it."

"Sounds familiar. Not the first time you've heard it. Jeff would want you to move forward. He wouldn't want you sitting in that house, cleaning it day after day, giving up your career, your friends, your life so that you could try to stop time from moving forward."

"I'm not doing that." Olivia also knows me well enough to know that I spend my days cleaning 3,000 square feet of emptiness. After giving up my job and shutting myself in, it's the only thing I have control over, even if I don't want to admit it out loud.

"Really? You know, Parker, it may not be a bad idea to make a new friend, especially someone who might know a little about what you're going through. Any idea why he was at a bereavement support group?"

Good question. I was so caught up in my own crap I didn't even think about his. I sit back down and rub my eyes, regretting calling her and trying to have a conversation about this. She doesn't understand. Nobody does. So I do what I always do: deflect. "Don't know. Enough about me. What's new with you?"

CHAPTER 4

Olivia fills me in on the past three guys she's dated and dumped. Apparently, it's been a while since I've asked about her life. Jeff would have been annoyed that I stayed up late talking with Olivia. They loved each other because of me, but they never saw eye to eye.

I walk to the sink to wash out the glass of vodka. I study the floor and decide it's time to change the towel stopping the leak underneath the sink. I wipe away the dampness and wring out the towel. I try to remember the last time I changed it. I keep telling myself that I need to get a calendar to keep track of things, important things like towel switching and bathing. It seems so pathetic. I used to keep a schedule of eight to ten meetings a day. Now I can't remember the last time I washed my hair. Or changed a towel on the floor. If it was yesterday, then the leak is getting worse.

I place the towel directly beside the kickboard and then center it between the two cabinet doors underneath the sink. It took me several months and numerous types of towels before I figured this out. I now use the Super-Duper absorbent towel that I bought through an infomercial during one of my sleepless nights. I thought *what the hell* and took a chance. Worked perfectly for what I needed, so I ordered four more.

Washing my hands, I reach for a paper towel and glance at Jeff's Honey Do List on the refrigerator. At *fix sink leak,* the perpetual knot in my throat rises to the surface. Tears spring to my eyes. I know better than to look at that. It's a trigger for me, but let's be honest, what isn't? Before I dwell on it for too long, I rush upstairs to drift into another sleepless night.

* * *

I AWAKE to knocking on the front door. My mother knows not to use the doorbell. She knows it's another trigger for me. Since that night, whenever the doorbell rings, all I picture is two police officers standing in front of me about to deliver the most devastating news of my life.

Even if she didn't know, she couldn't miss the fact that the doorbell was ripped from its cradle. A few weeks ago, the delivery man rang it twice. Anger took over and I lost it. The butter knife I had in my hand at the time helped me take care of it so it wouldn't be an issue in the future.

She knocks again. I can tell it's her knock from the hesitation. One knock and then, as though she's rethinking it, two softer ones. After the third round of this, I decide to get up. I wasn't asleep anyway, and her next move will be to use her key. Which reminds me, I need to get that back from her.

Throwing my legs over the edge of the bed, I make my way downstairs, throw open the door, and head toward the kitchen without a word. Coffee. I need coffee.

"Well hello to you too, dear. Were you still in bed?"

Dumb question number one. Where else would I be? "Yes mother."

She steps over the threshold. "I see you've cleaned again."

Always armed and looking for a fight. I don't understand why she brings this up *every* single time. I've explained it repeatedly. There is only so much one can do in the same house day in and day out. It's one small thing that I have control over in this world. For the love of God, let it go, woman.

"Yes, I cleaned again. What are you doing here, Mom?" I hope she can hear the frustration in my voice.

"I wanted to see if you'd like to go to lunch with me. We could invite Julia or another one of your friends if you like."

"Lunch?" Dumb question number two. I look at the clock on the microwave and groan. I slept in again. More specifically, laid in again. I will never understand it. Either I can't sleep at all, or I go for what seems like days and do nothing but sleep. I can't seem to find any kind of routine or normalcy.

"I just got out of bed, Mom. I'm not in the mood for lunch. And as I've told you before, Julia was Jeff's friend, not mine." I was never crazy about the fact that my husband's best friend was a woman, but we were always cordial with one another, and she's tried to be supportive since Jeff's death. But I've done a great job of keeping my distance from her for the past nine months. "Is that the only reason you're here? Because if so, you can go."

"I wanted to check on you, see how you're doing."

"Mom, I'm the same as I was yesterday. And the day before that, and the week before that." I glare at her. "Please, this has to stop. I just need some space and some time, okay?" I angle my face away from hers to avoid the wounded look on her face.

"Jensen, it's been over eight months since you were released from the hospital."

"Yep. What's your point?"

"Mr. Thompson called your father yesterday."

I stop searching for the coffee filters, cross my arms, and look at my mother. "Why is my boss calling Dad?"

She clears her throat. "He said he's been calling you and leaving messages, but you haven't returned his calls."

I start digging for something, anything. "That's because I

assume he wants to discuss when I'm coming back to the firm. I'm not ready yet."

"Jensen, that may have been why he called two months ago, but that's not why he's calling now."

"What's your point?" I rattle the bowls and plates in front of me, trying to drown her out.

"Honey, he called to make one last attempt to get you to come back to work, but your father told him you weren't ready."

"So what's the problem?"

"Jensen…" She clears her throat. "Sweetie…."

Finally finding the coffee filters, I throw them on the counter. "Oh for Christ sakes, Mom, just spit it out. Stop treating me like a child. What?"

"They had to let you go."

Fired? They fired me? My stomach clenches and I feel nauseous. I grip the side of counter and stretch out my arms. Jeff's face flashes before me. I waited until he came home that night to tell him I had landed a job at one of the top law firms in Kansas City. He smiled, picked me up and swung me around, and then insisted we go out to dinner to celebrate. I miss him being proud of me. I lower my head and focus on the tile grout in the kitchen. I need to clean the grout. It's been a few weeks.

I lean down, open the cabinet underneath the sink, pull out my grout cleaner and toothbrush, and sit them on the counter so I don't forget to add them to my cleaning rotation today.

"What are you doing?" My mother asks.

"Just sitting this out so I don't forget later."

"So you have no response to what I just told you?"

"He's right."

"Who's right?"

"Mr. Thompson. It's time." I pick up the coffee filters and meticulously try to separate them. "They haven't been paying me for months anyway, so we might as well make it official."

"You're not upset that you were fired?"

I shrug my shoulders. "No. I wasn't planning on going back anyway. Do you want a cup of coffee?"

"Jensen, come on. That is your dream job. You're just going to walk away from it?"

The coffee filters aren't cooperating, so I shove them aside and move on to the coffee scoop. I focus on leveling the scoop so I don't say something to my mother I'm going to regret. Why she doesn't understand that I no longer care about that job is baffling to me. It's like saying the same thing over and over in a foreign language. A language called grief. It doesn't matter how I say it or how often, she hears what she wants to hear.

She starts rambling on again about the sacrifices I made for that career, for that particular job. Things that don't matter in this world anymore. Her voice becomes muffled and she sounds like she's in a tunnel far away. I feel my face warm and I try to slow down my breathing. She's my mother. She's only trying to help. It's me, not her. Don't get angry.

But it doesn't work. I slide the coffee cup across the counter, willing it to shatter, just so one more thing can be broken in this house. "Jesus, mom! I don't give a shit about the job! Why don't you get it? How the hell could that possibly matter after everything I've gone through?"

"Jensen. Please don't get angry again. What's happened is… tragic, but I'm afraid you're starting to actually make the situation worse. Making it even more tragic."

I squeeze my eyes shut. *Breathe Jensen, breathe.* "How am I making it worse, Mom?"

"By not moving on. You know you can't afford this house without Jeff's salary. And his life insurance was gone months ago. After the funeral and other expenses, and with no money coming in, you won't be able to live here much longer."

"Mom don't start on this again. I don't want to have the 'how irresponsible' conversation *again.*" Jeff and I didn't have a lot of life insurance. We were young and focusing on our mortgage and trying to build our life. We never dreamed that we would need it. Until I got pregnant. We started talking about it then, but I was only three months along. We thought we had time. Time to do a lot of things we never would.

"Jensen, I don't want to fight. But I'm not going to sit back anymore and let you sit in this house with no job, no husband, no children, and no future. This isn't the life I want for you."

"He was my life! What's so tragic about not leaving him behind? Without him, I'm nothing." My throat burns from the sudden increase in volume leaving my mouth.

"Really? Where's that stubborn daughter I raised? The one who was strong-willed and wouldn't take no for an answer. You remember, the one who dreamed of becoming a lawyer, to help people and to make a difference in this world. You were something before him, and you can damn well be something after him!" She picks up the coffee cup from the floor and slides it back in my direction before marching through the dining room and slamming the front door behind her.

I stand, unmoving. My mother yelled at me. I don't think that's happened since I was four years old and decided to glue her new, custom-made drapes together. I rush to the front door to apologize, but she's already gone. Yep. I'm still an asshole.

Coffee calls as I shuffle back into the kitchen. I need to make some decisions about my future. A future I never imagined. But it's easier to avoid it and pretend that it will work itself out. Especially since I don't care. Knowing what this day will hold for me, I march back up the stairs. Yet, instead of turning left toward our bedroom, I find myself turning right and standing at the entrance of a closed door.

I don't go in here often. I'm not strong enough. But since my mother already broke me today, I turn the knob, focus on the hard steel, and slowly open it. My senses are overloaded, and before I can even process it, a tear is running down my face. I see the crib that Jeff put together two weeks before he died. We settled on a dark cherry wood since we didn't want to know the sex. I couldn't wait to get the nursery together. We were so excited.

I cross the room and pick up the stuffed Sluggerrr mascot Jeff brought home the first day he found out I was pregnant. He'd always been a Royals fan and told me it didn't matter if it was a boy or a girl, they would be too. I hug it to my chest as I sit down in the glider and take in the room around me.

The changing table still sits in a box next to the closet. Jeff was going to put it together the weekend he died. A package of newborn diapers sits off to the side. It shows a young, beautiful mother with a baby in her arms. Her face is in awe of the little person she holds in her arms. Those diapers were the first thing I bought after finding out I was pregnant. I shake my head realizing how stupid I was to purchase those first. Not clothes or even something fun or memorable, but something that would be thrown away and forgotten. But instead of being used and thrown away, they sit there, frozen in time, just as I am.

CHAPTER 5

*B*efore I became a widow, I led a charmed life. Some might say predictable, maybe even boring. But that's what I loved about it. It was everything I had dreamed of since I was a little girl. A good job, a good husband, a child on the way. Stable. It was so good that I still spend a lot of time in that life. I often wonder what Jeff and I would have been like as parents. I wonder what choices I would have made as a mother: organic, soy, strict routine, or wandering around so blissfully happy none of it would have mattered. How often would I have put my child above my husband, my career, myself? But now there's no one to put above myself, and the choices look a little different: should I shower, should I clean, should I eat? Those choices, which probably seem simple to most, are almost too much for me to bear on most days.

So is deciding if I'm going to group. Nash's crooked smile flashes briefly through my mind. I don't want him to be a factor in my decision. I tell myself it's only curiosity, considering how we left things.

I go through my normal motions. I get in the car. Drive to the church and back into my usual spot. I begin the countdown. Five minutes. And here he comes. He pulls into the lot like last time. But as soon as he spots me, he pulls forward and slowly backs into the spot next to me. This time I'm ready for him. I watch him climb off his bike and place his helmet on the back. I expect one of two things from him. Either he'll lean down and try to talk to me through my window again, or he'll ignore me and walk in. I can't decide what I wish for more.

I have a fluttering feeling in my stomach as I watch him cross in front of my car and lean down to talk to me through my passenger side window. I follow him the whole way so we're looking at each other as he says, "Unlock the door, Jensen."

I do, even though I'm confused by my willingness to be so accommodating. He climbs in, and suddenly I'm very aware that there is a man in my car. He smells clean, like hanging fresh laundry on a line to dry. He pulls his sunglasses off and tucks them into the collar of his shirt. He then angles his body to face me and says, "Hi."

I don't ask him what he's doing in my car. Or yell at him for what he said to me last week before he walked away. I respond with my own "Hi."

"How are you today?"

I shrug my shoulders. "Same as every other day."

The muscles in his jaw clench as he nods. "Figures." Several moments pass, and I realize he's not going to say anything. I glance at the clock. Three minutes.

"So, mind telling me why you're sitting in my car?"

"I'm waiting."

I glance around. "On?"

"You."

My mind starts to race. "What about me?"

"What choice you're going to make."

"Choice?" His steady stare is unnerving and welcoming all at the same time.

"To see if you're going to walk in or not."

He surveys the parking lot as I study his profile and his five o'clock shadow. "And if not?"

"If not, I have a different idea." He pins me with his eyes, and I shift in my seat with anticipation. "But I want you to make the decision for yourself, without any help from me. It's your choice, Jensen."

I look over at the door to the church and see Larry helping Mrs. Olsen up the stairs. I have no desire to get out of this car. "Why do I need to make the decision for myself?"

"Making decisions gives you control, and I want you to have something in your life that you control."

"What makes you think I'm not in control?"

"Just a wild guess." He continues to stare while waiting for an answer. "What's it going to be, Jensen?"

I already knew the answer the moment he gave me a choice. "I'm not going in."

"That's what I thought." He's then out of my car, walking back to his bike. He starts it up he yells, "Follow me."

And I do.

* * *

FOLLOWING NASH, I try to keep a safe distance from his bike. I sit up tall in my seat to make sure I can see clearly. I'm relieved when he puts on his turn signal in front of McFadden's coffee shop so that I don't have to worry about running into him. But as soon as I park, I rub the back of my neck and rethink my answer to his question. Even though I don't like group, I'm not forced to talk no matter how hard Pastor Paul tries. But having a cup of coffee with Nash, sitting one-on-one with him, is going to force me to go even further outside of my comfort zone. He's going to ask questions I don't want to answer. He's going to want to discuss things I don't want to discuss. I'm just about ready to step out of my car and tell him that I changed my mind when he steps off of his bike.

He motions for me to roll down the window. "You have another choice. Get out, or stay here. I've just pulled a twenty-four-hour shift, so I'm going to get some coffee and read the paper. You can join me if you like." He then walks away again.

Why can't I ever predict what this man is going to do? It's not like me. Part of being a lawyer is always being a step ahead. I've always had a keen sense for how people are going to react or respond to situations. But Nash keeps tripping me up. Then I dwell on something he said: twenty-four-hour shift. I wonder what he does for a living. Before I can change my mind, I shuffle out of the car and follow him.

I walk up behind him as he's placing his order. "Large coffee, black." He glances over his shoulder. "And whatever she's having."

"This isn't a date, so that's not necessary."

He pulls out his credit card. "Suit yourself." He hands it to the barista, and she grins at him and then drops his card, picks it up, and drops it again.

"I'm sorry...sir." Her face flushes bright red. She then says under her breath, "I'm such a klutz."

"Don't worry about it sweetheart." He winks at her, and I step forward to make my presence known.

"Thanks." She hands him his card back. "They'll have it down there for you."

He smiles and saunters off to retrieve his cup of joe. I wait a few seconds and finally clear my throat. Her eyes finally leave Nash, and I order a caramel macchiato.

Nash already has his coffee in hand and is making his way to a booth in the back by the time I get to the pick-up counter. I snatch some sweetener and join him. He's holding a newspaper, and his face and the upper part of his body are hidden behind it as I sit down.

I wait a few minutes and then sigh heavily. Nothing. Finally, my patience gives in. "Excuse me?"

He lowers his paper and his eyes gaze over it. "Hmmm?"

"Well?"

"Well what?"

"I thought you said you had a better idea? Is this it?"

"I said 'different,' and yes." He then resumes reading his paper.

"Okay *different*, so…."

He sighs and lowers the paper once again. "You had a choice, right?"

"Yeah, so?" I hit the packet of sweetener against my hand a few times and dump in its contents.

"And you chose this as opposed to group, right?"

"Yeah." I take a sip of my coffee. "Unfortunately."

"Would you rather be stuck between Mrs. Olson and *Larry* right now?" He says his name as if it's a bad word.

I squint and feel the wrinkles forming in my forehead. I used to try to avoid that because I didn't want premature wrinkles. But that whole not-caring side effect has prevented me from thinking about it in a long time. So why am I thinking about that now?

Nash stares at me, and when I don't say anything, he slides the Lifestyle section of the paper over and disappears again behind his own paper.

I sit for a few minutes, staring at the other side of his paper.

He finally says, "Pick up the paper, Jensen. Read something, just for a little while. Forget where you are, forget who you are. Try it."

The fact that a total stranger, who is barely paying me any attention, has dragged me to a coffee shop and convinced me to do something I don't want to do is unnerving. But I do it anyway. I can't remember the last time I read a paper. I have no idea what's happening in the world outside of my life. And it's a nice reprieve. A reprieve from the grief and the worrying about the future, and most importantly, a reprieve from the guilt that eats at me every hour of every day.

CHAPTER 6

*B*efore, I never would have been the type to sit in a coffee shop and read a newspaper. The hustle-bustle life of a lawyer never gave me the opportunity. Which is one of the many reasons this has been hard. After I lost the baby, I went into a treatment facility for depression. Even there, my days were scheduled. Group therapy, one-on-one therapy, horseback riding therapy, yoga, meditation, and the list goes on and on. It was all pretty much crap, but it kept me busy. When I was released I came home to nothing but silence and emptiness. Which is why my house is so clean. I had to find something to pass the time. When I was a lawyer, I always worried about when I would find time to clean our big house. I think about how ironic and ludicrous life can be. Before, it mattered and I didn't have time; now, it doesn't and I have all the time in the world.

At some point, Nash and I started exchanging newspaper sections, and I'm almost out of things to read. Before I can dwell on it, Nash is out of his seat ordering more coffee. He comes back with two cups, sets one in front of me, and throws down a sweetener packet and a stirrer.

"Is this for me?" I ask.

He laughs. "I don't see anyone else sitting here." He takes a sip of coffee, and his eyes lock on mine. "Don't worry, I'm aware that this isn't a date."

If he only knew my story, he would understand why I'm so sensitive right now. But it's nice to talk to someone who doesn't automatically think *widow*. He doesn't look at me as sad and pathetic, and I think that's what I like best about him. I'm someone else, even though I don't know who she is.

"Jensen!"

I realize I've been staring at him and not listening. "I'm sorry, what?"

"I asked if you were okay."

"Yeah, yeah...I'm fine." I pick up my paper and go back to reading about March Madness. As I scan the article I'm not interested in, Nash peeks over my paper. I scoot a little to the right, trying to ignore him, but his eyes follow me. I shift to the left and he follows me again. He starts to chuckle, and I finally throw the paper down. "Why is this so funny?"

He continues to laugh before saying, "You're so easy to rile."

"Thanks for that." My voice is laced with sarcasm, but he deserves it. "Most people walk on eggshells around me. They're afraid what will happen if they get a rise out of me."

"How does that make you feel?" His U-turn almost gives me whiplash. One second he's giving me a hard time, and the next he's getting all introspective on me. "How does it make you feel when people treat you differently because of what you've gone through?"

"Well, I...I don't like it, actually."

"If you're expecting that from me, you're going to be waiting a long time. I'm not going to treat you like you're glass, waiting for you to break."

I wait a few moments before I respond. I study his body language and expression, but he gives nothing away. "Why not?"

"You're already broken. Others don't get it, but I do. Doesn't mean I'm going to make things easy for you." He takes a sip of his coffee and leans back in his seat. "I'm going to push you in ways that others haven't because they don't understand."

I pause, waiting for him to say more, but he doesn't. I want to ask him a million questions. But I don't. I'm not sure I'm ready to know. I fiddle with my empty sweetener packet, but it's too quiet between us. "How did you know what I like?"

"I overheard you order it, and I saw what you put in it." He shrugs one shoulder like it's no big deal.

"That's pretty observant of you."

"Observation is part of my job."

Relieved that the subject has changed, I commit to it and move on. "What do you do?"

"I'm a paramedic," he says and then takes another sip of his coffee.

"Oh, so like looking for injuries and stuff?"

"That and knowing your surroundings. We're called to a lot of different places, not all of them safe. It's important to understand what you're walking into, for your safety as well as for the patient you're working on."

"That makes sense. And you just got off a twenty-four-hour shift?"

"Yeah."

"Aren't you tired?"

"Yes, but it takes me a while to wind down after coming off a shift."

I smile. "And black coffee helps?"

He smiles back. "Not exactly, but I don't sleep all that much anyway."

I want to move the conversation back to the questions I have, like why he doesn't sleep, why he was at group, why he's bothering with me, but I don't. I hate when people force me to open up, and I won't do that to him. He'll tell me if he wants to and when he's ready.

We sit in silence for several minutes. I feel as though we're sizing each other up, but I don't know why. He smirks at me, but I lean my head away as I feel my face warm. As I do, I analyze our surroundings. It's been a while since I've been out in public for this long. Beside me, I see a couple snuggled up. The man has his arm over her shoulder and is whispering in her ear. She laughs and looks up at him while he kisses her temple.

"You okay?"

Something brushes against my hand, and I realize it's Nash's hand. I pull away like I touched something hot and squeeze my eyes shut.

I felt in control of my surroundings at some point tonight, but that feeling is gone and I want to run back to the fort and hide. I try to get control of my breathing as my limbs begin to tingle and the lights brighten. I feel an anxiety attack coming to the surface, and I'm scared I won't be able to stop it.

"I'm sorry, but I'm not feeling well. I need to go." I gather up my purse, and Nash rises with me.

"No, please don't leave on my account. Jensen, I'm here because of you."

What? I fumble on my way out of the booth. Instead of focusing on the anxiety, I focus on my anger. "Would you please stop doing that?" My voice rises as I try to untangle my purse strap.

"Stop doing what?"

"Throwing me off. I never know what you're going to say. Or do. It's making me uneasy."

"Sorry. Not my intention. You should probably know that you've never met anyone like me. I'm not..."

I lift my hand up before he can say anything else. "I realize that, okay? You don't have to state the obvious. I have to go." I back up and run straight into a chair, knocking it over. Nash is at my side in an instant, helping me to right it.

"Jensen, it's okay, I'll get it."

I take a deep breath, "Stop. Just stop. You don't get it, so please don't try to pretend, because then I'll lose all respect for you." I glance into his eyes, "And you're the first person I've met in a long time that I actually respect. So just don't!"

He bites his lower lip and nods but doesn't say anything. Nor do I. I rush out of the coffee shop, throw myself into my car, and squeal my tires as I pull out of the parking lot.

CHAPTER 7

I should be embarrassed by my outburst, but I simply don't care. It's been three days since I spent time with Nash at the coffee shop. Three long days. I've shut the rest of the world out again. I spent most of those seventy-two hours in bed, unable to function. Why did I think I could try to jump back into a normal life without being reminded that I'm a widow? That I'm alone. Seeing other people who aren't alone brings feelings to the surface I don't want to face. It's more than jealousy. More like desperation.

After Jeff died, a numbness took over. It's like when your leg falls asleep, and you get up and try to walk on it, but that sharp, tingly feeling knocks you over instead. That numbness had taken permanent residence in my life. But Nash has forced that stinging to return, and I feel as though I've been knocked down all over again. I know that's not his intention. He's only trying to help, although I don't know why. Pity, I guess.

Light trickles in from behind the white plantation blinds in my bedroom, so I roll the other way and face the wall. When I do, my gaze lands on a picture of Jeff and me when we were in Jamaica for our honeymoon. Bronzed skin, leaning into one another as close as we could get, and sitting on the beach drinking daiquiris without a care in the world and nothing but hope for our future. Life without hope feels like someone is holding you down with their foot while pouring water down your throat. You gasp for air, but at some point, you know the fight isn't worth it and instead of struggling, you begin to gulp the water and pray for it to end.

I squeeze my eyes shut and start to count to five. I tell myself to look at something else the moment I open them. I get to three before I hear knocking at the front door.

I'm going to kill her.

Motivated by white-hot anger, I throw my legs over the bed and stomp down the stairs. I don't even bother to put on pants or a robe. I throw open the door, and so many feelings wash over me when I see him standing there. Confusion, doubt, rage, embarrassment.

I really should have put on pants.

Gripping the hem of Jeff's favorite Royals shirt, I pull it down, willing it to grow in order to conceal my bare legs. "Nash! What are you doing here?"

"Thought you needed a choice this morning. Looks like I'm right. Still in bed at…" He brings up his wrist to note the time on his watch while I glance across his chest. Tight shirt again, this time black but no leather jacket. I spot a tattoo peeking out from underneath his sleeve, but I can't tell what it is. "Ten 'til ten? You usually sleep this late?" His eyes gawk at my legs, and it seems like an eternity before they rise back to my face. I should be offended.

I pull at my shirt and again try to hide behind what little clothing I have on. "Depends on what kind of night I've had. Why are you here?"

"Checking up. You left in a hurry the other night."

"Yeah, I'm sorry…I…."

"I don't want an apology, Jensen. The sorrys of the world can't change the facts."

I grip the doorknob tighter, embarrassed for other reasons than what little clothing I have on. "I'm sorry." And then roll my eyes. I really am pathetic.

"You apologize a lot."

My eyes shift downward. It feels as though time stands still. He's right, I do. I can't apologize to the one person in this world that I need to, so I apologize for everything else. Then I feel a rough, calloused finger under my chin, moving my face upward as Nash looks into my eyes. His hand then moves under my chin to the back of my neck, and warmth surrounds me. I lean into his hand and feel my eyes closing. When they do, Jeff pops in my head, and I immediately jump back. "Nash..."

His hand retreats and the feeling of despair returns. "I'm sorry." He takes his own step back and I wrap my arms around myself at a sudden chill.

"How do you know where I live?"

He smirks. "Let's just say I have my ways. And I thought you could come with me to a motorcycle show."

Is he serious? He looks serious. He sounds serious. He chuckles. "You'd be surprised. I bet you'll like it."

I pull my long sleeves down to my wrists. "You don't know me at all. Do I seem like the type to know anything about motorcycles?"

"I didn't say *know*. I said *like*."

"Yeah, not so much. You're the first person I've ever known who rides one."

"Doesn't mean you've never been curious."

"Well, I haven't."

"Okay, sweetheart, whatever you say. My motives are selfish anyway. Need your help to negotiate a deal. You're good at that sort of thing, right?"

I feel a tingle in my stomach at the prospect of playing hardball with someone. I'm caught off guard, since I haven't felt the excitement of the back and forth since before Jeff died.

"Now there's a genuine smile."

I touch my fingers to my lips and feel my smile widen. "Wait, how did you know I was good at negotiating?"

Nash looks away from me, sticks his hands in his pockets, and rocks back on his heels as he glances around my subdivision. His eyes finally land back on mine when he says, "You mentioned you were a lawyer at the coffee house, remember?"

"No."

"Yeah, in passing. If you want to go, we need to head out. The show is at the convention center, so we're going to hit traffic."

My instincts are telling me to press him more on the issue, but the prospect of getting out of the house is suddenly appealing, so I let it go. "Yeah, okay. I need about twenty minutes to get ready."

"All right, and I need gas. I'll be back to get you." He saunters off, and I close the door, resisting the urge to watch him go.

CHAPTER 8

*M*e attending a motorcycle show is laughable. Motorcycles mean outlaws, rule breakers, leather-clad hoodlums. Jensen Parker Landry doesn't associate with those types of people—until now apparently. I watch Nash through the side window of the front door as he backs out of the driveway, thankful he brought his truck instead of his motorcycle. I may go to a motorcycle show, but that doesn't mean I'll ever ride one.

I rush back up the stairs and head to the closet. Skidding to a stop, I change course, go to the bathroom, and look in the mirror. Although I shouldn't be shocked, I am. My eyes are puffy and my face has red blotches on it. Hopefully I'm done crying for the day. My long brown hair looks like I stood in a puddle and stuck my finger in a socket. There's not enough time to shower, so I'll have to do my best with what I have.

I grab a brush and begin to rake my hair into a ponytail. Stopping, I realize it hasn't been cut since Jeff died. Ten months without a haircut. Or a brow wax, for that matter. My God, my hairdresser must wonder what happened to me. I used to set up my appointments a year in advance on a three-month cycle. That would be the only way I could fit them into my schedule.

I throw down the brush and dig around my makeup bag for my tweezers. Unable to find them, I rip open the door to the linen closet and stop. The first thing I see is Jeff's razor, shaving cream, and aftershave. I close my eyes and take a deep breath. What did that shrink tell me after Jeff died? Something about not being able to change my circumstances or my surroundings, only the way I respond to them? A panic attack rises in my chest. I controlled the one in the coffee shop, but I'm not strong enough to keep this one at bay.

The room warms, and sweat trickles down my neck. Flashing white lights pierce my eyes, and I grip the vanity top, grasping my way over to the toilet. I fumble for the lid and lower it to sit. With my eyes closed, I try to control my breathing, reminding myself I'm in control. Nash's voice seeps into my head *It's your choice, Jensen.*

Gradually, my breathing slows and returns to normal. I feel my skin cooling at the same time the fog clears in my head. *My choice.* The doorbell rings again.

I rush into the bedroom and look at the clock on the nightstand. Has it been twenty minutes? I used to be a prompt person. That was when time mattered and I had places to be. Time, like a lot of things, doesn't matter anymore. But I don't want to keep Nash waiting, so I yell down "Five minutes." and zoom into the closet. I don't have time to think about what I'm wearing, so I grab a pair of jeans and a long, gray, cowl-neck sweater. Back in the bathroom, I grab an elastic hair tie and pull it onto my wrist. Some foundation and eyeliner come next. Then I dash back down the stairs to grab my purse.

I sprint through the dining room and round the corner to the kitchen to grab my keys, when I slide on a small puddle of water. I look down and realize the puddle that usually keeps itself under the sink has now made its way about four feet to the right. I don't have time to clean it properly, so I grab a kitchen towel, mop up the excess that I slipped on, and rush to the front door. Before I open it, I glance in the hallway mirror and sigh. I don't even recognize that person in the mirror, so I don't know why I bother looking. I move my hand under my eyes and try to blend my makeup to conceal the dark circles. I then throw the wet towel down by the door and step onto the porch where Nash is sitting.

He stands and gives me a shit-eating grin. I narrow my eyes at him. "What's that look for?" I ask.

He shrugs. "Nothing, just excited. Been waiting a long time for this."

"Yeah?" after locking my front door.

"I have an old motorcycle that I've been tinkering with for the last three years." He then climbs into his truck and I follow. He rambles for ten minutes about his bike. It's the most I've heard him talk. Where he bought it, how it was a total piece of junk, how he meticulously searched for and bought every single part for it and rebuilt it from the ground up. "I call it Shirley." He removes his eyes from the road to look at me, and I can see a twinkle in them.

My face tightens into a grin. "Shirley? Why Shirley?"

"During the summers, my sister and I would watch re-runs of Laverne and Shirley every day in our pajamas. She liked Laverne, I liked Shirley. Got a thing for brunettes." He turns to wink at me, and my face betrays me and flushes.

Focus, Jensen. I clear my throat. "You have a sister?"

His eyes shift to his rearview mirror, and then to his side mirror, and back to the highway in front of him. "Um, yeah."

"What's she like?"

"Nothing like me. You have siblings?"

"Nope, only child. My parents both retired shortly after I got married and moved here to be close to Jeff and me." Is that the first time I've mentioned Jeff to Nash? He doesn't question me on who Jeff is, so I assume I've already mentioned him. Nash nods and focuses on the road ahead of us.

Several minutes pass, and both of us relax into the silence. There is a lull in the conversation, and it seems that both of us are in different places. Then Nash flips on the radio.

"Please shut that off."

He glances at me before turning back to the road. "What? Don't like hard rock? Let me guess, you're one of those pop princesses, yeah?"

"Nash, shut it off." His head jerks to look at me and his mouth is open, but nothing comes out. "Sorry, there's something about music that makes me emotional. I haven't been able to listen to it for some time now."

"Fair enough." His hand reaches over and flips off the radio. Before he can pull it back to his body, I grab it. His knuckles have scabs running over them.

"What happened? Did you get into a fight?"

He chuckles, tugs his hand out of mine, and then returns it to the steering wheel. "No, I don't fight people anymore."

"*Anymore?*"

His eyes shift again to the rearview mirror and he hesitates before looking at me. "Story for another day."

I frown and wish he would say more, but he hasn't pushed me when I haven't been forthcoming, so I let it go. Almost. "Where did the cuts come from?"

"Wanted to feel the sting of the bag." He then moves on as if that was a normal statement. "Have you been to the convention center?"

Last time I was there, Jeff and I went to a concert. That was what, a year ago? No, a year and a half. I glance out the window. "Yeah, but it's been awhile."

He changes lanes for the exit and then says, "Here's what I need from you. I'm a little impatient and therefore not great at negotiating."

44

"*You?* No!" I smirk and he smirks back. For whatever reason, it seems like we've had a heavy morning between one another. I'm glad to lighten the mood a little.

"Funny. Anyway I have an idea of what I want. The question will be if she's here or not."

"She? Are you serious?"

"Heck yeah. I'm looking for Shirley, Jr. It can't just be *any* bike. I need to feel a connection to her."

I mutter "boys and their toys" under my breath as we exit his truck and walk up to the counter to buy a ticket. I reach into my wallet, but before I can pull it out, I feel Nash's hand on my arm.

"That's okay, I got it. I'm the one that dragged you here."

I think too hard and too long about him touching me. His palm is warm and callused. He slowly slips it away, and I remember what I was going to say. "No you don't. I got it. You're ahead on coffee, so let me get this."

"Jensen, this is way more than coffee."

"Nash, stop. I'm taking your advice. This is what friends do, right? And I think we both know I need a friend. Just let me, okay?"

He relents and as we come around the corner, I'm shocked at the view before me. Every make, model, color and size of motorcycle is in this arena. There is so much chrome, I need sunglasses. Nash doesn't agree with me, according to his face. His eyes have glazed over, and he looks like a prosecutor who has just been told the defendant will take the plea deal. A mix of awe, contentment and satisfaction. A laugh rises in my stomach, but it comes out as a snort.

"What?"

"You look like a cat in catnip heaven."

He nudges me with his shoulder and says, "Shut up."

I shake my head. "So, where do you want to start?"

"Let's just go in a circle. I don't want to miss anything."

CHAPTER 9

*W*e stroll down the aisle on our right. I've never seen a man walk so slowly. I can see the wheels in his head spinning, taking it all in. We don't do a lot of talking. I'm not sure what he's searching for, so I just look around and try to learn something—anything—about the fascination he seems to be experiencing.

We come across two that Nash seems particularly interested in. Before we can fully make our way into the booth, the salesman is on him like cream cheese on a bagel.

"Well, hello there. You look like a fella in the market."

Nash plays it cool. Although I'm not sure he ever plays it any other way. He walks in a circle around the bike with his hands behind his back. "Maybe."

I follow his lead.

The salesman smiles. "Well, we've got a couple of beauties here." I bend down and pretend to check out something on the motorcycle as the salesman continues. "But from the look of it, you're no stranger to beautiful things." Glancing up, I watch as Nash glares at him with his eyebrows pulled in and follows the guy's line of sight as it then lands on me, bent over, looking underneath the bike. Everything happens quickly after that. Nash stalks toward the salesman and grabs the collar of his cheap button-down.

"What the hell did you just say?" Nash's voice is tight and controlled. But the rest of him is like a wild animal.

The salesman's feet come off the floor, and his arms grip Nash's as he speaks in a hushed tone. I rush over and knock Nash off balance, forcing him to release the salesman.

"Nash, stop!" My hands push back on his chest, and I'm having a hard time understanding how so much muscle could be concealed under his shirt. His chest rises and falls, but his eyes never leave the salesman.

"He owes you an apology."

I glance over my shoulder and watch the salesman swallow and straighten his tie. "It's fine. Let's just go." I push against Nash, but he still doesn't move.

"You heard me." Nash's hard eyes are focused directly on the salesman. My hands rest on his chest which is still sharply rising and falling. I'm ashamed and uncomfortable, so I slowly remove them, but Nash steps forward again. "Don't make me say it again."

"All right, all right. I'm sorry. I was just trying to pay your lady a compliment. No need to get all bent out of shape about it." Nash glances at me, but neither of us correct the guy about me not being Nash's lady. "I'm sorry, okay? Now, how about we try to make a sale here?"

I spend too much time dwelling on being called someone else's. Growing up, I never thought I would be that kind of girl. And I didn't think I was, until after Jeff was gone and I realized that I no longer belonged to anyone. It was one of the things I missed most.

Nash smiles but it doesn't reach his eyes. He strides toward the salesman, who retreats a few steps and glances to me as if I can protect him. Nash gets within four inches of his face and says, "I wouldn't buy anything from you if you were the last

BROOKE MCBRIDE

salesman in this room. Next time, think about how you treat a woman. That's someone's daughter, someone's wife...." And then he stops and looks at me before lowering his head with a sigh. He runs his fingers through his hair and mutters a profanity as he walks away, guiding me out of the booth with his hand at the small of my back. And suddenly, I'm reminded of something else I miss about Jeff.

CHAPTER 10

*W*e walk in silence for several minutes, nudging between several women in skimpy bikinis. I don't realize I'm staring until Nash tugs on my arm. His eyes are wounded as he walks to the side of the aisle and I follow. People of all shapes and sizes walk past us as I wait for him to say something. He rubs the back of his neck and finally says, "I'm sorry I lost my temper back there."

I don't know what to say. I've never had someone stick up for me before like that. Jeff was protective, but his blood didn't run as hot as Nash's. If that had happened to me with Jeff around, he would have gotten me out of the situation first and then commented on what an idiot the guy was later. "It's okay."

"It's not. I...look..." He sighs again. "It's been a while since I've lost my temper like that. But when I saw him looking at you like that... I—I don't know. I felt the need to protect you."

Protect me? My stomach knots itself up. I don't know what else to say but what I already said, so I say it again.

"It's okay." I doubt I've convinced him, but I want to move on.

Nash must sense my hesitation because he says, "We can go if you want. I'm sure this isn't what you had in mind today for our little outing."

"No, please." I don't want to leave, and as hard as it is to admit to myself, it has nothing to do with the bike show. "You said you needed help, right?"

"Yeah, but I ruined the day. Let me just take you home." He moves around me and turns to walk away, but I grab his arm. His eyes briefly close, and as he opens them, he steps toward me. I let my hand drift back toward my body.

"I don't want to go home, Nash. It's my choice, right?"

That little-boy grin creeps back on his face. "I may have created a monster here."

I grin too. "You brought me to negotiate. You haven't seen nothing yet." I feel him fall in step behind me as we move back down the aisle. As he does, the tension drifts away and the comfortable silence returns. As he takes the lead, I fall in step behind him. He checks on me occasionally making sure I'm keeping up, but in all honesty, I couldn't pull away even if I wanted to. Nash brings a sense of security that I haven't felt in a long time.

As we come to the end of the second aisle, Nash slows and then stops altogether. I come up beside him and feel the heat radiating from him. He whispers, "That's her."

I follow his line of sight to what looks like every other bike in this joint. He said he would know when he saw her, so obviously there's something different about this one. The salesman spots us, so I kick into negotiation mode. "Play it cool. You start by asking the questions you want answered and then follow my lead."

We make our way into the booth and casually look around. Finally, the salesman approaches Nash. "You in the market?"

Nash pauses several beats and then says, "Might be."

"I see. Well, we've got a lot of great deals today, so I'm sure we have something you're interested in." The salesman follows Nash like a little puppy. Nash looks at several bikes, asking questions here and there, and then stops at the one he's interested in. "Now this one is fresh off the line."

Nash tries to stay quiet, nodding his head. He makes it all of three seconds before diving in. "What's her horsepower?"

"122 with eighty-six pounds of torque. It's also got our new security fob that arms and disarms it as you walk away."

Nash leans down, and a small smile starts to form on his lips. I realize why he brought me. The guy can't bluff to save his life. I'm up.

I walk up to the bike and start examining it myself. "You're not considering this blue one, are you?" Nash glances over his shoulder and then stands up. His eyes dart to me and then to the salesman.

"We can order it in pretty much any color you want, ma'am." The salesman is talking so fast I barely understand him.

I step in front of Nash, forcing him to back up a few steps, "Is that so? Well, I want purple. Does it come in purple?"

"Purple?" The salesman peeks at Nash over my head.

"Don't look at him. This is as much my bike as much as it is his. What, you think because he's the man, he has all the say?"

"No, no! I just...I guess I uh...wanted to see what he thought of purple."

Nash steps forward, and his chest brushes my back. "If she's happy, I'm happy."

Goosebumps travel down my arms as Nash's breath caresses my neck. I ignore both his statement and his proximity to me by circling the bike like a shark. I run my hands across the smooth leather of the seat before throwing my leg over and sitting down. I'm off in three seconds flat. "I don't like it. Let's move on."

Nash stares at me but doesn't move. I wave my hands in front of his face. "Hello? Did you hear me? I don't like it. I like the purple one we looked at earlier."

"Ummm." Lovely. Nash has gone stupid on me.

The salesman violently flips through a catalog before finally stopping. "Ma'am, it comes in burgundy. How about burgundy?"

I want to throw him off his game a little, so I walk closer to him and he leans away, gaping at Nash like he's afraid of me. Good. "I take it you're not married. Because anyone who was married and had a woman in their life would know their colors, and burgundy is not purple."

"No of course it isn't. But this is an amazing bike, and I wouldn't let color get in the way of..."

"Of what, my happiness?" I shift back to Nash, who is still dumbfounded. I wink at him now that my back is to the salesman, and realization drifts across his face. "Do you believe this guy?"

Nash steps toward me and runs his hand down my arm before grabbing my hand. "I think you're being a little harsh on him. He's just saying that the ride isn't necessarily about the color of the bike."

Now I'm the one that's dumbfounded. I pray that Nash didn't feel the goosebumps he left on my arm as he was running his hand down it. I pull away, needing some distance, and make my way back over to the bike. "I get that. But this one isn't as pretty as the other one we looked at." Nash walks around, looking at the bike and holding his chin in his hand. He then mounts the bike, and all the air leaves my lungs. It never dawned on me how good he looks on a bike. I can't have that image in my head, so I look away and focus back on the negotiating.

"What's the fuel capacity?" I don't even listen to what this guy is telling me, but I'm trying to act more and more displeased with everything he says. I don't know enough about bikes to ask any more questions, so Nash finally takes over. For every two of the three answers the salesman gives, I find something to complain about and keep going back to the fictional purple hog that I'm supposedly in love with.

Finally, after twenty minutes of questions and answers, I can tell Nash is starting to lose his patience. It's time to talk numbers. I mount the bike one more time, trying to act a little more interested so this guy will start to work with us. I feel the handle bars in my grip and fantasize about what it might be like to drive one of these. I then force myself to focus. "He obviously likes this one, but I still like the other one, so what's the best you can do?"

"You know, I like you. You're one of those take-charge kind of women, and I admire that. She's something, isn't she?" He angles toward Nash and smiles.

Nash crosses his arms and leans back on another bike before saying, "She asked you a question."

"Right. So, the best I can do on this one is nineteen."

I watch Nash smile, and thankfully the salesman is looking for my reaction. I immediately shake my head and dismount the bike. "No way. For that kind of money, I want the purple one."

Nash's eyes morph into bowling balls and he shakes his head in just the slightest way so it's barely noticeable. I wink at him again, and he takes a deep breath then stands upright. "Okay."

He starts to walk away when the salesman yells, "Wait. Okay, okay. I can do better. What if I also throw in a cover and an extra twelve months of warranty coverage?"

Nash's back is to the salesman, but he's facing me and a grin develops on his face like he's just won the lottery. Before he can agree, I say, "Take $2,000 off, and you've got yourself a deal." Nash's smile fades, but I give him a stern look and watch him hold his breath.

The salesman sighs. "I need to get a manager's approval for that."

My eyes never leave Nash's. "Okay. We'll wait."

"All right, I'll be back." He pulls his cell phone out and walks behind a table where a computer is set up.

Nash glows at me and whispers, "I knew I brought you for a reason."

"Really?" I flutter my eyes at him in a dramatic way. "I thought it was for my charming personality."

"That too. I think he's as low as he'll go."

I shrug my shoulders. "I took a chance. Sometimes you have to walk away for people to realize what they're missing."

Nash continues to glow. "I'll have to remember that."

The salesman walks toward us, and I move away from Nash to put some distance between us. "You have a deal. But there's a minor problem."

Nash asks, "What's that?"

"We don't have stock on that particular bike right now, and there's a six-week delay."

Nash curves around and smiles at me. "That's okay. Most good things in life are worth the wait."

Heat rises to my cheeks, and without my approval, my body responds with an instinctive smile. I'm not sure what he meant by that comment, but my body, my soul, and my heart all seem to be on the same page, and they all approve. It's my mind that is drawing a pause. Nash continues facing me without looking at the salesman and says, "And I got the lady to agree on black. So before you write it up, make sure you get the color right."

The salesman walks over with a clipboard and asks, "While we're doing a custom order, are you interested in an adjustable suspension, since I'm assuming you'll ride it without her sometimes?"

I want to correct the salesman and tell him that I won't be riding it at all, but I can't seem to form the words on my lips. Nash glances at me, and his face lights up with joy. "That's a great idea. Let's go ahead and add that feature." He says.

"It's another $1,000."

Nash winks at me. "That's fine. She's worth it." He turns back to the salesman. "Where do I sign?"

I'm thankful he moved away from me. I'm having a hard time processing what I'm currently feeling. Maybe this wasn't a good idea. Luckily, Nash takes several minutes to sign all of the paper-work, and I have some time to myself.

He finally comes toward me and sticks the paperwork in his back pocket. "What?"

I smile at him. "You seem pretty excited."

"Absolutely. Even if I have to wait a little longer."

"I hope you didn't add that feature thinking you would guilt me into getting on that thing." I also hope he didn't add it for someone else. I immediately regret the thought.

"Jensen, I don't know a lot about you…yet. One thing I do know is you're stubborn." He takes a step forward, then another until he hovers over me. His voice lowers, and it's more rugged when he says, "I also know that I will get you on that bike, come hell or high water."

I want to argue with him and tell him he's wrong. But I'm no longer convinced he is. I don't know why I'm drawn to what he wants me to do, but me on a motorcycle, with him, sounds so appealing that now I'm not sure I can wait the six weeks it will be before he can make that happen.

CHAPTER 11

*W*e proceed through the arena, watching different demonstrations of the latest and greatest bike gadgets. Nash checks out a few things seriously. But he appears to be daydreaming and enjoying the high from his recent purchase.

"How many bikes have you owned?"

"Oh gosh..." He hesitates while he does the math in his head. "Eleven."

"Eleven?"

"Yeah, but the other nine were junk that I rebuilt and then sold. The one I have now is on its last leg. Shirley Jr. will be my first one that is new." We're at the end of the last aisle in the convention center when Nash asks, "Wanna grab dinner?"

"Dinner?"

"Yeah. You've got to eat, right?"

Something in the air has shifted, and my chest tightens. It feels wrong to be here, with another man. And to be considering eating dinner with him. I feel Nash's hand on my arm.

"Hey, where'd you go?"

I pull away from him and say, "I'm not sure that's a good idea."

"Why?"

"It's hard to explain, Nash. It's just that...I don't know if it's appropriate."

"Appropriate?" He squints at me and then takes a step back. "Okay, help me understand. What's inappropriate about it?" I don't respond, because I don't know how to. Nobody tells you how to handle being a widow, and certainly no one tells you how to behave as one. The old--time rules of wearing black for a year are no longer a requirement. But I would prefer it because then there would be guidelines for me to follow. I don't have those rules. But hanging out with a man I find attractive, less than a year after my husband died, screams inappropriateness. "Jensen?"

"I'm sorry. I don't know, I just think that coffee and hanging out is different than dinner?"

"Because dinner is more like a date?" I nod my head. "I get it. Was your husband the type to not let you go to dinner with a friend...a guy friend?"

"No, of course not, he wasn't like that! In fact, his best friend was a woman, so we didn't have those jealousy issues." I'm not sure if it's my imagination, but something passes over his face when I mention Julia, and then it's gone.

"If it didn't matter while he was alive, it sure as hell shouldn't matter now that he's dead."

I glare at him as my body tenses at his brashness. I sometimes think anger is a synonym for grief, and just like a warm blanket, I'm draped in both. "You don't have to be so crass about it."

"Sorry, was I? Wasn't my intention. I thought I was just stating a fact."

"Yeah, but still."

"But what? It's a fact, Jensen, and the sooner you accept it, the easier it will be. Trust me."

CHAPTER 12

*S*omehow, he talked me into dinner, but I insisted we go Dutch and he agreed. We're seated in a booth as I take in the restaurant's surroundings. The lights are dim, instrumental music is playing in the background, and I try to drown it out by focusing on the sounds of glasses, silverware and plates being moved about. The aroma of fresh spices and sizzling food assaults me as I try to force my eyes away from all of the happy couples out on a Saturday night.

"Jensen?" I glance back over to Nash, and my eyes fall to the waitress who has joined us. "What would you like to drink?"

"Oh, sorry. Um, water. Water's fine."

Nash smiles and says, "Two waters please." His attention focuses back on me as she walks away. "Have you been here before?"

I'm perusing the menu and thinking about Jeff. He's never far from my thoughts, but this feels different. I can't do this, so I close the menu and get ready to tell Nash that I need to go, but as I look up he cuts me off. "Tell me about him."

"What?"

"Jeff. Tell me about him. You're obviously thinking about him right now. And that's okay. I want you to know it's okay to talk to me. About anything."

"I don't think I'm comfortable talking about him."

"Why not?"

I fidget with the paper strip that was wrapped around the silverware. I rub it between my fingers, pull it tight so that it makes a small cylinder, and then unwind it again, only to repeat this process. A glass of water slides in front of me and I gulp down half of it.

Nash says, "We're going to need a few minutes."

He's just trying to help. All he's done is try to help me. I take a deep breath and open my mouth, but then close it again. I try to think of what I want to say, but it's harder than I imagined. "I haven't talked about him to anyone in a while. I mean, I think about him. About our life. Most days it consumes me."

"Where did you meet?"

A tiny smile starts to form until I remember Jeff usually tells this story. He loves to tell the story because he comes out looking like the hero. I squeeze my eyes shut, forcing the tears to stay away. I struggle to speak until I feel Nash's hand grip mine. I clear my throat and say, "We met at law school. First semester torts class." Nash's thumb gently rubs across my hand once, then twice, and then he pulls away. I open my eyes.

"We didn't pay much attention to each other until the end of semester after we had to work on the same group and give a presentation together. Once the semester was done, we went out to celebrate with some other people in the class. But it didn't take long for Jeff and me to end up by ourselves talking." I start to laugh. I can't believe I'm about to tell Nash this story. "My drink of choice at the time was lemon drop martinis. Let's just say I was enjoying myself. I'd had one too many drinks and I knew it, but there was no way I was leaving. I remember his hand brushed up against my leg, and his voice grew quieter until I had to lean closer for him to talk into my ear in order to hear him. I couldn't tell you what he said, but it didn't matter. He had me, and he knew it."

"Sounds like a pretty cool night."

I start to laugh. "Well sort of. The beginning was."

"What happened after that?"

"There's a lot about that night I don't remember. But I'll never forget throwing up all over his legs."

Nash starts to cough and wipes away remnants of water dribbling down his chin. "What did he do?"

I beam, thinking back and remembering the look on Jeff's face. "We both sat there in shock. I had tears running down my face, and I thought about running to the bathroom to hide until Jeff started to laugh."

"He laughed?"

"Yep. He used to tell his friends that he had been chasing me all semester and that he wasn't going to let a little vomit get in his way."

Nash is still laughing but takes a break to ask, "Then what?"

"The rest is history. After that he never called me Jensen again. It was always Lemondrop."

Nash's eye contact is steady as large pupils stare back at me. "Lemondrop," he says with a nod. "He was a lucky guy."

I shake my head. "No, I was the lucky one."

Nash leans over, grabs my hand again, and squeezes it so hard I almost pull away…almost. "No, like I said. He was a lucky guy." We stare at each other until the waitress interrupts us.

"You guys ready to order?"

Nash slowly withdraws his hand, looks down at his menu, and says, "Ladies first."

CHAPTER 13

*a*t one point in my therapy, my doctor said new opportunities would present themselves. She told me it would happen sooner or later, and that when it did, I should focus on the present and not dwell in the past. So I do. I tell myself I haven't been out to eat for months, and it used to be one of my favorite things to do. Nash is great company. There is an easiness about him and about us that I enjoy, and it's a nice change of pace for me. I also tell myself it's normal, even though it feels anything but.

Once our meals arrive, I relax a little. We spend the rest of dinner talking about Nash's bike and how he's planning a long trip now that he has a reliable ride. We also talk about his job and some of the people he works with. The dinner goes quickly, and even though I'm surprised and don't want to admit it to Nash or myself, I have a good time.

He pulls into my driveway, kills the ignition, and we sit in silence. Finally, he says, "Let me walk you up."

As I walk to the door, I search for my keys and step up on the porch. I regret not wearing a jacket as the chill in the March air envelops me.

"Thank you for your help today. You were a good negotiator." Nash says.

I smile as I'm still digging in my purse and then pull my keys out. "Not a problem. It was fun. I haven't done that in a while." I unlock the door, step in, and fumble for the switch. I glance down and see the wet rag on the floor from earlier.

"Goodnight, Jensen." Nash moves and takes a few steps down from the porch.

"Wait!"

Nash shifts back around with his hands in his pockets and then steps back up on the porch. "Yeah?"

I glance down at the rag again and then back to Nash. "Well, I was wondering if you could…"

He takes a step closer, "Yeah?"

"Well…I hate to ask you, but…"

One more step closer. "Jensen, what do you need?"

"My faucet's been leaking. I've been meaning to call a plumber, but Jeff usually took care of those things, so I don't even know what to ask, or what a good price is, and then I was worried about being alone in the house with a stranger, so I've been using these rags that I bought on an infomercial that are supposed to soak up twice their mass, or is it three times their mass? I don't know, and they work well. Or at least they did work, but it seems like the leak is getting worse, so I…"

"Jensen!"

"Hmmm?"

"I said I'll look at it, but you have to stop rambling and let me in."

"Oh, right, of course." I open the door wider and step aside so he can come in. He glances up and around while I close the door. He then looks at me with his hands in his pockets once again and rocks back on his heels. I look down and fiddle with my hands.

"So…"

I glance back up at him. "So…"

"Is this leak in the bathroom?"

Mentally, I slap my hand to my forehead. "Sorry. No, it's in the kitchen. I'm sorry, it's been a long time since I've had someone in the house. Well, besides my mother. But she doesn't count. Plus, she usually just lets herself in anyway. Well, after knocking several times, but I've learned to ignore it...but that doesn't help, because she has her own key and she uses it whenever she pleases." I shut up and see he's grinning at me because I rambled. I sigh. "It's this way."

I walk past him, flipping on lights as we go through the dining room and into the kitchen. I flip on the last switch and take in the sight before me. I love this kitchen. Well, I loved it when Jeff and I bought the house. I loved to cook and bake and entertain. But I haven't done any of those things since he's been gone. Plus, food hasn't been much of a priority for me, so this room is barely used anymore.

Nash is still looking around. "This place is amazing."

"Oh, yeah...thanks." I brush past him and open up the bottom cabinet doors. "The leak is over here."

Nash walks around the large marble island and over to the sink. He kneels and runs his hand along the base of the cabinet. "Yeah, there is definitely moisture here. Looks like your wood has warped a little."

"That's not good."

"No." He leans down and motions to underneath the sink. "May I?"

"Yeah. If you want to hand me stuff, I'll get it out of your way."

He starts to unload the items, handing them to me above his head. When everything is removed, he asks, "Got a flashlight?"

"Um, I'm sure we do. Well, here..." I pull out my phone from my back pocket and bring up the flashlight app. I kneel and try to angle it so he can see. "Is that better?"

"Yeah, thanks." He pauses for a few moments. "It looks like your connection to the valve is leaking. Do you have a wrench?"

"Probably." Jeff was always asking for tools for Christmas, even though he wasn't great at using them. But he was learning. "How big?"

Nash scoots out until his face comes into view. "Probably on the smaller side. Do you want to bring me a few and I'll get an idea what I need?"

"Yeah, they're in the garage. I'll be right back." I go directly to Jeff's tool chest, and it takes me several minutes to finally locate the wrenches. I grab the smallest three and head back to the kitchen. I kneel back down next to Nash. "Will one of these work?"

He tries one but tells me it's too big. He tries another, same thing. He finally asks, "Do you have one that is a tad bit smaller than this one?"

"Yep, it's the last one I brought." I hand it over to him and wait while he tries it.

"That's it. Let me tighten this, and then we'll see if that makes a difference." Metal clanks against metal, and I start to feel flushed as Nash flexes his bicep, which makes a peak so beautiful I look away. He continues to grunt and groan. Maybe I waited too long? He grunts one more time and then asks, "Can you move the light a little to the right?"

"Your legs are in the way." I attempt to get out of his way. "Here, let me go this way." I hover over him with the light and then bend down and move my hand farther into the cabinet.

"Stop. Right there." He grunts again. "Damn, this thing isn't budging."

Then all hell breaks loose. Water sprays Nash in the face and then all over my legs. I scream, "Oh my God!"

"Shit!" Nash scurries out from underneath the sink, practically knocking me over in the process. "Where's your shutoff valve?"

"What's a shutoff valve?"

"Shit! Where's your basement?"

"Right there, second door on the right."

Nash takes off and throws open the door. He gallops down the stairs and frantically searches for something. I realize it's the light switch.

"On your right," I yell.

Once he finds it, he runs away, presumably looking for the shutoff valve. I can't help him with that one.

Several seconds later, the water that was gushing under the cabinet turns into a drizzle and stops altogether. Nash takes the stairs two at a time while he wipes his face with his shirt sleeve. He reaches the top of the stairs, and I move out of his way. As he runs across the kitchen, he starts to go down right as he heads to the island. There's a squeal that reminds me of a teenage girl, and then it all happens so fast that I barely have a second to process that he may be hurt.

Running toward him, I grab the counter before I fall myself. "Oh my gosh, are you okay?" He's lying on his back with his arm across his face as his body shakes. "Nash, say something! Are you hurt?"

He moves his arm and I look for blood, bruising, anything to get an idea of what injury he's hiding. But he's laughing, and he laughs even harder when he looks at me. I glare at him and then start to laugh myself, releasing all of the tension and worry that I was feeling just ten seconds earlier. He's okay. I laugh so hard hot tears run down my face, and I grab my stomach because it hurts to laugh this hard. This goes on for what feels like hours. I let go of everything...the grief, the anger, sadness, frustration, sorrow. Pure joy feels good. Nash is still laughing, soaked from head to toe.

"You look like a drowned rat," I say through fits of laughing.

He takes a deep breath and finally stops laughing enough to talk. "I could say the same for you. Think we should have called a plumber."

"Apparently."

"Sorry."

I cover my face and try to get my breathing to return to normal. But I think about it again and laugh some more. "I saw you going down, and it was in slow motion. And I'm sorry but…" I start to laugh again and can't get it out.

"What, Chuckles?"

"That squeal you made." I clutch my stomach and rock back and forth.

"Thanks a lot."

"I'm sorry, I just…" I have to stop again. "You sounded like a teenage girl. I haven't laughed like this in so long." When I look back to Nash, he's no longer laughing, he's staring with a wide grin on his face. As we look at one another, his breathing slows and the grin on his face relaxes into a calm smile. He stops blinking, and I begin to feel that he is no longer looking at me, but in me.

I feel my face flush and my smile fall. My throat tightens, and I move my hands to cover my face. You would think I would be used to this onslaught of conflicting emotions. Since Jeff died, it's the one constant I'm familiar with. I don't control my emotions any more than I control the weather. I don't want Nash to see me cry. My shoulders shake up and down, and I feel him scoot closer to me. I wish he wouldn't. Lord, how I wish he wouldn't.

His arm wraps around my shoulder as he pulls me to his chest. "Jensen, it's okay to laugh."

He says it as a whisper, and my cries morph into sobs. He makes no other movements and says nothing more. He lets me cry in his arms, the one place I shouldn't be, but I make no attempt to move away. I cry for what could be minutes, or hours, I don't know. But finally my breathing starts to calm, and I remove my hands from my face. Staring back into his eyes, the look of endearment that was once stretched across his face has been replaced with pity. I hate that look. Out of all the looks people give me, that is the one that bothers me the most because it's a reflection of how weak and helpless I feel. That's a reminder I simply don't need.

I shake my head at him and scoot away. "I think you need to go."

His head jerks back as if he's been hit. He takes a deep breath and closes his eyes before staring into me again. "Jensen. Don't... don't shut me out."

He doesn't understand. I don't do this anymore. I don't lose it in front of people, because when I do, it makes them uncomfortable, it makes me uncomfortable, and it gives them an idea that I need to be fixed or I need to be helped. But I just want to be left alone. Except I don't want him to leave me alone. I'm so confused. He shouldn't be here. I shouldn't have let him in. And I certainly shouldn't have asked him to fix something Jeff was supposed to fix. I resent Nash for it, even though I put him in this situation.

"Nash, you need to go." I stand up crossing the kitchen, hanging onto the counter as I go so I don't slip. I grab a towel, wipe my arms down, and then hand it to Nash.

He stands and starts to wipe stuff down. "At least let me help you clean up this mess."

"I've got it. Just go."

"Jensen, please. I'll help you."

I don't mean for it to happen, but sometimes the anger has a mind of its own. "Just go!" I scream.

"Jensen, I can't." I can tell he's trying not to scare me more than I already am. His voice is soft and slow. "I had to shut the water off. I need to fix the valve so that I can turn the water back on."

My back is to him as my hands grip the edge of the counter. I hunch my shoulders and hang my head. "Don't worry about it. I'll call someone first thing tomorrow morning."

"Tomorrow is Sunday. You'll never get someone out here to fix it, and I won't leave you without water."

"Then I'll go to my parent's." I whirl around and try to conceal my anger. I asked for his help. This is my doing. "Please leave. I never should have asked you to help me."

"Jensen..."

"Nash, *leave*. Now!"

He hesitates and sighs but finally says, "Okay."

My eyes squeeze shut, and once again I give him my back. I fight the tears, wanting nothing more than to be left alone. His footsteps retreat down the hall, and then I hear him punch the lock on the handle before he closes it.

CHAPTER 14

*O*nce the door latch clicks, my body sinks to the floor, where I clutch the towel to my chest and cry as loud as I can until my throat is too raw to make any more sounds. I lie on the cold, wet kitchen floor and run my fingers through the puddled water. I wish I could feel it. I wish I could feel anything besides guilt. The guilt of Jeff's death, the guilt of our baby's death, and now the guilt that I let another man into our home and then laughed with him like nothing in my life had changed. Like my whole world wasn't spun upside down. Like the air hadn't been sucked right out of me.

I have no idea how long I've lain on the floor, but I calm down, pick up all of the towels I threw down earlier, and take them to the laundry room. At the front door, I see that Nash must have locked it as he left. I flip the deadbolt and take my clothes off as I walk up the stairs. Since my clothes are soaked I throw them on the bathroom floor before crawling into bed.

My skin is cold, my mind is racing, and I can feel my heart beating. It takes several hours before sleep finds me.

* * *

MY CELL PHONE RINGS, and I swear there is a freight train running through my head. I reach for it, yank on it so that it comes unplugged, and answer it without bothering to see who it is.

"Hey, Parker. How the hell are ya, kid?"

"Lovely."

"You hung over?"

"What? No."

"That's your hung-over voice."

"I am not hung over. Just didn't sleep much."

"Me either. I'm calling you from the on-call room because I can't sleep. You okay?"

"Mmm hmm," I mumble into my pillow.

"Well, you should get the award for the person fullest of shit."

"What else is new?" I throw my arm over my eyes, knowing she's right.

Unfortunately, she's one of those people that is always right and she knows it, so she's never been afraid to throw it in my face. She's also one of those people who has always had her life together. Ever since we met, she told me she would be a doctor. She is. She told me she would move back to the East Coast the first chance she got. She did. And she swore she would never settle down, and she hasn't. We're different, especially in that area. She could always be single, not have a date on Valentine's Day or New Year's, and be totally okay with it. Of course, that just made guys want her even more. I've always envied that about her. I wish more than anything I could be okay without someone, especially now.

"That doesn't sound like my best friend. One of the things I love about you is that you're rarely full of shit."

"These days I'm not quite myself." Just talking to her makes me feel even more pathetic about my life. I dig a little deeper and somehow find the energy to walk to the bathroom and at least try to do something with myself.

"Okay, spill. What's going on?"

I grab the handle of the faucet, but, I have no water. I rub my temples and go back to bed. I throw my body down and stare up into the ceiling. "Rough night, rough week, rough year. I don't know."

"What makes today different then?"

"Well, let's see...for starters, I invited a man into our house last night."

"That a girl! And Parker, I mean this in the kindest way possible kid, but there should be no *our* in that sentence."

"What did you just say?"

"You said into *our* house. It's *your* house."

"Not that. The first thing you said. Did you just encourage the fact that I brought a man into our house?"

"Yep. And you just did it again. There is no *our* anymore, Parker."

I cover my head with the pillow. "I know."

"What? Your voice is all muffled."

I pull my head up and out of the pillow. "I said *I know*."

"I'm sorry. I'm not trying to be hurtful, but I do want you to start to face reality, kid."

"I know that too."

"So let me guess, support group man?"

I sigh. "Yeah."

"Have you gotten his story yet?"

"No, and I'm not going to push."

"Can you at least tell me what he looks like?"

"My God. Are we back in high school? Is that all you still care about?"

"Honey, the important things never change. We'll be having this conversation when we're eighty, except at that point I'll also ask if it still works."

I laugh a little and then realize she thinks that I'll be alone at eighty. "Wait, eighty?"

"Not you, kiddo, me."

"Oh. Why you and not me? I'm the widow here."

"Exactly."

"I'm confused." I roll to my stomach and try to ignore the picture of Jeff and me on the nightstand.

"Parker, you're meant to be with someone. You always have been."

"Then I lost it."

"You'll find it again."

I squeeze my eyes shut as tears start to form. "Liv, don't."

"What?"

"Please don't talk like that. It's disrespectful."

"To who, Jeff?"

I sit straight up, wanting to reach through the phone and wring her neck. "Yes, Jeff!"

"Come on. Do you think Jeff would want you to be alone for the rest of your life?"

I have thought about this so many times. But it doesn't matter. I don't want to move on, not after what I did. So I lie. "Yes."

"There you go again, full of shit."

"Why did you call again?"

"I called to say hi, to shoot the breeze, to check in. But now I want to talk about the man you *confessed* to bringing into your home. The same man you've been spending time with and who seems to be making you happy even though your life has been total hell this past year. *That* sounds like a way better conversation than what I had planned."

"Olivia...my husband died." It comes out in a whisper.

"Yeah...almost a year ago."

"Ten months." And eighteen days. "Do you really think that's an acceptable amount of time to get over it?"

"Parker...you know that you'll never get over it. How could you? You guys were in love. You shared a life together, a child. No one expects you to get over it."

Silence stretches between us. I hesitate before asking my next question. "What do you expect, then?"

"To move forward, to live, to try to find something in this world that makes you happy. So it's been ten months. Is it okay if it's ten years? Please, fill me in on the rules here."

I don't respond. I can't imagine truly being happy again. I'm sure there will be moments when I'll briefly laugh or days I might get through with no tears. But happy? Happy is a sustained feeling that you have when things in your life are good.

"Parker?"

"Yeah?"

"Do something for me, will ya? I want you to find something, just one thing, every day that makes you happy."

I inhale and exhale. "I'm sorry Liv, I can't promise you that. I see the world differently now, and it's a lot harder to find things, even simple things that make me happy."

"Okay, then give me one thing a week. Come on, you can do that."

I'm not one to make promises I don't intend to keep. One thing a week, can I do that? A month ago, I would have said probably not. But that was before Nash. Before I was finally rid of my job. Before I started venturing out of the house to run errands. I want to, I do. I just don't know if I'm capable. "I'll try."

"Atta girl."

After hanging up with Olivia, I pick up my wet clothes from the floor and go downstairs to start laundry, but I have no water. I spend the next few hours tracking down a plumber. By that evening it's fixed, so I start to clean up the kitchen. Cleaning the kitchen leads to cleaning the dining room, which leads to cleaning the family room, and so on and so on. Cleaning has always calmed me. I spray some cleaner on a towel and dust the coffee table when a smile stretches across my face. I think back to my first date with Jeff. I wasn't sure I was going to hear from him again after he spent the night in my apartment. I tried not to overthink it, but the night before our first date, I was so nervous that I got up at 2 a.m. and started cleaning.

Shortly after the bar incident, Jeff had asked if he could take me out for a real date. I of course said yes, and he told me he wanted to take me to this Italian restaurant downtown. He showed up at my door with a bouquet of flowers. I smiled and said thank you, but he noticed something was off.

"What's wrong? Do you not like roses? I thought it was carnations women hated?"

I laughed. "They're very pretty, and they're a wonderful gesture. But I don't like flowers."

He stepped into my apartment with a confused look on his face. "You don't like flowers?"

"No. But it was very sweet of you. Here, let me take those."

He pulled them back and smiled at me. "What's not to like about flowers?"

I shifted my weight and crossed my arms. "Several things, actually. For one, I would rather spend money on something that's going to last instead of something that's going to be dead in a week. And as they're dying, they make a mess with their leaves and flowers falling all over the place."

He smirked at me. "Yes, but you get to enjoy them for a couple of days before those things happen."

"Yeah, but that's when their smell is at their highest, and I hate that smell."

He shook his head before smiling again. "You hate the smell of fresh flowers?"

"Yes."

"Why?"

"Because they remind me of funerals." Jeff stared at me, and his expression turned from confusion to longing.

"You're one of those."

"One of what?" I asked.

"One of those women most men have only heard about but have not actually experienced."

"What do you mean?"

"A woman who is full of surprises, challenging, but so refreshing and adorable you can't help but want to be near her."

My whole body began to tingle as he leaned in and gently kissed me. When he pulled away, I already saw the love in his eyes, and I felt the same thing. I went to grab the flowers again, but he leaned back out of my reach. "I have a better idea. Come on, we're going to be late for our reservation."

I tilted my head and gave him a questioning look, and then grabbed my purse. He held the door open for me. "I don't understand, what are you going to do with those?"

"Give them to someone who will appreciate them."

I slapped him on the arm. "Hey!"

"Well...?"

"I just wanted to be honest with you."

He walked closer and slid his arm to my lower back. "I appreciate that, and it was cute. I never thought about it like that. And I promise for the rest of my life, I'll never buy you flowers again."

Blushing, I asked, "The rest of your life, huh? You seem pretty sure of yourself."

He hesitated and then said, "Yes, I am." I smiled and we walked out of my apartment building. As we did, we passed a little boy who was probably seven or eight dribbling a basketball, and his mom was nearby reading a book.

"Hang on just a sec, okay?" Jeff said.

Jeff walked up to the little boy and talked to him for a few minutes. The mom sat up taller and paid a little more attention to her son. She glared at me, but I smiled, trying to reassure her. We both turned back to the little boy and Jeff. The boy yelled, "Okay." and Jeff handed him the flowers. The little boy, now bursting with excitement, ran over to his mom and gave her the flowers. She laughed and hugged her son.

With a huge grin on his face, Jeff walked back over and took my hand. "Ready?"

I squeezed his hand. We never talked about it again, but Jeff kept his promise. In the several years we were together, he never gave me flowers again. He sent me balloons on birthdays or cards on special occasions. For our first anniversary, he actually sent me a singing quartet to work, but that was just to embarrass me. Jeff always kept his promises, except the one where he promised to grow old with me. I hate him for breaking that promise.

I sit the bottle of cleaner as well as the towel down on the coffee table. I'm haunted by the silence of our house as well as my own beating heart, because that means I'm still here and they're not. I make my way back upstairs, climb back into bed, and throw the cover over me, hoping that sleep comes.

CHAPTER 15

I'm not even sure why I came back to McFadden's. We mentioned in passing our first night here that we could make this a weekly occurrence as opposed to going to support group. But that was before I had yet another breakdown in front of him. I don't even know if Nash will show up after I kicked him out of our—*my* home. I grab my coffee and stand up to leave when I see him walking through the door. He gives me a tight smile, and I sit back down.

"Didn't know if you'd be here," he says.

My eyes stay glued to the table. "I wasn't sure I would come myself."

"You okay?"

"Can we just forget it?" I ask.

"Jensen."

"Nash, please."

He nods but doesn't say anything. He then jumps out of his seat and walks to the counter. I get up myself and walk to the magazine rack. I pick up several, not knowing how long we'll be here or even if I'll be able to focus. I used to love to read, and watch TV and movies. I noticed after Jeff died that most stories revolve around love, couples, happily-ever-afters. Doesn't matter if it's a cop show, sci-fi, or even the news. People live for their love stories, and I can't stand those reminders. At least in magazines I can look at pictures. Pictures of clothes that I no longer care about, gadgets I no longer want to buy, and health concerns I no longer worry about treating. Why bother worrying about taking care of yourself when you have no one to take care of?

Nash slides back into our booth with our coffees. "Did you get your water turned back on?"

"Yeah. I found a plumber that came out on Sunday. He told me that the valve was pretty corroded, so it could have happened to anyone."

"I really am sorry." He rubs the back of his neck.

I swallow hard and try to ignore his fidgeting. "I never should have asked you. It's my fault."

His head slightly flinches. "Why is it anyone's fault?"

"You know what I mean."

"Not really."

"I shouldn't have asked a strange man into my home."

"Strange man?"

"I didn't mean it like that..."

"Why can't you see our relationship for what it is? We're friends."

I pick up my coffee and blow on it before taking a sip. I gently sit it down and rotate it in circles, back and forth, back and forth.

"That's not how you see us?" he asks.

I force my eyes and hands away from my cup and give him my attention even though I don't want to have this conversation. He deserves at least that from me. "That's what scares me, Nash. I don't know how I see us. It's been a long time since I've had a guy friend that wasn't connected to my husband or wasn't one of my girlfriends' significant others. It feels...wrong." I can't look at him anymore, so my eyes dart everywhere but toward him. It doesn't matter though, I can still feel his eyes raking over me.

Several beats pass before he says, "Like you're cheating?"

I don't say anything for several moments. I finally give him a curt nod and feel a tear run down my face. It only makes it half way down my cheek before his thumb brushes it away. I pull back and my eyes fall to his. I'm not sure why he looks so wounded. Shouldn't I be the one wounded in this scenario?

"Jensen, I just want to be here for you, in whatever way you'll have me. I'm trying to be a friend and help you through this." He pauses, I assume to make sure I hear him over the doubts in my own head. *Can I do that?*

He continues, "Let me give *you* what I didn't have when I was going through something similar."

Something similar? "We never talk about you."

"It's not important right now…one day, but not today." Not the answer I wanted, but I said I wouldn't push. I flip a couple of pages of my magazine. I wish he would share something with me. It might make this easier, the grief, the getting to know each other, becoming friends. "We all have a past, Jensen."

He has no idea. I'm sure if he knew how I played a role in my husband's and child's deaths, he wouldn't be sitting here with me. "Some more tragic than others." It leaves my lips before my brain can even process it. I move my hand in front of my mouth as his eyes meet mine.

His head tilts to the side, and then sorrow wraps around him. A few seconds pass before he says, "Yeah, something like that. So…maybe friends isn't a bad idea after all?"

"I'm sorry about how I acted last Saturday. I'm sure that was uncomfortable for you."

"Want to talk about it?"

I run my hand along the table, wiping away remnants of the sweetener I placed in my coffee earlier. No, but I should. I owe him that. After all, I'm the one that invited him in. "I guess I owe you an explanation."

"No."

My head shoots up. "What?"

"Grief is not explainable."

I sigh. "It was the first time I really laughed since Jeff died. I mean, stomach hurting, eyes watering, something-is-truly-funny laughing."

"And you felt guilty?"

"Yes. I felt horrible. How could I laugh after everything that has happened?"

"How could you not?"

I shake my head. "You don't get it."

"I guarantee I get it better than you think. This shit's hard. But you're still here. You lost your husband, but you can't lose yourself too."

I scan his face, his five o'clock shadow, a small scar above his right eye. I want to look him in the eyes, but I can't. I shift my eyes back to the table as I say, "That's not all I lost..."

"Sure you don't want to talk about it?"

I shake my head. "Not tonight."

"Want to go hiking this weekend?"

I bark out in laughter before asking, "What?"

"Hiking." He has a wide grin on his face.

I begin to fidget. "That was random."

"Not really. I think it'd be good for you. Get out of the house. Get some fresh air, get your lungs moving. Ever gone hiking?"

"No."

"Might be good to try something new. I'm already planning on going, so you can join me if you want."

Butterflies soar through my stomach as I ask, "Would it just be the two of us?"

"Yeah, sorry. I typically don't hike with others. It's more therapeutic that way. Want to invite someone?"

"No, that's not why I was asking."

"Oh? Why then?"

I feel a slight surge of adrenaline, like when he told me we were going to the motorcycle show. I want to look away but I don't. "Because I want to go if it's just you and me. I don't feel like being around other people."

"Just you and me."

I'm not sure I'm the hiking type. But he's right. I need a friend. I need a distraction. I need to take a step, even if I already feel as though I'm too close to the edge. "I don't have hiking gear. Do I need it?"

"Only thing you need is decent hiking shoes. I have everything else."

"I can run out to get some tomorrow."

"Okay." He picks up the paper that I grabbed for him, and a grin slowly spreads on my lips.

We relax back into our comfortable silence and eventually call it a night. As I'm driving home, I think about what this weekend may bring. I typically don't think much about the future. Why focus on something that consumes you with fear? Yet I'm looking forward to a hike. I need a change of scenery, and I trust that Nash can provide that for me.

CHAPTER 16

J'm sitting at the dining room table looking out the window again. This is a pretty typical spot for me. For some reason, I feel closer to Jeff here. We liked to cook together, and we made a point to eat at the table almost every night and enjoy the time with one another. We would also spend time on the weekends at the table working on our respective cases.

After going to the mall today to buy hiking shoes, I needed a break. I felt overwhelmed at all of the options. I texted Nash asking him what exactly I should buy, but I never heard back. I've never been much on outdoor activities, or outdoor anything for that matter. But when Nash mentioned it, I realized that was the old me. And at this point, I'm sick of being alone. It's ironic since I'm the one that pushed everyone away. But my family and friends all look at me like I'm broken. Nash doesn't. I'm lost in thought and startled when I hear my phone ring.

"Hello?"

"Hey."

"Hi." There is something about Nash's voice on the phone. I feel guilty for the desire that begins to spread. His voice encases my ears and oozes strength and confidence. I envy that about him.

"Just got off work and read your texts."

"Oh." I chuckle and try to push down the feeling of rejection. I have no right to that feeling. "I thought maybe you were ignoring me."

"No. Can't have our phones in the field. Too many distractions."

"That makes sense."

"Seems like you need some help making a shoe decision."

I roll my eyes. "I can hear you snickering."

"Sorry. I think you're making it more complicated than it needs to be."

"I didn't make it more complicated. The shoe companies made it more complicated. Why does there need to be so many options? I mean low-cut, mid-cut, full-grain, split grain...seriously! My head hurt when I left."

"I take it you didn't buy anything?"

"Oh, no. I bought eight pairs, and now you have to help me choose."

"Eight?" I hear him break out into full laughter now. "You're joking?"

I fold my arms across my chest and wait until he stops laughing. "No, I told you. I've never been hiking and have no idea what I'm doing."

"Have you eaten?"

"No, why?"

"I can grab a pizza and come over to help you choose. That okay?"

I feel a slight flutter in my stomach, but I don't want a repeat of last Saturday. "Do you mind if I come to you?"

"Sure. I'm still at work and need to shower. Give me thirty minutes or so?"

"Great. That will give me time to change and call it in before I come over. Any preferences?"

"Anything with meat on it."

I smile. Typical male. "I'll grab a salad too. Dressing preference?"

"Italian."

"I need your address."

"I'll text it to you so you can use GPS."

"That would be great, thanks."

"See you in a bit."

Thirty-five minutes later I walk up to his house and manage to ring the doorbell with my pinky finger while juggling a pizza box, a six pack of beer, and a grocery bag around my arm.

I hear him yell out, "It's open." But my hands are full so I ring it again.

The door opens and his eyes grow wide. "Oh, sorry. Let me help you."

"Thanks."

He grabs the pizza box and beer. "I love Primo Pies. Good choice."

I kick my shoes off and follow him into the kitchen. "I didn't know we lived so close to one another."

"Yeah, should have told you that the other night." He sits the pizza box on the counter and I follow with the salad. "Would you like a beer?"

"Sounds good." He walks to the fridge and pulls out one bottle. I sit down on the barstool while he opens it for me. I guess he's not drinking. I take a sip and then ask, "How was work?"

He grabs a bottle of water. "Boring."

"I didn't think that happened in your line of work." I watch him move about his kitchen getting out paper plates, napkins.

"When it comes to action in my job, it seems to be feast or famine."

"What do you do when you're not on calls?"

"Restock or clean the truck, complete paperwork. Stuff like that." He has a pained expression on his face while he says it.

"I take it you don't like that part of the job?"

"I don't *hate* it, but it's not why I got into my line of work. I like to stay busy. Time flies when we're trying to help someone as opposed to restocking."

"I get it." I walk over and grab a plate. "Where's your silverware?"

"Whatcha need?"

"Salad tongs and a fork."

He smiles. "No salad tongs. How about two forks?"

"Sure. Typical bachelor," I say and then nudge him.

He gets out the forks and hands them to me. I put some salad on my plate and then do the same for him, but then I stop. This is too easy, too familiar. It's a simple gesture, but there is nothing simple about the meaning of putting together a plate for someone. Couples do that, friends don't. I take a deep breath and close my eyes. I feel hot and my breathing becomes ragged. I then feel someone touch my shoulder.

"You okay?" He gives me a gentle squeeze, and my first instinct is to pull away. Instead, my gaze locks with his. "There you are. Where'd you go?"

"I'm sorry. I just… It's nothing." I pick up a piece of pizza and grab a fork. "Where did you want to eat?"

He pauses. I can tell he's trying to decide if he wants to push me on the issue. I smile and raise my eyebrows.

He scrunches up his lips and narrows one eye at me but then shakes his head. "Outside on the patio? The sun is on the front of the house, so it should be cool."

"Sure." I walk to the sliding glass door. "I'll come back for my beer."

"I'll get it."

"You can't carry all that."

"Watch me." He picks up his plate, his water, my beer, and the salad bowl and shuts the door behind him with his foot, smiling.

"Thanks."

We sit down at the glass patio table and start to eat. "So, you've never been married?"

He laughs. "I knew this conversation was coming after you said the word *bachelor*."

I shrug. "You don't have to answer if you don't want to. I thought that was a mutual understanding between us."

"It is. Just giving you a hard time. But no, never married."

"Ever lived with someone?"

"Nope. You and Jeff live together before you got married?"

"Are you kidding me? No! Our parents would have had a fit. I'm not opposed to it. It's hard to suddenly be married and share your space with someone."

"Meaning?"

I wipe my mouth and try not to dwell on the fact that I feel as though it's someone else's life I'm talking about. I guess if it were someone else's, it wouldn't hurt to talk about. "I mean, it was new and exciting, but some of your independence is gone. I remember the first night I stayed late at the office after we were married. I lost track of time and forgot to call him. He called me in a panic wondering where I was." I exhale while shaking my head.

"What?"

The last moment I saw Jeff flashes in my mind. A few moments pass before I can find the courage to keep talking. "I should have been up pacing that night worried about him, but instead I was asleep in bed."

"Would it have changed the outcome?"

I sigh. "No, but I wouldn't feel like a total asshole for not knowing that my husband wasn't in bed with me where he should have been." I've never had to tell this story to someone before. Everyone who knows me has already been briefed on the circumstances before I even get the chance. I've never been thankful of that until now. I clear my throat and attempt to continue. "Do you remember hearing about that high-speed car chase after a man robbed the convenience store over on Oak? It wasn't quite a year ago."

He inhales a large breath before releasing it. "Yeah," he says.

I try to detach myself as I explain what happened. But how do you detach yourself from the most painful experience of your life? "That's who shot my husband. Jeff had left to buy a gallon of milk. The police told my father that the robbery was already in progress when Jeff walked in. He walked up behind this guy, and the worker there told the cops that the robber freaked out. Jeff struggled with him, and he shot my husband in the head." I set my piece of pizza down. I hadn't realized I was still holding it. "He didn't even take the money. The clerk called the police, and I guess they tracked down the car and chased him for a while before they got close enough to shoot his tires. He shot himself."

I avoid Nash by focusing on the trees that are lush and green and just beginning a new season in bloom. A couple of doors down, kids are screaming and laughing.

"How do you feel about that?" he asks.

My head jerks toward him. "The fact that he was so desperate he committed a crime and then took his own life?"

"Yeah."

"Nothing. I feel nothing for him."

"Really?"

"I mean, I don't think good things about him, but to be honest, I don't think about him much. I got a letter from his widow a few months later. She apologized, said that he had been out of work and that they had a three-month old at home and they were having a hard time putting food on the table. She said she knew it didn't excuse his behavior, but she wanted me to know he wasn't a bad person. I guess we all make mistakes. Plus, hating is such a useless, crippling emotion. It won't change the fact that my husband's dead and I'm alone."

"Doesn't mean you'll be alone forever, Jensen." His hand holds mine, and instead of pulling away, I grab on. He squeezes and the guilt slowly creeps in, so I pull away.

I shrug and tilt the bottle back, tasting the bitter fizz of my beer. I sit it down. "I *want* to be alone."

"Being alone won't bring him back."

Looking back to Nash, I say, "I have no plans of ever being anything but alone."

"Why the hell not?"

"Because he took all of the good in me with him when he died. My strength, my passion, my sense of humor. Now all that remains is a bitter, selfish shell of who I once was."

"You're strong enough to live without him."

I wish he was right. But he doesn't understand. No one does, and I can't explain it. Instead of arguing with him like I have with my mom, my dad, Olivia, and even Julia, I shrug and try to move the conversation back. "I figured you were curious about my story and how I ended up at group so...that's it, that's my story." It's not the whole story. Like why Jeff was out that late or the fact that I was three months pregnant at the time, but it's enough. It's all I can share at this point.

He takes a deep breath, and as opposed to pushing me to say more, he chomps down on his pizza and angles his body away from me.

The sun has set, and it's starting to become a little chilly when he finally says, "Thank you for telling me. I know it wasn't easy."

I don't respond. I pick up my plate and head back inside. He follows and we both move around the kitchen as though we've done it a thousand times. He's so confusing. One minute I feel the tension between us, and the next we're covered in utter silence and it feels completely normal. But there isn't much about me that's normal these days, and I kind of have a feeling Nash is in the same boat. I just don't know why.

I lean against the counter and watch him clean the surface

with a sponge. His black hair is cut short, and he has a combination of charm and easiness about him. Yet, there are times I see that easiness weighed down by something that I can't pinpoint. It's almost like he struggles with making up his mind which person he wants to be.

"Where are these boots we need to check out?" He's put everything away while I've been freely staring at him.

"Oh, they're in the car. I couldn't carry them with everything else. I'll go get them."

"Need help?"

"Nah. I'll be right back."

I walk through the front door to my car and take a deep breath as I lean against it. I take a few more for good measure. *How did I get here?* I don't know this man. But for whatever reason, my walls haven't been up with him. I've always been a person with walls. Tall, thick ones. And with Jeff dying, my heart has been protected like Fort Knox. But Nash is the first person I've met and befriended who didn't know Jeff. Maybe that makes it easier. Or maybe harder. All he knows of me is my current, pathetic self. How could he say I was strong earlier? He knows there is nothing strong about me. He's seen it.

"Jensen?"

My head whips up and I see Nash standing in the driveway next to me. "Huh?"

"You were out here for a while, so I came to check on you. Here, let me help you." He pauses, silently asking for permission. I step aside and let him lean into the backseat to grab the boxes. He gets all but one bag, so I grab that one while he waits for me to cross in front of him back into the house.

I plop down on the floor in the family room and remove box after box. He sits across from me and does the same. After all of the boxes are on the floor, I locate the ones I like best, strictly on looks because I have no idea how any of them are different. "I like the look of these the best."

He examines them. "These look like backpacking boots. What does the box say?"

I pick up the box and read the label. "Yep, is that bad?"

"Not necessary for what we're going to be doing. The midsoles are stiffer and they're typically heavier, which means they'll just slow you down. What else you got?"

For the next twenty minutes, we look over my selections and settle on a mid-cut boot in full-grain leather with a waterproof lining that Nash says I need just in case, whatever that means. But I trust him, so I go with it.

"Thanks for your help." I start to pack up the rest of shoes and return them to their boxes. "Now I can take the rest of these back. When did you want to leave on Saturday?" I'm sad that we have to wait forty-eight hours to spend more time together.

"Around 8:00 a.m. We can spend as much or as little time there as you like. I need to take my truck so that we can haul all the gear."

"Any update on the bike?"

"Yeah, it's going to here sooner than they thought. Next few weeks, actually."

I chuckle as his eyes light up. "I know you're anxious to get it."

"Yes ma'am, I am. You should be anxious too, you know."

"Really, why is that?" I reach down to grab the bags, but Nash beats me to it. He grabs all of them but one again and smirks at me.

"Because you're finally going to get to ride a motorcycle."

I shake my head. "Yeah, we'll see about that." But he's right, I am a little curious.

CHAPTER 17

*N*ash pulls into the parking lot and I gape at the trail. My head then turns toward Nash.

He smiles. "What?"

"Um, that seems steeper than I was expecting."

"You afraid of heights?"

"Nash, one thing you'll learn about me sooner or later is that I'm afraid of a lot of things, even moreso now. I'm not much of a risk taker, not a fan of adrenaline, and I pretty much hate anything outside."

He laughs. "Wow, so glad I brought you." I roll my eyes and he continues. "Duly noted. But the trail is away from the ledge. At least until we get to the top, but the view is worth it."

We grab our packs, secure everything, and head toward the trail as the crunch of the gravel steadies our feet. "So, how long does this take to get to the top?"

"On a good day, three to four hours. Even though it's March, you'll heat up, so we may need to rest here and there."

The trail starts to climb, and I feel a slight burn in my shins. I'm out of shape. I try to focus on the soft breeze and the chirp of the birds in the distance. Spring blossoms perfume the air, and dew sparkles on the leaves of the trees.

We climb for several minutes before Nash breaks the silence. "So, you mentioned your parents?"

"What?"

"That night I was at your house. Do they live here?"

"Oh, yeah. In fact, they live about four blocks from you, over on 15th street."

"Is that where you grew up?"

"I'm not originally from here. I grew up in Springfield, Missouri. Once Jeff and I decided to stay here after law school, they moved here to be closer to us. My mom had been a stay-at-home mom, and by then my dad was retired and they wanted to be closer, even though Kansas City is only a few hours away." I hesitate and take a deep breath. "They wanted to be closer to their grandkids."

I feel the blood drain from my face. I don't look at Nash. I keep my head down and focused on where I'm walking, and he doesn't respond. I'm not sure he heard me until I feel the tension radiating between us. I'm used to it. People don't know what to say when I say things like that. I don't mean to make people uncomfortable; it's just the uncomfortableness of my life. It's amazing how talking about mundane, everyday life can detour into sad, uncomfortable, can-we-please-talk-about-anything-else things.

We climb for a few more minutes, and then he changes the subject. "Did you build your house?"

I internally thank him. "No, it was in the process of being built, so we got to pick out the finishes and colors and do some upgrades we wanted, which was nice. But it was stressful."

"Stressful?"

"Very. Every decision you make feels so permanent, and you can't see it all put together until everything is done. It was overwhelmingly stressful."

"I can see that."

As we proceed on our hike, we go back to our comfortable silence and enjoy the scenery around us. That is, until we continue to climb and the trail turns narrower. I realize I've started to inch closer to Nash as the edge of the cliff has become more visible.

Nash starts to shift to my other side. "Here, why don't you switch sides with me, so I can be closer to the edge?"

"No!" *Where did that come from?*

"You sure?"

I move my hand to my mouth and smile. "Sorry, I didn't mean to yell."

He chuckles. "That's okay. But you don't look comfortable over there. In fact, you look pretty terrified."

I stop to catch my breath and look over the cliff. "I kind of like it."

He walks up behind me. Heat radiates from his body. Nash isn't as sweaty as me but I still smell a hint of it. His ragged breathing brushes against my neck and a shiver runs down my spine. Then I feel him take a step back, and I wish he wouldn't.

"Why?" he asks.

I place my hands on my waist and try to figure it out. "I don't know. I guess it's a different kind of scared." I turn back to him. "And a nice reprieve from what I usually feel. Maybe that was the intervention I needed as opposed to the one my family and friends gave me."

"Intervention?"

"Oh, sorry." I wave my hand and begin to walk again. "Yeah it's a long story. Basically, my family and friends thought they needed to step in and help me. Needless to say, it backfired."

"Well... I, um...I'm sorry to hear that." He breaks eye contact with me and shifts his weight before clearing his throat and for the first time on our hike, he walks ahead of me. I'm a little jarred by the distance he's placed between us. But I shrug it off and try to catch up.

After a few minutes, he stops and looks over his shoulder before saying, "Hope I don't turn you into an adrenaline junkie like me."

"Well, I see the fascination now. Nice distraction."

He strides toward me closing the gap. "So I might just get you on Shirley Jr. after all."

He's determined to get me on that bike. I tell myself to take a step back and put some distance between us. But my thoughts and feelings aren't on the same page, not even the same book. The fascination is growing on me, but he doesn't need to know that. I lean in and whisper into his ear, "Never happening." Then I take off in a sprint up the hill.

"Yeah, yeah, run away because you know I'm right." He yells.

I giggle and hear him sprinting up behind me getting closer and closer.

Thirty seconds later we're both winded and tired so we ease into our normal pace and we continue to climb. I kept my spot on the outside, and I'm enjoying the view. It's breathtaking. I can't believe I've never seen this before. I try to focus on those views as the sweat drips down my neck and back. With my sleeve, I wipe the sweat that has also formed on my brow. "Man, it's getting hot."

"We're almost there." Nash took the lead about thirty minutes ago. He was probably afraid if I continued to be in the lead we would never get there.

"How come we haven't seen anyone else out here?"

He glances at me. "I think this path is a lot less traveled than the others because of how close to the edge it is."

"How often do you come up here?" My shins are now officially on fire, but I'm trying to focus on his deep voice as opposed to how much I would like to lie down and die right now.

"Couple times a month."

The climb is growing steeper, and my steps have slowed considerably. "I'm sure I'm the slowest friend you've ever brought up here." I try to say it without being winded, but I fail.

He switches directions and closes the distance between us. Perspiration runs down the side of his face and disappears under his chin. "I told you, I usually do this alone."

I stop. I need a breather. I tell myself it's from the climb and not the proximity of his body to mine. "So you've never brought anyone else up here?"

"Nope." He rummages in his bag and pulls out a bottle of water. His Adam's apple moves up and down after each gulp.

"Why am I the first?"

He hands the bottle to me. "I thought it might help."

I take a sip. "Why?"

"Because it helped me once…" He's also breathing hard. "Like an old friend who gave me comfort when I didn't know where to turn. It's peaceful. Gets your blood pumping, and then you see the view." He shrugs. "I don't know. It helped me see things differently…clearer, so it was just a little bit easier to face the day."

His description was simple. Nothing special about it, except to me. I feel like he described a salvation I've been searching for. I run past him, almost knocking him over. If I thought my legs and lungs were burning before, I was sorely mistaken. I hear my heart pumping. I feel as though my mouth has never tasted water, and everything burns from my thighs to my shins to even my feet. But I don't focus on that. I focus on the part that could help me. Something that could help me face the day.

My legs pump, my breath struggles, but I push and push and finally see the crest of the hill. Nash's boots thump behind me, and I can feel him right there with me. I see the sky line, but I want to see more, so I take off in a sprint. And then it's before me and I stop, chest heaving. My body tingles as Nash stops at my side, and I get a slight whiff of the scent I associate with him: an earthy cedar combination that brings a sense of peace.

"Jen, meet my friend. A friend who doesn't talk, doesn't judge, doesn't offer advice, doesn't even show pity. Just gives you the most breathtaking view and calming feeling you could ever imagine."

"Wow, this is amazing." *Did he just call me Jen?* I like that he's comfortable enough in our friendship to give me a nickname.

He faces me. "You're right...it is."

I don't turn toward him—I can't. Something in his voice changed, and I don't have the courage to look into his eyes. Our normal ease no longer feels comfortable, so I walk closer to the edge. "You can see the whole city from up here."

He follows me. "You can."

It no longer looks like the city where I met Jeff. Or the city where we fell in love. Or the city where I planned to raise a family. My mind drifts to the land of I Wish. I wish he was still here. I wish we didn't fight that night. I wish I didn't hate him for dying. I wish I didn't hate myself. I wish I hadn't lost our child before he or she ever got an opportunity to take a breath in this world. But those wishes won't come true because what's done is done. Nash's knuckles lightly skim my arm and my hair stands straight up in response. I sigh. I must have been in the land of wishes too long, because it feels like he's attempting to pull me out of it. But let's be honest, no one is strong enough to do that. Maybe temporarily, but I always end up back there. In my daydreams, in my nightmares. It's now where I call home.

"I've always wanted to come up here at night," Nash says with a gleam in his eye. The same gleam he had when he was at the motorcycle show.

He's baiting me with a distraction, and I take it. "*That* we have to do." I wonder what it would feel like and look like and smell like at night. How different just a few hours could be. I inch a little closer to the edge.

Nash grabs my arm. "Hey, not too close."

He's protecting me again. It feels good to be protected. And not in the way my family and friends are trying to protect me since Jeff died. It's almost as if they don't want me to feel the pain. They never talk about what happened. They never talk about him. They never talk about how I lost him. And then our baby. He was already gone, so I can't blame him for that. The second worst thing that ever happened to me, and the lucky bastard had already left me behind. I reach down and put my hand over Nash's on my arm. "Thank you."

"For what?"

"For bringing me here. For reminding me of a world bigger than the four walls of my house." I glance back over the edge. "A world from this vantage point that I don't hate."

He squeezes my hand, and I feel it all the way to my heart. "You're welcome."

I appreciate that Nash knows when to stand in the stillness. He doesn't know much about me, but in a way it feels like he knows everything there is to know. The only thing about my old life he doesn't know about is the loss of my child. And there isn't much to know about my new life. What there is to know, he's already seen. He's lived it with me.

There should be another category in there somewhere. A future category. But how does one even start to think about a future when the only future they ever dreamed of, ever worked for, was taken from them before it even started?

ash's posture is relaxed, and his eyes sparkle with a weightless gaze. It's a look I rarely see him wear. He seems at peace here. "How did you ever find this place?"

"A buddy of mine." A little bit of that easiness drifts away as he sits. "A friend of his in juvie told him that they found weed growing up here once, so he came to check it out. He told me about the view and...the steep cliff." He closes his eyes, and now there is nothing but tension. Between us, in the air, in his muscles, in his jaw. He finally takes a deep breath and turns toward me as his eyes drift down. I don't even realize what I've done until his eyes shoot back up to mine. I have scooted closer to him so there is no longer any space between us.

I should be embarrassed, maybe ashamed, but I'm not. The contact feels good. "Are you okay?" I ask. He swallows hard and then gives me a curt nod. I should pull away, but don't. "Do you want to talk about it?"

One thing I love about Nash is he always looks me in the eyes. Yet right now, he's looking anywhere but. His head bows as his shoulders curl over his chest. "I...don't know. I...Jen, I...I've never told anyone."

He called me Jen again. I like it. "It's okay, take your time."

"I...when I hiked this cliff for the first time, I was on a mission. So desperate. Desperate for the pain to stop, for something, anything to change. I wasn't strong enough to live with what had happened, so I came up here to end it." The last few words come out in such a hurry that I barely understand him. It's almost as if he never wanted them to reach me.

"At the time, I didn't think about it as ending my life. Just ending the pain and the guilt. I couldn't take one more day of having to face it. I felt out of control all the time. On a good day, I tried to live with it. On a bad day, I saw myself as a pathetic loser whose one wish in life was to have died that night too. I was in a constant battle with myself because I survived."

His story comes to a grinding halt. I remain quiet, hoping he's going to say more. I hug my legs to my chest and rest my chin on top. I feel the need to shield my heart from whatever else he's about to say because he was obviously hurt by it. But I'm smarter than that. There is nothing you can truly do to protect your heart. It beats on its own, whether you tell it to or not. It can also speed up, crack, and even fully break without being told. He makes eye contact with me, and I smile to reassure him that I'm here. His shoulders relax, like he's relieved to have finally told someone one of his darkest secrets. I envy him, because I wish I could do the same.

"What stopped you that day?" I say it calmly, making sure my voice is even. No judgment or pity, just curiosity.

He grimaces while looking down the trail we climbed. "Couldn't believe it. I actually still can't. I brought up a piece of paper and pen to write a letter to my family. I didn't have the guts to do it until the bottom of the cliff was staring me in the face. But as I sat down to write it, I only got four words into it when I heard a child screaming, followed by a woman screaming for help. My instincts kicked in, and I dropped the pen and paper and ran toward the screaming."

"What happened?"

He points and says, "I ran down that hill and rounded a corner when I saw a woman trying to get her son's leg free. He'd tripped on a fallen tree and got his foot wedged underneath it. To this day, I don't know how he fell in that position. She told me he was running up the cliff when he tripped and tumbled backward. He was unconscious when I reached them. He had a huge gash on his head and there was a lot of blood. I came to her side, and it took both of us to free his leg. Once we did, we both knew we needed to get him down the cliff and call for help. She had forgotten her phone in her car, and I hadn't brought mine." He looks over at me and shrugs. "I didn't think I would need it. I told her to run ahead and get help and that I would carry her son down. The ambulance was arriving as I came down with him. I handed him to the EMT, and the mom threw herself into my arms crying and thanking me for saving her son's life. And in that moment, I knew. I knew that if I had thrown myself over that cliff, it would have been *another* waste of a life, and that wasn't the answer. It felt so good to help someone. Almost like I might be able to save myself by doing so. I realized *that* was the adrenaline rush I wanted every day. The next day I went to Crown William University and talked to an advisor about being a paramedic, and that focus stayed with me until I graduated. It stays with me every day I go into the field. It gives me something to hold on to, knowing that I can save a person or at least make a difference in their life. Even if I hold a kid's hand while someone checks him over after falling off his bike, I know it made a difference to that kid."

I regret not pressuring him to tell me what led him to the cliff in the first place. But I won't break our mutual understanding, and I won't push him to open up to me. Even though I can't fathom how someone like Nash could ever think about killing himself.

"Can I tell you something?" I ask.

"Yeah."

"I think you're pretty amazing, and I'm glad that you didn't do it. And you don't only help people in life or death situations, Nash. You've helped me just by being my friend."

He smiles at me, a fascinating smile to match a fascinating soul. "Thanks."

The comfortable silence returns, and we both move our eyes to the view in front of us.

"I was pregnant." I say it quietly, but it's out of my mouth before I have a chance to stop it. I don't want to hear it; I don't want him to hear it. But I want him to know. It's important to me that he knows. "You don't have to say anything." I focus everything I have on the view. The unbelievable view I'm supposed to be finding some sense of joy or comfort in. Yet I no longer feel it.

"I lost the baby a few days after Jeff died. The doctors tell me it could have happened without the stress. That we would never exactly know why..." I talk about it with no emotion. This part of my life feels detached from me. I can grieve Jeff. That I understand. We had memories that I can lean on. I knew what I loved about him, and even the things I didn't but still accepted. I wonder if it would have been the same as a mother. That there are things you love about your children and things that you wish you could change. Or is it really unconditional, no matter what, because they're your flesh and blood? I don't know, nor do I think I ever will. When our baby died, those feelings and the sense of wonder died with them. I no longer wish to be a mother. If I lost another child, I wouldn't need a cliff to jump over. I would already be dead.

I don't notice him stand up. I don't notice him step in front of me. But I do notice when his hands grab my arms and pulls me up to his chest. I lean in and hug him back. He tenses at first, but then he inhales and moves his face into my hair. And I hate the fact that there is something so right about being in his arms that I slowly run my hands down his back, and return them to my side where they should be. He pulls back and looks down at me, and then he gives me a tight smile as we walk down the cliff in silence.

CHAPTER 19

*W*e finally reach the truck. Nash walks around to the bed, takes his pack off, and then grabs mine. He reaches into a cooler to hand me a water. "Here, nice and cold."

"Thanks."

He pulls one out for himself, and then climbs into the truck as I follow.

"Man, I'm looking forward to a shower. Good thing I got my water fixed," I say.

"No kidding. Do you want to grab a bite or anything?"

"Oh...well, we can if you want. It's just that I'm pretty sweaty and tired. I think that's the most physical activity I've gotten since Jeff died." His head whips around, chin on his chest. And I realize what I just said. "Wow, um, that came out wrong. I meant that you know...I used to exercise and stuff, but since Jeff died it hasn't been a priority, so my body is out of shape and I'm not used to the grunting and groaning that comes with physical exertion. Oh my God! Wow. I'm going to shut up now."

He laughs and lightly brushes my shoulder, "It's okay. I knew what you meant."

I can't help but laugh at the awkwardness of the situation. "No you didn't. I saw your face whip around when I said it."

He chuckles. "Okay, yeah maybe. Makes sense now. It just came out...a little wrong, that's all."

"Yeah, tell me about it." Heat covers my face as I blush from embarrassment. But there's nowhere to hide, so I might as well try to find the humor in it.

Nash turns the key over and pulls out of the dirt lot and onto the main highway. We sit in silence. I'm not even sure where we're going. He mentioned a bite to eat, but after my mouth vomit he didn't mention it again. And I'm not sure if I want to get a bite to eat with him. We've had a great day, but I need a time-out. A lot has happened today, and I don't know how to feel or what to think about any of it.

He must have sensed my reservation about dinner because he pulls into my driveway, and I feel my body relax at the prospect of being by myself. He turns off the truck and leans back against his door. He opens and then closes his mouth as a pensive expression crosses his face. The weight I saw lifted from his shoulders on the cliff has now returned, and I'm not sure why. Maybe now that we're back in the real world, he's uncomfortable about what he shared? I hope not, because I'm not. I'm glad he knows. He knows everything now. Well, almost everything. But the guilt I carry, and the why of it, I will take to my grave.

"Nash, seriously, thank you for today...for taking me to the cliff, for opening up to me. Your friendship means a lot to me."

He runs his hand through his hair and says, "You're welcome. I'm glad I opened up to you too. It's been a long time since I've done so...but...you make it easier."

"I know what you mean. I don't really talk to anyone either...well, my best friend Olivia, but she's not here, so I don't get to talk to her as much as I would like."

"Where is she?"

"She lives in New Haven, Connecticut. She's a doctor at Yale."

"Wow."

"Yeah, it's kind of a dream job for her, and she's one of the youngest doctors there, so her schedule is a disaster. We sometimes go months without talking to one another, but we always pick up right where we left off. Well, we used to go months, but now she checks up on me more. But not much has changed in my life in the past nine months or so." He slowly nods. And then I realize how that sounded. "Oh wow, that came out wrong too. I didn't mean that." I bury my face in my hands. "Man, I'm putting my foot in my mouth today."

He laughs. "It's okay. I knew what you meant."

"No, really." I look back up at him. "I talk about you all the time to her. Well not all the time, but...wow. Okay, Jensen, shut up."

"Jen, it's okay. You're cute when you're nervous and rambling." I jerk my head in his direction and see his face flush with embarrassment. "Wow, it's contagious. Now I'm saying things I shouldn't."

My hand fumbles for the door handle. I finally reach it and throw it open before saying, "Um yeah...okay...well, I guess I'll see you later." I jump out of the car, grab my backpack from the truck bed and run up the porch steps as fast as my sore body will allow.

CHAPTER 20

$\mathcal{I}$ set my backpack on the dining room table, unzip it, and begin to remove its contents, unable to get what Nash just said out of my mind.

It was just a friendly thing to say. He didn't mean anything by it. Why am I making it a big deal? I've learned that if you keep moving and do something, you can trick your mind into focusing on something else. So I empty my bag, carry it upstairs, and throw it in the closet before heading to the shower.

But in the shower, my mind drifts back to Nash. I'm surprised at how he opened up. Nash doesn't seem like the type of person who would ever consider suicide. But unfortunately, I now understand what grief can do to a person. As I'm getting out of the shower and wrapping the towel underneath my arms, I can't help but to wonder what could have happened for him to even consider that.

Even though I've been consumed with grief and guilt, I've never thought about taking my own life. Are there days that I wish I were dead with them? Absolutely. But thinking about actually taking my life has never been a viable solution. I couldn't put my family and friends through any more grief than what they've already experienced.

I'm trying to be as patient with him as he's been with me, but I wish he would open up more. I don't know why he was at a bereavement support group. I don't know anything about his family and friends. But it's not like he's hiding something. We've been in public together. He's invited me over to his house. He just seems really private and I shouldn't pry. He hasn't asked me things about my life that I didn't want to share, so I should do the same and respect that mutual understanding between us.

After talking about Olivia to Nash, I realize it's been awhile since I called her when I'm having a good day so I take the opportunity to do it now.

"Hey, hooker," Olivia says.

"Well, I take it you're not at work answering like that."

"Nope, you happened to catch me on my night off. I'm hanging out with some of the nurses from work, trolling for guys. What are you doing?"

I sigh. I'm constantly forgetting that other people's lives are still going on. I can hear the music in the background as well as voices. "Oh nothing, but I can let you go. I just wanted to say hi."

"Hang on a sec." I hear Olivia tell her friends she's leaving and will see them tomorrow at work. "Okay, I'm all ears, kid. What's going on?"

"Liv, don't leave on my account. I can talk to you another time."

"Bullshit. I want to talk to you. Plus I already got my coat from the coat-check, and I'm hailing a cab. So spill, sister. What's going on?"

"Nothing. I really am just calling to say hi." I can hear Olivia moving around on the other end of the phone.

"110 Church Street. Sorry. So, you're okay?"

I feel guilt that she assumes the only reason I call her is when I need her to comfort me. "Yes, I'm okay. I actually had a pretty good day."

"Were you with Nash?"

"Yeah, how'd you know?"

"I don't know, maybe because he's the only one you ever talk about anytime we text."

I yank the pick through my hair as it gets stuck on a tangle. "What does that mean?"

"What?"

"What's that supposed to mean, Liv?"

"It's not supposed to mean anything—unless you want it to."

"I feel like you're insinuating something."

"Nope, I thought I was just stating the truth. Is there a problem with that?"

"Seriously Olivia, you don't waste your breath unless you're trying to make a point, so what is it?"

"I meant nothing more than what I said. You don't talk about anything else when I talk to you. It's not a bad thing."

"Yes, it is. You're making it seem like...I don't know...that...I don't know, I just don't like what you're implying."

"I'm making it seem like you might have feelings for him, is that what you wanted to say?"

"No! Olivia I don't have feelings for him. We're just friends."

"Okay."

"That's it? That's all you're going to say?"

"What do you want me to say?"

"I don't know."

"Thanks, keep the change." I hear a car door slam and Olivia walking up the stairs as her breathing becomes more labored. "I'm glad you had a good day. What did you do?"

"He took me hiking and..."

"Hiking? You don't hike!"

"I realize that, Liv, but there's lots of things I do now that I didn't use to, like go days without showering or eat cookie dough for dinner. Do you really want to get into all that?"

"No, keep going."

I sigh heavily. "Anyways, we went hiking and there was something therapeutic about it. Parts of it were narrow, and the edge was terrifying, but I liked it. The view was amazing. It's the first time I've felt some peace...since Jeff died." I want to tell her how Nash was protective when I got closer to the edge or how it felt being in his arms. But I don't. Because then I would have to admit out loud what I felt, and I don't want it to be true.

"I can't imagine you hiking, but if it helps I'm glad."

"It did. And I even think it helped Nash a little. He finally opened up to me."

"*Finally*. What kind of dirt did he give you?"

"What is wrong with you?" I hear the faint sound of a cork being popped, and as usual Olivia is opening a bottle of wine to settle into our conversation.

"What kind of best friend would I be if I didn't help you analyze the crap out of his twisted past?"

I shake my head at the humor in her voice. "You would think after all these years you wouldn't still shock me."

"You would think."

"He doesn't have a twisted past. Well, I don't think anyway."

"Parker, everybody has a past."

"I'm aware of that, painfully aware. I made an ass out of myself tonight in reference to my past."

The gulping on the other end stops when she asks, "How so?"

"When we got back to the truck, I put my foot in my mouth and said something about not getting that physical since Jeff died."

I hear Olivia splutter and then start to laugh. "You just made me spit out my wine. You're joking?"

I walk into the bedroom and flop onto the bed, covering my eyes with my arm. I didn't realize how bad it sounded until I said it out loud. "No, I then started rambling in the car and put my foot in my mouth again, and then he told me I was cute." I wait for Olivia to say something, but she doesn't. "Well?"

"Well what?"

"Well, isn't that wrong? I mean, telling the grieving widow she's cute?"

"You can't be a grieving widow forever."

"What's that supposed to mean?"

"Exactly what I said."

I feel my face flush, and that anger I've grown so accustomed to is starting to announce its unwelcome visit. "So, you think it's okay for him to be hitting on someone whose husband hasn't even been dead a year?"

"Was he hitting on you or paying you a compliment?"

"I called you so that you could help me, not confuse me more."

"I'm sorry. But I don't think you're confused. I just don't think you're ready for what's happening. And that's okay."

"What are you talking about?"

"You're my best friend, and I love you more than most of my own family members, but haven't you lost enough?"

"I don't understand."

"You lost your husband and your child. You gave up your career and pretty much every one of your and Jeff's friends, and you barely talk to your family anymore. Are you going to give up every chance at happiness for the rest of your life?"

I squeeze my eyes shut. She's trying to help, but I don't want to hear this. Olivia doesn't understand the guilt I carry. They wouldn't be dead if I hadn't been so selfish, so yes, I will give up every chance because I don't deserve to be happy.

"Jensen?"

"Don't call me that. It's weird. You never call me that."

"Kiddo, I don't want to upset you, but you also know I'm going to tell it to you straight."

"I know." I desperately need to change the subject. This conversation is over. "So, how's work?"

"Is that really what you want to talk about?"

"Yep. I called to check in to see how my best friend is doing."

"If you want to change the subject, I'll let you...for now."

I listen, reply when necessary, and act interested in what Olivia's saying, but I'm relieved when the conversation finally wraps up. We've been at different stages in our lives for quite some time now. She's busy with her career and still does the bar scene when she has time. She's also tried online dating, but overall Olivia is one of those people who doesn't need someone in her life to be happy. She has a career and great friends and could survive on the occasional one-night stand here and there. I have never envied that about her because I'm a relationship girl. I've never had a one-night stand and never even casually dated. I had a boyfriend in high school and one in college, and besides a few dates for sorority parties that my friends set up, that was it besides Jeff.

Yet I now find myself stuck in this in-between of never imaging myself in a relationship again while knowing I can't live my life alone either. One of those stupid grief books my mom gave me showed a chart about how people who were happily married when their spouse died have a greater chance of getting remarried. That doesn't make sense to me. Wouldn't those people be so devastated that they wouldn't be able to move on? Or is that just how I feel? Or is that the guilt talking?

I climb into bed, wet hair and all. I hope that the hiking has made me tired enough to get a good four to five hours of uninterrupted sleep. I get the covers just right when I hear a text come through on my phone. I figure it's Olivia texting to apologize for being so blunt. But I don't feel like talking any more tonight, so I ignore it. It beeps again. Annoyed, I lean over and pick up the phone from the nightstand. I'm surprised to see Nash's name on the screen.

Hey...hope you're not sleeping...

I was laying here trying to sleep and I couldn't stop thinking about what I said. Sorry I made you uncomfortable. We had a good day today, and I didn't want that to be the last thing that I said to you. I'm sorry. See you Tuesday.

I read it and immediately feel ashamed of how I handled the situation. I don't want to make him feel bad. I need to get over my own issues. He's been nothing but supportive and nice to me, even when I haven't deserved it.

Hey. I'm awake. I should apologize to you. I overreacted...I'm sorry. It's been so long since I've had a guy friend and I've forgotten how to do this. And there's all these other feelings I'm trying to work through, but I think today I realized...you're my best friend and it scares me.

I don't want to put myself out there like that, but it's a little easier since it's through a text and not face-to-face.

Why does that scare you?

I debate how honest I want to be. I know what Olivia was trying to get me to admit. I'm battling with why I'm so defensive. Because it's not true or because she couldn't be more right?

I don't know. I'm still trying to figure that out. I'm not going to pretend that I'm easy to like. Most days I don't know up from down. But one of the few things I do know is that I appreciate your friendship...and I don't want to lose it.

I'm nervous when Nash's response takes longer to come back than the others. I'm ready to jump out of bed when he finally gets back to me.

Jen, you're so easy for me to like that it scares me too. I opened up to you so easily and I can't explain it. You're my best friend too so you're not going to lose me. I know things are hard now but it won't always be this hard. I'm sure that's difficult to hear and even more difficult to imagine but you have to start to believe it.

I read the text three times, and I can feel the apprehension in what he's saying. I feel better hearing him say he's not going anywhere. I can't lose him. I also don't know if I have the strength to totally let someone else in, knowing that in the end, that's exactly what could happen. I think about that longer than I should because he texts me back before I respond.

Please tell me I didn't upset you with my last text?

I respond. *No, sorry...just thinking. Thank you for being honest, that's all I ever want you to be. But right now, I can only see the day in front of me and when the sun goes down and the lights go out, I see nothing ahead of me, only what was behind me.*

That's okay. You haven't let go yet.

If you're telling me I have to let go of my past to jump into my future, I'm not sure I'm capable.

I know it feels like that right now...

But what if it always feels like that?

I don't know Jen. I don't have the answer to that, I think only you do.

A sudden coldness envelops my body. This is the first time that Nash hasn't imparted some great words of wisdom, and it scares me. I don't have the answer to that, either. I know Jeff is gone, and I know my child is gone. What I don't know is where that leaves me. So, if I'm supposed to have the answer, I'm screwed.

I set my phone down and throw my body under the covers, praying for sleep.

CHAPTER 21

*J*t's been over two months since Nash and I first went hiking. We've never talked about it again, any of it. I'm waiting, trying to be patient for him to tell me more, but he hasn't yet. We've hiked several more times and have done numerous things around the city as friends, but we've never shared like we did that day. Most of the time we just enjoy the peace in the quiet that we both seem to be comfortable with.

I haven't been back to support group either, but my mom no longer fusses about it. She's mentioned to me that I've put on some weight and that my dark circles aren't as pronounced. I also laughed the other day in front of her when she drank expired milk in her coffee. The look on her face was priceless. She looked happy, like she just saw me take my first step. Maybe in a way I did. It was the first time I laughed with someone besides Nash since they've been gone.

Even though Nash and I never attended support group again, we've never missed a Tuesday. Even with his weird schedule. Sometimes we've done breakfast after he got off of work, or we even went at 4:00 p.m. one day before his night shift. I guess you could say we started our own little support group.

I'm already in the back at our normal table when he pulls up on Shirley, Jr. He walks in, confident as always, and heads straight for me.

"Hey you," he says.

"Hey." I slide his cup of coffee toward him. We've gotten into a habit of whomever gets here first makes the first purchase. He usually beats me, and I think he secretly tries to one up me.

He looks at me with concerned eyes. "You seem upset today. Something going on?"

"That obvious?" Maybe the dark circles and the slightly greasier hair is a giveaway.

"The red nose and puffy eyes don't really suit you."

"Sorry, you're probably embarrassed to even be seen with me." I wipe my fingers under my eyes and try to make myself look more presentable. I tried before I left the house, but I guess I wasn't successful.

"Jen, I could never be embarrassed by you. Okay, that's not true. I was embarrassed when you accidentally leaned against that wall with the "Wet Paint" sign. Then you walked through the restaurant with it down your side." He starts laughing, and I kick him under the table.

"You promised you would never bring that up again."

He raises his hands in the air. "Okay, okay, you're right. Sorry. What's going on?"

I feel the smile fade as my lips turn inward. When I saw the date on my phone this morning, I couldn't believe it. Six days. In six short days, it will have been a whole year since he's been gone. "The one-year anniversary of Jeff's death is coming up next week...."

"Oh."

It didn't seem possible. But the past few months have been a lot different than the ones right after. At that time there was a chaos that surrounded me. Nothing mattered. Nothing made sense. And I refused to accept it. But now I've settled into widow life. It's not a place I can stay in forever, nor do I want to. I will eventually have to step back into the land of the living and at least start earning a wage again. But I will always be a widow. I will always be a mother without a child. And I can't continue to live in a house I can't afford. Even if I don't know what the next step is.

"Yeah." I sit my coffee on the table and then lean in, like I have a secret to share. "But a part of me is relieved."

His cup was almost to his lips, yet he hesitates and glares at me before sitting it back down. "Okay, why?"

"I know that's horrible. It's just that I've read so many of these damn books, and they all talk about how the first year is the hardest. The first birthday, the first Christmas, the first anniversary of their death. So my mind is telling my heart that there's just one more hurdle to get through before this starts to get easier. And it's stupid. It's not like I'm going to wake up the day after and everything will be fine. Plus, I lost the baby a few days later, so..." I haven't mentioned the baby since the hike. Talking about Jeff is hard, but talking about our unborn child will always be unbearable to me.

"I understand and I'm not judging you. Life is hard enough without people judging you through it. I also don't think you being relieved is a horrible thing. But I'm glad you realize that everything won't be fine. It will be another hurdle, but it's not going to make all the pain go away. Time won't even do that Jen, but you know that."

"I'm no longer Jeff's wife..." That's the first time I've said that out loud.

"No. You're not."

"So who am I?"

"Maybe it's time for you to figure that out."

"How? How do I do that? I don't want this life."

"But you have it, whether you want it or not."

I place my head in my hands. I think back to law school, when

I was truly finding out who I was, and I can't help but think of Jeff. I grew into a woman with him. Every decision I made was influnced by his decisions. I became the type of lawyer I did because he wanted to be a trial lawyer. I knew one of us would need a more flexible schedule if we wanted kids. We stayed in Kansas City to be closer to his family. And since I was an only child, my parents moved here to be closer to me. I made a lot of sacrifices for him and for our future, and at the time, I didn't consider them sacrifices because I loved him. I sigh and take a sip of my coffee while Nash stares at me. "We all have forks in the road in our lives that we have to choose, and once you do, you can't go back."

"You don't need to go back, you need to go forward."

"What are you saying?"

He scrubs a hand over his face. "What do you want me to say?"

I scoff. "You and Olivia both! Can't either of you give me a straight answer when I need it?"

"I'm sure you feel lost, Jen. I understand—I do. But only you can find your way back. And when I say back, I mean back to you, the *new* you."

I close my eyes and try to drown out the hum of laughter and talking. I focus on the aroma of coffee and take a deep breath before saying, "But it's all gone."

Nash grabs my hands and moves them toward him. "You! You're not gone, you're right here."

I sigh. "That's a little cliché."

"It's not." He nostrils flare, and I can tell he's trying to remain patient, but I don't know what he expects me to say. There's too much fog to make my way through.

"I don't know, okay! I mapped my life out, worked hard, got everything I wanted, and then in one brief moment, it was all gone."

"I get that. So what do you want now?"

"Besides what I had?"

"Yes, Jensen. If I could give that to you, I would. But…you know that life is gone."

Glancing around the coffee shop, I see a few people staring at us. I must have been talking louder than I realized. Tears prick at the back of my eyes, but I manage to hold them back "I know…I just…I don't know how to live without them."

"It's going to take time. But you have to acknowledge they're gone and accept it before you can move on."

"What if I don't want to move on?"

"I'm sorry, but I just don't believe that anymore."

"What the hell is that supposed to mean?"

"Jen, I've seen you make so much progress these past few months. You smile, you laugh, you shower. We hang out. You're able to function in public. When was the last time you had a panic attack? I can't imagine you going back to drifting through life like when I met you. Is that what you want?" He proceeds without waiting for a response from me. "Is it going to be hard? Yes. Are there going to be days that guilt takes over, that anger takes over for being in this shitty situation in the first place? Yes. And I can guarantee there will be times you'll be so sad you don't want to get out of bed. But I don't believe that you're not going to fight your way through it, because that's not who you are."

I take a deep breath and slowly release it. "I guess…"

"Let's just focus on getting through next week, okay?" I nod and then watch him force himself up and out of the booth. He moves away and navigates the entire distance of the coffee shop. He paces in short spans before he returns to the booth. When he sits, he's his normal, calm, cool and collected self. What he has to be mad about, I have no idea.

CHAPTER 22

*I*t's anniversary day. I've always thought of anniversaries as happy occasions. Not today. I'm in bed, but not sleeping. I knew today would be hard. How do you prepare for something like this? I was very clear with my mother that I didn't want her checking on me. She's been talking with Doris, Jeff's mom, and they've been pushing me to go through his things. I get it. I'm sure there are things of his she wants. But it must be in my time, and I'm not ready.

My mother asked me earlier in the week what I planned to do today. I looked at her like she was crazy. What's the protocol for officially being a widow for a year? I guess I can go back to bright colors and life just moves on, right?

The clock reads 2:38 a.m. It's the same clock I looked at the night I heard the doorbell ring. For some reason, the doorbell ringing is what I remember the best. I don't remember running to the door. I don't remember letting the two police men in. I do remember holding on to my stomach, trying to protect our unborn child because I knew my life was about to change forever. My parents showed up at some point. I know my mom put me to bed. I know they called my OBGYN and she made an unheard-of house call and told my family to watch over me and do whatever they could to take the stress off me. But I remember none of this.

The next thing I remembered was the closet light shining in my face. I glanced around. The room was dark, but I could see light lurking beneath the shades. I heard someone rustling through the closet, and then my mom walked out with one of Jeff's suits.

I sat up and felt my face flush with anger. "What are you doing?"

My mother, clearly startled, jumped back. "Honey, I thought you were sleeping."

"What are you doing, Mom?"

"Well, honey, the funeral home...they need...honey, they need something to bury him in."

"And you didn't think I should have a say in that?"

"Oh honey, I didn't want to bother you with it."

I threw the covers off and walked up to my mom. "Give me that." I ripped the suit from her hands and walked back into the closet. I rehung the suit and went to the end of the row where Jeff kept his favorite suit. It was the first one he had splurged on when he won his first big case. I then grabbed the blue pinstriped shirt that he liked to wear with it as well as his dark gray tie. I picked up his favorite cufflinks and his black shoes. I walked out and handed them to my mom. "Here. He should wear this."

I walked over to the dresser and pulled out a clean pair of boxer briefs and black socks. I held these out for my mother to take and avoided eye contact with her. I was angry with her for a long time for that. I couldn't believe she would make a decision like that without me. But looking back on that time in my life, I wasn't capable of making any decisions.

Everyone was trying to protect me since I was three months pregnant. We had just told our family and friends I was pregnant only two weeks before. In the end, it didn't matter. I'm not sure which day was worse. The day I lost my husband or the day I lost our baby.

I don't remember much between the time I picked out Jeff's suit and the day of the funeral. There were lots of things that happened in between. People came by. They dropped off flowers, which I demanded be removed. They dropped off food I never ate. They offered condolences I didn't want.

I do remember walking into the funeral home the morning of his funeral and being knocked in the face with the overwhelming smell of flowers. I remembered when Jeff promised to never buy me flowers as long as we were together. I guess he kept that promise. But I never envisioned being surrounded by them on the day I would say goodbye after spending such a short time with him.

My mother was annoying me that morning because we were running late and she was making a big deal about it. My mom led me or, more accurately, dragged me into the lobby and told me that we were in the large chapel. As I turned the corner, I saw the pastor from our church marching toward us.

My mother had made all of the arrangements, so I let her continue to run the show. I remember her saying, "Good morning, Pastor. I'm sorry we're running late."

"That's okay, I understand." He released my mother's hand and reached for me. "Jensen, my deepest sympathies. Jeff was a wonderful man and will be truly missed." I didn't take his hand, and he finally moved it back to his side. "If you don't mind, there are some details of the service I would like to go over with you before we begin?" I felt him come around to my side, and he placed his hand on my elbow and I stepped away from him as fast as I could and followed him wherever he was leading us.

"Please have a seat. I just want to make sure I have some dates correct, names, those sorts of things." The pastor pulled out a piece of paper and laid it in front of me.

As I scanned it, I realized it was my husband's entire life laid out before me. His birth date and place. His parents' names. His sister and friends. When we met. The day we married. And then, there in black and white, read a list of survivors. My eyes found them like they were jumping off the page: "Survived by his wife, Jensen Parker Landry and his child, Baby Landry, both of the home." I reached down and grabbed my stomach and finally felt the tears start to flow. They came in such a rush. I couldn't stop them. For the first time since Jeff died, I cried. I sobbed so hard that I couldn't catch my breath.

My mother grabbed my shoulders and wrapped her arms around me, "Oh honey, it's okay...it's okay..." She said as she shushed me.

But I didn't want to be shushed. "It's not okay. Nothing will ever be okay again." I picked up the piece of paper and waved in front of her face. "Look, his whole life fits on one little piece of paper. It should be a book. He was so amazing and didn't get to do all the things he was supposed to do. His child will never know the type of person he was or how much he loved them." Screams erupted from my lungs and took over for the sobs that had been escaping. The pastor walked over and tried to calm me down. But it had no impact. The only thing I could focus on was the fact that my husband was gone. He had left me to care for our unborn child alone.

My father rushed through the door. I looked at my father and saw heartbreak as he watched me. I should have stopped, but I couldn't. "He's dead, Dad. He's *dead!*" I screamed as loud as my body would allow. Everything that I had kept pent up for the past few days came out. The anguish and guilt that he was at that damn convenience store because of me.

I began to hyperventilate, and my father rushed to my side. "Calm down, Jensen. Breathe."

"I don't want to calm down. He's dead."

"Shhhh, shhhhh. I know sweetheart, I know." My dad

wrapped me in his arms and tried to soothe me, but I pushed back.

"You don't know. I'm twenty-nine years old and my husband is dead. He was the love of my life. How am I supposed to go on without him? How am I supposed to raise a child without him?"

The door flew open, and Jeff's family as well as Olivia came rushing in. Jeff's mom, Doris, pushed through everyone. "We heard her screaming. What's going on?"

I had never seen Doris look that way. She had a hard life raising Jeff and Jeff's sister, Megan, all by herself. She was a strong woman and had done a great job. But on that day, the day that she was to bury her son, her baby, I watched her break. She broke as she watched her son's wife, pregnant with their unborn child crumble into a pile of nothing.

I began to pace back and forth and sob, asking why over and over. Doris walked up to me and tried to console me, but I pushed away from her too. Olivia was the only one who kept her distance.

I heard the pastor say, "I'm going to tell the guests we're going to start late." He walked out of the room while my family continued trying to calm me down. Then everything stopped and it got very quiet. A wave of pain rushed through my abdomen, and I cried out. I bent over and grabbed onto a chair to balance myself, feeling as though I couldn't stand up anymore. I heard my family members rush to my side, but my mother got there first.

"Jensen, honey, what is it?"

I didn't reply. I was hunched over and let out another cry. This wasn't normal. This wasn't about grief. "Something's wrong...something's very wrong."

Megan gasped, "On my God, look at the floor." All eyes shifted to the floor, and I watched as everyone went pale. Looking back on it, I already knew what was happening, but I refused to believe it. It wasn't until I followed their line of sight, and saw the stream of blood that I had left in my pacing wake, that reality started to sink in. I moved back and looked at my legs. Two red streams trickled down both legs. Everyone was frozen with shock until I heard a bloodcurdling scream.

"No! Oh God! No!" It was me screaming.

I heard my mom tell my father to call an ambulance. I watched him take off running into the hallway.

I fell to my knees and clutched my stomach while still screaming, "God, no...please no!"

I felt light headed and started to sway. Megan's husband, Todd, scooped me up. "There isn't enough time. The hospital is only two miles away. I'm taking her." My family watched as he carried me out of the room like a rag doll.

I remember drifting into unconsciousness, but before I was completely gone, I heard a male voice stop Todd and tell him that he was a paramedic and could help.

My eyes were closed and Todd's voice was distant, but I remember hearing him say, "No, we're just going to take her to the hospital, she's losing too much blood. We have to get her there now."

* * *

I ROLL over and look away from the clock. Time is not my friend, and I don't want to be reminded what today is. I've relived those days so many times in my head it's like a horror movie about someone else's life. But as much as I wish that were true, it's not. It's my reality. And even though it's been a full year, everything inside of me feels the same, even though everything has changed.

CHAPTER 23

J glance at the clock again. It's now after 9:00 a.m. The one thing I was clear on was that I didn't want to see anyone. So I'm confused and angry when I hear a car pull into the driveway. It idles for a few seconds before the ignition shuts off. I'm tempted to climb out of bed and glance out the window to see who it might be. But then I don't care. I have no plans to answer the door no matter who it might be.

Another car pulls up, but this one is louder. It also idles for a few seconds, but as opposed to the ignition turning off, it remains idling. I hear a car door open and shut, and then a trunk closes, followed by another car door. I sit up in bed when I hear Nash's voice. It's muffled and I have to strain to hear it, but I would recognize it anywhere.

"Who are you?" he asks.

"The best friend. Who are you?" *Olivia?* Olivia is here? I have the inclination to jump up and run down to the door and let her in. I haven't seen her since the funeral. She stayed with me until they put me in the hospital, but after that no one could reach me, and she had to go back to her job. She told me later she felt horrible about leaving, but I reassured her. I didn't want her here. It was bad enough having other people see me absent and broken. I didn't need her seeing it too.

"The other best friend," Nash responds. Hearing him tell Olivia that he's my best friend does something unexpected to my stomach. Tack it on with the other emotions I'm feeling today. I feel a light twinge of guilt eavesdropping, but Olivia will tell me about it later anyway.

"Ah, you must be Nash," she says. I hear her luggage rolling closer to the house. I can't help but climb over the bed frame and peek out the window.

"And you must be Olivia." Nash extends his hand toward her. "Nice to meet you."

"You too."

"Sorry...Jen didn't tell me you were coming."

"Jen? Hmmm...interesting. Anyway, she doesn't know."

"No?"

"Nope. She's so stubborn that she would have just argued with me and insisted I stay home. So, I basically saved us an argument." She's right, on both accounts.

"I see. I was sitting here debating on how I was going to get her to let me in. I figured even if she did come to the door, she would tell me she was fine and make me leave."

"Sounds like you know her well."

He sticks his hands in his pockets and nods while leaning back on his heels.

"Well, she can't tell me to bug off. I don't have anywhere to stay. So, let's go, shall we?" She begins to walk toward the house before Nash stops her.

"Here, let me help with you that." He grabs Olivia's luggage and lets her pass in front of him before starting toward the front door.

"Well, well...I guess you're living up to that reputation."

He stops and asks, "What reputation would that be?"

"Oh nothing, Parker just told me you were a gentleman. That's all."

"Parker?"

"Yeah, her maiden name. I've called her Parker since we were seven years old. No one has ever called her Jen before." But I don't get to hear his response since Olivia is banging on the door. She then says, "Here we go."

Even though I'm excited to see them, realizing why they're here makes me feel sick to my stomach. I had planned to spend the day trying not to dwell on what we were doing a year ago. But, I wanted to do it alone. Or at least I thought I did. Now that they're both here, I feel somewhat relieved. I won't face the day by myself.

Olivia bangs on the door again, and I sigh. I have to get up. I have to let them in. And I have to continue to breathe and survive this day. I just don't know how to do that. But if anyone can help me through it, it's Olivia and Nash.

I get up and walk to the bathroom. My eyes are puffy and red. As usual, my hair is a disaster. At least it all matches the dark circles under my eyes. I look ten years older. But I don't have time to dwell on that realization. I hear more pounding. They're getting impatient.

I glance at my pajamas. I have on an old shirt of Jeff's, his favorite, and a pair of black yoga pants that are a little loose on me. This is as good as it gets today, and I can't stall anymore. I shut off the light, take a deep breath, and head down the stairs. Halfway down, I see Olivia's face pressed to the glass with her hand over her forehead. Her face lights up, and then as I get closer, her smile fades.

By the time I open the door, she recovers and hides it well. "Hey, gorgeous." She steps forward and leans into me for a hug.

"Very funny." I say. I look over Olivia's shoulder and give

Nash a small smile. He smiles back. I pull out of Olivia's arms. The tears are already starting to flow, and I need a few moments to gather myself. I move back toward the dining room, knowing Olivia will make herself at home.

Behind me, she says, "I guess that's our cue."

This is the most company I've had in over a year, and of course the house is not clean. Or at least not my definition of clean. Cleaning has lost the ability to calm me or take away my thoughts this week, so I finally gave up. I've focused so much on this day, it was like I wanted to be enveloped by chaos so that my surroundings would match what was going on in my head and my heart. I sit down and bring my foot up to the seat and clutch it to my body.

"Well, it looks like you've got all your best friends here." Olivia starts looking at the bottles on the dining room table. "Jack, José, Jim...little early isn't it?"

"It's a little late since I started about twelve hours ago."

"You've been drinking since last night?" Nash asks.

"Yep." I rest my cheek on my knee. "Seemed like a good idea."

"Well, I agree. Let me catch up." Olivia walks into the kitchen and grabs a glass out of the cabinet. "Care to join us, Nash?"

"I actually...um, I had something else in mind."

He made plans for today? I thought he knew me a little better than that. I have no intention of doing anything, except finding the nerve and strength to finally visit Jeff's grave. I haven't seen it since I missed his funeral. I've avoided it, not confident I could handle it. But I owe him, *them*, that much.

Olivia sits down at the table and pours herself a shot. "Oh yeah, what's that?" She leans her head back and downs her shot.

"I thought we might go hiking, get you out of the house and get some fresh air?" He's looking at me, talking to me, and barely acknowledging Liv. He's focused on me, but he's restless and moving back and forth on both feet.

"Hiking, huh?" Olivia looks between us. "You guys still doing that?" She downs another shot. Her eyes rest on me, looking for an answer.

My eyes drift between her and Nash. "Yeah, it's kind of our thing. It relaxes me."

Olivia takes a different bottle and pours herself another shot. "Okay, I can hike."

I can't help but laugh. "You? Hike?"

"Sure, why not? But we need to take this with us." She grabs the bottle of José.

Olivia has no idea what she's in for. Nash either, for that matter. Taking Olivia hiking is like taking a pig to Rodeo Drive. But now that Nash has mentioned it, it sounds like something I should do today. I don't want to sit in this shrine to my former life and make wishes about things that I can't change.

"How about we hike first, then drink? There are some pretty steep cliffs where we hike, and I don't want anyone getting hurt." He's going to regret that. If anyone is going to need a drink, it's Nash. I've learned to tolerate Olivia and her quirks over the past twenty years because I love her. But most people can only take her ruthless honesty in small doses.

"You're right, Parker. He is the overprotective type."

I dart my eyes to Olivia as my adrenaline spikes. I'm going to kill her. Now he's going to know that I've been talking about him. I don't want him getting the wrong idea. And I know Olivia. She'll do anything, say anything to get my focus off my dead husband. *Dead.* Even saying that word in my head causes my chest to clench in pain. You would think after a year of Jeff being gone, something would be familiar about the fact that he is no longer here. But it's not. I still reach for the phone sometimes, wanting to talk to him. I still hear his voice and his laugh.

"Jen?"

Nash snaps me out of widow-land, and I come back to both staring at me. "What?"

"Your boy here wants to take us hiking, so let's go."

Yep. I'm going to kill her.

I give Olivia a death glare. "I'll go hiking. But I need to make a stop first." I made myself a promise that no matter what happened today, no matter how hard it was, I would go to the cemetery. And if I can't do it with my two best friends by my side, I'll never be able to do it.

"Whatever you need," Nash says.

I push back from the table and walk over to Olivia. She already knows what I want, what I need, to get that little bit of courage to take the next step. She pours me a shot, and I tip it up to my lips and try not to smell it. I down it and feel the tingle and burn, hoping to take the focus off the pain inside of me. But it only works for a split second before the ache in my heart returns.

Olivia takes the glass from me, and I glance down at my clothes. "I guess I should change. And Liv, you can't wear that. Come upstairs and I'll get you something to put on and some better shoes."

We walk past Nash and head upstairs. As she closes the door to the bedroom, I walk into the closet to find something for her to wear. I'm digging through a drawer looking for a pair of old yoga pants when I notice she's quiet. I look at her, and she's smiling like the Cheshire Cat.

"What?"

"You didn't tell me he was gorgeous."

"Who?"

"Come on Parker, don't play coy with me. Nash. My God! And it's not just his face, but that body. What does he do for a living? Stripper?" She's trying to get me to smile, but I'm not in the mood.

"Liv, don't. Here, wear these." I throw a pair of pants at her and start looking for a shirt.

"Parker, sweetie. I know you're a widow and all, but your ovaries still work, which means you still have hormones, which means there is no way you're going to stand there and tell me that you've never noticed how fine that man is?"

I turn my back to her because I don't want her to see my face flush. "I don't look at him that way." She laughs but doesn't say anything else. I continue to dig through a drawer to find a shirt that will cover her boobs. Olivia and I are stacked a little differently. Something loose on me would show the goods on her, and I don't want Nash to see her like that. I freeze.

I don't want to care if Nash finds her attractive, but I do, way more than I should. Every guy I was interested in growing up, Olivia got them. That's just the way it worked. Not only is she gorgeous, but she puts herself out there and oozes so much confidence that guys can't help but trip all over themselves to get to her. It's been like that since we were kids.

Except with Jeff. Jeff was the first guy who stared at me and my body when Olivia and I were together. The first time all three of us hung out may have been the night I fell in love with him. It's as if I was waiting to put Olivia in the same room with him to see how he responded.

I then remember why Olivia is in my closet in the first place. Jeff, my dead husband. It's been a year. A whole year of him not being in my life.

"Earth to Parker? What is with you drifting off?"

I don't know where it comes from, but I take a shirt and whip it right at Olivia's face. She didn't see it coming, so it hits her directly in the eye, "Ow! What the hell?"

I storm into the bathroom and slam the door. I grab my hair and pull. I watch my chest rise and fall rapidly and hear my breathing. I take a deep breath and hold it before releasing it and then do it again.

I do this for several moments as I hear Olivia outside the door. "I never promised to not be an asshole." I shake my head. Olivia never apologizes for who she is. Take her or leave her. She taps on the door. "Come on Parker, open up."

I hesitate before opening the door, but it doesn't matter because she lets herself in and slides down on the floor opposite me. "What's going on with you?"

I glare at her in the mirror. "What kind of question is that?"

"I guess I should have listened to your mom after all."

I spin to face her. "What are you talking about? When did you talk to my mom?"

"Right before the intervention. She told me things were bad with you, but I guess I didn't believe her. I've been around your mom enough to know she's a worrier. I thought she was just blowing things out of proportion. But now...seeing you today...I realize I should have come sooner."

"What did you expect me to look like?"

"Not this. I knew you were in bad shape. Who wouldn't be after everything you've gone through? But...I wasn't expecting this."

"What? To have puffy eyes and be in pajamas? I'm sorry I'm not living up to your expectations. I don't know how I'm supposed to act. My widow handbook must be lost in the mail."

"It's not only how you're acting...I just didn't expect you to look like this."

I glance down at my pajamas and grab the hem of my shirt moving it away from my body. What's she talking about? No holes or stains.

"I'm not talking about your clothes. How much weight have you lost?"

I take a deep breath, walk to her, and slide down next to her. "I don't know. I didn't notice until a few months ago that my clothes were falling off me. Trust me, it wasn't intentional." I start to laugh.

"It's not funny. It took everything in me not to gasp when I saw you."

"It's a little funny considering I've been on a diet since I was in the sixth grade. Looks like I finally found one that took." As soon as the words are out of my mouth I want to take them back. I squeeze my eyes shut, but a tear escapes anyway. Olivia puts her arm around my shoulder. I lean into her and clutch her shirt in my hand. How could I joke about this? About my husband's death? On the first anniversary of his death?

"Jeff would have laughed at that, ya know?"

I pull away and wipe at the tears on my face. "Don't!"

"What? Talk about him or give you an excuse to cut yourself some slack?"

"Both. I can't believe I joked about that!"

All of a sudden my hands are yanked away from my face. "I can't believe you're acting like this. Jeff is probably rolling over in his grave right now for the way you're behaving."

"Screw you, Olivia!" I push off the floor and stomp toward the bedroom. I begin to pace like a caged animal. Olivia leans against the bathroom doorframe with her arms crossed and a blank look on her face.

"Why did you come here if you were just going to make the day worse? I don't need that, not today." I want to get back downstairs since Nash is waiting for us. I don't feel like having a heart to heart.

"I didn't come here to make your day worse. But I had no idea what the hell I was walking into. I didn't know that you would look like a skeleton or act like a zombie. And I sure as hell didn't know that you haven't properly grieved for your husband and your child. I thought you were in therapy getting help. I thought you were going to support group. I thought you were befriending a man because you know you're not the type of person to go through life alone. I didn't realize that you had already given up. I wasn't in support of that stupid intervention your family and friends did, but now I get it. My God, Parker!"

"Don't you dare bring that up. You know how pissed off I was at everyone for that. That was the last time I saw most of my friends. They betrayed me by telling me I needed to go back into that hospital. Back to therapy. They don't understand. No one understands. I don't know what I'm supposed to do."

She rushes toward me and grabs my shoulders. Her nails dig into my skin, and I want to scream but I don't. "Fight, damn it! This isn't who you are. They love you. They're worried about you, and now I see why."

I shove past her. "This is who I am...now, without them. This is all I am." I cross my arms and keep my back to her. I'm so angry I can't look in her direction.

"Is that what Nash would tell me?"

I wheel around. "What?"

Her voice is quieter, and I watch her try to calm her breathing. "What would Nash tell me about you?"

"I don't know. You would have to ask him. But I don't care what he thinks of me. He's free to leave anytime. I didn't ask to be friends with him. He's the one that latched on to me."

"And why do you think that is?"

I throw my hands up in the air. "How the hell am I supposed to know? I don't even know why he bothers to continue to come around or why he's here today."

"Maybe because he sees something in you right now that you don't see in yourself."

"What are you talking about? What does this have to do with anything?"

"That's for you to figure out, Parker. For some reason, your whole life you've thought you were invisible to men, and you always hid behind me. Until Jeff came along. And now he's gone, so there is nowhere for you to hide except behind yourself."

"I don't know what the hell you're talking about. But I do know this isn't the day for it. This day is about Jeff, and you've been here twenty minutes and have already made me forget that. Can you please be the best friend I need right now and support me through this?"

"Fine. I get it, Parker. But just remember, I see you. Nash sees you, and even if you don't want to see it for yourself, you can't ignore it and you can't hide forever. I came here to support you, I did. And I'm going to let you mourn Jeff. And I'm going to let you mourn your child. But if you think for one goddamn second I'm going to let you mourn them like this for the rest of your life, then you're seriously mistaken!" She then storms out and slams the door behind her.

CHAPTER 24

J sit on the bed, my weight pulling me down. I lean back, fold my arms across my chest and stare at the ceiling. What the hell is she talking about? I don't see why Nash is a factor in any discussion we're having today. I hear them talking downstairs, but I can't make out what they're saying. I don't trust Olivia right now. So I force myself off the bed and into the closet to change.

I make my way downstairs and see that Nash is now sitting at the table. He stands as he sees me approach. "You okay?" he asks.

I give him a tight smile and walk toward Olivia. She gives my shoulder a tight squeeze and then pours me another shot. "One for the road," she says as she hands it to me.

I take it from her, down it, and sit the glass on the table. "Just leave it. I'll clean it up when we get back."

"Or we'll just pick up where we left off." Olivia winks at me and manages to make me smile. We're back to normal.

"Can we all fit in your truck, Nash?" Olivia asks.

"Yeah. It will be a little tight, but we'll fit. All of the gear is in the back anyway."

"Okay, let's go. You two can introduce me to your hiking world." Olivia takes off toward the front door.

I step to Nash's side. "Sorry, she can be a lot to take."

"It's okay. I'm glad she's here for you."

"Me too...I'm glad you're here, too." I never would have asked him, but having him here is more comforting than I would have imagined. "I need you to take me to the cemetery before we go. Do you know where Ashland Memorial Park is?" I ask. I watch as the color drains from his face. I reach over and touch his arm. "You okay?"

"Jeff is at Ashland?"

"Yeah. Have you been there before?" I watch him as his eyes drift away from mine. "Nash?"

He continues to stare at the floor. "Jen, there's something that I need to tell you...but not today, okay?"

I'm about to ask him to tell me now when we hear a car horn. "She's so impatient." I stare out the front door as I struggle to put one foot in front of the other. But I made a promise, and it's something I need to do.

The shock of Nash's hand grabbing mine throws me off balance. "Take your time. She can wait. But just remember, we're both here for you."

I squeeze back as I feel the tears form in my eyes. I whisper, "I can't believe it's been a year. In some ways, it feels like yesterday and in others..." My voice trails off. I squeeze his hand again, and I feel a tear trail down my cheek. "And in other ways, it feels like he's been gone forever." I'm barely whispering, and my voice is shaky, but Nash threads his fingers through mine so I know he heard me. "There are things I'm starting to forget about him..."

I then feel the heat radiating from his body as he leans over and brushes his thumb over my cheek and wipes away a tear. "You'll never forget him Jen, you know that. But that's a part of grief. You'll never move forward if every memory remains vivid in your mind."

"I'm not ready to move forward."

"Maybe not today, but someday."

More tears fall. "I'm still not sure I want that." I'm caught between two worlds, one world where the guilt and grief hold onto me so tight that everything reminds me of him, of what we had, of what we lost. But I don't want to live in that world. It's too hard, too painful and as scary as it is, life goes on. They're gone, but I'm still here, and everyone keeps telling me I don't have a choice but to move forward. I just don't know how.

I glance at Nash and see that his eyes are also full of tears. He clears his throat, and then slowly releases my hand and moves it to the small of my back. "Let's go. It will do you good to get out."

I don't move until Nash's hand pushes me forward, forcing me to take that next step. I walk out the front door and see Olivia leaning against the passenger side door. She puts out her arms and I walk into them. I climb into the truck next to Nash and wait as Olivia slides in next to me. I'm thankful she's here for me to lean on, even though she can be a pain in the ass.

CHAPTER 25

The three of us are silent as we drive. After sniffling a few times, Olivia's hand finds mine. I grab onto it, having second thoughts about going to the cemetery. But before I can vocalize it, Nash turns into the cemetery and stops. "Jen, which way am I going?"

I shift in my seat and look at the cemetery. I don't know. My parents and Jeff's family picked out the plot, and since I didn't attend the funeral, I have no idea where he is. Where they are. I place my face in my hands and start to cry. How can I not know the final resting place of my husband and child?

Olivia wraps her arms around me and pulls me to her. "Parker, stop. Take a deep breath." I try and do what she says, but I can't seem to focus on anything. "Again." I feel the air enter my lungs, and then release, and enter and release. I pull away from Olivia, and Nash is holding a tissue for me. I look at him after grabbing it and see tears in his eyes again. I've never seen him so somber. I stare at him for a few moments before he looks away.

I wipe my tears and take a deep breath.

"Are you sure you want to do this?" Olivia asks. "We can come back another time."

I shake my head. "No. We're already here." Nash is still turned away from me, looking out his side window. "Nash, can you take me to the office so I can find..." I'm not able to finish that sentence. There is a reason my parents and Jeff's family had to do this. I wasn't strong enough.

He turns to face me, but before he can respond Olivia says, "I know where they are." Her voice hitches but she continues. "Go straight and take a right. Past the grotto."

I feel the truck shift beneath us as we move down the narrow path, further into the cemetery. I look down seeing that Nash is holding my left hand and Olivia is holding my right. I'm not sure if I grabbed on to them or they grabbed on to me, but either way, I'm thankful to be drawing strength from them.

The truck stops, and I look to Olivia. She's looking out her side window, and then she looks at me with tears in her eyes. Olivia never cries. In the twenty plus years I've known her, I can count on one hand how many times I've seen her cry. "Top of the hill, on the right." I barely hear her because she's speaking so quietly. "Your mom told me they would be able to watch the sunset...together." It's a beautiful thought. Or it would be if she wasn't talking about my husband and child.

At the top of the hill, I see green grass, coral blooms on trees, and a statue of a woman, cloaked in cloth and flanked by wings. She's perched on top of a square pedestal that raises her far above the headstones that surround her. Neither Olivia nor Nash have moved. Almost as if they're trying to protect me from what awaits. But no one can protect me. This is something that I have do. I grab Nash's arm.

"Remember the first day we met, and you told me there wasn't a way out...only a way through?" My eyes gaze out the front window.

I hear his door open and feel him shift next to me. I look to my left and see him standing with his hand outstretched toward me. I take it, and his strength pulls me out. We walk to the front of the truck, and Olivia joins us. I want nothing more than to take both of their hands and have them escort me to the gravesite. But this is about *my family*, and it's something I have to do alone.

I let go of Nash's hand, grab Olivia's for a split second, squeeze and then release it. "Give me a few minutes, okay?"

"Sure, take your time. We'll be right here," Olivia says. I don't turn around. If I do, I might stop. Now that I have forward motion, I have to keep going.

I crisscross around headstones, while my heart beats rapidly in my chest. I make my way up the hill. Olivia didn't tell me which one it was exactly, but it doesn't take me long to see the name "Landry" on top of an arched headstone. It's steel in color, and so shiny I can see the reflection of other headstones in it. Underneath our name it says, "In loving memory of Jeff and Baby Landry. Joined together for eternity. Gone, but forever in our hearts." I walk closer and then fall to my knees. I raise my hand in front of me and my fingers drift along the cool, slick surface.

As my fingers roam over "Baby Landry" my heart stops. I remember Jeff. I know what his voice sounded like, I know what he smelled like, I know what made him laugh, made him tick. I know how much he loved me and me him. But I know nothing about our baby. I don't know if they would have been the creative type, the one with a quick wit and sarcastic sense of humor, the competitive athlete or the boisterous extrovert. I don't even know if they were a boy or a girl. That's the real tragedy. I have nothing of my baby to hold on to. It's almost as if they never existed, but they did, and I know they did because there is a hole in my heart that will never be filled. I'll never know what their voice sounded like, what they smelled like, what made them laugh or what they were passionate about. And they'll never know how much we loved them. We knew they were a part of us and we already loved them, unconditionally.

I hear leaves rustling behind me. I turn and find Olivia

walking toward me. She sits down next to me and grabs my hand. We both stare ahead, lost in thought. Minutes pass before either of us says anything.

"You know they're together, right?" she asks.

I wipe away my tears and nod. "It's a beautiful spot."

"I'm glad you like it. Your mom was a mess that day. And Jeff's mom wasn't much help. Megan and I were the ones who made the final decision."

I turn to her. "You and Megan?"

"Yeah. It was a little awkward. We hadn't seen each other since we were bridesmaids in your wedding. But she handled it well considering she had just lost her brother."

"Thank you."

"For what?"

"For doing that. I guess I never thought about that stuff. I was too consumed with what was going on with me that I haven't thought about everyone else and what they lost. I've pushed everyone away."

"Don't do that. They know, okay? They get it."

"But at some point, I'm going to have to reach out to them. I cut everyone out of my life." Olivia stands and then gives her hand and helps me up. She wraps her arm around my waist and we turn and walk back toward the truck. I silently thank her because I didn't know how to put one foot in front of the other in order to leave them both behind. She's knows me better than I give her credit.

"Yeah, but you know how people deal with death. I mean, I'm sure they still care and think about you, but they're probably relieved they don't have to do the whole awkward grieving widow thing." I stop and gape at her. "What? Too soon?"

I roll my eyes and keep walking. I hear her mutter "sorry" as we continue to walk.

I sigh. "I know what you mean. The first few months after I

got home from the hospital, people would come by and my mom would let them in."

She shakes her head. "Of course she would."

"And all of the conversations would start the same way, 'I'm sorry. He was a great man'. Blah, blah, blah. Like I needed them telling me he was a great man. I was the one who married him." I sigh again, and my pace slows. I look over my shoulder and glance at the headstone one more time before walking away. "They all finally gave up. Well, except Julia."

"Oh, Jeff's best friend Julia. How I've missed her."

I can't help but laugh. "You never did like her."

"Hey man, I was fine with her until the day of the wedding when she started encroaching on my Maid of Honor duties."

"She was just trying to help."

"She was meddling, as usual. To be honest with you, I never understood their relationship. I don't believe men and women can be friends. Either sex has already gotten in the way, or someone wants it to get in the way, or it gets there on its own."

"Stop. It wasn't like that and you know it."

"I guess, but you have to admit, you never liked her either."

She was never a real threat to our relationship but we never hung out unless Jeff was with me. "Disliked is a strong word. She's a good person, we just never became good friends."

"Have you heard from her lately?"

"Nope, not since the night of the intervention."

"I'm sorry I wasn't here to defend you. I didn't really think your mother meant an intervention. I didn't know she would invite everyone you know and corner you."

"Me either. At least after that they all backed off. Of course, my mom still thinks I'm going to support group."

"Have you told her about Nash?"

"Nothing to tell. Plus, she wouldn't understand why I would want to go to a coffeehouse and sit in silence with someone as opposed to going to a support group where Pastor Paul could watch as I vomit up my feelings."

We reach the bottom of the hill and see that Nash is nowhere to be found.

"Speaking of Nash, where did he go?" Olivia looks around and I do the same.

"I don't know."

Olivia looks down at her watch. "God, how long were we up there?"

Running my hands through my hair, I blow out a breath. "I don't know. I'll go look for him. He couldn't have gone far."

"Okay, I'm going to stretch out in the cab. I'm exhausted all of a sudden." I watch her climb into the truck and her feet dangle over the seat.

Cocooning my stomach, I walk and search for Nash. I listen to the birds chirp, and I take a deep breath and the smell of pine overwhelms me. Off to my right, about 100 yards away, Nash is knelt down in front of a headstone. He didn't mention visiting anyone while we were here. I debate if I should walk toward him or give him a moment. But my feet have a mind of their own, and before I've even decided, I'm standing behind him.

I look over his shoulder and read the headstone he's cleaning with his thumb. It reads:

Mark Summers
Beloved Son
You were gone too soon
Like a shooting star passing over the moon
We love you, forever
Mom and Dad
April 16, 1985 – April 4, 2002.

Nash shoots up and looks behind him. "Hey." He places his

hands in his pockets and rocks back on his heels, avoiding eye contact with me.

"Hey. We came back to the truck and you were gone." I take a step closer. "Are you okay?"

"Shouldn't I be asking you that?"

"Better now." I glance at the truck and up the hill where a part of my heart will always be. I then turn back to Nash. "Thank you. You and Liv being here made this easier. I couldn't have done it without you."

"You're welcome. But you're stronger than you realize."

I give him a small smile, but he's avoiding eye contact again. I look at the headstone in front of us and I can't help myself. "Who's Mark?" I ask.

His eyes find mine, and he takes two slow and steady steps toward me. He takes my hands into his and says, "Jen, I promise you that one day I will tell you, but today's not the day." He glances at the grave and then back to me. "Can you trust me on that?"

If there is one thing I can relate to, it's grief. And it has to be in your own time. Nash has never pushed me to tell him things I wasn't ready to tell him, so I'm going to respect his wishes. "Of course, Nash, you don't have to ask. If you're not ready to talk about it with me, then you don't have to."

He releases air that I didn't know he was holding and gives my hands a quick squeeze. "Thanks. Are you ready to go?"

"Yeah, Liv's in the truck waiting for us."

We ride in silence to the trail, and even though I'm heavy-hearted, I'm thankful to be sandwiched between my two best friends. Going to the cemetery felt right. I've put off going convincing myself I don't need to be there in order to think about Jeff or our baby. But today, it's where I needed to be. I relax into my seat and for the first time in a long time, I live in the present without the weight of the past or the future.

$\mathcal{W}$e pull into the gravel lot, and a sense of calmness pours over me. If I have a happy place, this is it. It's too extreme to call it happy today, of all days, but I'm grateful that Nash thought of this.

"This is it?" Olivia asks.

I look at Nash, and he smirks at me as though a secret passes between us. "This is it," he says confidently. This place means as much to him as it does to me.

"It's a little more rustic than I envisioned. Like the Clampett's backyard."

"It's not supposed to be a five-star resort, Liv. It's a hiking trail."

She climbs out and mutters, "I knew I should have brought the liquor."

Nash and I look at each other and grin. "Prepare yourself." I say to him. "If you thought I was clueless, just wait."

"All right, I've officially been warned. Let's get packed up." Nash says.

I climb out of the truck and stretch. My goal is to make it through the hike without crying. I was giving myself a pep talk on the way here. I hope I can do it. I walk to the bed of the truck and grab my pack. Nash helps me as usual, and with the extra weight, I topple a little.

"You okay?"

I don't want to tell him that I'm still a little buzzed from this morning. He wouldn't let me go if he knew. "Yep, ready to roll." Nash begins laughing, and I turn to see Olivia swatting away some type of flying bug that's buzzing her head.

I smile, "Are *you* ready to roll, Liv?"

God bless her. She tries to hide it when she says, "Can't wait."

Nash walks beside me. "Come on. You lead. We'll put her in the middle just in case."

We're not more than 10 minutes in when she asks, "So, how far does this trail go?"

I wait for Nash to respond. Stupidly, I never asked that question.

"It's about four and half miles."

"Oh, well that doesn't sound too bad." There's that confident Olivia I love, even if it's all for show.

"One way." Nash says.

Smart ass. He did that on purpose. He laughs but then stops and says, "What?"

I look back and see that Olivia is no longer moving. Her hand is on her popped-out hip, and I can only imagine the death glare she is giving him.

She yells up to me. "Parker, you didn't tell me Casanova was a smart ass." My smile falls as she pivots her body to face mine. My body tenses as she smirks at me. She's not going to start this, so I turn and keep walking. A few moments later I hear them bickering back and forth about something, but I focus on my own thoughts. I don't know why she insists on trying to make something out of nothing. Yes, Nash and I are friends. Very good friends. I can't imagine these past few months without him in my life, but she wants to make it something it isn't.

I'm pulled back into their conversation when I hear Nash say, "Because I've only known you a few hours, but I already know you butt your nose in where it doesn't belong." Wait, what? I wheel back around to see them standing across from one another. Nash has his hands on his hips and his legs spread wide while Olivia is a making exaggerated gestures with her hands and arms.

"I told you, my nose does belong there, and even if it didn't, who cares. I'm entitled to my opinion," Olivia yells while Nash lowers his head shaking it back and forth.

"Yeah, that doesn't mean you have to share it with everyone. There's this thing called a filter. Ever use it before?"

"You're just pissed because you know I'm right. I can see it on your face."

"For someone who thinks she knows everything, you sure as hell don't know shit about me." Nash brushes past her and keeps his nose to the ground.

But Olivia is quick on his heels. "Then why the hell are you so mad and so determined to deny it?"

They both stop once they realize they've caught up to me. "Deny what?" I ask.

They look between each other and then at me. In unison they say, "Nothing!" And Nash weaves around on my left while Olivia weaves around me on my right, leaving me behind. I try to remember what they were yelling about before when I was paying attention, but I have no clue. Nash's voice brings me back.

"Jen, you coming?"

I start to climb again, and they both let me cross in front of them and resume our previous positions. Except for our ragged breathing, we're all silent on the way up. I stop occasionally for Liv. I see Nash do the same and our eyes meet, and he winks at me. A slow smile spreads across my face and my body floods with warmth.

When we finally reach the top, I sigh, thankful for this

moment. There is nowhere else I would rather be. I turn and see Olivia looking at the view and Nash looking at me.

"You were right." Olivia looks at Nash. "This view is amazing...and worth it." She says as she swipes sweat from her brow.

"I have a feeling I might never hear those words come out of your mouth again, so I'm going to say thank you." Nash says.

Olivia glances in my direction with a smile on her face. I take a few steps closer to the edge and sit with my arms stretched out behind me. Liv sits to the right of me and Nash follows to the left side. I lean my head back and let the sun warm my face. Jeff comes into view, holding a baby. It's not the first time I've had this vision. I've dreamed about it too many times to count. I smile, watching both of them smile. They smile at me, then at each other, and then they're gone. I wipe a tear from my cheek. So much for not crying.

Nash's pinky finger lingers over mine. I grab on. I can't imagine where I would be without these two people, especially Nash. He's been here for the day in and day out. He's pushed me when I didn't want to be pushed. And he's done it with nothing but patience and kindness.

"You ready to head back?" he asks. I nod and we all take a few sips of water before loading up our gear again.

Nash is helping me with my pack when Olivia says, "Hey Nash, do you want to be my knight in shining armor and carry me down the hill?" She snickers as she starts to walk down the hill.

Nash steps into my eye line and glares at me. I'm laughing with Olivia until I see the look on his face. He's pissed. The last time I saw that look on his face, he had a salesman by the throat.

"What?" I ask.

He doesn't respond, so I look to Olivia and she also asks, "What?"

Then it dawns on me. His story of carrying the little boy

down the hill, he thinks I told her what he told me that day. "Nash, no. It's not what you think."

I watch his lips thin as he shakes his head in disbelief and then gives me a last hard look before he retreats down the trail. I go after him. "Nash, wait!"

My chest tightens as I run to him and try to walk backward so he'll look at me, but I quickly realize that's not going to work. "Jen, face forward before you get hurt!"

"Okay, then stop! Let me explain."

"What's to explain?"

"Nash, it's not what you think."

I hear Olivia running, trying to catch up behind us. "What the hell is going on?" She yells down at us, her breathing forced.

"Misunderstanding," I yell up at her because she won't stop asking until I answer her.

Nash cuts in with a flat tone. "Seems pretty clear to me, Jen."

"Nash, I didn't tell her anything."

He abruptly stops, and I catch myself so I stop with him. "I don't want to fight with you, Jen, not today. Let it go and we'll talk about it later."

"Nash, seriously. There is nothing to talk about. I didn't tell her."

Olivia finally catches up to us. "Tell me what?" I watch Nash narrow his eyes at her. "What the hell is that look about? What did I do?"

"Nothing. I guess I shouldn't be surprised since you guys are BFFs. Obviously, women talk and don't keep anything to themselves even if it was told in confidence." He then glares at me and says, "Didn't know that was the type of person you were." The coldness in his voice chills me.

Nash moves forward and Olivia gapes at me. "What's he talking about?"

I grab her shirt by the shoulder and pull her down with me so that we can catch up to him. "Nash, please stop and talk to me."

He keeps walking. I yell again, "Nash, stop!" At this point Olivia is starting to fall behind, so I leave her and pick up the pace to reach him. "Nash!" I finally start to run down the hill, which is harder than I expected. "For crying out loud, would you st—" But before I can finish, I start to fall. Although it feels like slow motion, I can't get my hands underneath me in time and I start to tumble. I vaguely hear Olivia yelling, and by the time the trees are upright again, I see both of them running at me.

Nash reaches me first and slides in the dirt next to me. "Are you okay?" Olivia's not far behind.

Olivia pushes Nash away when she reaches me. "Are you okay?" Before I can respond, they're both bickering at each other. "Nice going, dick!" Olivia yells and pushes him away from me.

He rights himself before yelling back, "What is your problem?"

"You wouldn't stop when she asked you to. What did you think was going to happen?"

"Obviously not this!"

"You know what? I take back what I said earlier. Why don't you just stay the hell away from her?" Nash clenches his jaw and sighs. We're all breathing hard, and I'm trying to figure out what just happened.

He then starts to move his eyes down my body, followed by his hands checking for injuries. "Are you hurt?" he asks.

"She fell down a cliff, dumbass. Of course she's hurt." Both of their hands are frantically moving as Olivia assesses my injuries.

Nash moves Olivia's right hand off my leg, "Would you get out of my way!"

"You get the hell out of my way. I'm the doctor here."

"What's that supposed to mean? That you're somehow smarter than me right now, out here on a cliff? This isn't Yale. I'm the paramedic. Move!"

"Both of you, shut the hell up!" I yell it louder than I intended, but at least they both stop. "I'm okay." I talk quieter now that I have their attention. "I just scraped my knee and hands." Nash picks up the knee that has a shooting pain rushing through it. I then feel Olivia move his hand away. He blows out a breath, closes his eyes briefly, then opens them. He then moves to my hands and lifts them up looking them over. He takes out his water and pours it over them as I hiss out in pain.

"Sorry." He says.

"It's okay."

"I'm out of water. Can I borrow that?" Olivia asks. He hands it to her without taking his eyes away from mine.

I jump a little when Olivia pours water over my knee. It doesn't hurt, but I wasn't prepared for the cold. She examines my leg, pushing with her fingertips in certain spots, checking things over. She finally says, "You'll live." She stands up and brushes off the dirt from her clothes. "I'm going to jump ahead and give you guys a few minutes."

Nash's eyes still don't leave mine when he calls out, "You know where you're going?"

"Yeah, I think so. But if I'm not at the bottom by the time you guys get there, send a search party."

Nash asks me, "Should I tell her to stop and wait for us?"

I hesitate but Liv's smart, she'll find her way. I shake my head. "No, she'll be okay."

"Are you okay?"

"Yeah." I try to brush the dirt off me, but it's difficult with the cuts on my hands. So, Nash does it for me and then stands. He reaches for my arm and pulls me up. I gaze into his eyes and see pain staring back at me.

"I'm sorry." He tucks a piece of hair behind my ear, and I can feel the heat and tension radiate from his body.

I want to take a step forward, but I don't. "It's okay."

"No, it's not. You could have gotten hurt and it would have been my fault."

"It wouldn't have been your fault, Nash. I was the one that was running and lost my footing."

"Because I wouldn't stop."

"So? That doesn't mean I had to run."

"Yeah but…"

"Stop. I'm fine." He nods his head, looking back up the cliff. His shoulders are tight and his eyes stare, frozen in place. He finally blinks and I continue. "I didn't tell her, Nash. She was trying to be a smart ass."

"What?" He looks back to me frowning.

"That's what I was trying to tell you. I didn't tell her what you told me that day. I would never do that."

Nash rubs at the back of his neck before saying, "I guess I just assumed by what she said."

"No, she's trying to push us together. She's been doing it all day. Like when she called you Casanova. That's just who she is. She thinks if she throws it in my face that I'll see what she's been talking about and tell her she's right."

"Right about what?"

"Come on, Nash. From that little fight between the two of you, I know she already said something to you. When I was upstairs?" He hesitates but finally nods. "I knew this would happen when I opened the door and saw the two of you standing together. I just figured it would come out at dinner when she had alcohol in her system."

"Well, to be fair, she did a few shots, remember?"

"Yeah, but that's not enough for her to run her mouth without thinking about the repercussions."

He's looking everywhere but at me. "I don't think we should talk about this today."

"I agree. But I want you to know, I did not break your confidence. Even though she's my best friend, I wouldn't do that. You're my best friend too, remember?"

His eyes finally reach mine again. "Sorry. I just thought…I

thought you told her by what she said. I should have known you wouldn't do that."

"I understand. I would've thought the same thing."

Nash then steps closer and pulls me into his arms. I can feel his heart racing. He whispers into my hair, "I was scared when I saw you falling. I'm sorry." He takes a deep breath but before I can respond, he continues, "I'm glad you're okay." Then he releases me. Some may say pushed. Some may say shoved. Either way, he forces us apart.

"Should we go?" He asks.

"Yeah."

"You okay to walk?"

I stretch my leg, bend my knee and take a few steps. It burns a little, but I don't want to make him feel any worse than he already does. "Yeah, I'm good. Let's go."

We reach the bottom of the trail, and Olivia's nowhere to be seen. My heart races for a brief moment until her head pops up in the bed of the truck. "About time."

Nash looks to me and then to her before asking, "What are you doing?"

"Trying to get some rays. This was supposed to be a vacation. I was supposed to spend the day drunk with my best friend, and instead I spent it on a mountain. A beautiful mountain, mind you, but it was still a freaking mountain." Nash and I look at each other and then burst out in laughter. "Glad I amuse the both of you. Can we get the hell out of here and go get that drink?"

We're both still chuckling as we climb into the truck. Nash leans over the steering wheel looking at Liv and me. "How about I take you ladies out for dinner?"

"Well, I think it's the least you can do for yelling at me and throwing her down a cliff." Olivia winks at him and Nash smiles.

CHAPTER 27

"*W*hen you said take us out to dinner, I was thinking wine and steaks, not beer and peanuts." Leave it to Olivia to complain about a free meal.

"You're not dressed for wine and steaks, sweetheart." Nash flashes a smile at me with a twinkle in his eyes. I can tell they already hate each other so much they love one another. "Plus, this place has the best fish and chips in town."

Olivia scrunches her face, until a cowboy at the bar makes eyes at her.

She gives him a little wave and says, "You're right. Parker's never brought me here, and it's important to check out the local scenery. I'll buy the first round. What will it be?"

"No thanks, I think I've had enough for one day." The need to spend the day numb in a drunken haze has left me. The hike got my blood pumping and reminded me that just as I need to climb the hill, I have to keep putting one foot in front of the other, even if there will be times when I fall flat on my face.

"And I'm driving, so none for me," Nash says.

"Oh, you can have one, Nash." Olivia looks over her shoulder

and smiles again at the cowboy. "Plus, we might be here a while."
I know what she has in mind. I'll let her play, but if she thinks
she's bringing that drunken idiot back to my house, she has
another think coming.

"No! I don't drink and drive."

I look at Nash as the tone of his voice catches me off guard.

"I didn't say you had to get drunk. I said have *a drink*."

"I heard you. I don't drink and drive. Drop it."

Olivia looks at me with outstretched arms and her palms
facing the ceiling. I shrug my shoulders and shake my head. I
don't know why that seemed to upset him so much.

"Fine. Didn't realize I left the house this morning with two
stick-in-the-muds. I'll be at the bar." I watch her saunter to the
bar and shake hands with the cowboy. He pats the bar stool next
to him and she sits down.

I laugh and say, "Well, you're going to get your wish, because
we probably won't see her for the rest of the night." When Nash
doesn't respond, I turn back to him. He elbows are on the table as
his head rests in his hands. I reach across the table and lightly
brush his arm. He jumps back. "You okay?"

"Yeah. What are you having?"

He won't tell me even if I push the issue so I let it go.

"Nash, you don't have to buy us dinner."

"I don't have to, but I want to." He looks up from his menu
and smiles at me. But I can tell it's forced. "It's been a long day."

"Yeah." I pick up the menu and start perusing it.

"How you holding up?"

"As well as can be expected, I guess." I look at him and smile,
trying to reassure him. "Thank you for taking us hiking."

"Glad I could be of some help."

A few brief moments pass and then Nash's back straightens. I
glance over my shoulder and see Olivia sucking face with the
cowboy.

Nash clears his throat. "Um, that was fast." He returns to his menu.

I yawn and say, "That happens. She's gorgeous, wicked smart, and a rich doctor. Who can blame him?"

"I take it there is no one serious back home?"

"Not that I'm aware of. That's not her thing, though. Olivia isn't the relationship type."

"So you're opposites in that regard?"

The cowboy is now whispering in her ear, and she gives him her best fake laugh. "You could say that. Olivia's never had a problem getting guys interested in her. But I've had to work at it. Plus, I never wanted guys. I was looking for *the guy*. She gets bored easily."

"And you don't?"

"Not usually. I haven't been in a lot of relationships, but the few I have been in, I made sure to not take them for granted. I know you have to work at it." I take a sip of water. "She wants the fairytale, and I already know it doesn't exist."

"Maybe it does." He says, sweeping his tongue over his lips.

I chuckle and push the menu away, no longer hungry. "Not for me."

Nash slides his hand across the table and grabs mine. "Your life isn't over, Jen."

My eyes flash to his as I pull my hand away. My muscles tense and my stomach feels heavy. "I think I need some air." Standing, I head to the door in the back and walk out to the covered patio. There is a couple off to the side, in their own world. I step down and stride toward the back parking lot, needing to get some distance.

My head is spinning, and that perpetual ache of being alone suddenly feels more prominent. There're too many emotions. Too many questions. I kick at the gravel underneath my feet and head back to the patio. But I'm not ready to go in, so I change directions and round the corner, out of sight.

Leaning my head against the wall, my eyes close as I cross my arms. Nash is acting weird and I don't know why. He's hiding something from me. He told me he needed to tell me something. What could that possibly be? And who is Mark? I noticed by the date on his headstone that he's about Nash's age. But he's never mentioned him. Just like he's never mentioned other friends or even family, except a sister that he never talks about.

The door squeaks open, and I hear Olivia's voice. "Hey, where ya going?"

"I came out here to find Jen." Nash's boots scurry around frantically around the patio.

"She's pretty amazing huh?" Olivia asks. She's slurring her words, so I know she's already had too much to drink. I start toward them and come out of the dark, but their conversation continues, so I resume my spot and listen in.

"Yeah. She's holding up pretty well. But she's been out here awhile so…"

Before Nash can finish, Olivia interrupts him, "How long have you been in love with her?"

His footsteps stop. "What?"

"I see it when you look at her." Silently, I will her to shut up. She's taking this too far. It's bad enough she's trying to force it with me, but she needs to leave him out of it. He doesn't see me in that way.

"I told you, I don't know what you're talking about. We're just friends." He told her already, when?

"So you said. But I see that you want more. Look, I'm not judging. In fact, I think it's a good thing, or it could be." I should show myself, put an end to this for Nash's sake, but I'm paralyzed against the wall.

"Just drop it, Olivia!"

"You and I both know she can't hide behind widowhood forever." I angle my body closer to them and strain to hear without being seen.

"I don't think she's hiding behind anything. I think she's grieving."

"Yeah, she's grieving all right. Trying to be an expert at it, like everything else in her life."

"What's that supposed to mean?"

"She always gives 100% to everything she does. But I'm not going to sit by and let her throw her life away."

Nash sighs and I wish I could see him. "Why are you telling me this?"

"Because the two of you have a connection. She's told me that when she's around you, you don't pity her. You understand her grief and you let her be."

"Isn't that a good thing? Why do you sound angry about it?"

"Because I don't think you're pushing her. Her grieving has gone on long enough! I think you're coddling her, making it too easy for her."

"Too easy? Are you kidding me? Her husband was murdered, and she lost her unborn baby days later. All before she was thirty years old. How could anyone possibly coddle someone who has lived through that?"

Olivia raises her voice. "I know what she's been through, but at some point, she has to come out on the other side of this. When she started talking about you a few months ago, I thought you would be the person to help her do that."

"I'm trying."

"No, you're not. You might have been at first, but now you're scared. You're afraid you'll hurt her."

"Hell no, I don't want to hurt her! She's been through enough."

"No, she hasn't, because she hasn't done the hardest thing yet."

"Which is?"

"Let them go. Nash, for her to move forward, she has to let them go. She has to look at that life and she has to walk away from it because it no longer exists. Someone has to help her find who she is without them….and I'm not here to push her."

"What do you want from me?" Nash no longer sounds angry, just tired.

"I want you to help her. Help her find out who she is without them. Neither of you will get what you want if you don't." Footsteps echo across the wood, and then a door slams. I slowly peek around the corner. I can barely make Nash out in the moonlight. The couple on the patio is now gone, and so is Olivia. Nash's arms are leaning on the railing and he has his head hung low. He sighs, pushes off the railing, and walks inside.

I fall against the side of the building and decide to go around to the front. I don't want either of them knowing I overhead them. Just as I'm walking in, Nash is walking out, and we practically run into each other.

"Hey. Where'd you go? I went out back to find you and I started to get worried."

I want to wrap myself around him and I don't know why. I run both my hands down my pants to wipe the sweat away that has appeared. I don't understand the emotions that are running through me. "Sorry. I just took a walk."

Heaving a sigh, he runs his hands though his hair. "I ordered you a burger. It's on the table. I need to get something out of my truck." He steps around me and is out the door before I can respond.

Returning to our table, I throw myself in the chair. I push the burger away. I should eat after the day I've had, but my appetite is gone. I'm fighting enough battles within myself. Forcing myself to eat isn't a battle I'm willing to fight.

I glance over and see the cowboy running's his hands up Olivia's back. She leans into him. I feel my stomach harden and I look away. I can't believe I'm feeling jealous over Olivia being pawed by a man she doesn't know. Closing my eyes, I try to focus on something else when Nash's woodsy scent invades my space.

"What's wrong?" He asks.

I open my eyes and shake my head. "Nothing."

"You're not going to eat?" I shake my head again. "Jen, you haven't eaten all day."

"Nash...please don't."

His posture goes stiff as his biceps clench. But he doesn't push it. He takes the napkin that's wrapped around his silverware and unfurls it before laying it in his lap. He brings his burger up to his lips but stops and flexes his jaw.

I start to laugh. "Has she gotten to you, or are you looking out for her?"

He looks back to me. "Huh?"

"I see you watching her. I can also see you're pissed. I'm just not sure if you're pissed at her or him."

"She's drunk. And so is he. Plus, there's no way he's coming back to your house."

"Agreed. But believe me, she could have that guy on the ground with one swift kick."

"Oh, I don't doubt it. Still, I want to keep an eye on her."

I grin. "I know. One of the many reasons I love you."

He drops his burger as his eyes dart back to me. "What did you say?"

I've caught him off guard and he starts to blush. "You heard me." I say. I feel my smile start to grow. "What's with that face?" I didn't mean to say it, but it's what came to mind. And I'm okay with it now that I've said it out loud. His reaction is priceless. I figure I might as well tease him about it. The day has been too serious, for all of us.

He shifts in his chair and moves his attention back to Olivia and the cowboy. "Nothing."

"Oh, I get it. You're a guy and guys get weird talking about feelings." I nudge his shoulder. "Friends love each other, right?"

His hands clench and unclench while resting on the table. "Friends...right." He says. He's now the one pushing his burger to the center of table. He then throws his napkin down. Before I can ask what's wrong, Olivia arrives and practically knocks over the table when she bumps into it.

"Oops. My bad." Her butt finds a chair, and she smiles at both of us. "You guys look deep in thought. Deep thoughts, ha!" Her words are slurred more now than on the patio.

"Oh my. You know, you were supposed to get drunk with me, not without me. Wasn't that the point?"

"Yeah, but you didn't want to drink, so I found someone else to party with."

"Yeah, and he looks high class," Nash says.

Olivia laughs and nudges Nash's hand. "He does, doesn't he?" She obviously missed the sarcasm in his voice.

The cowboy calls out across the bar. "Hey, sweet cheeks. Why don't you get your fine self back over here?"

Olivia giggles and starts to get up, when Nash stands and gently pushes her back into her seat. "Hey, what're you doing? You're an ass!"

"I may be an ass, but this ass is saving you."

"What?" She tries to stand again but sways and Nash gently pushes her back down again.

"Why don't you sit here and keep Jen company? I'll be right back," he says.

"No!"

I can feel the situation rapidly spiraling out of control. "Liv, please? I don't want to be by myself. Come on, sit with me."

"No!" She gets up and grabs Nash by the shoulder as he's walking away. "You're supposed to be saving *her*, not me."

This time instead of forcing her to sit down, he pulls her toward him.

"That's enough. Let's go," he says.

"Go? No! I don't want to go, I'm having fun."

I rise to go with them when I see the cowboy making his way over. "Just where 'n the hell you think you're going with her?"

"Home. Now get the hell out of my way." Nash attempts to step around him, but the cowboy steps in his path.

"I don't think so, pretty boy. I've been feedin' her drinks all night. She's with me."

Nash steps the other way. "No. She came with me, she's leaving with me." The cowboy grabs Nash's shirt. Bile rises in my throat as I rush over to them.

Nash glowers down at the guy's hand and then steps toward him. "I suggest you let go of me. *Now!*" Nash is still holding Olivia's arm, and she's looking back and forth between the two of them. "The lady's going home." The expression on Nash's face is cold and hard and dangerous.

Too drunk to see the threat, the cowboy saunters closer to Olivia. "You don't want to go home with him, do you sweet cheeks?"

She looks in my direction and I give her a death glare making it clear it's time to go. I can tell the encounter has sobered her, as she's no longer swaying. She looks back to the cowboy. "Yeah, I do."

"Bitch."

The cowboy reaches for Olivia's arm, but Nash steps in front of him and shoves Olivia into my arms. "You *really* don't want to do this." But the cowboy lunges, and Nash sidesteps him. Nash puts his arms up, but it dawns on me he's not swinging.

Cowboy lunges again, but Nash moves back, then trips into a chair and loses his balance, letting the cowboy get a swing in. His knuckles crack against Nash's chin and I cry out, "Nash!"

Nash recovers but still doesn't swing. The cowboy tries one more time, but before he can get to Nash, the bouncers arrive and tackle him. Nash straightens up and lets out a sigh. He rubs his chin and I see a trail of blood on his lower lip. I rush over to him.

My heart feels like it's about to explode. "Are you okay?"

He rubs his jaw and I lightly touch the blood on his lip. "Yeah, is she?" He looks over at Olivia who is covering her face with her hands and sliding down into a chair.

"Yeah, she's fine. But it's time to call it a day."

"I agree. Let's go."

I grab a napkin from the table and dip it in my ice water. "Hold still." I touch Nash's lip with it and he briefly closes his eyes. "You sure you're all right?"

His eyes open, and I can feel his breath on my face. The world disappears around me. He brings his hand to my face and moves it to my ear, where he tucks a piece of my hair behind it. "You know, you and I ask that too often of each other."

I take a deep breath and try to focus on the task at hand. But then I'm staring at his lips, so I focus on his eyes. That's not any better. I swallow. "I agree. I think we're both just doomed." He smiles. "Let me go grab the pain in the ass so we can finally get out of here."

I then realize that while I was taking care of his lip, his other hand made its way to my waist. He doesn't move. Neither do I. I should move. Nash's eyes roam down my face, and then they shift over my shoulder. He pulls away and the loss of him sends a cool breeze down my body. "I'll pay our bill and pull the truck around. I want to make sure that asshole isn't waiting outside."

As Nash heads outside, I yell, "Watch your back." He gives me a wave over his shoulder and walks out.

My pulse is still racing as I spin toward Olivia who is smirking at me. "What the hell is that smile for? He could have gotten hurt because of you."

"It wouldn't be because of me. He was doing that for you."

"What are you rambling about?"

"You think a guy protects a girl's best friend like that just because?"

"Yeah, most decent men would."

Olivia shakes her head. "You're still blind when it comes to this crap."

My body tenses as I drag my hands through my hair and look away from her. "Nash is bringing the truck around. Let's go." I throw the napkin on the table, grab my purse, and start to walk toward the door. I notice she isn't following me so I turn back. She's still sitting. "Are you in shock or just deaf? I said let's go."

"I'm sorry," she says.

I release a ragged breath as I make my way over to her. Kneeling, I take Olivia's hands and realize I feel sorry for her. My life is screwed up, but so is hers, just in a different way. She thinks I'm hiding? She's the one who has hidden behind one-night stands and superficial relationships her whole life. She doesn't even know what I've lost because she's been too afraid to have it for herself. I'm not sure what's worse. The fact that I had it and lost it or the fact that she doesn't even know what it feels like to be in love. I can't blame her for how she grew up. Her mother's revolving door of men didn't teach her anything about having a good relationship. She's never actually seen it up close.

"It's all right. But you owe Nash an apology. He defended you and got popped in the chin because of it."

"I feel terrible. I didn't mean for that to happen."

"What got into you tonight? This isn't like you."

"I...I just...." She leans her head into her hands and stares down at the table once again.

"What?"

She then leans back in her chair and says, "I miss him too, you know. I miss who you were with him. And I can't stand to see you in this much pain."

I need to stop forgetting I'm not the only one that lost him. I'm about to say just that when I see Nash in the doorway. "Come on, we can talk about it when we get home."

I help her up and let her cross in front of me toward Nash. "You okay?" he asks her.

She nods her head. "Yeah. You?"

"I'll live." He tries to look angry and intimidating, but

repeating the words she used on me earlier shows he's not. "Come on sweet cheeks, let's go." She smiles weakly, and I know they'll be fine.

We all climb into the truck and pull away. Olivia's fidgeting next to me. She knows she needs to apologize to Nash, but she doesn't want to. I finally nudge her and glare.

She blows out a breath. "Nash, look, I'm sorry. I didn't know it was going to escalate to that."

Nash chuckles to himself. "It was nothing compared to the hits I used to take in juvie."

Both Olivia and I say "Juvie?" at the same time. She and I look at each other and then to Nash, where his mouth hangs open in shock. He mutters a curse word under his breath.

What is he talking about? He's never mentioned anything about juvie before. I remember him saying he had a friend who went to juvie, but I didn't know Nash was in there with him. Why has this never come up before today? "What were you in juvie for?" I ask.

"Ah, hell Jen, haven't we been through enough today?"

Olivia picks this opportune moment to chime in. "Hell no, I want to hear this."

I see Nash plead with his eyes to let it go, and after everything he's done for me today, it's the least I can do. "He's right, Liv. We've all had a long, hard day. Let's drop it."

Olivia groans and sits back against the seat with her arms crossed. I glance at Nash, and he mouths *thanks*.

I want to smile but I don't. I simply nod and focus on the road ahead of us. His past is a mystery, and I'm starting to feel uncomfortable with the accumulating questions. I don't want to push him to tell me things he's not ready to reveal. But on the flip side, I wonder what he's not telling me.

I decide to let it go as we pull into the driveway. Today wasn't what I expected, but I wouldn't have had it any other way. I'm thankful I didn't spend it drowning in pain. But as Olivia and I shuffle out of Nash's truck, that ache in the back of my throat returns. Am I ready to walk back into the shrine where time doesn't move? Even though Olivia's a pain in the ass, she's right. Something has to change.

CHAPTER 28

I walk ahead of Olivia as Nash backs out of the driveway.

Olivia lightly chuckles. "I've got to tell you kid, I don't get what you see in hiking." I love how she starts a conversation like nothing happened back there.

Jabbing my key in the lock, I walk through the door and wait for Olivia to follow. She saunters into the dining room, where she picks up a shot glass and pours herself a drink. "Don't you think you've had enough for one night?" I ask.

"Not really." She picks up the glass and downs it and then pours me one. "Wasn't this the plan?"

I walk around her and pick up the shot glasses, including the full one, and move to the sink where I throw it down the drain. I move back to the table and pick up the bottles, shoving the caps on them, and put them away.

"What's eating you?"

I swirl around and glare at her. "Me? Do you mind telling me what the hell all of that at the bar was about?"

Olivia leans against the doorframe to the kitchen and crosses her arms over her chest. "What? I thought we were supposed to be getting your mind off things."

"You think trying to pair me up with Nash is going to help me get over my husband?" She stares at me silently. "And I don't know what you said to him while I was upstairs, but I heard you guys bickering about something on the trail. Then I overheard you on the patio at the bar. Care to fill me in?" She doesn't move. Not her body. Not her face. Not her eyes.

Dropping into a chair, I unlace my shoes and kick them across the floor. "Fine. I bet I can guess." I grasp the edge of the table and lean forward.

Lazy steps drag Olivia to the chair, where she leans back and slams her shoes on my expensive dining table. She moves her hands behind her head and glares at me. "Try me."

"You're trying to play matchmaker!" We stare at each other as I clutch my fist until my nails dig into the palm of my hand. Heat is rising in my neck. "You're not even going to bother to defend your actions today?"

"Which actions are you talking about?"

"Oh, I don't know, the knight in shining armor joke, or the Casanova comment."

"Just trying to lighten the mood, kiddo. Didn't know it would bother you so much."

"Bull. After our conversation upstairs, you knew exactly what you were doing. I don't understand why you felt it was necessary to start this crap, today of all days."

Dropping her feet to the floor, Olivia leans onto the table, so our eyes are level with one another. "And what about today?"

"What?"

"Say it. What about today?"

"What do you mean?"

"What is it about *today*, of all days, that is so hard for you?" I laugh because I don't trust myself not to pop her in the face. Tears well up in my eyes and I look away. "Parker?"

I gaze out the window, but it's too dark to see anything but our reflections. I watch as she leans over and reaches for my hand. Snatching my hand away, I whisper, "Don't."

"I'm not trying to hurt you."

"Well, you are."

"I think you're doing a pretty good job of that yourself."

I turn around and wipe at two stray tears. "And how am I hurting myself?"

"You're not addressing what's in front of you."

"What, you think Nash has feelings for me, is that it?"

"That's not what I'm talking about."

I rest my forehead in my hands and have this uncontrollable urge to pull at my hair. "My God, Olivia. I swear, would you just spit out whatever it is you want to say!"

"There's something I want you to say first. That you *need* to say and that I *need* to hear you say."

"What? What is so damn important for me to say? What!" Shoving myself out of my chair, I start to pace the room. I want to break something, damage something until it's as broken as I am.

"Why are you getting so defensive?"

Her calmness is only making me angrier. "I don't know what the hell you want from me. This is worse than the damn intervention my family tried to pull on me. At least with them I knew what they wanted me to do. I wouldn't do it, so I walked out."

"What did they want?"

"Go into therapy, get help, deal with my grief."

"And why did they want that for you?"

"I don't know. I didn't understand it then, and I don't understand it now. Everyone wants me to respond or react in a certain way, and I'm sorry, but I've never been a widow before, so I don't know how I'm supposed to be acting."

Olivia has turned her body and leaned her arm on the back of the chair as I pace around the room. I'm tempted to get the booze back out, but it will only prolong this conversation. I just want it to be over. I want this day to be over. I sit next to her as my chest feels constricted. She scoots her chair closer and grabs my hand. "Parker."

I take a deep breath, and then another one trying to calm myself. I don't even know what's got me so worked up.

"Parker, I'm genuinely frightened."

I remove my hand from hers and wearily, I lay my head down on the cool wood of the table and angle my face toward her. "You? What could possibly be scaring you?"

"I'm scared for you." She looks around the room, and her eyes land on the picture above the mantel of Jeff and me on our wedding day. "I've always been jealous of you."

My mouth falls open. "What are you talking about?"

She smiles. "I've hidden it all these years because we each had a role to play in our friendship. I was the loud, outspoken one who put myself out there for guys because I knew I would never let them close. So it didn't matter to me if they were in my bed at night and out the door the next morning. I've never been the type of girl who needs a guy, but I've always envied that about you."

"Envied me? I thought you saw that as weak."

She laughs. "Weak? You have to be strong to allow yourself to be vulnerable to completely give yourself to someone. You have to be strong enough to trust them with your life, your future, with the worst of you. You have to be fierce with your heart to completely give it over to someone. But *you* do that. You've always done that. You can count the number of friends you have on one hand because once you let someone in, they're in. They've broken through your walls, and they're never going to let you go because it was so damn hard to get there in the first place." She shakes her head. "I let people in easily because I know I'll be able to handle them walking right back out. You're not built like that. When you love someone, it sticks."

For the second time today, Olivia wipes away tears on her face. "But Jeff left you. Your baby left you. Not by choice, but they left, and I'm not sure anymore that you're going to survive that." Her face crumples as tears streak down her face. I reach out my arms and she falls into them. I soothe her hair and try to focus on the irony of me comforting her when she sniffles.

"I don't even recognize you. Not just physically. But your passion, your humor, your fight...they're gone. I don't know who this person is."

"Liv, sometimes I feel that there is no *me* left—just this empty, hollow shell."

She pulls back and grabs my shoulders. "Do you think this is what Jeff would want for you?" She shakes me. "Well?"

I whisper, "No." We sit in silence. "I haven't quite figured out how to live without them yet."

"I get it. I see you struggling. But I think you need to find out who you are without them. You have some hard decisions to make. And it's time, Parker."

My eyes shoot up to Olivia's. "Any suggestions?"

She looks around. "Like what you're going to do with this house. You know your parents can't continue to pay the mortgage on this. Plus, I don't know how you stand it." She shoves herself away from the table, and now she's the one pacing. "It's hard for *me* to even be here. Everything reminds me of the two of you. And I walked by the nursery when I was putting my bag in the guest room. Even though the door was shut, I know what's in there. Just the idea made me want to crumble onto the floor and cry. I don't know how you can continue to stay here; the damn place is like a mausoleum."

In despair, I run my fingers through my hair and squeeze tight. "It's all I have left of them."

"That's not true." She squats in front of me. "You have pictures. You have mementos, you have memories."

It's not enough but she's right. I need to accept that's all I'll ever have.

"Are you going to join another firm?"

"No." I shake my head. "I'm done being a lawyer."

"Then you know you can't afford this house."

"What do you want me to do, Liv?" I'm pleading for her to be specific.

"I want you to give yourself a break. Accept the fact that you're no longer going to be a lawyer and that's okay. And accept the fact that you can't keep this house, or Jeff's things, or the things in the nursery, and that's okay."

My throat thickens as two tiny tears fall from my eyes.

Olivia walks over to me and wraps me in her arms. "No one is going to think less of you. No one is going to judge you. But Jeff would want you to move on. You have to move on."

I push away from her. "How can you say that? You don't know what Jeff would want for me."

"Yes, I do, and so do you. I don't know why you're punishing yourself. He would want you to be happy."

Olivia doesn't know the truth. She doesn't know that I'm the reason both Jeff and my unborn child are dead. If I hadn't been so stubborn and so selfish, Jeff would never have gone for a drive that night. I don't deserve to move forward. But she's right about the house. I've been avoiding reality. I can't imagine packing up our belongings and leaving the house behind, but there's no way I can keep it. But today, of all days, is not the day to think about it.

I've had enough. I've dreaded this day for so long, but I survived and I'm beyond exhausted. "Liv, I'm tired. I'm going to bed." I brush past her and make my way through the dining room.

"Parker, wait!" She comes trailing after me. "Please don't shut me out. You know I love you and I don't want to hurt you."

"I know." I move toward the stairs and don't stop when she calls out.

"I'm only trying to help you."

"Goodnight, Liv."

"I'll be right down the hall if you need anything, okay?"

I don't bother to answer her. She's trying to help, but bringing up Jeff and what he would want for me was the last straw. No one knows the full story of what happened that night. I haven't been able to bring myself to tell anyone, and I doubt I ever will. It's a secret I plan to carry with me because I could never trust anyone with it. If someone knew that about me, they would never look at me the same way again. I didn't gamble. I played it safe by getting married, getting a good job, and getting pregnant. It wasn't risky, but I lost it all anyway.

I strip off my clothes, climb into bed, and move my body away from Jeff's side. I remember lying in his arms just a year ago. Then we argued about what our future would look like. Over the past year, I've reflected on every fight we ever had, and I wish nothing more than to take them back, all of them. But that fight, that night, will haunt me until the day I die.

I'm ready for sleep to come. Just as I'm about to drift off, my phone dings. I reach over and pick it up.

"I wanted to let you know how proud I am of you. I can't begin to imagine how difficult today was and I know you still have hard days ahead. But I wanted to tell you that I see you getting stronger each day. I see you smile and laugh, and I know Jeff would want that for you. I hope you enjoy your time with Liv but if you need anything, you know where to find me. Good night Jen. ~ N."

I throw the phone back down on the night stand and ignore how that text made me feel.

CHAPTER 29

I flip through a magazine, not looking at anything in particular, when the bell on the door rings and Nash walks through it.

Tension rolls off his body. His smile looks forced and his eyes are jumpy. He immediately sits down and I slide the coffee I ordered for him to the center of the table.

"Rough day?" I ask.

He looks up from the table before saying, "Hmm?"

"I said, rough day?"

"No. Yeah. I guess."

"Wanna talk about it? Did you lose a patient or something?"

"What? No, nothing like that. It's not work related."

"Oh." Nash still hasn't shared a lot about his personal life. Olivia and I were both curious about his juvie comment. Olivia even tried to find something online the next day, even though I tried to explain the whole purpose of being charged as a juvenile was so your record didn't follow you around the rest of your life. But as usual, she didn't listen. She wasted two hours and found nothing.

"Did Olivia leave?"

There is something off about him today, but as usual, it's like working with the CIA. I'm always on a need to know basis, and whatever he's struggling with, he apparently doesn't think I need to know. "Yeah, she left yesterday. She only had the four days off."

"Oh. I guess I assumed she was still here since I hadn't heard from you."

"No, I had some stuff to think through."

"Anything you want to talk about?"

I hesitate. Once I say it out loud and to someone else, it's out there, and I can't take it back. I take a deep breath. "I think I need to sell the house."

Our eyes meet, and his forehead scrunches together. "Whoa, where is that coming from?"

"Hurricane Olivia."

He laughs and cocks his head to the side. "What?"

"She means well and I love her to death. Probably one of the things I respect most about her is that she tells it like it is. But her approach can be a little harsh sometimes."

"She loves you."

"I know, and she's right. It's just hard to hear."

"What exactly did she say?"

"That I need to move on, that Jeff would want me to be happy. If I'm not going to be a lawyer, then I can't afford to keep the house."

"Are you're sure that's what you want?"

"Nash, I'm not sure of much, but I'm confident that I will never practice law again. It just doesn't feel right anymore."

"Have you thought about what you *do* want to do?"

"Nope. That will come, but I need to take care of some other things first. And I guess the best place to start is selling the house."

"How can I help?"

"I don't know yet, but thanks."

"When you're ready, let me know. Did you have a good visit with Olivia?"

"I'm glad she came, but we fought quite a bit so it was kind of hard."

"What did you fight about?"

I chuckle. I've never lied to him before, so there is no point in starting now. "You, actually."

"Me?"

"Yeah. I didn't appreciate what she was trying to do. She told me that she confronted you about our friendship."

"Oh." His eyes roam around the room and he shifts in his seat.

"Why didn't you tell me she confronted you?"

His eyes return to mine and his shoulders slouch. "I don't know. I guess I didn't want you thinking...I don't know...that..."

"That you put that idea in her head?"

"Basically."

"I wouldn't. I don't. I know her. She means well. She only wants me to be happy. But she also knows you can't force something between two people."

"*Force?*" Nash jerks upright and leans back, crossing his arms across his broad chest. "Maybe she just sees something you don't."

"What's that supposed to mean?"

Nash runs his right hand through his hair and pulls on it. He shakes his head and forces a smile back on his face. "Nothing. I didn't mean anything by that. I didn't mean to be the cause of tension between the two of you."

"It's not your fault. She doesn't understand our relationship, and she was butting her nose in where it didn't belong, but that's Olivia for you. She thinks I can just click my heels and move on to a different life. But this isn't a fairytale. Not all stories have happy endings. That's not how life works."

Nash's eyes roam over my features and land back on my eyes. His jaw works back and forth, and he opens his mouth only to shut it again and look away. As he does, my eyes move down and land on his hands resting on the table in front of me. They're clasped in one another and gripping each other so hard that all his knuckles are white. An uncomfortable tension washes over me, and I don't like it. This isn't how things usually are between Nash and me. I've said something wrong but I'm not sure what.

Is he offended somehow? Does he feel rejected? That's it! He's not the type to be rejected by women. I reach for his hand, hoping to break the tension. He pulls back like I've lit him on fire. He forces a smile and puts his hands where they were before.

I try to lighten the mood. "She should know better. No offense, but you're not my type." I try to be playful. It's not a side of myself I'm used to anymore, but I'm trying. Some things Olivia said to me this past week did break through my cold, dead surface. The only way I'm going to continue to move forward, is to try.

He smirks and all of the emotions that were previously reflected in his eyes are gone. "Oh yeah, why is that?"

I lean in and he follows. I whisper, "Well, I'll let you in on my secret. I usually go for tall and handsome guys." I purposefully leave out dark because if there is anyone who fits the epitome of tall, dark and handsome, it's Nash.

He smirks at me and then asks, "Did you just call me short or ugly or both?"

I laugh and pull back. Suddenly I don't want to be that close to him. "You're definitely not ugly or short, but the motorcycle and tattoos would be a first for me."

"You know, change isn't always a bad thing." He winks at me. "Besides, I will get you on a bike one of these days." He's right, change isn't always a bad thing, and there are numerous things about my life that need to change. Starting with our house.

CHAPTER 30

$\mathcal{I}$’ve always been someone who, once I put my mind to something, there is no stopping me. Which is why I was probably so successful at grieving. It took me a whole year to realize I didn't want to be an expert at grieving. So once I decided to take the next step, it was like a whirlwind. It took me several days, but I managed to go through what I needed to go through. It was probably the most painful part of the process. There were a lot of tears, and some alcohol involved. But I did it. Another step that I had to take.

I knock on the door, anxious as the first day I met her. Except on that day I had Jeff to support me. He told me, "Don't worry babe, she's going to love you." The door opening pulls me back to the present, and Doris smiles at me.

She sighs. "Jensen."

"Hi Doris."

She steps down and gives me a hug. "It's been a while."

There's something about her embrace that reminds me of Jeff. "I'm sorry. I don't have a good excuse."

"Yes, you do. I know it's hard to see me without him. It's hard for me to see you without him." She touches the end of my hair and smiles. "You grew your hair out. Come in."

I pick up the box and walk inside. I follow her into the family room as my eye wanders. Nothing has changed. Jeff's high school graduation picture is still on the mantel. Another picture of him and Megan, his sister, smiling before her prom. Jeff and Doris hugging before she left him at college.

"You can just sit that down by the couch."

"I have a few more in the car."

She walks over to the box. "May I?"

"Of course. He would want you to have these things. I found some of his old trophies and grade reports. Some things I assume he made. I kept some things, so if there is something specific you want and it's not in any of the boxes, let me know. I have a pretty good idea now where everything is and I can get it to you."

"I'm sure what you have brought is fine."

I swallow trying to push back the unease. "I also brought some of the baby's things." My voice starts to crack but I continue on. "The teddy bear you bought and the onesie that says, 'I Dig Grandma.'"

"Oh." She grabs my hand and squeezes. "Thank you, sweetheart." I look away not able to face the sadness on her face or the tears in her eyes. The whistle of a tea kettle breaks the silence. "Let me go grab the tea."

I sit down on the couch and run my hands over the fabric. I remember the first night Jeff brought me here. After his mom had gone to bed, we stayed up late and talked.

"I told you she would love you." he said.

"I know, but she's your mom. I wanted to make a good first impression."

"Babe, you've never made a bad first impression, and tonight was a great first impression. Thank you."

"For what?"

"For taking the time to come here and meet her and my sister. It means a lot to me."

"Of course." He started to play with my hair and then leaned down to kiss me. After a few minutes, we both pulled back breathless. "Stop. We can't...not in your mom's house."

"Oh, come on. I was too scared to do it when I was in high school."

I couldn't resist those eyes. I remember him gently laying me on the floor and hovering over me with a look of such happiness that I wanted to freeze time. When we had finished, and he wrapped me into his arms, he whispered, "I'll never be able to look at this floor again without blushing."

"Jensen?" Doris' voice snaps me back to the present.

I turn and feel the smile as well as the blush on my face. "Sorry..."

"That's okay, you're smiling. It's been a long time since I've seen you smile." My smile fades. "No, Jensen. I'm sorry. I didn't mean to make you feel guilty."

"No, that's okay. I shouldn't be smiling."

"Oh, sweetheart..." She rushes up to me and grabs my hands. "Jeff would want you to be happy."

"I know."

"I'm not sure I believe. It's obvious you don't believe it yourself. But it's going to take time. You're going to be okay, Jensen." I try to reassure her with my smile as she gently lets go of my hands. "I made some sandwiches. Do you want to join me for a little bit?"

I know that we'll spend the time talking about Jeff. I'm better now at getting through conversations talking about him, about us, without breaking down. So, as I look at Jeff's mom and see his eyes staring back at me, I say, "I would love to." And I mean it.

* * *

I CLIMB into bed exhausted but relieved to have spent the day with Doris. We laughed, we cried, she told me stories I had never heard of about Jeff. She told me more about Jeff's dad, Derek, who walked out on them when Jeff was three. I could never get Jeff to talk about him much. But Doris told me how much in love they once were. They were young and poor. Jeff was three and Megan had just been born. She said it was just all too much for him and one night he didn't come home. Doris wished she didn't still love him. But she always would.

And then she said I would always love Jeff too, but that I was too young, smart and pretty not to love again. I told her that I didn't think I had it in me, but she just smiled and said, "Jeff always talked about your big heart. I know there's room for someone else in there."

$\mathcal{I}$ pull up outside the house I found to rent. It's by no means my dream house. But it only took me two weeks to find and they allowed me to sign a month-to-month lease in case my house sells fast. The paint is faded, and the roof is on its last legs. But I was drawn to the craftsmanship and charm that it had to offer. The past few weeks have also been the first time I'd started to think about money again. It may not be the nicest, but it's all I can afford.

"Here it is." I lean back against the driver's seat door and look past Nash out the passenger side window.

He looks over at me. "What?" And then out his window. "Here?"

"Yes. What's wrong with here?"

"Are you serious, Jen? This isn't the best neighborhood."

"Oh, stop. It's fine. Plus, I don't have a lot of choices until the house sells. The only equity I have is tied up for the time being. Once it sells I can look at something else." Thankfully, the market is up and with a little luck, I can make some money on the sale.

"But I'm called to this area a lot, and it's not for heart attacks. This is a rough part of town."

"You're overreacting. Plus, you haven't seen the inside. It's quaint. Very kitschy chic."

"Kitschy what?"

I sigh. "Come on."

Climbing out of the car, I head for the front door. Nash is behind me, taking his sweet time scoping the place with his brows pulled in and tension in his arms. I place the key into the lock. It won't budge, so I jiggle it.

Nash comes up behind me, and the heat radiating from his body causes me to pause. He leans over my shoulder and his breath brushes against my neck. "Is it stuck?"

My hair stands up on both arms. I close my eyes, take a deep breath, and move closer to the door to put some distance between us. "No, it's just a little tight, that's all."

"Here, let me try." I step aside to put even more distance between us. His muscles strain as he pushes harder against the door. He jiggles the key a few times until the door finally opens. "Well, there's something I'll have to fix. After you." He steps aside and motions for me to walk ahead of him.

"See, it's quaint. I love the lead glass windows." His gaze flits around the room as he scans everything from floor to ceiling.

"Did you ask if the fireplace is safe to burn in?" he asks.

"They told me not to use it, so I take that as a no."

"Hmph…"

"The kitchen's back here." I escort him down the narrow hallway and point out the floor as we walk, "Look at the hardwood floors. They're original."

"Yeah, I can tell." I try not to let the sarcasm in his voice bother me.

"This is the kitchen."

He walks in shaking his head. "Jen, seriously?"

"What?"

"How old are these appliances? They look like they're from the 1950's."

"That's because they are. I think they're cute, retro. They don't make them like this anymore."

He paces around the kitchen, which doesn't take him very long. "I don't see a dishwasher."

"There isn't one. It's just me. What do I need a dishwasher for?"

He circles back to me. "There's no room for a kitchen table."

"Sure there is." I walk around him and say, "If I get a bistro set and push it up against the wall here." Nash moves across the kitchen to the back door while I lean against the counter. "What is it Nash?" I ask.

I wait while he gathers his thoughts. "I'm sorry. I'm trying to come up with something positive to say...but..."

"But?"

"It's not what I was expecting." His lips purse in thought. "I can't picture you living here. Is this really what you want?"

I cross my arms as well as my legs and lean back on the counter. "It's not ideal, but it'll work."

"You can ask for help sometimes, ya know?"

"No, I can't. My parents carried my mortgage for over a year, and they're going to have to continue to carry it until it sells. Who knows how long that will take? *And* they're loaning me money to cover rent. Any money that Jeff and I had is tied up in that house, so until it sells, I need to watch my money. This will be fine." I move away from the counter and pace around, looking at what needs to be done. "It needs some work, but it's my first step, Nash."

"Do you need money?"

I open my mouth and realize I'm about to say something mean. He's only trying to help, not make me feel as small as possible, "No Nash, I don't need money. I need my best friend to support this decision."

He scratches at his five-o-clock shadow before saying, "On one condition."

"Yes?"

"Before you sleep here, let me fix the front lock." He walks to the back door. "And let me replace this back door since the top half is glass. Deal?"

I don't want his help, but he has a point. If anyone would have asked me two years ago if I would be living in this neighborhood I would have called them crazy. "Deal."

He smiles, looking pleased with my answer. "Well, are you going to show me the upstairs?"

"Sure." I walk back toward the front door and up the stairs. "There are only two bedrooms, but they're pretty good size, which is nice considering the downstairs is a little tight. The master bedroom is…" I hear a crack in the wood and yell "ouch" before looking down. My foot has gone through the top stair.

Nash rushes up beside me. "Are you okay?"

I start to laugh. "Yeah, but my foot is caught." My right foot and half of my calf is lost beneath the stair.

"Let me help you." Nash leans down and wiggles my foot around, finally pulling it out. "You cut the crap out of it. We need to clean it off."

I start to walk again, but I feel shooting pain and I go down. "*Ow.*"

"What is it?"

"I think I might have twisted it."

Nash leans down. "Yeah, I think you're right. It's already swelling."

I take one more step but stop, hissing out in pain.

"Here, let me." Nash walks over to me and scoops me up into his arms.

"Nash, I can…" But before I can finish, I'm enveloped by Nash's arms. I feel his breath on my face and take in his scent. He smells like fresh cut grass on a sunny day. His eyes are steady with a small amount of blue peeking out behind large pupils. They move downward to my lips, and I want to take up permanent residency in his arms. He leans his forehead onto mine and closes his eyes before taking a deep breath. Slowly he opens his eyes, and then I'm wishing for something more. I lick my lips as he studies them, but then abruptly looks away.

"Where's the bathroom? I need a better look at it." His voice is strained, almost angry.

I clear my throat. "Second door on the left."

When he reaches the bathroom, I fumble with the switch as he lowers me to the countertop. Swiveling, I peer into the empty medicine cabinet to distract myself. I didn't like how good it felt to be in his arms. Or maybe I did, and that's the real problem. *Focus, Jensen.* I turn and our eyes lock. I clear my throat again and say, "Looks like water will have to do."

Nash looks around the very small and very pink bathroom. "There's no toilet paper. Is there anything in the kitchen?"

"No, I haven't had a chance to bring anything over yet."

His eyes frantically move around the room and then he hesitates. His eyes hold mine as he grabs the back of his shirt and swiftly pulls it over his head.

"What are you doing?" I scoot forward to jump down from the counter when his hand lands on my waist and pushes me back. He leans over me, and my heartbeat rushes through my ears. The water starts to run and my head hits the mirror behind me. He cocoons my body as he wets his shirt. His neck is three inches from my lips and I swear I can see his pulse throbbing. I keep my hands flat against the cool counter, not trusting them to go anywhere near him. I take a few deep breaths but immediately regret it when his scent assaults me.

"I need to get the dirt and blood off so I can see what I'm working with." The breath from his mouth caresses my neck, and my body jumps forward again. His hand moves back to my waist and this time he leaves it there. "Would you stop? Sit still."

Do I want to run? *Yes, into his arms, idiot.* I shake the thought from my head as his body comes back into view. I try. I really do.

To not stare. At his shoulders, a yard wide and molded like bronze. At his chest, broad and tempting as my eyes trail down to his six-pack. My hand inches away from the cold counter, wanting to feel heat. The heat his body is giving off. The heat my body is producing in response. My fingertips prickle with anticipation as they're drawn to the tribal tattoo that runs down his left arm and continues along his shoulder and back. They begin to lightly brush against it, and he stills. He inhales a sharp breath but continues looking at my ankle.

"When did you get this?" I ask as my fingers continue to trail over his warm skin. I feel like a child exploring a present on Christmas Eve. Just because you know you shouldn't do it doesn't mean you can stop yourself.

"Different life. Different time. I know tattoos aren't your thing."

"I like it. It suits you."

"Jen." His voice has a struggle in it I've never heard before as he moves away from me. When he does, my eyes pull away from his tattoo and land on the lower part of his abdomen where a mix of healed wounds live. There is one main line that is jagged and curves like a river, with smaller rivers breaking away from it in every direction. It's about twelve inches long with faint tick lines along it like a ruler. Each line is symmetrical to another line across from it. The skin underneath it doesn't match the rest of Nash's unblemished core. This skin is an angry pink and mottled. Some areas are raised in mangled bumps while others are taut and smooth.

"What happened?" I whisper.

His eyes follow my line of sight as his jaw tenses. They quickly move back to my leg. "Can we just focus on what's in front of us? Give me your foot!"

I wrap my arms around my body in response. The feelings of warmth and desire have been extinguished.

He then leans over me, both hands flat against the counter, pinning me in. "Hey," he whispers.

But I make no movement to respond. I then feel his finger running underneath my chin, moving my entire face so that we're now eye to eye with one another.

"It's not something I like to talk about. Especially right now while you're bleeding and in pain. Can you please give me your foot so I can try to help you?"

I raise my leg as Nash's eyes roam over my face. He finally pulls away and takes my ankle in his hand. He begins to rub the dirt and blood off my foot, and a new pain overtakes me.

I jerk my leg back in response.

"Sorry. That hurt?"

"Ya think?" But I'm happy for the distraction. Heat is flushing through my body at the realization that he is definitely hiding something from me. I cross my arms over my chest and dig my fingernails into my palms.

"Please tell me you haven't already signed a lease and put a deposit down?"

"Yep!" I say, popping the *p*.

He glares at me before saying, "Why didn't you wait until I had a chance to look it over for you?"

"Because you're not my dad."

"Speaking of, what did he have to say?" He's still cleaning my ankle, but now that he has gotten the worst of it off, his fingers are light and gentle as he works. I take a few deep breaths watching him work. He's focused and meticulous and caring. The only way he's ever been with me. The tension in my body starts to fade. He's trying to take care of me while I'm trying to get him to tell me something he obviously doesn't want to tell me. And that's not fair. There has been one constant between Nash and me since we met: a mutual understanding that we don't have to talk about things we don't want to.

"My dad hasn't seen it either."

"Really, Jensen?"

"You're acting like I'm a child, Nash. I can make my own decisions."

"Apparently not. This place is a shithole in a shithole neighborhood. I'll never sleep knowing you're living over here by yourself."

"My God, you're being dramatic. It's fine. I'll be fine."

He looks up at me. "Yeah, you really look fine with your ankle the size of a cantaloupe."

I glance down at my already swollen ankle. I'm sick of him handling me with kid gloves. I'm sick and tired of everyone handling me that way. I've never been a wallflower, but ever since Jeff's death that's how everyone treats me.

It's time for that to change. "I'm fine." I jump down and try to put weight on my foot before tumbling over into Nash's arms. My hands have somehow found their way again to his bare chest, warm and solid. Everything around me fades, and all I hear is my labored breathing. His finger tenderly traces the line of my cheekbone and jaw. His strength supports my weight and I feel safe. But as our eyes meet, I see hesitation staring back at me. So I pull back and try to retreat on one foot.

He laughs. "Stop being so stubborn. Let me help you."

"Whatever." I glare at him and will that smirk right off his face. That's the feeling I'm trying to focus on, not the empty feeling of no longer being in his arms. Or that distant look in his eyes.

His voice is quieter as he grips my arms. "Does that mean you don't want my help?"

I should *want* to push away from him, but that's what I'm feeling. And since my body won't do what I want it to, I use my mouth to push him away. "Would you stop being a cocky ass?"

"If you'll stop being a stubborn one!"

"Did you just call me an ass?"

"I believe I did."

"Ugh! You're bothering me." I can't stand being this close to him anymore.

"Come on, let me help you."

I walk away from him. "No, I can manage on my own."

I squeal as he comes up from behind me and hoists me into his arms. "Nash stop!"

"I'm not letting you walk back down those stairs on your own."

I try to wiggle out of his arms, but it's no use. I finally relent and wrap one hand around his neck and place the other one on his chest. My eyes move back to his face, where the shadow of a beard gives him an even more masculine appearance. He stops moving and ducks his head almost as if he's trying to hide the effect I'm having on him, but he's doing a lousy job. Without warning, we're moving again as he's rushing down the stairs. He sits me down and leans me up against the railing. "You stay put. I'll get the lights."

He comes back, and I realize I'm still holding onto his shirt. "Want your shirt back?"

"Thanks." He puts it back on, wet and filthy from the blood and dirt he wiped off of my foot and ankle. "Do you want to lean on me or do you want me to carry you?"

"I'll lean. I guess you're going to have to drive my car though since it's my right foot."

A smirk sneaks onto his face. "Too bad we didn't bring my bike."

"You know you're never going to get me on that thing, right?"

"We'll see."

CHAPTER 32

$\mathcal{N}$ash pulls into my driveway and walks around the passenger side to help me out. Leaning on him, I walk/hop up the path to the front door. I put the key in the lock and open the door.

"Thanks."

"Do you need anything before I go?"

"No, I think I can manage." As I turn to move into the house, my hand instinctively lands on his chest. He looks down at it and back up at me.

He steps closer. "You sure?" He asks.

"Yeah, thanks." I pull out of his grasp and am assaulted with a sudden chill even though it's June.

"I'll come by tomorrow to see if you need an X-ray."

"I can't afford that."

"Don't worry about it. I have a buddy at work that owes me a favor. But we'll wait and see what it looks like. Don't forget to alternate between ice and heat tonight. Start and end with heat, and keep it elevated. Do you have a heating pad?"

"Yeah, it's upstairs in my bathroom."

Nash looks up the stairs and then back to me. "You know, you're going to need help getting up the stairs."

I falter but he's right. On the ride home, it felt as though my ankle was tighter, and I'm in a little more pain than I expected. "I guess..."

He steps closer and then asks, "Are you incapable of asking for help?"

My eyes shift to him and then up the stairs before landing back on the floor. "It's not that, it's just...."

He puts his finger under my chin, leveling my eyes with his. "What?"

"I don't know, you've never been upstairs, it's a little too...."

"Intimate?"

I swallow and mutter, "Yeah."

"Do you want me to call your parents? They could help."

"No, it's late."

"Jen." He inhales and pauses. "Do you want me to carry you?"

I search for an excuse, any excuse. I'm not sure I can handle being in his arms again. But there isn't an alternative. "Please."

"Before I do, what do you need from down here besides ice?"

"There's a book I'm reading on the coffee table. Can you grab that, please?"

"Sure. Anything else? Water or something to eat?"

"I'm not hungry, but a bottle of water would be good."

"Where's your aspirin?"

"Upstairs in the linen closet."

"Okay." He leans down but angles his face back up to me like he's asking for permission. I answer with a curt nod, and he grabs me around the waist and behind my knees. I close my eyes and force myself to remember that I'm in Jeff's house. That this man should not be carrying me into our bedroom. But I can't focus on that. All I feel is Nash's body securely wrapped around mine as he carries me up the stairs. He abruptly stops, and I'm forced to open my eyes. I then realize he doesn't know where he's going.

"That's my bedroom." The moment "my bedroom" leaves my mouth, I think of Jeff. That's the first time I said mine, not ours. Even though it's correct, my stomach rolls with nausea. I switch on the light, and we both gape at the neatly made king size bed. Our eyes seem to find each other, like two magnets drifting toward each other. He quickly looks away and starts to make his way to the edge of the bed. He gently sets me down and then moves to the top of the bed and begins to pull down the sheets for me but I grab his arm. "That's okay. I can get it."

"Right. I'll go down and get some ice and water and be right back."

"Thank you."

After he leaves the room, I sit there, frozen. My stomach is still quivering at the thought of another man in my bedroom. So many feelings flash through me: embarrassment, guilt, desire, confusion. I try to shake off the feelings by focusing on the task at hand. I shimmy up the bed and manage to get to my knees without putting weight on my ankle. I move the pillow so that it's pressed against the headboard and rest against it. I can't believe I did this. Plus, that stair now needs to be fixed before I can move in. And what if the other ones are in the same condition? And how am I going to finish packing and move with a bum ankle?

"Jensen, stop!" Nash's voice startles me.

"What?" I ask.

He has a bottle of water in one hand, a bag of ice in the other and my book tucked underneath his arm. He strides over to me and sets the water and book on the nightstand. "What are you worrying about?"

I shake my head. I don't want to admit he's right about the house.

"Jen, what?"

But I also don't want to lie to him. "The house. Now I need to fix that stair, and I'm worried about the other ones. I mean, if that one is rotten the rest probably are too. And how am I supposed to pack and move with one leg?"

He scoots closer to me as his eyes bore into mine. His hand drifts toward my face and he gently rubs his thumb along my cheek while cupping my face. I lean into his hand. "Don't worry about the house. I'll help you, and we'll make sure everything is safe before you move in. And I think the ankle will be okay in a few days. But you're going to have to stay off of it. Don't push it or you'll make it worse." He reaches over me to grab the other pillow and I inhale his scent again. It's a scent I've grown accustomed to over the past few months, but for some reason it's more noticeable tonight and I can't help but lean further into him. "Lift." Nash grabs my leg and places it on top of the pillow. He moves it around and looks at it again.

"Ow! Do you mind?"

"Stop being a baby and let me look at it."

"Ow! Seriously? I can't believe you do this for a living. You think you would be more careful."

He smirks. "You really can be a pain in the ass, you know." I roll my eyes. "Where's the aspirin again? And your alcohol? We need to properly clean it."

"Bathroom, in the linen closet." Nash walks across the room to the bathroom, which gives me time to realize how uncomfortable I'm starting to feel with him here.

He walks back to me and holds out his hand. "Here, take these."

My uneasiness drifts away and is replaced with a light-hearted feeling. I've been through a lot, but I'm thankful that unimaginable circumstances led me to Nash. He's always so patient with me, and he's the only one that I feel like myself around anymore. I'm no longer the person I used to be, and although I'm still not sure who I am, when I'm with him, I'm hopeful and confident that I can figure it out.

"Thanks."

He smiles back and sits down on the edge of the bed to grab the water. As he does, I notice him staring at a picture of Jeff and me at our engagement party. Julia and Travis stand next to Jeff while Olivia and her boyfriend at the time stand next to me. He continues to stare at it, so I say, "That's at our engagement party." I lean over to pick it up so he can see it better. "That's Jeff's best friend Julia and her husband, Travis. She met Jeff in grade school and they were best friends for years. And then you recognize Olivia. That was her boyfriend at the time. I think his name was Tom." I look up at Nash, who has his eyes closed tight. Leaning over, I touch his arm. "Hey...you okay?"

"Jensen...I need to tell you something." He takes the picture out of my hand and sits it down on the bed. He then stands and moves toward the end of the bed.

"Okay." I pick up the frame and place it back on the night-stand. I then give Nash my attention as he paces at the foot of the bed. "Nash, what is it?"

"I, um…I need to tell you something, and you're not going to like it." I hold my breath as he continues.

He continues to pace. I've never seen him so wound tight. "Just say it, Nash."

He stops and comes back to my side of the bed and sits down next to me. He reaches over and grabs my hand. His hands are clammy, and it's such a foreign feeling I want to rip them away. But before I can, he squeezes mine tight. "Jensen, I know Julia. I'm her brother."

I continue to hold his hand, but the room tilts on its axis. *Her brother?* I knew that Julia had a brother. Jeff mentioned him early in our relationship. They never really got along. Her brother was overprotective of her, so they kept their distance from one another. He also told me Julia's brother had a rough time in high school, had gone through something traumatic and wasn't ever the same. Julia brought him up once in passing conversation, but it was by accident and she quickly changed the subject. But I had met him, hadn't I? Nash isn't him. And his name is Jack.

"Say something...please."

My focus is on our hands, and my knuckles are white from holding onto Nash. I jerk my hands away. "What are you talking about? Julia's brother is named Jack. And I've met him. At Julia and Travis's wedding...I met him."

"That was me. Don't you remember? I missed the rehearsal dinner and showed up right before the ceremony. You and the other bridesmaids had already been drinking."

My pulse starts to race as my heartbeat becomes more prominent.

"Jensen. You and I have met before. I'm Julia's brother, Nash. My family calls me Jack, but I haven't gone by Jack since...since high school. I knew Jeff. We grew up together because he was friends with my sister."

I still feel as though the room is spinning. I don't understand. If he knew me, why did he pretend like he didn't at group? And why has he lied to me all this time? "Wait, did you just now figure out who I was after seeing your sister in that picture?"

"No, I've known all along who you were."

"Nash, I don't understand. When? When did you figure out who I was? And why didn't you say something?"

"Jen, I went to that group because of you. After the intervention they had with you, Julia called me. She asked for my help. They were worried about you, so they wanted someone to check in on you and make sure you were getting help. Julia told me about the support group. When I went that night, I wasn't supposed to be an active participant. I was just supposed to make sure you got out of the car and went. Your mom knew you weren't going as much as you should. But that day, when I saw you...I saw how angry you were and I...I stepped in. I was afraid if I told you who I was, you wouldn't give me a chance."

He pauses as if he's waiting for me to say something. "Then

the first night we went to get coffee and sat in silence, something changed in me. I enjoyed your company, even when we weren't talking to one another. Then we became friends and I saw you opening up to me. I knew you weren't doing that with anyone else, and before I knew it, I was in too deep. I didn't want to risk our relationship, so I didn't tell you. Jen, I meant what I said when I told you that you're my best friend. There are so many things I need to tell you, but what I need you to know right now is that I'm sorry. I shouldn't have kept this from you. But I got scared because I can't imagine you not being in my life. Something changed when I met you. You make me feel alive, like I deserve something better. It's been a long time since I've felt this way." He exhales before continuing. "And while I'm coming clean, there's something else I need to tell you."

"You lied to me." It's hardly a whisper. I can't believe what he's telling me. Not just that he's a liar. But that my family and friends lied to me too. And they betrayed me. They've had someone watching me this whole time. That's why everyone backed off.

"Wait! Hear me out. After the intervention, your family…"

"You knew about that…before I told you about it?"

"Yes, Julia called me the night you stormed out of the intervention. She thought that with what I had gone through I might be able to help you. I saw what happened to you at Jeff's funeral."

A bitter tang rushes into my mouth. "You were there?"

He swallows before whispering, "We heard you screaming. Julia went running and Travis followed." He pauses, tightening his fists, and takes a few deep breaths. "But it was the first time since I became a paramedic that I didn't run toward someone who needed help."

I feel a tear fall past my eyes and I brush it away. "Why?"

His body moves away from me as he leans his elbows on his knees. "Because I knew whatever was happening was breaking someone already broken. And I was too familiar with that feeling. I didn't want any part of it." He turns back to face me. "But I finally found my nerve and offered to help when Todd was carrying you out."

I think back to that day. That voice. *His* voice. "That was you?" The words rush out. Nash's eyes respond. "You lied to me." My voice is no longer a whisper.

"And it ate me up every day. But I had a *good* reason, and then we got close and I knew I couldn't bear to lose you. I had finally started living again, and after what had happened to me in high school…"

"You lied to me!" I find my voice, and I'm pretty sure the whole neighborhood can hear me. "Get out! Now!"

"Jen, please! I understand you being angry, and you have every right to be, but please just…"

"I don't have anything to say to you. Get out." I cross my arms over my chest refusing to make eye contact. I wait, but he doesn't move.

Finally, I hear him exhale and the bed shifts underneath me. Making sure he's leaving, I watch as he walks to the door with his head hung low. Stopping, he turns back, but I look away. I can't face him. I won't. I pick a spot on the wall to stare at until I hear the front door shut behind him. Then I pick up the picture again and throw it against the wall, and it breaks into a million pieces, just like my heart…all over again.

CHAPTER 33

I stay in bed for the next three days. On the third day, my stomach starts to hurt so I manage to slide down the stairs to protect my ankle. I eat some crackers, and then crawl back up the stairs and collapse on my bed. My chest hurts. My lungs hurt. My heart hurts. It's all eerily familiar to how I felt after losing Jeff. And Nash was the only one that truly helped me out of that. He helped me to at least want to try. But the emptiness I had finally let go of has returned, and I dwell in the uncertainty of what I'm going to do.

By the fourth day, the sadness has transformed into anger and motivation. I'm mad at myself for comparing the feelings of losing Nash to those I had when I lost my family. I haven't even known Nash for a year. I've made too much progress to regress because someone that I thought was important turned out to be a liar.

Climbing out of bed, I switch my phone on for the first time in four days. I have over two dozen voicemails and texts, but I delete them all. I can only imagine that Nash has come clean to everyone, and they are circling the wagons. Their little plan of sending in a spy to check up on me just blew up. I wonder how many of them were in on it. Olivia wasn't. She would never go for that. But the rest of them—my parents, Jeff's family, our friends. Well, they all can go to hell!

I tried to put weight on my foot yesterday and it was still too painful. I slowly rotate it and try again. It's not 100%, but it's going to have to do. I'm no longer going to be the pathetic girl who just lets life happen to her. I wasn't that girl before Jeff, and I'm not going to be her after Nash. Enough is enough. I shower, get dressed, do my hair, and even put on makeup. I then call a moving company and set up a time for them to come this weekend.

Once I hang up with the moving company, I draft a text to my mom.

"Can you and dad come over Friday morning?"

"Sure. :-) Everything ok?"

I huff at the smiley face. Yeah, Nash told her what happened. *"There's something I would like to discuss with you."*

"Ok, we'll be there."

CHAPTER 34

"Knock knock." My mother's voice drifts in as the door squeaks open.

"In the dining room…"

My parents walk in and halt, taking in their surroundings.

Everything is packed—every last dish, picture, memento. Some of it will go to the rental with me, and some of it will go to a storage facility until I find a more permanent place. Movers will physically move me, but I went through the painstaking process of packing up my family's life all on my own. I was driven by pure anger and hatred, which is better than the grief that would have consumed me. Knowing that not only did my family and friends deceive me, but also the one person I had grown close to these past few months was all it took. I finally did it.

My mom gawks around the room. "What's going on? Why is the house destroyed?" She asks.

"It's not destroyed, mom. It's called packing. I'm moving today."

"Is this why you called us over here?" my mom asks.

"Yeah, why did you think I called you?"

My parents exchange glances with one another as my mom says, "Because we heard from Julia. Nash called her and told her what happened. We thought you wanted to talk to us about it. And we know you're upset, but honey we *didn't* have a choice. You weren't listening to any of us, and you refused to get any sort of help. We couldn't continue to watch you waste away. We were desperate."

I'm glad I have my back to them as I stare out the window. Desperate? She doesn't know the meaning of the word. I try to remain calm by taking a few cleansing breaths before turning to face them. "Let me tell you how this is going to go. I've hired a moving company to move everything for me, so the two of you don't need to do anything. They'll be here in an hour."

"Oh Jensen, now come on honey, let's sit down here and talk before you go and make any rash decisions—"

I interrupt my mother. "I wasn't done talking, but you are. So again, let me tell you how this is going to go. I've hired a moving company to move me out of here and take everything to the new place. I don't need the two of you to do anything, but I at least wanted you to be aware that this was my last day here. I'll call you when I'm ready to talk."

My dad finally decides to join the conversation as opposed to hiding behind his wife. "Jensen, we know this must be hard..."

"Hard? You know, Dad, I'm running out of adjectives to describe how painful my life has been for the past year. But *just* as I was starting to turn a corner, I find out that the person I've grown closest to is a liar." I laugh and then clap my hands together. "And the cherry on top is he was sent by my family and friends to deceive me. So, yeah, you could say my life is a little hard right now. I'm also a little pissed!"

My mother clears her throat. "Please don't be angry with Julia or Nash. They were just trying to help. We were all just trying to help and..."

"Help? You call this helping? This didn't help. I found

someone who I thought understood me. Someone I relied on and trusted. I was also starting to enjoy life again after losing everything. But then I find out he's not who I thought he was. That my family and friends felt the need to dupe me so they could *help*!"

"I can understand why you're angry, but we love you and were only trying to do what we thought was best. We know it was unimaginable circumstances, but we thought that with what Nash had gone through himself, he might be just the right person to help you."

I shake my head, fumbling with my words. "Wha…what are you talking about?"

My mother's eyes move to my father's, and he responds by shaking his head at her. What the hell does that mean?

She looks back to me and squares her shoulders. "Well dear, I think that's his story to tell."

"Of course!" I throw my hands up in the air. "More secrets, just what I was looking for from this conversation. You know, it doesn't matter, and I don't give a damn. I can see the two of you aren't interested in being honest with me, so you can go."

"Jensen, I really wish you would calm down so that we could have a mature and reasonable conversation. We only did what we thought was best because we love you and—"

I cut her off. "If you truly love me, you'll get the hell out."

"Jensen! That's enough! I know you're upset but you don't speak to your mother like that."

"I wasn't just talking to her, I was talking to you too, Dad. Get out! NOW!"

My parents shoot daggers at me. I haven't seen that look on their faces since I was sixteen and lied about the scratch I put on my dad's new car. My chest tightens, so I turn away. I can't look at them anymore.

"Jensen." My mom speaks softly, like she's talking to someone with a bomb stretched across their chest. "We don't want to leave you, not today. We know how hard this is going to be for you."

Slightly hysterical, I start to laugh. "This is easy after what I've been through. I don't want you here. I don't want any of you here. I will do this on my own." My body twists to face them one more time. They're frozen in place, unsure what to do. I know the feeling. But not today. Today, I know exactly what to do. "You need to go. I'll call you after I have calmed down."

Several moments pass, and then my dad finally speaks. "Linda, we need to go. Come on, let's give her some space."

I know my mother wants to support me and help me through this. But unfortunately, not only do I not want her help, I can't have it. I'm going to have to make this move on my own if I ever want any chance of truly moving forward. She hesitates before saying, "If that's what she wants."

Even if I wanted to tell them to stop, I can't. There's nothing left to say. Once the door closes behind them, my body falls into a chair and I focus on trying to survive the day.

CHAPTER 35

*N*ine hours later, it's done. My life with Jeff was packed up and moved like it never happened. But my heart knew better. A piece of me, of us, will always live in that house. But it's time to leave it behind.

"That should be all of the information we need, ma'am. Typically bills go out two to three weeks after delivery, and it will come to your new address."

"That will be fine. Thank you." The empty two-wheeler clatters down the stairs as I close the door behind him. I lean against it, trying not to feel overwhelmed. There are boxes everywhere. I'm thankful that I had them take several loads to the storage unit or else I wouldn't be able to walk in here. I knew there was no way a 3,700-square foot house would fit in a 900 square foot house, even after giving a lot of Jeff's things to his mom and sister. But I'm too exhausted to do anything else tonight, so the room will have to stay this way. I sit down on the one cushion of the couch that isn't covered in crap and look at the clock. I ordered pizza twenty minutes ago, so it should be here any minute. I'm ready to eat and head straight to bed.

I sit in silence and listen to the new sounds the old house

brings. I hear the hum of the refrigerator and a dog barking outside. I didn't notice it before. Does it bark all the time? The moving truck rumbles as it's pulling away, and I hope that's why he's barking.

I never got used to the noises our house made after Jeff was no longer in it. Everything seemed so much quieter after he was gone that I'm now appreciating this change. This space doesn't remind me of Jeff; of his smell or where we made love or had a fight. Yet with that comes a sense of closure and sadness. I'm not sure I'm ready.

The buzz of my phone startles me, but I have no desire to look at it. There is no one I care to talk to right now. Even Olivia. She didn't betray me like everyone else, but I still don't feel like talking. It buzzes again and I pick it up, intending to turn it off. As I do, I see Nash's name.

"I know I'm the last person you want to hear from but I just want to make sure that you're okay. Julia talked to your parents and she told me you moved today. How did it go? How is the ankle?"

I snort since I had forgotten all about the pain. Anger drove me today, but now that he mentioned it, it does hurt and it's still swollen. Why did he have to bring it up? I also love how they still all seem to be talking about me behind my back. They need to get lives. At least I have an excuse for not having one. I'm about to shut off my phone when the doorbell rings.

I grab my purse, now nursing my ankle a little more than I was. I look out the peep hole and see a teenager holding up a pizza box, bouncing on his feet as he surveys the neighborhood. I open the door and smile.

"Hi."

"Hey. It's twelve bucks."

"Okay." I dig in my purse, pull out the twelve dollars, and then go back to find a tip when he snatches the money from my hand. He pushes the box into my arms and runs back down the stairs. "Wait! Your tip…"

He yells back, "Don't worry about it," sprints back to his car, and speeds away.

Good grief. I walk into the kitchen as another text comes through, but I'm definitely going to ignore it now that I know who it is. I'm starving, and he's going to be waiting a long time for a response.

I dig into one of the boxes and pull out a paper plate and paper towel. I grab a beer from the fridge and walk back to the couch. I turn my phone over, resisting the urge to look, and eat my pizza. I take my time eating not one, not two, but three pieces of pepperoni with extra cheese. I wipe the crumbs from the coffee table that missed my plate and walk back into the kitchen. I put the rest of the pizza in the fridge and spend the next hour unpacking boxes in the kitchen and putting things away. I look for any excuse to keep myself busy so I don't read that text. But after another hour, I can't resist anymore.

"Please don't ignore me. Just let me know you're okay and I promise I will leave you alone."

I huff—I held strong for two hours for *that*? Does he really expect me to be okay? I press the top button on my phone and then slide the red arrow to power it off. I'm going to let him stew.

I make my way into the family room and move some bags off the couch and boxes out of the way so that I don't feel like I'm in a fort. I grab the book I'm reading from my purse and lie down on the couch. Before I open it, I look up at the ceiling and see water stains that I hadn't noticed before. I drop my arm over my eyes and sigh. *How did I get here?*

CHAPTER 36

After my first night in the new house of trying to sleep but failing, I get up and go to turn on the shower. I pull my hair up in a bun because I'm not in the mood to fix it today. It's just grocery shopping. I stick my hand under the water and pull it back. It's ice cold. I double check that I have it all the way on hot and start to undress before checking it again. Still cold. I groan and turn it off. Add that to the list of things I need to talk to my landlord about.

In my room, I dig through three boxes before finding underwear and a somewhat presentable outfit. I walk down the stairs, grab my purse, and head out the front door. Halfway down the driveway I stop. Clenching my teeth, I shake my head, open my car door and throw my purse into the passenger side seat. I slam the door and head to the street, where I start pounding on Nash's driver's side window.

He jerks awake and frantically glances around before his eyes finally find me.

"What the hell do you think you're doing?" I say, louder than necessary.

His truck door opens, and he climbs out, popping his neck. "Hi."

"I asked you a question."

"I was making sure you were okay. I guess I fell asleep."

"How long have you been out here?" I put up my hand before he can answer. "Never mind, I don't care. As you can see, I'm fine, so if you don't mind…"

His eyes rake over my body. "Are you heading out? Do you want to grab breakfast?"

I grumble and twist away from him. I'm having a hard time staying mad at him. His eyes are weighted down by pools of darkness. His clothes are wrinkled and his normal five-o-clock shadow looks more like a two-day shadow.

I stop as I realize I'm acting childish by not speaking to him. I turn around and walk back to him, trying to let go of the tension. "Look Nash, please don't make this any harder than it already is. I don't want to fight with you."

"I don't want to fight either."

"Great. We're on the same page. Can we just let it go?"

"And what…never speak to each other again?"

I cross my arms in front of my chest before putting all my weight on my good ankle. "Something like that."

He runs his hand down his face and scratches at his beard. "Jen, please, I'm sorry. I *know* I should have told you sooner, but there never seemed to be a good time in the beginning. Julia asked me for a favor, and I was just trying to help my sister and someone she cares about. And then it got harder and harder. I didn't know how to tell you. I told you that day before we left for the cemetery that I had something to tell you. It was killing me! But I didn't want to tell you that day. Then you told me you were going to sell the house, and I don't know, I just…" He looks to the ground and sticks his hands in his pockets before looking back up at me. "I didn't know how to say it. But you know I never meant to hurt you."

"I know that, but the fact is you did." We stare at each other without speaking. He makes no move to leave, and I don't have anything else to say. "I need to go. I have a million things to do."

I start to walk away when he asks, "Did you have someone fix your stair?"

"Not yet. I have a list of things that I need to talk to my landlord about."

"Jen, just let me fix it. And whatever else needs to be fixed. I don't want some random guy in your house when I can take care of it for you."

I don't stop as the need to put distance between us grows. "No thanks. That's one of the perks of renting. Someone else handles the maintenance."

He yells, "Okay, I'll talk to you later." I get in my car and pull away without giving him a glance.

CHAPTER 37

*M*y phone rings and I see that it's my mom, *again*. I can't keep avoiding her, so now is as good a time as any. I'm in my happy place.

"Hello?"

"Jensen, thank God." My mother exhales a whoosh of air on the other end.

"Oh mom, stop being dramatic."

"*Dramatic?* I haven't talked to you in almost two weeks. You up and move away, and then won't pick up the phone. I understand you being mad, but seriously, what is wrong with you?"

I cross my legs and pick at the dirt by my shoes. I used to think of this as Nash's place. Yet I'm here on my own so often lately that I don't think of him. Or try not to. But a tiny part of me wonders if that's the *only* reason I come here. "You act like I moved out of state or something."

"That's a possibility for all we know. We have no idea where you live. It's like you did it on purpose! Are you trying to cut us totally out of your life?"

"Nothing gets by you."

"Jensen!"

"Mom. Look, I needed some space, and you're not capable of giving it to me. Plus, I don't want to be judged by you and Dad on where I'm living."

"Oh honey, we would never do that. We're proud of you for taking a step forward."

Yeah, she says that now, but once she sees the place she'll change her tune. "So, what's up, Mom?"

"Where are you?"

"I'm hiking at Pierman's Point."

"Oh, are you with Nash?" Her voice rises as she asks.

I have no problem crushing her dreams. "Nope. Why would you ask me that?"

"Because you usually hike together. You're not hiking alone, are you? Jensen, that's dangerous!"

"And this would be why I haven't picked up the phone. I'm not with Nash. I'm fully capable of hiking alone. In fact, I've discovered these past few weeks that I'm capable of doing a lot of things *alone*." Even though it's not what I prefer, it's my life now, and I'm slowly learning to accept it.

"So, I guess that means you still haven't talked to Nash."

"Actually, I'm kind of shocked he hasn't told you where I live."

"Oh, I've tried to get it out of him *and* Julia, but no luck."

"Well, at least they're loyal, even though they're both liars."

"Oh, Jensen," she says after sighing.

"You're ruining my hiking buzz."

"I'm sorry. I miss you. Can we come over and see the house sometime?"

I rub my fingers across my forehead, knowing I can't hide from them forever. I've also felt guilty with how things have transpired between us. They're my parents and they love me. And just as I didn't know how to handle myself in this situation, they didn't know how to handle it either. They lost a son-in-law and a grandchild. And their daughter in a way. That woman is gone and I don't know who stands in her place. But, I'm determined to figure it out. "How about I come to you? I need to go check on the other house anyway. They've shown it a few times, and I want to make sure it's still clean."

"I'll take what I can get. Tomorrow night?"

"Okay Mom. I'll see you around 6:00 p.m."

"Dad and I look forward to it. Jensen…we love you."

"I love you both too, Mom. Bye."

As I sit and look out over the horizon, I rub my hands up and down my arms. I can't help but think of Nash when I'm here. My phone still sits in my hand and I want nothing more than to call him. To hear his voice. But I don't. Because there isn't anything left to say.

* * *

I WIPE my mouth and lay the napkin on the dining room table. "Thanks, Mom. It was nice to have a home- cooked meal."

"Are you not taking care of yourself?"

"I am, but it always tastes better when someone else makes it."

My dad leans over and looks at me before saying, "You look like you've put on a little weight."

"Geez, thanks Dad."

"Oh honey, it was a compliment." My mom picks up my plate and takes it into the kitchen. "You were getting pretty thin there for a while. You're looking a little more like yourself is all he means."

"I've been hiking almost every day, so I think a lot of it is muscle."

"Are you enjoying that?" my dad asks.

"I am. It's not something I ever saw myself doing, but it relaxes me and at a minimum gets me out of the house."

My mom sets brownies on the table. "I'm glad to hear that dear, I really am. You know we love you. And we're sorry for how we handled the Nash situation."

"I know what happened wasn't your intention. And it's his fault for not saying something as we grew closer to one another. And I'm sorry for how I've treated you both. I know I haven't handled this situation very well. But, I am trying to move forward."

"Honey, your mother and I know that. But we worry about you."

"Dad, I get it, but there's nothing anyone can do. I'm the only one who can do this."

"Well…" My dad says as he seems to stumble to find his words. "I was hoping that maybe I could do something."

My mother gives him a death glare. "John, we talked about this. I don't think she's ready."

My eyes bounce back and forth between them. "Ready for what?"

"Why don't you let her make that decision, Linda?"

"Because I don't want her to feel pressured."

I'm still looking back and forth between them. "Pressured about what?"

"That's for her to decide. She can say no if she wants."

"Guys! I'm in the room here. What are you talking about?" They both stop and look at me and then each other.

"Okay." My mother shrugs. "Go ahead and tell her."

My dad scoots closer to me as my mom continues to clear things off the table. I've known her long enough to know that whatever he's about to say, she doesn't support. But I also know he's going to say it anyway. "Do you remember Kevin Talbot?"

"Yeah, you guys golf together. Why?"

"His daughter, Tara, is the director of the Hope Project. They're a non-profit group that works to place foster children in permanent homes."

"Isn't that what social services is for?"

"Yes, but there are so many cases that this group formed about seven years ago to help. They help with the really difficult cases of children who have been in the system a while and can't seem to find a home."

"What does that have to do with me?"

"Well, recently their lawyer took a different job, and they've been desperately looking for another one for almost three months. Since they're a non-profit, the pay isn't great."

My stomach twists as I realize what he's asking me. "Dad, no. I told you, I'm done being a lawyer."

"Jensen, I know you've said that. But you just said that you're ready to move forward. This would be a great first step."

"I'm sorry, Dad, but I'm done practicing law."

"I don't believe you. It's the only career you've ever talked about. You're sure you just want to walk away from it?"

"Quite sure." I cross my arms and lean back in my chair, glaring at him.

"I was hoping that this would help you. It's not full time. It's around twenty to thirty hours a week. They just need someone to make sure the legal formalities are followed. Kevin was talking to me about it while we played golf last week, and I thought it would be a great opportunity for you."

"Yeah, except I'm not looking for *that* kind of opportunity."

"Okay, okay. I'm not going to push you. I just wanted to mention it. If you're not interested, that's fine."

"Well, I'm not." He looks down, shakes his head, and then takes the glasses into the kitchen where my mom is loading the dishwasher. I sit at the table by myself and try to ignore my blood pressure rising. I pick up my glass of water and take three large gulps. It's times like these I miss Nash. I would have felt comfortable talking with him about this but no one else. He would have understood and sympathized with why I'm not interested. I pull the glass from my lips as I realize that's not true. Nash probably would have challenged me on why I wasn't considering it. Jeff would have sympathized with me. My heart starts to palpitate realizing that for the first time since Jeff's been gone, I didn't wish he was here, I wished that Nash was here. How can I sit here and want to talk to the guy who deceived me instead of my loving and loyal husband?

I shove back from the table, needing some air. I grab my purse, yell out to my parents that I'm leaving, and run out the door. I get into my car and pull away as quickly as possible. I pass the street I should take to my old house, so I can stop and check on it, but I don't care.

I drive around for a while trying to calm my nerves and somehow end up at Nash's house. I park on the street about three houses down and kill the engine. I sit, trying to figure out why I came here of all places. My hand hovers on the door handle, but once the cool steel touches my sweaty hands I realize I've made a mistake. Going to him now would be unfair to him. He's kept his distance from me like I asked him to do weeks ago, so I need to respect that he's moved on.

I'm numb as I drive back to the rental. The gravel crunches under my tires as I make my way through the narrow alley. The neighborhood is quiet and dark as I walk up to the back porch. I delay unlocking the door when I hear a noise around the side of the house. I debate on rushing in and locking the door behind me so I feel safe. Or being a grown-up and walking around the side of the house to check on the noise. But I'm a chicken and I get inside the house as fast as I can. I deadbolt the lock and then peer out the window. Nothing. I laugh at myself. I'm getting worked up over nothing.

I walk through the kitchen, bypass the family room, and walk up the stairs. As I reach the top, I look down at the now-fixed stair and think of Nash. I hate myself for it. It's been two weeks since I caught him sleeping in his truck, and I miss him. I can't control what happened to Jeff. But I'm in total control of what I'm doing to Nash. I'm sick of hating myself or feeling guilty or wanting a life that I can't seem to have. A shiver moves throughout my body as I walk into the bedroom and reach into the drawer for my pajamas. After washing my face and brushing my teeth, I climb into bed.

Sleep comes easily as I'm exhausted from guilt and self-doubt. I feel guilty that Jeff is no longer here. I feel guilty that Nash is no longer in my life. I feel guilty that I think about Nash more than Jeff. I feel guilty that I no longer feel as if I was ever a mom. I feel guilty that I think the person I was, who I worked so hard to be and who I was proud of, is gone. That person no longer exists, and I have no idea who stands in her place.

CHAPTER 38

I wake up with dry mouth and reach for my water on the nightstand, but I didn't bring one up with me. The clock on the nightstand reads 2:57 a.m. I rub my eyes and climb out of bed, walk down the stairs, and grab a bottle. The bottle stops at my lips when I hear my neighbor's dog, Chief, barking. That's probably what woke me up. I scan the backyard but I don't see anything. I turn to make my way back upstairs, but I linger in the hallway because Chief usually doesn't bark at nothing. I walk back to the door and look out again, searching a little harder this time. I still see nothing, and I can't see Chief. I can only hear him. I wait a few seconds and then decide it must be nothing and head back to bed.

As I climb the stairs, I hear a noise that sounds like something being dragged. I freeze and try to make out where the sound is coming from. A few seconds later, I hear it again. It's coming from either the side or back of the house. Something then hits the back-porch door, and my adrenaline spikes as fear paralyzes me. The noise comes again, and I race up the remaining stairs into my bedroom to grab my phone. I skid to a stop, pluck it from my nightstand, and hit my favorites list, praying he's not on duty. He picks up on the second ring.

"Jen, what's wrong?"

"Nash! Something's on the back porch!"

"What kind of something?"

I hear scuffling in the background and I hear him start to pant. "I don't know. Almost like someone pounding on the back door."

"Jen, hang up and call the police. I'm already to my truck and on my way."

"No!"

"No? Jensen! This isn't the time to be mad at me. Do as you're told."

"No, I mean I don't want to hang up. Nash, I'm scared, don't leave me!"

"Jensen, call the police. I'm already on my way, but they'll get there faster."

"What if it's nothing?"

"What if it's not!"

He's out of breath and his voice trembles with fear. I realize I'm scaring him and I don't even know what I heard. I take a few deep breaths to calm my racing heart and turn back toward the door. "I'm going to go downstairs and look,"," I whisper.

"Jen, no! Where are you?"

"In my bedroom."

"Stay there and lock the door. Don't do anything until I get there."

"Nash, just let me go look."

"No! Damn, you just won't listen."

I can't help but grin. He's right about that. I creep out of my bedroom and look down the stairs. Everything looks normal, so I make my way to the stairs and creep down them one by one, looking around as more of the room comes into view.

"Jensen! Why are you so quiet?" I ignore him so I don't make any noise. "Jensen. Son of a bitch! Answer me."

"Shh...I'm looking around."

"Seriously? Are you trying to kill me here?"

I walk into the kitchen and take a deep breath. I pull back the curtain and look into the yard. Again, everything seems fine, but Chief is going crazy. I can hear him running up and down the length of the fence and barking non-stop. What is he barking at? I glance down to the landing of the patio, and then I scream. In the process, I drop my phone. A raccoon chews on something with a tail hanging outside of its mouth. I start to laugh. The laugh gets louder when I remember Nash is still on the other end of the phone. I pick up my phone and stare at a cracked screen. Crap. I try to turn it on, but nothing happens. As I'm fiddling with it, I hear a crash at the front door. I rush to the hallway just in time to see the woodwork crack around the frame. My adrenaline spikes again until I hear Nash screaming my name on the other side of the door. I yell back and run toward him, but I'm too late. The next thing I see is the door flying open as fragments of the wood door fall to the ground. Nash sails through it and zooms up the stairs.

"Nash, stop. Nash!" The stairs creak, and he runs back down.

"Nash, I'm okay."

He runs toward me and I meet him halfway. Our bodies collide, and he squeezes me, hard. His body is covered in cold sweat and his breath is ragged in my ear. His chest rises and falls sharply against mine. "You're okay?" he asks, rushing the words out of his mouth.

"I'm okay." He has my arms pinned to my sides so I can't hug him back. Right now, I want to. But I don't move. I let him hold me and then I feel him start to calm down. He pulls back and looks in my eyes. He moves a stray hair from my face.

"You're okay." He says.

I smile and shake my head. "I'm sorry."

"For what?" His breathing is still broken, but not as bad as it was a few minutes ago.

"For calling you in the middle of the night."

"Can you be sorry for hanging up on me instead of calling me in the first place?"

I laugh and then hold up my phone. "I didn't hang up on you. I dropped it."

"But I thought I heard you scream?"

"You did. Follow me." I lead him to the back porch, where my new friend is still munching on its snack. I motion toward the window. "Look down." He does and then looks back at me.

"You called me at 3:00 a.m. because a raccoon was eating a mouse?"

"No, I called you because I thought someone was breaking into my house. I screamed and dropped the phone because a raccoon was eating a mouse."

He slowly smiles and shakes his head. "I never pictured you as the type to get upset over a little spilt mouse."

"Oh my God, seriously? That joke was lame."

"Give me a break. It's three o'clock in the morning."

"I'm sorry for calling you."

He walks to me, and my stomach begins to flutter the closer he gets. "Jensen, don't ever be sorry for that."

I don't know what to say. But I immediately feel myself retreating. I rub my hands up and down my arms. "I think you'd better go."

His eyes focus on mine and he moves back. "Can I have a glass of water before I go?"

He's trying to stall, but I at least owe him that. I step around him to the refrigerator, pull out the water pitcher, and grab a glass from the cabinet. I move back to the refrigerator, and the slamming of the ice cubes against the glass breaks the silence.

When I turn, he's leaning against the door frame. He plays the part of the bad boy really well: confident, almost cocky, tight white shirt that shows off his tattoo and the outline of his pecs straining against it. He's wearing gray lounge pants and flip-flops, proving he left in a hurry. Tension stands between us as his burning eyes hold me still.

I shake my head, releasing myself from the draw he has on me, and hand him the glass. Our hands lightly brush, and my tongue darts out to lick my lips. I then back away and lean up against the sink. He takes a slow sip, never taking his eyes off of me.

We stand in silence for what feels like eternity. "Can we talk?" he asks.

My emotions are like a car driving on ice. My first instinct is to slam on the brakes and stop the conversation before it starts. But if I don't have this conversation, I won't have closure. Even though I'm not sure closure is what I want now that he's standing in front of me. "I'm not sure there's anything left to say."

"Oh, come on. You dragged my ass out of bed at 3:00 a.m.; the least you can do is let me talk to you."

"Why, so you can lie to me some more?" I cross my arms.

"I deserve that. But Jen. I said I was sorry. And my heart was in the right place. I've given you your space. What else do you want me to do?"

"Are you really sorry?"

"Why would you think I'm not?"

"I don't know, Nash. In fact, I don't know anything. I don't even know who you truly are."

"You're right."

"And how can you…wait, what?"

"You're right. You don't know everything about me because I don't let a lot of people in." He grabs his hair with both hands and pulls before saying, "I don't want to do this right now because I'm afraid to lose you again, but you need to know."

"Know what?"

"Who I truly am."

I think deep down I always knew he was keeping something from me, but I ignored it. There was too much other crap to deal with, and if I'm being honest with myself, I didn't want to know. I didn't want anything to jeopardize our friendship because I needed him. But we're past that. "Why don't you go have a seat. I'm going to make some coffee."

"Really?"

"Really. I owe you that after everything you've done for me."

"Can I help?"

"No, I'll just be a few minutes."

$\mathcal{I}$ carry a tray out of the kitchen with two mugs of coffee, a cup of sugar, and a small pitcher of creamer. As I make my way to the family room, I see Nash bouncing on his toes. His cool and confident demeanor is gone, replaced with wringing hands and wandering eyes. I'm so startled by his appearance that I stop at the threshold and watch him. He doesn't see me as he approaches the fireplace mantel. He picks up a picture of Jeff and me at our rehearsal dinner. It's my favorite picture of us. And it's the only one I put back out when I moved.

Nash sets it down and makes his way down the mantel to a picture of my parents and me from my college graduation, and a picture of Olivia and me at our senior prom. He then picks up a picture of him and me that Olivia took of us on our hike. It felt right to frame it and place it with all the other important people in my life.

He notices me staring and sets the picture back down. He moves to the couch, where he throws his body into a sitting position with his head in his hands and his elbows resting on his knees. I close the distance between us and set the tray on the coffee table. And wait. I'm not going to push.

His voice startles me. "I've never seen that smile on your face."

I have no idea where he's going with this conversation. And my gut tells me that whatever he has to say will change us. "Which smile?"

"The carefree one that I see from your wedding day, your prom. All of them, except the one of us."

"But I'm smiling."

He turns his body toward me, and this is the first time I've ever seen him broken. "I don't want to hurt you."

Something compels me to grab his hand. I squeeze and then look into his eyes. "I won't break."

"This place smells like you now."

He says it so seriously that I can't help but laugh. "I hope that's a good thing."

He takes a brief reprieve from being so serious and smiles at me. "It is. Your smell has always reminded me of the lavender bushes that used to grow outside my home as a kid. My mom would be gardening, and I would be running my trucks up along the dirt when she would shoo me away." His smile falls again.

I squeeze his hand again. "I like hearing you talk about your family, your life. Things that make you happy." The way he looks at me makes me want to run away and to never leave his side all at the same time.

"I don't talk about my family a lot. It wasn't just about hiding who I truly was."

"Why don't you?"

He stares at the fireplace as if there is a roaring fire to focus on. "Julia doesn't go around broadcasting my story." He then moves back toward me. "But Jeff knew my story. I'm surprised it's not something the two of you discussed."

I shrug. "It never came up. I don't have anything against your sister, but Julia and I were never close. I knew she had a brother, and Jeff had mentioned that he...I mean you, went through some hard times, but Jeff wasn't one to gossip or overshare. And to be honest, I never asked."

Nash takes a large breath and blows it out. He then turns away from me to stare at the pictures on the mantel again. His hands are cupped in one another and I see the color draining from his knuckles.

To give him a minute, I add sugar and creamer to my coffee until it looks like chocolate milk. The couch dips next to me as he leans further into it. Knowing he likes his coffee black, I pick it up to hand it to him, but he doesn't move. I gently touch his knee, and his eyes swing to mine with tears in them. I hold the mug out for him to take. But he doesn't. Instead he says, "I killed my best friend."

CHAPTER 40

*H*e says it so quickly I'm not sure I heard him right. He stands up and starts to pace again. My hands tremble, so I move the mugs back to the tray. "Do you remember that day at the cemetery? You found me at a gravesite and asked me who Mark was. And I told you that we would talk about it some other time?"

"Yeah?"

He moves to the front window and looks out. It's quiet and still, so quiet I hear Nash gulp before he says, "Mark Summers was my best friend."

It's quiet for a few more seconds, and I realize I should say something. Instead, I stand up and cross the room to be near him. I place my hands on his shaking back. "Nash, I'm so sorry. What happened?"

He pulls away, and I try not to take it personally. He once again walks to the mantel and looks at all of my pictures. He picks up our picture and grips it in his hand before turning back to me. "I don't want to lose you."

I cross to the back of the sofa and place my hands on it, gripping it for strength that I suddenly feel I'm going to need. "You're not going to lose me." I've been a baby these past few weeks, holding a grudge over something stupid. He was only trying to help. Plus, I've missed him.

"That's what everyone says, but in the end people pull away from me. Or maybe I pull away from them." He sighs, "Either way, what I'm about to tell you is the hardest thing I will ever tell you."

I move toward him, take his hand, and pull him back to the sofa. Tucking my legs into my body, I lean back into the arm of the couch and face him. Then I wait. I make a silent promise to myself not to speak again until he finds the courage to tell me whatever he needs to.

I hear the clock clicking on the mantel. The old house creaks as the wind slightly blows. Nash takes a deep breath and says, "Mark and I met each other when we were seven years old. He moved in down the street from me the summer before second grade. I was out riding my bike one day when I saw him throwing a baseball in the air and hitting it. I rode around for a while, watching him struggle to pitch to himself, and then he finally yelled at me." A small smile drifts to his face. "He asked me to pitch to him. We agreed I would pitch five, and then we would switch so we could both bat. When it got dark, we made plans to do it again the next day. Baseball led to bike riding, and video games, and we spent the next ten years together as best friends." He squeezes his eyes shut. "That changed the summer before our senior year in high school."

He glances over his shoulder at me and stares into my eyes. His gaze moves up to my hairline and then down to my jaw before finally landing on my lips. If I didn't know any better, I would think he was memorizing every line, every freckle.

I smile at him, trying to connect and offer him some reassurance, but he doesn't smile back. "We were two weeks into the summer. We'd both had some sort of job since we were fourteen years old so that we could buy decent cars when we turned sixteen. We had worked all day and then found out there was a party out on Walsh's road. Mark didn't want to go because he and his girlfriend had just broken up. He finally agreed to go, but only if he could drive so he could leave when he wanted to. I told him okay.

"When we got there, we were surprised his ex was there too. He was pissed because he didn't want to see her. They both created drama when they were around each other, and that night was no different. The second she saw us, she ran up to him and started punching him in the chest, telling him to leave. Her friends dragged her away and I dragged him away. I led him to the keg and handed him a cup to get him to focus on something else. He was always the responsible one between the two of us, and since he had driven, he had one beer and then walked away. But he continued to get irrirated as the night wore on.

"Toni started hanging on a guy we were kind of friends with, and after an hour or so, Mark had enough. He walked up to her and asked her what the hell she was doing. Our friend, Eric, got in between them and things got heated. I rushed up to Mark and told him to walk away, which he did after a few choice words with Eric. He then told Toni they were finished and walked back to the keg.

"It had been awhile since he had a drink, so I let him have it. I walked to the fire where our other friends were. Mark stood there with the same beer in his hand, drilling holes into the back of Eric's head. I knew Mark well enough to leave him alone."

He pauses as his jaw clenches. "I look back on that night and realize how stupid I was and what a shitty friend I was. As *soon* as that argument happened, I should have stopped drinking and focused on him instead of my own good time. But I didn't. I didn't need to remind him he was the one who drove us there. He knew that, and I trusted him. I trusted that he would know when he had had enough. We had gotten behind the wheel after a couple of beers before. But we were smart about it. Well, what a teenager would consider smart.

"And I didn't think I was drunk when Mark threw down his cup and stormed over toward Eric and Toni. Eric had his tongue stuck down Toni's throat, and I knew things were about to escalate, so I threw down my own cup and raced toward Mark. But he pushed me down and just kept charging toward them. When he reached Eric, Mark pulled his shoulder back and decked him. Toni screamed, and before I could get there, Eric's friends had jumped in and were getting a few good ones in on Mark. I finally pushed my way through, pulled Mark back, and told him we were leaving. He could barely hear me over Toni screaming."

He cracks his knuckles and his nostrils flare. "One stupid fight. Over one stupid girl who had been cheating on him for half of their relationship. I dragged his ass to the car thinking that the excitement had sobered me up. And it had. I felt okay enough to drive. I didn't realize at the time, but that's not how alcohol works. It was obviously still in my system and affecting my motor skills. But as I dragged Mark to the car, I realized he wasn't just shaken up from the punch, he was drunk.

"I asked him how much he had to drink, and his words were slurred when he said, 'Too much. I lost track watching them.' I knew out of the two of us, I was more capable, so I walked him to the passenger side. He asked me if I was okay to drive and I told him yes." Nash stops and tightly closes his eyes. "I looked my best friend square in the eyes and told him *yes*."

I know where this story is going, and I try to keep the water from cresting over my eyes. He opens his eye and frowns before saying, "That yes meant he could trust me. That I would take care of the situation and get him out of it. I had looked in his eyes a million times before and told him that for different reasons, and I had never let him down."

Nash gets up again, crosses back to the window, and faces away from me. "He handed me his keys and we pulled away. I didn't want to draw attention in the middle of the night after I'd been drinking, so I drove carefully. Or so I thought. I'm not even totally sure what happened. The rest of the night is fuzzy. I remember Mark bitching about Toni. I remember telling him he could do better.

"I vaguely remember driving along Winterman's Avenue. I'm sure you've been up there. It's winding and can be dangerous in the light of day. But, for whatever reason, that's the route I decided to take that night." He shakes his head as he continues watching nothing out my front window. "Instead of taking the longer, safer way home, I took that. I managed several of the curves fine, and then knowing me, I probably got overconfident." His voice is soft and fragile as he continues. "All I remember are the sounds and smells and the screams. And the panic. The realization of what was happening and that I couldn't stop it. I remember hearing metal screeching on metal. I remember smelling gasoline and oil. I remember Mark yelling 'watch out'."

I try to stop them but I can't. Hot tears run down my cheeks as Nash turns to me. He's kneeling in front of me in two seconds. His hand is rough but his touch gentle as he wipes the tears away.

"I don't deserve your tears, and I can't stand to be the reason you're crying."

I sniff and I don't mean for it to, but my voice breaks, "How can you say you don't deserve my tears? Everyone deserves compassion, Nash."

"No, they don't. Murderers don't deserve compassion."

I violently shake my head back and forth and whisper, "Don't say that. You're not a murderer."

He hits his fist against the coffee table and the mugs rattle against the tray as their contents spill over the edge. "The hell I'm not!"

I rush off the couch and place my hands on his chest. I feel his heart furiously beating. Then his hand grips mine and pulls it away from his chest.

"What are you doing, Jen?" he whispers.

I look up into his eyes, so haunted I can barely stand it. "Nash..." I move my hands down his chest trying to get closer to him and offer him some form of comfort.

"Don't pretend like this doesn't bother you."

"Of course it bothers me. I'm sorry you had to go through that. That you have to carry that with you."

"That's it? You don't want to scream at me for keeping something else from you?"

"What? No."

"I don't want your pity, Jen." He pushes away from me.

"Compassion and pity are two very different things." I go after him and move my body in front of his with my feet firmly planted on the floor. My shoulders are back, and I feel a small twinge of my former self. Confident and determined. "And I don't care what you want. I'm entitled to my own feelings."

His chest is still frantically rising and falling, but his eyes are now steady and focused. He lifts a hair that has fallen out of my ponytail and moves it behind my ear. I lean into his hand, not because I totally understand it but because it feels good. And it feels right. "I expected you to be angry at me for lying to you again."

He doesn't know about the guilt I carry about Jeff and our baby. How my life wouldn't have been irrevocably changed if it weren't for my own actions. But I promised myself I would never tell anyone about that fateful night, and it's a promise I intend to keep. "You didn't lie to me. Either time. You just didn't tell me your whole truth. I wish you had told me sooner, on both accounts. But I understand why you didn't." If he only knew how well I understood. Guilt is destructive to the soul, even if warranted.

He leans his forehead into mine and closes his eyes. His breathing gradually slows.

"I know this is hard, Nash, but I want you to finish it."

His eyes fly open. "What?"

"Your story. That's not the end of it."

I grab his hand again and move us back to the couch. I resume my position and then sprawl the blanket that was on the back of the couch over my legs. I want to lean into Nash and feel his warmth. To offer him comfort and strength. But I don't think that's what he wants or needs right now.

He mirrors my position on the couch so we're face to face. His eyes harden before he continues. "The next thing I knew, I was waking up in darkness. My eyes were trying to adjust to the light, and the first thing that hit me was the smell. Burnt flesh. I glanced around and saw that we were on an incline. I looked over my left shoulder and saw a cliff and a metal railing hanging from it. I knew we had gone over the side of the road, but I couldn't tell how far from where I was sitting. I moved to confirm I could and then realized there was a piece of metal sticking out of the right side of my stomach. Without thinking, I yanked on it and screamed from the pain. I went to toss it aside, and when I did, I noticed Mark wasn't there. And there was a hole in the front windshield.

"I remembered getting ready to go out that night and Mark picking me up, I remembered the fight between Eric and Mark. Then the night before the accident creeped in. My dad and I had gotten in a fight about me not taking out the trash again. Everything came rushing back, but it was in pieces and out of order. I remembered putting Mark in the passenger side of the car and realized I didn't buckle him in. Guys don't do that type of stuff. He would have called me a pussy for doing something like that. But I also knew he was too drunk to do it himself.

"Once I got my seatbelt off, I felt lightheaded and nauseous. My hands wouldn't do what my mind was telling them. I struggled and struggled and finally got myself free. I tried to open the door but couldn't. I punched through the side window, and it spidered out. My knuckles burned, but all I could think about was Mark. I finally pushed my body through the window and fell to the ground. I crawled to the front of the car. Only one of the headlights still worked. I couldn't see anything. I heard someone screaming and realized it was me, screaming for Mark, but he didn't respond. I tried to stand up and fell over again. I finally managed to get myself upright by leaning against the car. I remember the sound of my heartbeat as I frantically looked for him. I just wanted to lie down. I wanted to give up. But I kept looking.

"I looked around the car at least four times. Finally, I started to scoot down the cliff when I noticed a piece of green shirt that I membered Mark was wearing. He was 15 feet away from me, so I started to pick up my pace. As I did, I heard sirens in the background. I yelled to him that it was going to be okay. That help was almost here. My body finally collapsed once I reached him. He was lying face up, eyes wide open. His body was contorted in such a way that I knew he was in pain. One arm was under his body and his legs were bent in different directions. He had a large gash on his head...so deep that I didn't see red but white. I heard the sirens get very loud and then they stopped. I held his head in my lap and talked to him, reassuring him that help was there. But he never blinked, never looked at me.

"I heard someone yell down, and I yelled back up for them to hurry. I saw two men in bright yellow uniforms with bags in their hands maneuvering through the terrain trying to get to us. Once they reached us, they started relaying information over a radio. I heard him say white male, late teens, critical, broken neck, head wound, and then I stopped listening. The next thing I knew, I was in the back of an ambulance. I saw Mark lying in the street. The ambulance doors shut and I screamed, telling them we couldn't leave without Mark. The paramedic that was working on me said they were sending a chopper for him and that they needed to get me to the hospital. I begged them to wait, but they didn't. I lost consciousness before we arrived."

He takes a deep breath and pauses. His face is ashen and he looks tired. And defeated. I move down the couch and grab his hand. I then lay my head in his lap. I'm not thinking, only feeling. I'm not overanalyzing, I'm simply listening to my heart.

He starts talking again, and his body vibrates through mine as he talks. "The next thing I remember is waking up in the hospital. My parents and Julia were there talking in the corner of the room. My eyes felt heavy and the light was bothering me. I went to move my arm to cover my eyes and realized my arm was stuck to the bed. I looked down and saw my right wrist was handcuffed to the bed. The rattling of the cuffs against the metal bed alerted my family that I was awake. My mom and Julia had been crying, and my dad looked like crap. I immediately asked about Mark, and mom and Julia both started to cry again. Julia rushed out of the room as my mom grabbed my hand that was handcuffed to the bed. My dad was the only one who could get the words out to tell me Mark didn't make it.

"He told me I'd been arrested for vehicular manslaughter. It didn't matter. Mark was dead and I had killed him. That's all my mind could process at the time."

I squeeze his knee and then wipe a tear from my eye. "My parents mortgaged their house to get me a defense attorney who convinced the judge to try me as a juvenile even though I was seven months away from my eighteenth birthday. But only if I pleaded guilty to save Mark's family the turmoil of a trial. I didn't need a deal to plead guilty. I *was* guilty. I was in the hospital for three days and then went home for several weeks while I waited for my plea agreement to go through. I never left the house. I was too ashamed and too depressed. Mark was like the brother I never had, and knowing I was the reason he was no longer here was too much of a burden to carry. So I looked forward to being punished. It's what I deserved.

"Once I got to the juvenile detention center, I changed. I didn't have a choice but to fight for survival. I got jumped and beaten up repeatedly until I learned to fend for myself. After a year, I walked out of that place more broken than when I had entered. I had no idea who I was. I carried around so much anger that my own family didn't even recognize me.

"I couldn't hold down a job. I didn't have any friends anymore. And I couldn't stand the guilt...so I went to the top of that cliff to end it.

"That's really why I became a paramedic. The little boy on the cliff was the catalyst, but I feel as though I owe it to the world, to Mark, to try and give back and make a difference by saving lives."

"Because you couldn't save Mark's?" I whisper.

He nods his head, and then his hands slide under my arms and lift me. I move my legs so that they're straddling his lap, grounded to a place I'm terrified to be in, but have no desire to escape. Now that we're face to face, I see the remnants of his shed tears on his face. I move my hand to wipe them away, but he grabs it and rests it between us, slowly forming circles on it with his thumb. "Jen, I wasn't living. These past nine years, I've been punishing myself for what I did. I don't have any friends, and the only family I still talk to or hang out with is Julia and her family. I've never even been in love because I didn't think I deserved to be. He pauses while skimming his fingertips along my jaw line. "But when I'm with you, I feel alive. I'm not just existing, I'm actually happy. It's taken me a long time to come to terms with what I did. And if I could change places with him, I would...in a heartbeat. But I can't. You make me want to be a better person, not because I'm repaying a debt, but because I want to be a better person for you."

Tears flow over my face, and that's the only feeling I can process in this moment.

CHAPTER 41

"*J*ensen, say something. Please."

Something? What? How do I respond to that? He tells me that his friend died in a car accident when he was behind the wheel *and* that he has feelings for me...all within a twenty minute time frame.

I hold my breath, willing time to stop so that I can process.

"I wasn't strong enough to save myself before you," he continues. "But then you needed me. You needed someone who understood to be there for you. And I wanted to be that person. I needed to be that person...I still do. I want you to be able to move forward. You deserve more than the life you've been giving yourself, Jen."

The guilt and shame I see in his eyes reaches into me and moves me to act. I'm no longer paralyzed. I lean closer and lace my fingers with his, holding on so that our strength can move back and forth between one another like a current. "So do you. It was an accident."

"No, it was a mistake. Mistakes can be prevented."

I shake my head. He doesn't know it, but we're the same. Those feelings of guilt and shame for being the reason another person is no longer on this earth connects us in a way that other people could never understand.

I squeeze his hand. "Tell me about him."

"Mark?"

"Yeah, tell me about him."

"You're changing the subject so we don't have to talk about my feelings for you.."

"Nash..." I feel too raw, too exposed. Maybe I knew there might be more between Nash and me. But it wasn't the right time. I wasn't in the right place. I'm not sure I am now. I don't want to hurt him, so I choose my words carefully. "I don't think right now is the best time to talk about your feelings for me. I thought it might help if you had a chance to tell me about Mark."

"*My* feelings? Are they...just mine, Jen?" he asks in a grudging voice. I can't blame him. He just put it all out there. And I'm too afraid to tell him what I've felt between us. He watches me, waiting for me to respond but when I don't he says, "Mark was my best friend, and I've come to terms with the fact that if the roles were reversed and he was driving that night and I had died, I wouldn't want him wasting his life. He would want me to be happy because that's what I would want for him. So I know if he was here right now, he would tell me to shut the hell up about him and my *feelings* and worry about my girl. So that's what I'm going to do."

His girl? My stomach does flip-flops hearing him say that, and I can't help the flush that creeps up my neck and over my cheeks.

"Jen, I know you're scared. I am too. I know you feel guilty, like you don't deserve this. I do too. But we can't ignore it anymore. Admit it. Admit you feel it. What's between us..."

He grips my arms with both hands. There are two different people inside of me. The grieving widow who thinks she should pull away and remain alone, forever. And then there's this other person I am when I'm with Nash. I don't know who she is, but she wants to lean into him. She wants to feel his strong arms wrap around her back as he pulls her close to him, and never let her go.

But I don't think I can tell him that. I don't think I can say it out loud. And I feel like I need more time. My eyes shift to the clock as I think about time, and I see that it's almost 6:00 a.m. "Nash, it's almost six o'clock. Do you have to work today?"

He sighs. "Yeah, but I took Trent's night shift, so I probably need to get home and get some sleep."

"I guess you better go, then." I go to move my body so he can get up, but he pulls me back down.

"You're coming with me."

"What?"

"I broke your door. You can't stay here, not in this neighborhood. And knowing your landlord, who knows when he'll fix it. I can come over tomorrow after I sleep a little and fix it. And at some point, between then and now, we're going to finish this conversation."

I sigh. "I'm not sure what you want me to say."

"I just want you to be honest with me. If you can tell me right now that you've never had *any* feelings for me stronger than friendship, I'll walk out that door. I'll never mention it again, and we'll be friends."

As much as the grieving widow is screaming inside of me to say just that, my other persona wins out and shoves her back down so she can't be heard. But it seems that persona isn't ready to talk either, so I say nothing.

"That's what I thought. Let's go back to my place, get some sleep, and then we'll talk. I know I laid a lot on you tonight."

He rises and tries to take me with him, but I push off of him. I need some distance. He strides toward me but keeps his hands to himself. He then leans down so that he's eye level with me, and I watch as his pupils dilate when he starts to lean in. I feel my eyes close, and desire comes alive inside of me. The next thing I feel is his breath on my face before I hear him sigh. My eyes fly open in surprise and he grabs my hand. "Come on, you look like hell."

I laugh. "That's all you're going to say?"

"I told you where I stand, Jen. You know what I want. But you need some time to figure things out, so I'm going to give it to you. I also know if I don't drag your ass out of here right now, you'll spend the next hour analyzing the crap out of things, and we both need sleep. This mess will still be here when we wake up."

CHAPTER 42

I need a few minutes away from Nash, so I tell him that I'm going to run upstairs and grab a few things since I probably won't be back until late tomorrow.

"Do you need help?"

"No, thanks. I'll be right back." I take the stairs two at a time, run into my bedroom closet, and grab my overnight bag. I then sit on the bed for a few minutes and realize he's right. I'm starting to analyze so I stop. I throw in some jeans and a T-shirt, go to the bathroom and grab a few things, and then come back down stairs. Nash looks up at me and I smirk. "I'm not the only one who looks like hell."

"I bet. That's why we need to go. I need to get some sleep before I go in." He grabs my bag, and we walk out the front door. I go to lock it, but it will barely close, so why bother? I hope no one notices the broken door because anyone could come and go as they please.

"Do you want me to drive my car?"

"Nah. You can use my truck today or tomorrow if you need it, since I'll be working tonight. I'll take S.J." He winks at me and I smile back.

Fifteen minutes later, we're pulling into his driveway. He grabs my bag again and we head to the front door, where he unlocks it and guides me in.

He throws his keys on the table, and then he disappears down the hall with my bag. When he walks back out, he's carrying a pillow and blanket but doesn't have my bag.

"Where's my bag?"

"I took it to my room." He walks to the couch throwing a pillow and blanket down.

"Ummm."

He stops. "What's wrong?"

"I'm confused? Why is my bag in your room?"

"Because that's where you're going to sleep."

I feel myself start to panic. Or is it excitement? *What the hell?* But I'm afraid he's misunderstood the situation.

His eyebrows shoot up. "I'm sleeping out here, Jen, and giving you my bed. Sorry I didn't make that clear."

I exhale, relieved. Or disappointed?

"Wow, now I know how you really feel." I feel flustered as his comments are shooting at me faster than I can respond. He lightly touches my arm before saying, "Hey, I'm just messing with you. Go—I'm beat. I just washed the sheets two nights ago, so they're practically clean."

"Nash, let me sleep on the couch. You have to work tonight."

"Jen, I'm not going to make you sleep on this crappy couch, so go." He spreads out the blanket, making sure it covers the entire couch, and then he grabs the back of his shirt and pulls it over his head. My face flushes as arousal courses through my body. *Dammit.* I hate when Olivia is right. I try to ignore his muscles as they stretch and flex as he moves about getting situated for bed. He bends over to tuck the blanket into the side of the couch, and all of the air leaves my body. How have I never noticed his *butt*? I'm not sure it's even fair to the other butts in the world to call it a butt. I wonder how many squats he's done in his life to get that round mold just the perfect shape. I'm pretty sure it wouldn't jiggle even if he was covered in Jell-O.

"Did you need something?"

Oh dear Lord. How long have I been standing here staring at his ass? Wait, do I *need* something?

"What? No! What! I just…um… no. I don't know!" I back up, willing my feet to find the hallway, when my own butt runs into a lamp behind me, knocking it to the ground. I bend over to pick it up when I feel Nash's hand grabbing me by the arm and pulling me up.

"You're blushing," he whispers.

I'm unable to look him in the eyes. Instead I stare at his chest. His very tan, very defined and masculine chest. "You're practically naked," I whisper back.

I feel that chest vibrate, and I realize that both of my hands are gently resting on it. It's warm and smooth and making me rethink this whole *talk about our feelings later* situation.

"Sorry, I don't sleep in a lot of clothes. I still have pants on."

"Pants, yes I'm aware. It's like the pant company made those pants just for your ass." My eyes travel downward, where they be shouldn't be traveling, and he laughs again. And I want to die. What is wrong with me?

"Jen…go to bed. Now," he says with a strained voice.

I have the urge to pull him with me, but I don't. I force my feet to take baby steps. Steps that get me further and further away from him. Further and further away from the confusion and the desire. They finally make their way into his bedroom and I see my bag at the end of the bed. I remove my shoes and sit them next to it, and then lay my useless phone on the nightstand. In his bed, the smell of Nash engulfs me. The smell calms me, and I focus on that calm before my mind has a chance to spin. I force my eyes closed, knowing these feelings and the problems that come with them will be here when I wake up.

CHAPTER 43

I roll over and see Nash coming out of the closet with his uniform on.

"Sorry. I didn't mean to wake you."

I glance at the clock. "It's past 8:00 p.m.? I should probably get up." I sit up and stretch my arms over my head.

He laughs. "I was thinking the same thing. I've been waiting for you to wake up for hours. Did you have a hard time falling asleep?"

"No actually, and I slept really well. I didn't want to admit it to you, but you're right about the neighborhood. I haven't been sleeping much."

He walks over and sits on the edge of the bed next to me. "You don't have to stay there, you know."

I laugh. "It's where I live, Nash. Where else am I supposed to stay?"

"You haven't sold the house, have you?"

I sigh. "No, but I can't go back there. I'd feel like I was taking two steps back, and it was too hard to leave in the first place. I think the only thing that got me through it was that I was pissed off at everybody."

"Yeah, sorry about that."

I smile. "It's all right."

"Not really. But look, I'll buy a door in the morning on my way home and install it after I get some sleep. It should only take me a few hours. That way I can just take care of it, and we don't have to worry about your lousy landlord doing it."

"Nash, you don't have to do that."

"Yes, I do. I haven't slept much either since you moved into that place, so it's helping me too. There's food in the fridge or you can order a pizza or something. There's some money in the drawer by the refrigerator."

"Nash, I have money."

"I know, but we left in a hurry, so I didn't know what you had on you. But help yourself. My shift ends at 7:00 a.m., but it all depends on what's going on. I shouldn't be much later than that, though."

"Okay, I'm probably going to eat something, maybe watch some TV, and then go back to bed."

"I'll see you when I get home. Oh, and here…" He stands and sets a key down on the nightstand by my phone.

"What's that for?"

"Just in case."

"Nash, I don't need a key."

"Keep it. And don't take it the wrong way. It's just a friend giving another friend a key for emergencies. Oh, and I have a friend who may be able to fix your phone, so I'm taking it with me." He grabs my phone and heads toward the bedroom door.

"Nash."

He stops and looks back at me. "Yeah?"

I have a million things I want to say to him, but I don't know where to start. Neither my brain nor my heart have the nerve to say anything except "Be safe."

He smiles and says, "Always." And then he's gone.

I hear him walk through the front door and deadbolt it

behind him. After using the bathroom I move to the kitchen and find a frozen pizza. I eat, clean up the kitchen, and find nothing interesting on TV, so I pick up a newspaper lying on Nash's coffee table. I search for the section I need, and once I find it I throw the rest of the paper on the floor and spread out the paper on the table.

It's time. If I'm not going to be a lawyer, I need to do something to make a living. I have a college degree, so this isn't the best place to look for a job. But I need to start somewhere.

Scrolling through the classifieds, I see jobs for sales positions, childcare, healthcare, and numerous other things that I'm either not qualified for or not interested in. I remind myself to not be too picky. I've backed myself into a corner. As long as the house is on the market, I don't have much choice but to find steady work.

As I'm scrolling through the classifieds, my mind begins to drift back to this morning. I should have seen it. I should have known there was more to him. But I was too focused on myself and trying to survive. I can't imagine what he's gone through all these years. I start to feel sad. Sad for Nash. Sad for Mark's family. Sad for Nash's family. I may have had a little more compassion for Julia if I had known. But it wasn't her place to share that with me. I then wonder if Nash has told her about us. *Us?*

There's no us, Jensen. I lean my head onto my hand and rub my forehead back and forth before deciding to put the paper away. I lie down on the couch and snuggle under the blanket Nash used last night.

I'm startled by a warm touch on my arm. I open my eyes to Nash sitting on the edge of the couch and smiling down at me. "What are you doing out here?"

I look around and see the sunlight shining in. "I must have fallen asleep, sorry."

"That's okay."

"What time is it?"

"Almost 9:00 a.m. Sorry I'm late. My shift ended late, and then I picked up some stuff for your rental. And this."

He hands me my phone with a new screen, and I'm relieved. I feel like a limb has been reattached. "He fixed it?"

"Yep. I dropped it off last night on my way into work and picked it up just now.""

Propping myself up I say, "Thank you."

"Sure. Hungry? I was going to make some breakfast."

"Yeah, sounds good."

He moves into the kitchen. "I bought two new steel-enforced doors, new deadbolts, and locks for the first floor windows."

I stand and grimace. He lied about the couch being comfortable. "Nash, that sounds expensive and like a lot of work."

I walk into the kitchen and watch as Nash takes out eggs, milk, sour cream, and salsa, and sets it all on the counter. "What are you doing?"

He looks up at me like I have three heads. "Making breakfast?"

"Oh. You usually cook like this?" I ask.

"Yeah. I mean no, never. I'm doing this just to be a gentleman." He winks at me and smiles, and it makes me feel like I'm the most important woman in the world. I need some space from Mr. Wonderful.

I head toward the bathroom but turn around and say, "Well, whatever your reason, I'll take it."

I come back to the kitchen after freshening up to see Nash setting the table. "How was work?"

"Good. Nothing too traumatic. How about you—what did you do?"

"Ate some pizza and looked through the classifieds."

"See anything intriguing?"

"Nope."

"Do you have something in mind?"

"Nope."

He sits down and I follow.

He scoops some scrambled eggs out of a skillet onto a plate and hands it to me. "No biggie. It's not like you need to decide right now. You have time."

"I appreciate the support, Nash, but you're wrong. I do need to decide. It's doesn't have to be a life-long career decision, but it needs to be some kind of decision."

"Sorry, I didn't know what to say. You and I haven't really talked about this."

"Because I haven't wanted to talk about it. I've never seriously considered another career and don't really know where to start."

"Why did you want to become a lawyer?"

"After reading *To Kill A Mockingbird*." I shrug my shoulders. "I know, cliché."

"Well, what else inspires you?"

I chuckle. "It's been a long time since I've been inspired." His fork is midway to his mouth when he stops and narrows his eyes. A slow smirk forms on his face, but I have no idea why. "What's that face for?"

"I bet I know something that would inspire you."

"Why am I now scared?"

"Because I think you already know what I'm thinking."

"I do?" I haven't a clue what he's talking about.

"You do, you just don't want to admit it."

"Um...?"

"I think it's time I introduced you to Shirley, Junior."

"Nash, be serious." I rise to take my plate to the sink.

"I am!" He follows me with his own plate.

I turn on the water and rinse off my plate before placing it in the dishwasher. When I turn, Nash is in front of me with pleading eyes. I can't imagine him as a little boy and not getting everything he wanted. I cross my arms and lean against the counter. "How is riding a motorcycle going to inspire me?"

His body is still as he leans down, forcing us to be eye to eye.

He then places his arms on both side of me, pinning me in, and his chest lightly brushes up against mine. "Trust me."

I want to lean in as he licks his lips and then pulls his bottom in between his teeth. "Okay." I say. Because I do trust him.

He straightens up and leans back. "Really?"

"Yes."

His face turns playful as he grabs my hand and pulls me toward the garage.

CHAPTER 44

*a*s Nash wheels his motorcycle into the driveway, I question how I got here. But his smile gleams at me, and then I remember why I agreed to this. He looks like a teenager who just got his license, and I have to admit, it's damn hot.

"There are some things we need to go over to make sure you and I are both safe. First thing is I will always be the first one on the bike as well as the last one off. It's my responsibility as the driver to keep the bike balanced. So don't mount or dismount without letting me know. Secondly, even though you're a passenger, you have to participate. You need to pay attention to turns. Essentially, you need to lean with me and the bike and not make any sudden movements. Make sense?"

"It does now, doesn't mean it will once I'm on this thing."

"She has a name." He runs a blue cloth over what I assume is the gas tank and whispers, "Sorry S.J., she won't call you a 'thing' again." He gives me a glare and then continues. "You need to keep your feet on the footrests at all times, even when we're stopped." He walks over to the bike and points at the footrests. "And this is the muffler. Never touch it with your hands or legs. It will be hot and will burn you." I nod. "I don't have an intercom system, so if you need to stop you can tap on my leg and I'll pull over."

"How come you don't have an intercom system?"

He glances up from whatever he was tinkering with on the bike and smiles. "I've never had anyone ride with me before."

"*Never?*"

His smile fades and the playfulness is gone. "Never." The entire world around us disappears as he steps toward me and rests his hands on my waist. Neither of us says anything, but Nash and I have always been able to communicate in silence. Yet this feels like a completely different language, one that I'm starting to understand with total clarity. Adrenaline and fear course through my body, and a small smile appears on my face. His face mirrors mine and then he winks. He steps away to continue Riding Motorcycles 101. "The final part is the most important part. You're going to wear a helmet, and you're going to need to put your hair up so that it's out of the way. I also want you to wear jeans and long sleeves."

"It's July."

"I'm aware, but there's a reason bikers wear leather. It's not an image thing. It's a protection thing, and since we don't have anything leather for you yet, long sleeves and pants will have to do. Ready?" he asks.

I'm scared to death, but I don't want to tell him that. I keep reminding myself that I trust him…I trust him…I trust him. This is supposed to be fun, right? I say it before I can take it back. "Yes."

"Then let's go change, and we'll just start out around the neighborhood and see how it goes."

I can't believe I'm about to do this.

* * *

TEN MINUTES LATER, we're back in the driveway. "Okay, I'm going to get on, and then I need for you to get on. Don't worry about the balance—that's my job—but once you're situated, make sure your feet are on the footrests."

"Wait!"

"Don't get scared on me now."

"Tell me again how this is supposed to inspire me?"

He thinks for a minute. "Riding a motorcycle is freeing. Things are brighter, smell better, and that connects you to everything that surrounds you, including the person you ride with." He walks up to me and grabs my hand before continuing. "I've always thought it was romantic like that."

Well, when he puts it like that, how can a girl resist, even though a part of me thinks this is just a ploy to get me on his damn bike. But it worked.

"Okay, let's go." He climbs on, kicks up the kickstand, and tells me to get on. I move toward him and try to find a way to get on that won't require me to touch him. I soon realize that's impossible and try to not dwell on it. I place my right hand on his shoulder, throw my leg over the seat, place my left hand on the seat, and find the left footrest. I then sit down and find the right footrest. Now that I'm on, I don't know what to do with my hands.

Before I can ask, he asks, "Comfy?"

"As comfortable as I can be on this death trap."

He reaches behind him to grab my hands and wraps my arms around his waist. And I feel safe, content and happy. Like maybe I belong here, with him. His voice vibrates through my chest. "Don't worry, I've got you." And in that moment, I realize he's had me all along. Longer than I was willing to admit.

"Don't let go, whatever you do."

I nod but all I manage to do is bump our helmets together. He laughs. "You okay?"

"Yeah, sorry."

"You can talk when we're not in motion, and I should be able to hear you okay."

"Oh, okay."

"Ready?"

I'm not just answering if I'm ready for a bike ride. Am I ready to experience this...with him? To take another step out of my past into a future that's completely unknown? But I don't want to spend time analyzing it. I want to experience it. "Let's ride."

His chest moves up and down as he laughs, and then he picks up his feet and eases down the driveway. He yells back to me, "You're going to love this!"

I already do.

CHAPTER 45

$\mathcal{W}$e're so exposed, and I think about all of the horrible things that can happen: a car backing out of a driveway too fast, hitting a bump the wrong way, me leaning wrong and throwing off Nash's balance. But then I focus on how the ride feels. I close my eyes and feel the wind on my body, the sun on my face, and enjoy those things while pushing the anxiety away.

At some point, he turns his head and yells, "You okay?"

I yell in his ear, "Better than okay."

I can't see it, but I know he's smiling. I want to tell myself that he's smiling because he was right and I'm going to have to hear about it. But that's not true. He's smiling because he cares about me and he wants me to be happy. Everything he's ever done for me has been about wanting me to be happy. I want to sink into him a little more, and instead of debating those feelings or those actions like I usually do, I let it happen. I grab his waist tighter and inch as close to him as I can get. He briefly moves his hand to mine and squeezes it before gripping the handle again. I feel myself falling into him and then I let go. Of the pain, the grief, the guilt. I then recognize a feeling I almost forgot existed —happiness.

He leans back and yells, "Hang on tight, we're going to go a little faster."

Instead of speaking, I let my body do the talking and hold on even tighter. On my right, I see the sign for the highway. The throttle underneath us picks up speed and I want to throw my arms out to the side like I'm on a roller coaster. As he sways to the right and my body responds to the movements, my heart warms to the thought of doing this over and over with him. Jeff flashes in my mind. But I remind myself he's gone. He's been gone for over a year. Olivia's words crawl into my mind that he would want me to be happy, that I'm not moving on but moving forward. I close my eyes and press my cheek against Nash's back.

Riding on this motorcycle with Nash reminds me of the grief I've gone through in the past year. You don't know how it feels until you experience it, and once you're experiencing it, you have to brace yourself for the turns and the bumps along the way. But you have no idea where the road leads or if it will ever end. Will the pain ever end? Will you ever be able to appreciate the horizon without wanting to rip your throat out from crying? Will you ever be able to trust your heart again? I don't know. What I do know is something that has been asleep in me for quite some time has just awakened, and a new part of me has come to the surface. I grab onto Nash a little tighter. Even though I'm wrapped in uncertainty, there is nowhere else I want to be.

CHAPTER 46

*H*e exits the highway and pulls into a convenience store. I watch our reflection in the window, and I can't help but notice how good we look together.

He brings the bike to a stop, and I remove my hands from his chest and immediately feel a sense of loss. I try not to dwell on it as I tug my helmet off. I shake out my hair and then ask, "I get off first, right?"

He smiles over his shoulder. "Yeah."

I use his shoulders to push myself off, and then he removes his own helmet and grins at me.

I grin back. "What's that look about?"

"You look good on my bike." A small blush rises to my face. "And I told you that you had to ride to understand it."

I roll my eyes. "Fine. You were right, I was wrong. Are you happy now?" I say with mock frustration.

He approaches me with purpose, and then stops. I see conflict rush across his face, but I'm not sure why it's there. He then takes a deep breath and moves toward me, first taking my helmet and then wrapping me in a hug before whispering in my ear, "Yes, as a matter of fact, I'm happy. Thank you for doing that for me."

He starts to pull back, but I surprise myself by holding on tighter. He moves back in and sighs into my neck. A warmth spreads over me, and part of me wants to feel the guilt that I've become so accustomed to. Like I'm doing the appropriate thing by feeling guilty. But the reality is, I don't feel it. That feeling is gone, and it's replaced with something much stronger. I feel my face strain in a smile against his shoulder.

"You're welcome." I say.

We finally break away, and he looks into my eyes and smiles. "How about a bottle of water?"

"Sure."

"I recommend you walk around a bit. You'd be surprised at how sore you can be after riding a bike for the first time."

"Okay."

"Do you want anything else?"

"No, water is fine."

"Be back in a minute."

CHAPTER 47

J had a lot of time to think on the way back to Nash's house. Maybe too much time, because my head feels foggy and I'm not sure what I'm going to say once we're off his bike. I wasn't prepared for a bike ride to be emotional, but that's exactly what it was.

"Jen?" Startled, I realize we're now in Nash's garage and the bike is off. He rests his hand on my thigh and asks, "You okay?"

"Yeah, why?"

"Nothing, it's just we've been parked for a few minutes, and I was waiting for you to dismount before I did."

I recover and am off the bike in two seconds. "Sorry, just lost in thought."

He gets off the bike and puts the kickstand down. "No problem." We stare at each other for a few moments and it's too much. I turn away and take the time to study his garage. There are numerous tools neatly organized on a peg board next to a tool chest, a punching bag in the far-right hand corner, and boxes stacked along the side wall. I can still feel his eyes on me when he says, "Um, well if you want, we can go ahead and head to your house, so I can start to work on the doors."

I need some space before we do that. I need to talk to Olivia. "No, why don't you get some rest? You worked all night, and I know you didn't get the best sleep the night before."

"That's okay. I don't mind."

"No really. You're right. I'm feeling a little sore from the ride and I just need to rest."

"I'm going to hop in the shower and try to get a few hours of sleep, then."

"Sounds good."

He lets me walk in front of him to the kitchen. I wash my hands, and just as I'm grabbing a paper towel he asks, "You going to be okay?"

"Yeah. Sleep well."

* * *

I WAIT about a half hour after the water shuts off, hoping that Nash is asleep. I call Liv and pray that she picks up.

"Hey, Parker. It's been a few weeks."

"Yeah sorry, lots going on."

"Why are you whispering?"

I move to the sliding glass door to go outside, "Sorry, I'm at Nash's and he's sleeping."

"Nash's? I thought you weren't talking to him? Wait...sleeping in the middle of the day? Parker, you slut!"

"What?" Oh my God, no. "God, no! Are you serious?"

"Well, I thought maybe the two of you kissed and made up?"

"We did. Only not how you're thinking. But..."

"But...?"

"That's sort of why I called. I don't know what to do."

"Okay, back up. What happened?"

I tell her how I called him in the middle of the night and he came running. How I slept at his place and then we took a bike ride. I tell her I'm confused and don't know what to do. When I'm done, I'm out of breath.

"And?" Olivia coaxes me.

"And, what?"

"What does this mean, Parker?"

I don't want to say it. I'm having a hard time even thinking it, but the fact of the matter is, I feel it. Whether I am ready or not. "I care about him…as more than a friend." I wait and give her a moment to process what I said, but she doesn't respond. "Aren't you going to say something?"

"I love you and I'm proud of you." I let out a breath that I didn't realize I was holding. Lowering myself to the patio table, I put my face in my hands. As I do, I feel wetness on my cheeks. A fifty-pound weight has been lifted from my shoulders. The tears turn into sobbing. I think of Jeff and apologize in my mind to him for having feelings for someone else.

Liv tells me to let it out, and it's like someone just gave me a green light to fall into it. I start to shake and the sobs rush through my whole body.

"It's okay. It's going to be okay," Liv says.

"How do you know that?" I ask.

"Because I've seen you broken. I've seen you go to hell and back. And I've seen you with Nash. You're no longer broken when you're with him. Maybe still a little sad, but not broken. And you're not the Parker that I grew up with or who I stood beside when she got married. That person died with Jeff. But I see an amazingly beautiful and strong woman who is going to find her way. And I know you're scared, but you have to keep reminding yourself that Jeff would want this for you."

Air rushes back into my chest in ragged beats. "You say that, but you don't totally understand."

"You're right, Parker, I don't totally understand, and nobody ever will. But I knew Jeff, and he *loved you* more than anything, and he would want you to be happy. When you took those vows, you said until death do us part. You held up your end of the bargain. But he's gone. He wouldn't want you to be alone and afraid or feel guilty for moving on. Kiddo, we all want that for you, and I'm sure Jeff wants it more than any of us."

To hear her talk about Jeff in this way breaks my heart. She's right, but she doesn't know the whole truth. No one does. No one knows about that fight. No one ever asked me what the hell he was doing in that neighborhood at that time of night.

"You still there?"

My chest constricts as air tries to find its way back into my lungs. "Yeah."

"Have you told him?"

"Who, Nash? No. I don't want to say anything until I'm sure."

"About?"

"My feelings. He means so much to me that I can't imagine him not being in my life."

"He's not the type to turn his back on you, no matter what you tell him."

I lean back in my chair wiping tears from my face, when out of the corner of my eye I see something. I turn in that direction and see Nash leaning up against the sliding glass door frame. He gives me a tight smile and a nod. I smile back, glad that he's there. I can't avoid this any longer. He deserves for me to have this conversation with him, not with Olivia. "Liv, I need to go, okay? Can I call you later?"

"You okay?"

"Yeah, Nash is here, and we need to talk."

"Uh oh. I guess you should have kept whispering. Good luck."

"Thanks."

"And Parker?"

"Yeah?"

"Follow your heart, not your brain."

"Thanks." I press the end button and place my phone on the table.

Nash moves to sit next to me. "I'm sorry. I was trying to sleep and I opened the window to let the breeze in. I heard you crying and thought you were out here by yourself. I didn't know you were on the phone."

"How much did you hear?"

He sighs and then says, "Enough."

We sit in silence for a few moments. As we sit, I reflect on the many things that have held me back from even admitting that there is something between Nash and me. Guilt, shame, pride, confusion, fear. My feelings have been like darts heading for a dart board. Sometimes fast and harsh and stuck, and other times missing the target altogether and falling limply to the floor.

Nash grabs my hand. I close my eyes and he starts to let go, but I grab on with my other hand. I don't want him to let go. I don't want to let go. There is something else that's held me back this whole time, and it's time I tell him. I open my eyes and look deep into his. I see it. I've seen it for a long time. He loves me. He's in love with me, and he told me his story. It's time I tell him mine.

CHAPTER 48

I shift so that I'm facing him but I don't let go of his hand.

"There is something I need to tell you about the night Jeff died."

Instead of squeezing my hand like he always does, he laces his fingers through mine. And the intimate gesture soothes me. I know it's his way of telling me that whatever I tell him, it's going to be okay.

"No one ever asked me what Jeff was doing at that convenience store, in the wrong part of town, late at night. After we attended a dinner party at Jeff's boss's house, we left and had an argument."

"About what?"

I take a deep breath and then release it. "I didn't want to be a stay-at-home mom. We had been arguing about it for a few weeks, but I guess I wasn't hearing him. I didn't think much about it until I mentioned it to his colleagues that night. One of the partner's wives asked how much time I was planning to take off. When I said six weeks, Jeff got upset. He was concerned I couldn't handle both my career and our child."

"What did he do?"

"Nothing while we were there. But as any spouse can tell, I knew he was upset with me. He waited until we got to the car, and then we argued about it on our way home. By the time we had walked through the door, I had enough, and I told him it wasn't up for discussion. That I wouldn't even consider it." I pause thinking back to the words I used that night and the hurt on his face. "I didn't even hear him out. I didn't even respect his opinion. I didn't look at it from the vantage that it was *our* child and we were a team. All I saw was that he wanted me to give up my career and I wasn't going to do it. I had worked my butt off to get where I was. He wasn't the only one trying to make partner. He assumed since I was the woman, that I should be the one to take a step back. End of story.

"He blew up and decided to take a drive. I asked him not to, but he was mad, and he hated when he got mad in front of me. He was always the one who stayed calm in our marriage. It was a silent promise that he kept, never to raise his voice at me. But that night was different. This was a life decision we were making. The first as parents, and we weren't handling it well. I look back on that night and I realize how hurt he must have been. I wouldn't even consider it. I thought it was my decision and I had made it." I shake my head, realizing how selfishly I acted. He deserved to be heard even if I didn't agree with him.

"So he left. He told me he needed some space and was going out for milk."

I don't say anything for a few moments and neither does Nash. Not being able to stand the silence, I finish my story. "Nash, he's dead because of me. Because I wouldn't listen. Because I was too selfish to consider what he wanted for our family. Because I thought I was right, and he was wrong. He was trying to do what was right for our family, and instead I did the exact opposite, and now that family is gone."

I feel Nash's hand slip from mine. My heart breaks that he

sees me for what I truly am, for what I've been trying to hide all this time. I hear the chair scrape against the concrete, and I'm prepared for him to walk away when I feel his hands gently lift me and he pulls me into his chest. His head snuggles into my neck as he says, "I'm so sorry, Jen."

Wrapping my arms around him, I grab on, surprised he didn't run away from me. The sobs rush through my body, and my legs start to give as I see Jeff walk away from me for the last time. Me calling out, telling him I love him and hearing silence in return. I never saw him again.

Nash leans down and grabs me behind the legs and swings me into his arms. My hands clasp onto his neck as he slides open the door and uses his foot to slide it shut. My sobs continue as he moves down the hallway. Suddenly the bed is underneath me and he gently lays me down, placing his arms on both side of me. He takes my hair and moves it out from my face and leans down to kiss me on the forehead. It's the first time another man has kissed me since I met Jeff. I sob harder, hating myself for comparing the two of them. They both deserve better. Jeff deserved a wife who would hear him out, and Nash deserves someone who can give him what he wants and needs, to be loved whole heartedly. But selfishly I pull Nash down to me and grab onto him. He pulls me up into his arms and holds me as I finally come to terms with my past and watch it drift away.

$\mathcal{H}$e lets me cry. I don't think I'm capable of stopping. But Nash remains quiet and holds me. He whispers that it's going to be okay, that I'm okay.

"Jeff loved you, Jensen. He forgives you." After the words leave his mouth, I begin to shake. He pulls back and wipes tears from my face. His own tears fall and I mirror his motions, wiping them away for him before leaning back into his chest, where I take a deep breath and wrap my arms around him. I'm exhausted and my body starts to go limp. Nash must notice because he gently lays my head down on his pillow and brings the cover up to my chin. I breathe in his scent and relax.

His fingers lace through mine. "Sleep, Jen. I'm not going anywhere."

I close my eyes and start to drift before feeling his lips lightly brush against my forehead.

* * *

I roll over and look around the room. It's dark out, and as I sit up, I listen for Nash. But I don't hear anything. I walk into the bathroom and wash my face. I look like crap. My eyes are swollen and red. My hair is matted to my face from the dried tears. I stare at the person in front of me and as I do, I realize I finally know who I am. I'm staring at someone who is in love. For the second time in her life. I don't know when or even how it happened, but I let go of Jeff and the life we shared and feel in love with Nash. I'm in love with him.

I can't help but to chuckle. How can I be in love with someone that I've never kissed, never been intimate with? But maybe that's why this feels so strong. We don't need those things to feel the connection we have to one another.

I wait a few moments in the bathroom trying to figure out what I'm going to say to him when I see him. But it doesn't matter. He was waiting on me. And there's nothing left to wait for. I'm ready. I feel giddy and excited as a smile spreads across my face. I hear the garage door opening and I rush out to find him.

He's coming into the kitchen as I'm walking down the hall. He looks at me and then away. "Did you get some sleep?" he says over his shoulder as he washes his hands.

"Yeah. I just woke up. Where did you go?"

"I went to your rental and got the front door hung, but not the back. I wanted to head home and check on you." He turns to me as he dries his hand with a paper towel. "I can work on it tomorrow, but you're going to need to sleep here one more night." Sleeping here tonight quickly takes on a different meaning.

I stroll toward him as my mouth moistens. I'm in love with this man. And I'm ready for him to know. His hands abruptly stop drying themselves when I approach him. "I want to tell you something." I grab the paper towel out of his hand and throw it down on the counter as I lead him to the couch.

He stumbles right before we reach it but rights himself as he sits down. I scoot closer to him and place my hand on his knee. "Thank you."

He narrows his eyes. "For what?"

"For being there for me last night."

Relief floods his face as he says, "Oh, you're welcome."

My hands tremble with excitement as I notice his are starting to fidget and are sweatier than normal. But I ignore it, focused on what I need to say. Now that I've admitted it to myself, I can't contain it anymore and I want him to know. "And...I love you."

Those three words aren't all the way out of my mouth before he squeezes his eyes shut. His hand squeezes mine as his head drops and his shoulders slouch. I pull my hand out from his. The air fills with tension and uncertainty, and I don't understand what's happening. He wanted this. He wanted me. Us. Why is he grimacing in pain?

I lift my body from the couch and pace in front of the coffee table.

He then looks up at me, and I almost feel as though someone has slapped me. His eyes don't even have time to focus before he's looking back at the floor. But as brief as it was, I saw it. And I've never seen him look at me like that until now. I've seen it from others, but not him. Pure pity.

"I did a lot of thinking today while I was at your place." He's still not looking at me. "After you shared everything with me this morning, things started to make a little more sense." Finally he looks up. "I get why you were so angry at everyone. This whole time you've been blaming yourself for their deaths. And that's a lot to carry. I should know, better than anyone. We've been carrying around the same guilt. But...mine is warranted, yours isn't."

I go to interrupt him, but he stops me by putting up his hand. "Let me finish, okay?"

I say, "Okay" and let him continue.

He takes another deep breath. "Hearing you tell Olivia today that you had feelings for me…you have no idea how long I've waited to hear that."

He pauses as he studies me. "Do you remember when we went to dinner after the bike show and you told me how you and Jeff got together?" I swallow before nodding. "I knew he called you Lemondrop. I had heard Julia talk about that, but I never knew why. In that moment I was jealous. And then I realized there was no reason to be. I was there was because of Jeff. Because he was gone and Julia asked me to do something, which was to look out for you, to help you. Not fall in love with you. But I couldn't help it. I had already started to feel something for you and I didn't understand it at the time. We barely knew each other. But looking back on it, I know it's because we had experienced something so similar. That's when something changed in me. I started thinking about a future with you. A future that held hope and promise for a normal life." He looks away again. "And I still had that hope…until today."

The last sentence comes out in a whisper, but I feel as though it was shouted in my face. No. No! He can't do this to me, to us. I *just* let him in and he's shutting me out.

"Jen, look at me. Jensen!"

I try to control my breathing. I try to understand what I'm feeling. Hurt doesn't begin to explain what I feel inside. Rage is more like it. I take one more deep breath before I begin to say something.

"Wait! Hear me out." I begin to pace so I can keep my mouth shut until he's done. "As I was at your place today, I was looking at all of your pictures on your mantel again, and I realized I've been selfish. I'm so thankful you're in my life, but then I remembered why. You and I wouldn't have met if Jeff hadn't died. Or if Mark hadn't died. And those facts are feelings that we need to process. We have to remember that this isn't just about you and me. We've both been through something horrific, and I want to make sure we're both in the right place before we move forward.

I never got the help I needed, and I don't want you to make the same mistake."

I abruptly stop and face him. "What are you saying, Nash?"

He walks to me and grabs my hand. A part of me wants to shove him away but I don't. I let him hold me. "I'm saying I screwed up. You were supposed to be getting help, going to group and working through your issues in therapy. And I distracted you with us because I'm selfish. Because I started feeling something for you before we ever spent a day together. And I'm sorry. But I'm smarter now. My eyes are open, and I know that you need to focus on *you* before you focus on us."

"Why are you bringing up therapy now? We've never, *not once* discussed therapy since that first night in the parking lot."

"I know." He throws himself back down on the couch. "But I want to do right by you, and I know why you've acted the way you have. I think it's what's best."

My wall immediately goes up. I feel adrenaline rush through my body. I won't be pitied by another person in my life. Being pitied by him will destroy me. And I've been destroyed too many times in my short life. He may see me as weak and broken and scared, but that's not me, not the real me. There isn't much I control in my life, but this I can control, and I won't do it again. I won't let him see me as some pathetic, broken person, because once someone you love sees you that way, there's not much of a choice but to accept that as your fate or to walk away.

"You're right. I think that's a good idea." If there is one thing that God-awful rehabilitation place taught me, it's how to give people what they want.

His head jerks back in surprise, but then he releases a breath. "Good." He moves toward me and gives me a quick hug before he pulls back, fading away.

And the opportunity to be more fades with him.

CHAPTER 50

*a*fter that, I told him I was tired and was going to shower and then go to bed. He looked concerned as I walked down the hallway, but he let me go.

The next morning Nash walks in, and I pretend that I just woke up. But I never fell asleep last night. He's back on days, so he tells me he'll pick me up after work. I don't want to draw suspicion, so I tell him okay. He reminds me to use my new key for my front door. Then he asks, "You okay?"

"Yeah. I'm fine. Just ready for my own bed."

"Okay. I'll get it done before the night's over, promise. I'm going to take my bike, so I left the keys to the truck on the counter. See you later."

"Bye."

I wait until I hear the garage door open and close before leaping out of bed. I pack my stuff, and then get on my phone to find an Uber. Twenty minutes later, I'm walking up the path to my front door. I feel a pain in my chest as I see his handiwork, but I keep moving forward. I use the new key and drop my bag by the front door.

I head back to the kitchen on a mission. I walk to the fridge and pull down a business card. I dial the number and wait until a woman answers, "Gene's Home Improvement, how may I help you?"

"Hi, my name is Jensen Landry and I used one of your contractors a few weeks ago to fix a stair. I need some work done today and wanted to know if anyone was available.".."

"Landry, you say?"

"Yes." I wait a few moments as I hear typing in the background.

"Over on Market Street?"

"Yes, that's me."

"Looks like Tim helped you last time, but he's busy today. What did you need done?"

"I need an exterior door hung."

"Do you need parts?"

"No, the new door is lying on the front porch."

"Shawn is available today at 11:00 a.m. if that works for you."

"That will work, thank you."

I hang up the phone and lean against the counter. Nash is going to be pissed, but I need some distance. And I don't want to stay here without a new door. I might as well start to take care of things on my own.

The little boy who lives next door, Sammy, is outside playing with Chief when I walk out the back door to clean off the patio so Shawn has room to work. Sammy is laughing as he holds a stick over his head while Chief walks around on his hind legs. Sammy then bends over at the waist laughing so hard that Chief jumps up and grabs the stick. I walk down a few steps and sit, leaning my arms against the stairs. Chief comes back and drops the stick at Sammy's legs and does circles around him. Sammy says, "Okay boy," and he picks up the stick again as Chief dances around trying to reach for it. I giggle, and Sammy looks up at me.

"Oh, hi, Miss Jensen."

I get up and walk to the fence. "Hi Sammy. It looks like you guys are having fun."

"Yeah, we've been at this forever, and he's still not tired. I think he could do this all day." I laugh again as Chief falls over, desperately trying to grab the stick. "I sure wish I had a camera to take a picture of this. My mom would never believe what I taught him today."

I hate that Sammy spends so much time by himself. I've talked to his mom a few times and she's asked me to keep an eye on him since she's not home a lot. He's 10, so it isn't like he can't take care of himself. But kids need attention. With his mom working two jobs, I know he's not getting it.

"I have a camera." A nice camera, in fact. Only I haven't taken any pictures in three years.

"You do?" Sammy screams.

"Yep. Be right back." I head back inside and up the stairs. There's one room in the house that still has stacked boxes in it. There are dishes and kitchen equipment that I don't need every day but don't want to part with, as well as my winter clothes. The camera is in here somewhere. I just don't know where.

After 10 minutes of digging, I finally find it and run back down the stairs. I look out the window and see Sammy and Chief still playing. I pull out the camera and check the battery; dead. Great. I remember my spare in the bag and switch them out. The camera comes alive, and I rush out to Sammy.

I place the strap over my head, flick a few buttons, and then take their picture. I look down, and it's a great candid. Sammy didn't even see me coming. I'm looking at the picture as he walks up to me. "Hey, did you take something?"

"Yep, take a look."

"That's great. Can I get a copy? I'll pay you for it."

"Sure, but no need to pay me. Let me take a few more."

Sammy and I are laughing as Chief finally tires out and is slurping water everywhere.

"Are you Jensen Landry?" I turn and see a man holding a toolbox.

I run over to him and shake his hand. "Yes, you must be Shawn."

"Sure am. I almost left. I've been at the front door ringing the bell."

"Oh my gosh, I'm sorry, I must have lost track of time." I look down at my watch and see that I've been outside taking pictures for over two hours.

"Well, I saw the door lying on the porch so I knew I was at the right place, but your front door looks brand new."

My throat grows tight thinking about how upset Nash will be when he finds out I called a handyman to install the door he bought for me. But this is what's best for both of us, so I lead Shawn to the back door and show him what needs to be done.

"Did the person who hung your front door do a bad job?"

"Um, not exactly." I look away as Shawn sits his toolbox down and starts to remove the tools he'll need. "A friend hung it for me and doesn't have time to do the other one."

"Okay." He stands up and moves toward the door, inspecting the door jamb. "I can go ahead and get started then, if that's okay with you."

"Yeah, that would be great. How long do you think it should take?"

"Maybe an hour, depends on how much trouble it gives me."

"Sounds good." I'm hoping he'll be done by the time Nash gets off work.

CHAPTER 51

Shawn left around 3:30 pm. Apparently, the door did give him some trouble, but he finally got it hung. I spend the next hour cleaning up his mess and then clean the whole kitchen. I finally make it upstairs and take a quick shower. I have a plan for the evening and need to get out of the house.

I throw my wet hair into a ponytail, grab my camera bag, and dash down the stairs. I make sure the back door is locked and that all of the lights are off before walking out the front door. I lock it behind me and get in the car. As I'm backing out, I check the clock...5:45 p.m. Nash gets off work at 6:00 p.m. He won't have his phone on him, so by the time he gets my text, I'll be gone.

Something came up, so I won't be home when you get off of work. Had new door hung so you wouldn't have to worry about it. Talk to you later. ~ J.

I put my phone back in my purse and head toward a warehouse store to print the pictures I took today.

When I walk in, I head to the photo printer, thankful there isn't a line. I put my camera card into the slot and wait for the pictures to pull up. One by one, they load onto the screen. I see pictures of our house as it was being built, then pictures of Jeff standing in the driveway. There is a picture of my back, standing in between different paint samples on the wall trying to decide which one to go with. Jeff must have taken that without me knowing. I feel a rush of heat go through my body and remind myself I'm in public. I don't want to lose it, not here.

I hit "select all" and wait for them to print. I see several shots coming out of the printer of Sammy and Chief. Those I pick up and examine with a close eye. Sammy is laughing while Chief pants at his side. There's also one where Chief had run and knocked Sammy over, but Sammy laughs as if it's the funniest thing that's ever happened to him. Another where Sammy is kneeling on the ground while Chief licks his face. I blow that one up for him. As I'm waiting for the enlargement, my phone vibrates in my back pocket. I pull it out and see a text from Nash.

I got your text but came over anyways. Where are you? Why did you have the door hung? I was going to do it tonight???

A wave of guilt flashes through me. He's trying to help, but the only thing to do is to put distance between us. I tuck my phone in my pocket without responding and continue to wait for the photo enlargement. Once it's finally done, I ask the girl behind the counter for a photo holder so I won't wrinkle them, and then head back to the car. As I put the key into the ignition, my phone vibrates again.

You okay? You're kind of scaring me. Are we okay?

He needs to stop worrying about me. I'm not his concern.

Everything's fine. Over at my parents. Haven't seen them for a while. I didn't want you to have to worry about the door, so I just had the landlord take care of it – it's his job remember ;) Talk to you later. ~ J.

Glad to hear it. Tell your parents I said hi. Text or call me when you get home.

I hate lying to him, but it's for the best. He feels pity for me and a sense of obligation. He knows I don't have anyone else, but the fact of the matter is, I'm not his responsibility, and I don't want his pity. I'm strong enough now to handle things on my own, even if he doesn't believe it. I put my phone back in my purse and head toward the library.

Once I locate the photography section, I find several books I'm interested in. I fumble with them as I sit at a table. I pull out my notebook and pen and sit down to start flipping through them.

I've always enjoyed photography, but it was always just a hobby. I've been told I have an eye for it but haven't actually studied it since I took a class in college as an elective. Yet, today, there was something invigorating about taking pictures of Sammy and Chief. Like freezing a moment in time. That moment becomes a permanent memory that you can enjoy over and over again. Since Jeff has been gone, pictures of us have drawn out all sorts of emotions in me. Some sad, but mostly happy. Remembering who he was, who we were. Pictures of people who are gone start to impact your memories as they become foggier and foggier as each day passes. It helps to preserve something you didn't know you would miss.

I get lost in the books until the lights flicker. I look down at my watch and see that it's almost 9:00 p.m. I flip through my notebook and glance at the several pages of notes about aperture and lighting, shutter speed, the rule of thirds. I pick up the books that I am most interested in, take them to the front, check them out, and then head to the parking lot.

I pull into my driveway and look over at Sammy's house. I'm so excited to give him his pictures that I can't wait until tomorrow, and I rush up his front stairs to ring the doorbell. A little finger gently moves the blinds aside. "It's me Sammy. I have some pictures for you."

He gingerly opens the door, and once he sees me, he fully extends it. I see Chief beside him. "Hi, Miss Jensen."

"Hey. Here."

He opens the photo envelope, and his eyes shine as a smile breaks out over his face. "Wow, these are great. I can't wait to show my mom. Thanks."

"You're welcome. Glad you like them."

"I better go. I wasn't supposed to open the door since I'm home by myself."

"Lock it after you close it, okay?"

"I will. Bye, Miss Jensen."

"Bye, Sammy. Bye, Chief."

The door closes and I wait until the lock clicks into place.

As I walk up to the front door of my house, I feel a smile spread on my face just thinking about how happy Sammy was to get that picture. I let myself in and walk back to the kitchen, setting my purse down, and pull out the rest of the pictures. As I'm looking at them, I'm startled by a knock on the front door. I smile thinking it's probably Sammy, but as I open the door my smile fades.

"That's what I thought."

"Nash, what are you doing here?"

"I knew you were lying to me, but I was hoping you had a good reason. Seeing your smile fade tells me I'm wrong."

Sighing, I open the door wider for him to walk in.

Once inside, he asks, "What were you doing at your neighbor's house?"

"Checking on the little boy who lives there. He's home by himself a lot."

"Oh." He says as he places his hands in his pockets.

I wasn't prepared to have this conversation tonight, so I haven't totally worked it out in my head like I wanted to. I try to stall. "Do you want something to drink?"

"No, I want you to tell me why the hell you lied to me."

I walk to the couch and sit. He follows me. "I need some space, Nash."

"Why?"

"You and I have bared our souls to each other the past few days, and to be honest, it was too much, too soon."

I hear him release a breath. "Why didn't you just say that? I agree. We just need to take some time. Give each other a few days."

"No. I need more than a few days."

"Wait, what are you saying?"

What am *I saying?* I look at him and then I remember. Two eyes full of pity are staring back at me. He sees me differently, and I can't stand to look him in the eyes. *Do it quickly, Jensen, before you lose your nerve.* "I need some time, Nash. There is too much going on in my life, and I need us to take a step back."

The hurt is evident on his face. "How much time?"

Don't let him leave here with hope; it's not fair to him. "I think it's best if I spend some time alone and try to figure things out on my own."

He opens his mouth and closes it again, only to open it one more time. "I don't understand."

I know if I tell him the real reason, he'll deny it. He'll deny that he feels sorry for me. Or that he's somehow obligated to me because of a promise he made to his sister over a year ago. A promise he kept. He was there for me when I needed him most. "Nash, I'm still working through a lot of things. My house and my career...those things need to be taken care of before I can truly move on."

"Is this because I brought up therapy?"

I didn't want to lie to him. I also didn't want to hurt him. But it's apparent that he's not going to give up without a fight. And there's only one argument I can use against him that he won't try to win.

"I'll never love anyone but Jeff. I'll never move on from him. And now that I know how you feel, I can't be friends with you. It's not fair to either one of us."

He quickly moves closer to me and grabs my hands. I pull away.

"Jen, don't. Don't do this. You told me you loved me."

I lie again. "I'm so sorry. I let my emotions get the best of me the other day and I got confused. I was missing Jeff and used you in a way I shouldn't have." I swallow, trying to force the bile that is rising in my throat to go back down. "I can't give you what you want." I take a deep breath and brace myself for what I'm going to say. "So…I think it's best to part ways now before you get hurt."

His jaw tightens. "You're going to have to do a better job than that."

I push myself off of the couch. "I don't know what you're talking about."

"Yes, you do. Jen, I know you're scared. You're scared to move forward without Jeff. You're scared to move forward with someone who is nothing like Jeff. You're scared that one day you'll lose me too. But I also know you're strong enough to move past all those fears. You don't want to go to therapy, fine! Don't. I just wanted to make sure I gave you the chance to properly heal in order to move forward with me. I don't want to screw this up. But don't stand there and tell me that you don't have any kind of feelings for me!"

I have my back to him, and I know that when I face him, I'm going to have to give the performance of my life. All that is true. But what he doesn't realize is he's turned into everyone else in my life. They all see me as the poor little widow. It doesn't matter how much time passes, everyone who loves me sees me the same way. He *was* different. He didn't look at me like that. Now he does, and it forces me to do something I don't want to do. I can't be in love with someone who looks at me as broken. If I do, I'll always be broken.

I suddenly feel a surge of self-confidence, almost like my old self. With my shoulders back and my head held high, I turn and look him directly in the eyes. "I'm sorry you developed feelings for me, Nash. That was never my intention. The fact of the matter is, I love Jeff. Always have, always will. There is no room in my heart for someone else." I should be disgusted with myself for using my dead husband as an excuse, but I'm not. Because it's for the best, so both Nash and I can move forward.

For a split second, I'm proud of myself. I said it convincingly, because he steps back like he's been punched in the stomach. Pride quickly turns to shame once I see that I've hurt him. The pity he had for me just three seconds ago is gone. Now all I see is rage. His fists clench and unclench at his side. He continues to stare at me for a few moments, waiting for me to falter. But I don't. I hold my own because I don't want to hurt him any more than I already have. This needs to be over.

He starts to back up toward the door and says, "Sorry, my mistake." Turning, he strides out the door and slams it behind him.

I drag myself to the door and turn the deadbolt. The deadbolt that Nash installed to keep me safe. As I do, the strength leaves my body and I slink to the floor, knowing that the second man I ever loved just walked out the door. And just as Jeff did when he walked out that last time, Nash took a part of me with him.

CHAPTER 52

$\mathcal{I}$t's been three months since I've seen Nash. I got a phone call from Julia the day he walked out of my rental house. He filled her in on everything after apparently showing up on her doorstep drunk. I understood why she was upset, so I let her yell at me for forty-five minutes before she hung up on me. I haven't heard from either of them since.

But my life has been busy even without Nash. Two weeks after we stopped talking, I enrolled in courses at the local university to pursue an art degree with an emphasis in photography. I'm not fond of the other art classes I have to take to fulfill my requirements, but the photography classes make up for it. I've thrown myself into it, and I'm more passionate about it than I ever was about law.

I sold the house and made a nice profit, so I can go to school full time while also renting a place close to my parents.

I bend down to take out a plate wrapped in brown paper as my mom says, "Jensen, this place is great."

"Thanks, Mom. I'm pretty happy with it."

My dad walks into the kitchen where my mom and I are

unloading boxes. "Plus, you don't have to worry about maintenance and cutting the grass."

"Which means *you* don't have to worry about it, Dad." I wink at my mom and she smiles back.

They spend several hours helping me unpack as many boxes as we can. We focus on the immediate things, and then I tell them to go home. As they're leaving, my mom hugs me. "I'm so proud of you." She squeezes me tighter, and I squeeze back.

"Thanks, Mom. And I'm sorry. I know I haven't been easy these past few years. Thank you for loving me anyway."

She pulls back and looks me in the eyes. "That's what parents do, sweetheart." She leans over and brushes my hair out of my face. "But you'll see one day." I know she desperately wants grandchildren, and being the only child, I feel pressure to give that to her. But it's not something I can think about, not right now.

She steps away, and my dad gives me a hug, "Call us if you need anything, unless it has something to do with your condo, and then call the HOA." He steps back and winks at me.

"Yes, Dad."

I break down the last box for the night and peruse the takeout menus that were included in my welcome bag when I picked up my key this morning. Just as I decide on Chinese, I get a text message.

Hey, I heard you got a new number. Want to come grab dinner with us tonight? Just the old gang hanging out at Montgomery's Wine Bar...

Since I got a new number, I haven't had a chance to program in my old numbers, so I have no idea who texted me.

Who is this?

Oops...sorry Melinda

Melinda...it's been a long time since I've seen or talked to her. I think the last time was the intervention at my mom's house. I begin to type no thanks and then stop. I haven't gone out by myself or seen any of my old friends since Jeff died. It could be good for me to reconnect. Olivia hardly ever vists and now that I've cut ties with Nash I need to focus on building up other relationships. Thinking about Nash reminds me of Julia. Melinda and her husband, Colt, are close friends with Julia and her husband Travis.

Are Julia and Travis going to be there?

??? Don't think so...

I'll stop by for a little while. What time?

An hour?

See you there.

CHAPTER 53

I sit in the parking lot trying to get up the nerve to walk inside. This is the first time I've cared about what I've looked like in ages. I flip the visor up and shake my head, asking myself why I care. It's not like I'm going to try and pick someone up. I take a deep breath and try to give myself a break. This is a big step for me. It's been years since I've had to worry about walking into a social gathering by myself. Grabbing the door handle, I step out. Shoulders back, chin up as I remind myself these people are my friends. They love me even thought I haven't been a good friend to them.

I walk through the door and glance around. As I do, I see Melinda waving me down. Plastering a smile on my face, I take a deep breath and force myself to take the next step. As I come closer to the table, Melinda stands and Ryan, her husband, follows.

She reaches out to me and folds me in her arms. I relax against her. "It's so good to see you. You look great."

I pull back and genuinely smile. "Thanks, it's good to see you guys too. Hey, Ryan."

"Hey, beautiful." He hugs me, and I briefly think about Jeff.

These people were like our family. Dinner parties and holidays spent together. And I let it all drift away without Jeff. As I pull away from Ryan, I realize another couple Jeff and I were friends with is also here. Natalie walks up and gives me a hug, followed by her husband Robert.

Then I see a guy standing next to Melinda. He's around my height and is wearing khaki pants with a navy blazer and a blue and white polka dot bowtie. "And this is Stan." I notice Stan is alone, and I get a sick feeling in my stomach. *She didn't.*

I shake Stan's hand as he says, "Melinda's told me a lot about you."

She *did*. I give him a fake smile and look at Melinda as I'm still shaking Stan's hand, "Is that right?" Melinda's eyes shift toward Ryan, who gives a discreet shrug.

Yep, I've been set up.

"Well, nice to meet you, Stan. If you could excuse us. Melinda, would you like to go to the restroom with me?"

"Um...yeah, sure."

"We'll be right back, Stan." I say.

"Okay, take your time."

"Oh, we will." I grab Melinda by the arm and drag her to the back of the restaurant. She glances over her shoulder, and I follow her line of sight. I watch as Ryan mouths *I told you so* before he sits back down next to Stan. Furious, I pull Melinda toward the bathroom, trying to calm down before we get there.

I push her through the door and whisper through gritted teeth, "What is this?"

"I'm sorry, I didn't know what was going on with you and Nash and I had already told Stan you were going to be here. I've been talking about you for a few months, and he was interested in meeting you. He's a gr..."

"Wait, what does Nash have to do with this?"

"I texted Julia to make sure she and Travis weren't coming tonight after you asked and I..."

"You told Julia?"

"Yeah, but she…"

"Melinda! She probably told Nash I was going to be here. You better pray Nash is working tonight."

"Why?"

"Why? Because I'm trying *not* to see him. He doesn't have my new number or know where I moved. I'm putting distance between us, and I'd rather not rehash our problems in public. Not to mention, what on earth makes you think I would be interested in Stan?"

"Jensen, give him a chance. He's a nice guy, and he reminds me of…." She instantly stops.

"Of Jeff?" My voice flattens and all the frustration drains away.

Hurriedly she rushes on. "I just mean that I think you guys would really hit it off. He's sweet and like I said, he's been looking forward to meeting you. I'm sorry Jensen, truly, I'm just trying to help. We've missed you. It's been over a year and I thought…I don't know…we just want you back."

Melinda is doing this because she loves me and wants me to be happy, which is all any of these people have ever wanted for me. Before the anger, guilt and grief forced my wall up and I pushed everyone away. I can't keep doing that or I will be alone, all alone. I may never share my life with someone again in that intimate way, but I need my family and friends. Heaving a deep sigh, I walk up to her and she takes a step back.

"I'm not going to hurt you, silly." I wrap her in my arms, grateful for such a good friend. "Thank you, but I'm not ready."

She steps out of our embrace. "But Julia made it seem like something was going on with you and Nash."

"Not exactly. He's been a great friend, and he helped me through some stuff when I needed it."

"I'm glad to hear you've had a friend to lean on."

The bathroom door flies open, and Natalie walks through. "Um Jensen, I think you better get out here."

"Why, is Stan asking for her?" Melinda asks in a concerned tone.

"No, but Nash is."

CHAPTER 54

I march out of the bathroom as Natalie and Melinda follow in my wake. I round the corner and see Ryan trying to talk Nash down. As soon as Nash sees me, our eyes lock and he shoves Ryan aside.

"Nash, what are you doing here?" I ask, trying to keep my cool.

"Tracking you down since you moved and changed your number on me."

"This isn't the time or the place for this conversation." I attempt to brush past him, but he blocks me. I try the other way and he blocks me again.

Finally, Ryan chimes in. "Nash, don't do this man."

Nash keeps his eyes locked with mine. "This doesn't concern you Ryan."

"No, but it concerns me." Stan walks forward. *Oh, Jesus.* Nash's eyes narrow as they quickly shift and stare down Stan.

"You sure about that?" Nash asks.

"Yeah."

Nash reaches around Stan and pops a piece of his appetizer in his mouth before smirking at him. "Nice bowtie."

Stan attempts to take a step in front of me. Putting his hands on his hips, his jaw juts forward. "I think you need to go."

Nash takes a step toward him, but I intervene by putting my hands on Nash's chest. "Just stop. Don't do this."

Sneering, Nash glares over my shoulder as I feel his tension build. "No, I think we need to set your *little boyfriend* straight here."

I wince when he calls Stan little, but he's right. Nash has at least six inches on him and probably forty pounds of muscle. He could knock him out in one swift move. And with the anger that is oozing from his body, I wouldn't put it past him. I grab onto his shirt and hold his chin so that he's facing me again. "He's not my boyfriend, and you know it. Now stop."

"Stop what? Caring? Fighting? That's not me. And it's not you, either."

I take a few deep breaths trying to get a hold of my emotions. How dare he walk in here and cause a scene. Before I can say anything else, Travis walks up behind Nash and puts a hand on his shoulder. "That's enough, Nash."

Nash's eyes stay steady with mine. "Back off, Travis; this doesn't concern you either."

"Nash, stop." Julia walks up to him, but he doesn't falter.

"You too, Julia. She's going to talk to me."

Travis grabs his arm and Nash whips around. I see anger in Travis's eyes. I push my way in between both of them.

"All of you, stop it! This is ridiculous. We're adults, can't we try to act like it?"

They continue to stare at one another, each watching closely to see if the other is going to make a move. Nash looks at me and smiles. "You got a haircut. I like it."

Blinking, I'm momentarily unbalanced by the change in attitude. "Not the time for compliments."

"Just being honest. While we're on the topic of honesty, I have something to say to you. And I'm not leaving until I say it."

CHAPTER 55

" Fine. Please excuse us." I grab his upper arm and try to move toward the patio, but Nash doesn't budge.

"No. I want to say this in front of your friends. I want everyone to know how I feel about you. And I want them to hear the truth. Not some version of the truth you've made up in your mind.

"I don't do that!" One eyebrow raises in disbelief and he gives me a *yeah, right* look. I look around at my friends who are smirking. "I don't!" They continue to smirk, everyone but Julia, who is giving me a death glare. I take a deep breath and turn back to Nash. "Fine, let's get this over with." I cross my arms over my chest and wait.

"I get that you're scared."

I open my mouth to correct him, but he puts his hand up.

"Let me talk, and then you can talk." He sighs before beginning again. "You may not think you're scared, but you are. You're scared to let go of Jeff and your old life. You're scared to open your heart again because you know it makes you vulnerable. And you're scared because you feel the same way about me as I do about you.

"And I know you think you don't deserve this. I get it. Because I spent years there myself. That's why I don't know much about being in love. I never allowed myself to go there. But you...you make me *feel*, Jensen. Like I'm worth something. I'm no longer the guy that killed his best friend. But a guy who deserves a second chance. A chance to right a wrong that happened when I was seventeen years old. A chance to love and be loved, even though I feel like I don't deserve it. But I can't help it. When I'm with you, everything just makes sense. I could never be with someone who doesn't understand the grief and pain I've been in. You understand it, which means you understand me. And I *hate* that I love that about you. That you've been through hell and back and understand me. But without that, I wouldn't have found you, which means I never would have been saved." He walks closer to me, and his rough, warm hands embrace mine. He leans down so that we're eye to eye.

"I can't fix you, and you know what, I don't want to. And I don't want you to fix me. I need to live with this pain, or it's like it didn't happen. And it did. So did yours. I don't want you to forget the family you lost. I just want to quiet the noise and push away everything we both carry so that the love can come forward. I like that you're broken. Maybe our broken pieces can form a whole piece? I love you, Jen. All I am asking is for you to let me in. Take a chance and let me in."

Hot tears roll down my face, and his thumb brushes them away. I squeeze my eyes closed because it hurts to look at him.

He leans in and whispers into my ear, "Letting go isn't about forgetting them, it's about remembering you."

I open my eyes and stare into his. The rest of the room has disappeared, and all I see and hear is Nash.

"You will grieve forever, and nobody understands that better than me. But you have to find a way to close the wound even though the scar will linger. You'll never be the same person you were before them. Losing them made you who you are, who I love. And losing Mark made me who I am. Let me in Jen, please. Don't walk away from this because you're scared, or you feel guilty, or whatever excuse you want to give me."

He's threatening to rip down all the walls I've built. But in this moment, even though I can't explain it to myself, I can't let him. There's nothing left behind those walls, nothing left in me. He's lost enough. He would gain nothing by being with me.

I reach up and my hands move over his chest before I look into his eyes. The moment our eyes lock, he takes a step back. He knows. He knows I'm going to push him away. I have to. It's what's best…for him.

"You're wrong. Two broken pieces won't make a whole. All it does is put something together that is already weakened. Nash, you and I are too broken, too weak to ever make something whole."

I watch him stare at me, and I expect him to continue to be angry. But he isn't. Instead he walks up to me and leans into my ear. "I know you're a fighter, Jen. It's one of the things I love about you. But I wish you would stop fighting us. The loss between us can't define who we are." He pulls back, kisses me on the forehead, and strides out of the restaurant.

I hear murmurs behind me, and Julia starts after him before looking back at me. "Jensen, Jeff loved you. But he would be ashamed of the way you've handled yourself. And you don't deserve my brother." She then walks out.

I close my eyes, take a deep breath and turn to face the rest of our friends. Travis approaches me and says, "I'm sorry…for both of them." I shake my head and give him a tight smile. He says, "She didn't mean it. Nash has just been through a lot, you know? I've never seen him like this."

And in that moment, I feel confident that I've done the right thing. Julia's right. I don't deserve him. I meant what I said. The trauma that Nash and I have experienced would be a hindrance to our relationship, not something that would make us stronger. He's better off without me.

I look up at Travis. "Well, maybe this will give him the opportunity to open his heart to someone else. He deserves to be loved. But your wife is right, he deserves better than me. I don't have a whole heart to give him, and that's what he needs."

"Well, I'm pretty sure Nash would disagree, but it's not my place to interfere." He starts to back up. "I need to go after them. It was good seeing you." He turns and walks out.

CHAPTER 56

I look up and around at the separation of land and water. I can see penguins swimming both below the water as well as some wading above it. Stan is still talking. He talks all the time, incessantly. I nod and pretend to listen to whatever he is saying. But the truth is, I'm still annoyed that he brought me on a date to the zoo. He didn't bother to ask if this is something that I wanted to do. I hate the zoo. I've never been a fan of animals locked in cages while people pay to gawk at them. But I shouldn't be surprised. He never asks me what I want to do. I ask myself all the time why we still spend time together, but I already know the answer. So I'm not alone and because he's safe.

It's been almost two months since Stan and I met that night when Melinda introduced us. Two months since Nash walked out. He gave me a good two weeks before Julia was begging for my new number. Two weeks after that I finally gave in, and he started texting me. I don't ever text back. But he hasn't given up. He still texts me even though they're one-way conversations.

Stan continues to talk about some kind of formula he's playing with at work, and I nod while wrapping my arms around myself. It must be 15 degrees cooler in here. But I'm always cold around Stan. Especially when he touches me. His hands aren't warm like Nash's. Nor are they rough. In fact, I think they're softer than mine, and it of kind of creeps me out. I pull out my phone and read the last text that Nash sent me, three days ago.

Hey beautiful...miss me yet? I know you do even if you don't want to admit it. I miss you. It was a good day at work. I was able to resuscitate a four-year-old little girl that was pinned in her mother's car after an accident. Her mom walked away without a scratch. She threw her arms around me and thanked me. It reminded me of that day on the cliff and why I love my job. I wish you were here for me to share this story with you in person. So I could look into your beautiful eyes and see how proud of me you would be. I miss that, I miss you and I love you. I'm never going to be afraid to tell you that again. I don't care if you won't say it back. I'm still waiting on you to come back to me. I know we were thrown together for the wrong reasons, even though we're right together. I know you feel it Jen...come back to me...waiting, always. My love ~ N.

I have another ten or so texts just like that. He knows I'm seeing Stan. It would have gotten back to him by now. But I also know he's not doing this to compete with Stan. He told me so in the first text he sent after leaving me in that restaurant. He told me that he regretted not saying something sooner. That he needs to share these things with me. And if there are two people in this world who know that your life can shatter in the blink of an eye, it's him and me. And he reminds me often of that fact. Even though I don't need that reminder. I can't explain what I'm waiting for.

"Jensen?"

"Huh?'

"I asked if you think you'll be ready."

"Ready?"

"For your exhibit?"

"Oh, sorry. Yeah, I mean I think so. I've never done this before, but my professor assured me that I have enough pieces for a respectable showing."

"That's great. I'm proud of you and the fact that you've already been asked to be part of the university's photography exhibit."

"Oh, that reminds me. I need to run by Sammy's tomorrow and get his mom to sign a release since I'm using one of his pictures for the show."

"Who's Sammy again?"

I want to groan but I don't. I smile and try to be patient even though I've told Stan three times that Sammy is my former neighbor. "Remember, he's the little boy with the dog?" He still looks confused. "The one that was my inspiration...why I'm even taking this class."

"Oh right, Sammy. The boy with the Lab."

"German Shepherd."

"My administrative assistant has a German Shepherd. She lives alone..." I tune him out again. I miss the quiet of Nash. Of being able to sit next to him in total silence and feel like I knew exactly what he was thinking, and he knew exactly what I was thinking. "Olivia will be here Friday. I'm excited to finally meet her."

I tune back into the conversation at the mention of Olivia's name. *She's not excited to meet you. She's still pissed at me for pushing Nash away.* I respond with a smile.

"You're kind of quiet."

Finally picked up on that, did we Stan? Why do I bother? "I'm pretty tired. I think I should call it a night. I have a lot of work to do in the lab tomorrow for my class."

"Oh, of course." The disappointment in his voice makes me feel awful. "We'll come back another time to see the tigers."

"Thanks."

Fifteen minutes later, we're pulling up outside my condo. I hate this part. Two weeks ago, Stan caught me off guard and kissed me. I was in such shock that I just stood there, unmoving. It was like kissing a wet noodle. I've managed quick goodbye kisses since then, but I know he'll catch me off guard again. My body shakes uncontrollably as I think about it. "You're shivering. Here, let me walk you to the door."

"No! I mean that's okay, maybe tomorrow. Like I said, I'm tired and I have a long day tomorrow." I already know I'm going to cancel on him. The only reason I didn't cancel on him tonight is because I've canceled the previous two times.

"Okay, well get some rest, and I'll see you tomorrow."

"Good night."

I shut the door behind me and hurry inside. Throwing my purse on the floor, I fling myself on the couch. I pull out my phone to read the second to last text Nash sent me.

Good morning gorgeous, sleep well? I did...I had a fabulous dream of us riding across country. I showed you all of my favorite spots and you loved every one of them. I even let you drive Shirley Jr. If that's not love I don't know what is ;) Have a good day...I'll be thinking about you, always ~ N.

I smile to myself and pull up his phone number. My finger lingers over the 'send' button when my phone starts ringing. I just about drop it when I see it's Melinda. "Crap!" I'm not in the mood to discuss my relationship with Stan again.

"Hello?"

"What the hell is wrong with you, Jensen?"

"What?"

"Don't play innocent. I just got off the phone with Stan. He told me that you've canceled on him several times and that you guys finally went out tonight and you ignored him by reading text messages all night." I roll my eyes. Tattle-tale. But she's right, so I have no defense. "Well?"

"Well, what?"

"Jensen, the guy is trying. He knows what you've been through, and he's trying to go slow, but when you practically ignore him..."

I sigh and rub my eyes, "I know..."

"Is this about Jeff—or Nash?"

I sit up, offended she would even ask me that. "Maybe this is about *me*, Melinda."

"Okay, explain."

That came out before I could fully think out the excuse. Several moments pass without me saying anything. I'm too tired for this game, so I finally cave. "I don't know, okay?"

"I do. Cut Stan loose. Why are you playing this game with Nash?"

Now I'm pissed. "I'm not playing a game."

"The hell you're not. I know he's still pursuing you. He still has hope, and he knows you as well as I do. If you didn't have feelings for him, you would have already told him go to hell."

"Well how about this, how about I tell you to go to hell instead." Click. I drop the phone on the floor and lie down on the couch. "That was mature, Jensen. Ugh!"

I lay there for an hour and debate how to handle this mess I've gotten myself in. I'm painfully aware there is no chemistry with Stan, and I also know Melinda's right. I need to cut him loose. But now with the exhibit coming up, I can't. Olivia will be in town for my exhibit, and she can help me work through this mess and help me decide where I go from here. But I have to let Stan go—the man gets on my last nerve.

CHAPTER 57

I pull up outside Sammy's house and glance at my old place. I'm not sure what I was thinking. It's amazing the things you do when you don't have a choice. I grab the form and climb up to Sammy's porch. I called earlier today to make sure his mom would be home so that she could sign the release form.

I walk to the porch and smile when I hear Chief start to bark. I ring the doorbell and then walk to the right side and lean over the porch looking into the backyard. "Hey, Chief." He stops barking, and his tail starts to wag. As I walk away, his bark resumes, but this time it's a whimpering bark instead of a defensive one. As I head back to the door, I see Sammy looking out.

His face lights up when he sees me. "Hi Ms. Jensen."

I open the screen door and say, "Hey Sammy."

"Come in, Mom's in the kitchen making some lemonade."

"Sounds good." I follow Sammy back and see Regina standing at the counter stirring lemonade.

"Jensen, it's good to see you."

"Hi Regina. Thanks for seeing me on such short notice."

"Oh of course. I'm just glad my schedule worked out. I don't need to be at work for an hour, so Sammy and I were just going to have some lunch. Would you like a sandwich?"

"She makes a mean PB&J," Sammy says.

I laugh and watch as Regina gives her son an endearing smile. "No thanks, but I would love some lemonade."

"Coming right up."

Regina moves to get a glass, so I start up a conversation with Sammy. "So, how's Chief?"

"Oh, he's good. But he's been getting into some trouble. He keeps chewing up my baseballs. I think he gets mad when we stop playing."

"Oh yeah, I bet so. I know how much he likes to play with you."

"Yeah, Mr. Nash has to bring a ball with him every Saturday now. He keeps telling me to bring them in with me, but then he laughs about it so I know he doesn't mind if Chief chews them up when we're done."

"Nash, that's a...unique name. Is that a new boy in the neighborhood? Did he move into my old house?"

Sammy slaps his forehead and laughs. "No, silly. Your Nash!"

"My Nash?" I look between Sammy and Regina and I see her gently smile as she brings me my lemonade.

"Yes, when Sammy first told me he had let a man into our home, I freaked out. But then he told me he was a friend of yours."

"Nash was here, in your house?"

"Yeah, I told him about the pictures you took, and he wanted to see them, so I let him in. And then we played catch and he's been coming around ever since."

Still not processing what Sammy is saying, I start to fire off questions. "When was this? How long has he been doing this? He brings you baseballs every week, so you guys can play catch?"

Leaning against the counter, Regina chimes in, "Slow down, honey. He's only 10." She laughs, and Sammy follows. "It's probably been about two months. It was actually the morning you moved. He stopped by looking for you."

That would have been a few days before I changed my number and didn't tell him. "Every Saturday?" I ask.

"Yep, every Saturday." The little guy is practically dancing in place. "But he had to work one Saturday, so he made up for it by giving me a two-a-week. He laughed when he said it because it was supposed to be some kind of joke about two-a-days...I don't know, I didn't get it. Anyway, he started bringing me a baseball every time now since Chief chews them up. He even brought me a two-pack last week and said if Chief keeps chewing them up he'll have to buy a bucket, but I think he was kidding." Smiling at Sammy, I feel my heart swell. Sammy looks to the ceiling, think-ing, and then continues. "At least, I think he was. I don't know, sometimes I can't tell with him but he's funny. I can see why you like him. He talks about you all the time."

I feel my face blush and Regina turns her gentle smile on me. Great, a 10-year old knows more about my love life than I do. "Well, I'm...glad to hear that."

"I'll tell him that."

"NO! I mean, that's okay, he probably doesn't want to hear about our visit, so let's just keep it between us."

Puzzled, Sammy shrugs. "Okay."

Regina cocks her head to the side and smirks while looking at her child. She then looks at me. "So you said there was something you need me to sign."

"Right." I place the piece of paper on top of the table and pull out a pen from my pocket. "I'm taking a photography class at the university, and I was selected to be part of an exhibit at the downtown art gallery this weekend. One of the pictures in my portfolio that my professor loved was of Sammy and Chief. So, in order for it to be part of the showcase, I need you to sign a release form since he's a minor."

"Is it for sale?"

I wasn't expecting this question, but I don't want to lie to her, "Yes, it is. All of my pieces will be on display for purchase."

"Oh, so essentially some stranger could buy a picture of my son and take it home with them?"

I start to panic. If I don't have her release, I won't have enough pieces for the exhibit. My portfolio is not as large as the other students since I just started, but my professor took a chance on me. I swallow. "Yes, someone could buy it."

"Well, how much is it?"

I hesitate not wanting to tell her. "The price of all of the pieces will start at $1,000."

"Whew, that's a lot of money. Please tell me you get to keep some of that."

"Actually, no. The exhibit is for charity. It goes back to the university hospital for their pediatrics unit."

"Oh, well why didn't you lead with that?" She picks up the pen and immediately signs the release and then hands it back to me smiling. "There you go."

"Momma, are you gonna buy the picture?"

"No sweetie. That's too much money for us. But the good news is that some sick little boy or girl is going to get medicine they can't afford because of your and Chief's picture. Isn't that cool?"

"So cool!" Sammy jumps down from his seat and heads toward the back door, "Jensen, do you want to play with Chief before you go?"

I smile. "I would love to."

CHAPTER 58

*S*tan and I wait outside the terminal for Olivia. He insisted on coming, even though I was looking forward to spending some time alone with Olivia. "A woman shouldn't go to the airport alone," he told me. I waited until his back was to me before flipping him off. Once Olivia meets him, I'm sure blood will be spilled, and it won't be hers. She lacks that certain tact when it comes to people like Stan.

She knows I'm seeing someone but isn't happy because it's not Nash, so we don't talk about it. I hear Stan rambling about some flying statistic but I tune him out and watch for Olivia. Finally, there she is. Smiling, she breaks into a run. I do the same. I haven't seen her since the weekend she was here with Nash.

She falls into my arms and wraps me in one of her signature hugs and plants a wet kiss on my cheek. "Hey, hooker. You look like hell."

"Right back at ya."

Liv gives the best hugs. I've always loved them. Either you know how to hug, or you don't. Olivia has always known how to hug, uninhibited and full of love. Jeff knew how to hug. Nash knows how to hug.

I then hear over my shoulder, "Hi, I'm Stan." Stan does not know how to hug. Just like his kisses, there is something limp about it. I try to contain my laughter—that's probably not the only thing that's limp. Olivia gives me a funny look and then notices Stan.

She reaches out her hand tentatively. "Stan, is it?"

"Yes, hello, Olivia. Jensen has told me so much about you. It's so nice to make your acquaintance."

Olivia's eyebrows shoot up as her eyes fly open. "Oh Jesus, I'm going to need a drink before we leave the airport." And then she strides away.

With a quizzical expression, Stan watches her walk away and then looks at me. I respond with, "Nervous flyer." And walk away laughing.

After two drinks with Olivia ignoring Stan the whole time, we finally leave the terminal. We get to my car and they both walk to the passenger door. "How about you hop in the back, Stanley, and give us some girl time?"

"Um, yeah...okay, sure."

She is worse than I expected her to be. Stan leans forward and says, "Let me take you two lovely ladies to dinner."

Olivia's wide eyes shoot to mine. I open my mouth to respond but Olivia beats me to it. "Stan, thank you for the offer, but I'm just coming off two 24 hour shifts and I'm on East Coast time. This girl needs her beauty sleep."

"Oh, of course, of course. Jensen, what about you?"

"Oh Stan, I need my hostess to take care of me and tuck me in so she's going to have to pass too." She faces forward again before Stan can respond.

"Right, well okay." He leans back and is silent the rest of the way home. I pull up outside his house and drop him off. I should walk him to the door, but I don't. He climbs out and stands by Olivia's door. Leaning down, he motions to roll down the window. She looks at me like he has three heads.

"Olivia, stop!" I roll down the window from my side and Stan leans in. "Night Stan."

"Good night. Jensen. Do you want to call me when you get home, so I know you made it okay?"

"Oh, she's with me, big boy, so you don't need to worry."

I jump in, starting to feel bad for the guy. "We're probably going to be busy with girl talk, and then I need to get some sleep. I still have a little bit of work tomorrow before the exhibit opens."

"Okay then. Olivia, you're going to have to let me take you out for brunch on Sunday. Jensen and I go to brunch every Sunday, and we would love for you to join us."

Olivia plants on her fakest smile and her fakest voice. "I would love to, Stan."

She's on the verge of laughing in his face so I need to end this, quickly. "Great! Good night."

Olivia rolls up the window before he steps all the way back. I wave and finally pull away, leaving him standing on the curb.

"Brunch? What the hell is this, Parker?"

"What?"

"I can't believe Nash hasn't kicked the shit out of that wiener."

I can't help but laugh. "Oh, he considered it, trust me."

"I wanted to kick the shit out of him the first twenty seconds I met him. What are you doing?"

"Liv, don't."

"Oh hell no. Explain yourself."

"What? He's nice." I'm thankful I'm driving and don't have to look her in the face.

"What does he do?"

"He's an accountant."

"Shocker."

"Olivia—"

"Don't, Parker. You look like a fool."

"Excuse me?" I try to keep my eyes on the road, but I briefly glance at her.

"Seriously, everybody but him knows what you're doing. Hell, he probably even knows but is still following you around like a toddler follows their mama. He's just holding out hope you're going to change your mind."

"Can we please talk about something else?"

"I don't think so."

"Fine, I like him, okay? He's nice and funny and he treats me good."

"Oh yeah, what base you on?"

I groan, "Seriously, are we fifteen again?"

"I don't know, are we? I have a funny feeling you went further with Derek Nielson in 8th grade than you have with Stan the man there." Not being able to contain myself, I start laughing at the Stan-the-man comment. "Don't try to get out of this by laughing at me. I already know I'm funny. Now answer the damn question!"

I keep laughing, but she remains quiet. I look at her and her eyebrows are touching her hairline. She's not going to let it go until I answer her, so I finally give in. "Okay, you're right. Happy?"

"Are you?"

"Huh?"

"Parker, are you happy?"

"Yes, I'm focused on my photography and my classes. It's nothing like being a lawyer. I found something that brings me joy and even though my future is uncertain, I'm happy."

"Does that keep you warm at night?"

I pull into my assigned parking spot and shut off the engine. I lean my head back against the head rest and close my eyes. I wait a few moments before looking over at her. "What do you want from me, Liv?"

"I just want to understand, that's all, and then I'll drop it."

"How can I explain it to you if I don't understand it myself?"

"Exactly." I climb out of the car and hear her yell out, "Where are you going?"

"In the house. We can have this conversation in our pajamas with a bottle of wine."

"There's the girl I know and love."

I pop the trunk and yank out Olivia's suitcase. "You're going to be here for two days! Was all this crap necessary?"

"You already know the answer to that. Now, on to more important questions: red or white?"

We look at each other and say "white" in unison.

We change into pajamas. I grab a tub of ice cream and a bottle of wine and sit next to Olivia in the family room. I hand her a spoon, sit the tub of ice cream on the coffee table, take a swig of the bottle, and hand it to her.

"I've missed you, kiddo." She takes a drink and I smile even though she's been a pain in my ass these past few months. She hands the bottle back to me, but I decline. I move on to the ice cream. "So, you want to tell me why you're hiding behind that accountant geek when you could have prime-time, bad-boy hottie Nash?"

"This isn't about looks, Liv."

"Obviously! But it sure as hell ain't about chemistry either. I saw it between you and Nash. And even on one of the worst days of your life, it was there."

I shove the spoon into my mouth, missing part of it as ice cream melts down my chin. I wipe it off with the back of my hand and go in for more.

"You can shove that whole damn tub in your mouth as far as I'm concerned, she says. "I'll just sit back and wait until you answer me."

I sit the tub down and throw the spoon in it. "I don't know what to say."

She turns to face me, a serious look in her eyes. "All I want you to do is to tell me the truth. You do that, and I'll drop it."

"And what if the truth isn't what you want to hear? Are you really going to drop it?"

"Try me."

"I don't have feelings for Nash. Stan is nice, and we're taking things slow."

"Bullshit."

I roll my eyes. "See, I knew you wouldn't listen."

"That's because you told me you were going to tell me the truth. You might, MIGHT, convince me you don't have feelings for Nash. But you're sure as hell not going to convince me that there is any hope of a future with Stan." I hate her right now. I've held this conversation at bay with Julia, Melinda, my parents, and even Nash. I even managed to hold Liv at bay, but that was when she was on the phone. Now that she's here in person, I don't stand a chance. She knows me too well.

She yells, "Parker!" And I jump.

"What? You want me to tell you I'm in love with Nash? That I've been in love with him for months? That I'm terrified of being in love? For me to admit that I'm so damn scared to love him and so damn scared to lose him that I can't make a commitment either way? And who's to say he would even want me after everything I've put him through, put *us* through? Is that what you want to hear?" I stop screaming and try to control my breathing.

She smiles. "Yes."

"I really hate you sometimes."

"I know."

I start to cry and fall into her lap as she joins me on the floor. I grab onto her legs as she gently runs her fingers through my hair. She lets me cry until I no longer have any more tears in me. "Liv, I'm scared. Look at what happened before. My life was wrapped up in Jeff, and then I lost him and our child and my whole world crumbled."

She continues to stroke my hair. "Parker, that's what we do when we love someone. We give ourselves to them completely. You can't prepare for every what-if situation. You have to let go and love again and let yourself be loved. You know Nash loves you. Let him, Parker. Let him love you."

CHAPTER 59

I pull into my parking space, relieved I got everything done for the exhibit even though I'm running late.

Bursting through the front door, I trip over one of Olivia's bags and groan out in frustration. Olivia comes out of my bedroom, mascara tube in hand. "Hey Turbo, calm down, you still have plenty of time to get ready. These things never start on time anyways."

"I'm part of the exhibit, Olivia, I can't be late."

"I hung your dress out before I got in the shower. So it's ready to go. All you have to do is get yourself ready."

I kiss her on the cheek and yell over my shoulder, "You're the best."

I run into my bedroom and hear her call after me, "Yeah, just remember that tonight when I'm embarrassing you." I smile because she's right. She'll do or say something to embarrass me, but that's why I love her. She always gives me something to laugh at. I walk further into my room, pulling my shirt over my head, when flowers on the dresser stop me in my tracks. I walk over to them and smile. I then remember I told Nash the story about the first time Jeff took me out and how I hate fresh flowers.

"Looking for the card?"

I jump back, startled. "Geez, you scared the crap out me."

Olivia walks up to me and says, "Sorry."

I turn back to her. "Do you have the card?"

"Maybe."

"Did you read it?"

"Yeah, I wanted to see what dumbass doesn't know you well enough to know that you hate flowers."

"May I have it, please?"

She smiles and hands it to me, and then hovers as I read it: "Beautiful flowers for a beautiful girl. Good luck tonight. Stan."

"You look disappointed."

I lay the card down next to the flowers. "Of course not, who else would they be from?"

"Nash perhaps."

"Nash knows I don't like flowers. Plus, he doesn't even know about the exhibit."

"Oh, come on, you don't think Julia told him?"

"No, she promised me she wouldn't."

"And you believe her?"

"Yes. I asked her not to tell him because I didn't want any drama tonight. I just want to enjoy it."

"You shouldn't have invited me, then."

I look up and smile, "I realize. Momentary lapse in judgment, won't happen again." As I walk away she slaps me on the butt.

"There's my feisty girl. I've missed her." I turn around and chuck my shirt at her. She catches it and smiles back.

An hour later, I'm waiting in the family room for Olivia. "Liv, let's go. Traffic is going to be a nightmare downtown, and we still need to find a place to park." I wait a few moments but my patience is gone. "Olivia!"

She finally walks out. "Calm down, calm down, I'm coming."

I'll never stop being jealous of her. She's got legs for miles, she's witty, funny, and as smart as they come, not to mention gorgeous. And even though I know she's going to show me up, there is no one else I want by my side, or almost no one. I've thought about him all day. I've ached for him. I want to share this moment with him. All of this is possible because of him. He showed me how to live again, gave me a reason to get up and out of my house. Even if it was just to share a cup of coffee with someone, he did that, and I know I wouldn't be standing here without him. And I didn't even tell him about this. I look at the clock thinking he can still make it if I call now.

As I go to dial, Olivia walks up to me. "Ready?" I look at her and back down at my phone and drop it in my purse. I can't believe I almost did that. Way to send a mixed message.

"Yeah, let's go," I say.

She walks out first, and I try to maneuver my clutch purse, keys, and the end of my dress that I'm holding in my hand as I lock the door. I can't remember the last time I went to a black-tie event. I know it was with Jeff, but I try not to dwell on it. Tonight is about me, and I'm not going to be sad, not tonight. I finally manage to get the door locked, and as I turn to walk toward the car, I see Olivia standing next to a hummer limo. "Surprise. Now we don't have to worry about parking."

I smile and walk up to her. "You didn't."

"Hell yeah, I did! I was afraid you would kill us driving in those shoes."

I hug her.

"Come on now, Parker. We're all dolled up, and I need to land myself a man tonight. Plus, don't thank me just yet, there's one more surprise."

My heart starts to race, and my fingers tingle as I grasp the door to steady myself while I lean into the hummer. I hear "Surprise" and scan the interior. I see my parents, Julia and Travis, Natalie and Robert, Melinda and Colt, and Stan. My eyes continue to shift throughout the limo, and then I pull back and look at Olivia.

"What's wrong? You look disappointed."

"No, no! Gosh no! This is great, thank you."

"Oh shit, Parker, I'm sorry."

"What for?"

"You thought I meant Nash."

I don't try to continue to lie because she'll see right through me. "It's okay, this is great. Come on." I begin to climb in, but she grabs my arm.

"Parker, I'm sorry. Julia and I thought you didn't want him here, so we didn't invite him. I'm sorry, if I had known..."

"Liv, stop, you did the right thing. It's better this way. Now I can focus on the exhibit and not have to worry about what I'm going to say to him. Really. Come on, we're late." I climb in and put a smile on my face, thanking all of my family and friends for coming. Olivia climbs in behind me and squeezes my hand. I can't look at her because if I do, I'll cry.

CHAPTER 60

$\mathcal{B}$y the time we get downtown, my mood has lifted. Spending the last twenty minutes hearing my family and friends talk about how excited they are to see my pictures has made me almost giddy. My Dad tells me how proud he is, and my Mom can barely contain herself. I sit back and look at them and realize how blessed I am. These people stood by me when I was horrible to them, after I pushed them away and said things that I'll regret until the day I die. But they forgave me. I smile and think about Jeff. He would be so proud of me. He wouldn't have understood how I could walk away from being a lawyer, walk away from everything I worked for, but he would have supported me. It wouldn't have made sense when he was here because I was a different person. But I've made peace with the decision. It makes sense to me now, and that's where I need to live—in the present. I glance out the window realizing we're only about a block away and all I can think about is Nash. I wish he were here.

We pull up and have to wait several minutes before the limo can get close enough to drop us off. Usually I would say screw it and walk, but I'm going to be standing all night in these shoes, so I wait. As I do, I hear a cork pop and watch as Melinda's husband,

Colt, opens a bottle of champagne. Melinda is passing out glasses as he pours champagne in each one.

Once everyone has one, Julia gives a toast. "To Jensen. The girl who never stopped dreaming, never stopped fighting and found a life she never dreamed of. Thank you for allowing us to share your special night. And for all the ones who aren't here, remember they love you and they're here in spirit." She winks at me and then says, "To Jensen." And everyone says "To Jensen" as we clink our glasses. Julia texted me the day after Nash showed up at the restaurant and apologized. I immediately forgave her, not only because it's what Jeff would want, but because I know she loves her brother and was just trying to protect him. I also know that last part of her toast was about Nash just as much as it was about Jeff, but I'm glad she said it. It was just what I needed to hear before we exited. Now that we have, I feel like I'm going to throw up. I've stopped outside of the art gallery while my family and friends have started to make their way up the stairs. I look up and see a mountain ahead of me. Olivia turns back, realizing I'm not there, and comes back for me.

"You okay?" I can't find my voice, so I shake my head. "Yeah you are. Come on kiddo, just a few more steps. Once you get in there, the nerves will disappear." Is she *crazy*? I'm not going in there. What the hell was I thinking? I can't do this. "Parker? Parker, don't do this to me. I'll drag you if I have to."

"I'll take it from here, Liv."

I whip around and see Nash walking up beside me. My knees go weak, not because of my nerves but because of how good he looks in a tux. The pity that once made me run is gone, and now all I see is passion and a fight in him that makes me wonder if he'll ever let me go. My heart jumps and I exhale as I look him up and down. Olivia smiles and retreats into the gallery.

"Hey, beautiful. Looks like you're being a stick in the mud." A laugh escapes from my mouth. "Ah, there's my pretty girl."

"Your jokes get lamer and lamer." I look him over in awe that he is in front of me. He looks different with his close-cropped black hair. The type of hair you want to run your fingers through in order to feel the sensation of friction against your skin.

"Well, you haven't been around for me to practice."

"Nash…"

"Don't. This isn't the time or the place, and that's not why I'm here. We can deal with that later. Tonight is about you, and I wanted to be here for your first successful show."

"It's not a success yet."

"Sure it is. This is a huge step for you, Jen. Don't disregard it."

Hearing him call me Jen chips away at something I put up. I find myself reaching for him, but unlike other times, I don't stop myself. I cup his chin and watch him close his eyes. I move my hand down to his neck, and his eyes open and burn into me. My hand continues to move downward, and I straighten his tie, even though it doesn't need straightening. I touch him as long as I can before I finally have the courage to take the next step. My first instinct is to grab on to him and have him lead the way, but I realize that I have to take this step on my own. And as if he knows that without me having to tell him, he steps back until we're no longer touching and lets me go. Once I reach the first stair, I look back. "You coming?"

"Sorry, just enjoying the view."

"Flirt."

"Tease."

I smile but don't look back, afraid if I do, I might jump into his arms and demand he take me back to the limo. I've missed him, and now that he's so close I feel myself being drawn to him. As we reach the doors, I feel his hand at the small of my back, and I know he's not going anywhere. I push the heavy, ornate door and walk over the threshold. Just inside I see my family and friends smiling and laughing. I look up and see several of my photos scattered along the walls mixed in with other ones that I feel are so much better than mine. But I remember not to doubt myself and enjoy the moment. I turn back to find Nash and he's gone. I panic for a second and then see Professor Hagan approaching me.

"You're here. You look great." She says.

"Thank you, so do you."

"Thank you. Now remember what I told you. People buy the photographer just as much as they buy the photos, so put your best foot forward, but be yourself and don't worry. This is just the beginning for you. You always remember your first time, so have fun." I watch as she walks across the room calling after someone.

I glance around and decide to take her advice and try to mingle and sell myself. At one point Stan joins me, but I'm pulled away and his lips form in a straight line as I walk away. An hour later my face hurts from smiling, but I continue to do it to make sure I'm making good impressions. I'm listening to this same gentleman talk about the house he's been renovating for two years, and now that it's finally done he's ready to fill it with art but isn't necessarily a fan of photography. He's more drawn to oil paintings, so I really want to ask, "Why are you talking to me then?" But of course I don't. I try to keep eye contact with him when suddenly I see Nash behind the man who is droning on and on. He smirks at me, and I can tell by the look on his face he knows I want to get away from this guy. He has a glass of water in his hand, which he holds up and gives me a wink. I beam at him and then feel a touch on my arm. Professor Hagan is introducing me to another art gallery owner, talking up my work. I smile, shake their hand, and forget their name since I've met fifty people already. I glance over to where Nash was standing, but he's no longer there. I'm on my tiptoes looking around for him when Professor Hagan tugs on my arm. "She would love to, wouldn't you, Jensen?"

I smile and nod with no idea what I just agreed to. As I scan the room, I see Olivia flirting with an older gentleman and she catches my eye. She mouths *What?* And I mouth *Nash.* She looks around, shrugs, and then goes back to her conversation. *Geez, thanks Liv.*

As the night progresses, my eyes scan the thinned-out gallery, and I see my family and friends still mingling about. I have no idea what time it is, but by the ache of my feet, I would guess I've been here three hours. I haven't talked to anyone I know since I got here. That's not how I envisioned the night going, especially after Nash showed up. I continue to scan the massive room, knowing he's still here. I'm surprised at where I find him.

His back is to me, and I see that he's lost in one of my pictures. I walk up to him and run my hand down his arm. "I see you found my favorite."

He turns to me and smiles. "This is your favorite?"

"Do you really need to ask?"

We both look back at the picture and he continues, "Well, I thought the one of Sammy and Chief might be your favorite. Wasn't it one of your firsts?"

"It was *the* first. It's certainly what started this, but without our cliff and this view, I wouldn't even have known who I was."

He angles his body toward me, and his hand brushes against mine. "I like how you call it our cliff."

I turn to him and brush my hand against his. We look into each other's eyes, and then he looks back at the photo, as do I. A few moments pass.

"We still need to see it at night, you know?" he says and then winks at me.

A wave of desire rushes through my core. "I'm sure that can be arranged."

I drift toward him until I hear Professor Hagan yell out "Jensen!"

I stop, dragging my eyes away. I then realize Professor Hagan is pulling me away from Nash.

"It's okay, go."

"There is so much I want to say."

"I know, me too. But like I said, tonight's not the night. You know I'm not going anywhere." He leans over and kisses me on the forehead.

This time I follow my heart. I reach out and lace my fingers through his. "Thank you."

"For what?"

I can't put it into words, at least not right now. So I don't. I smile, squeeze one more time, and say "Goodnight."

He smiles. "See you soon, Jen."

I resist the urge to follow him out the door and instead walk with Professor Hagan.

"Jensen! You're not going to believe it. You set a record tonight."

Trying to focus on Professor Hagan instead of Nash, I shake my head and look at her. "A record? What are you talking about?"

"Your picture, it sold for $2,500." I see Olivia approaching with two champagne glasses in her hands. She walks past Nash, tilts one in his direction, and I see him nod at her before he walks out the door. She finally reaches me and hands me a glass. I take a drink. It's the first drink I've had all night. "Are you listening to me?"

"Sorry, what?"

"Your picture was the highest sale of the evening! In fact, of any exhibit we've had showcasing students."

"You sold something?" Olivia asks.

I take another swig and enjoy the refreshing taste of the champagne. "Apparently."

"That's awesome, how much?"

Beaming, Professor Hagan responds, "$2,500."

Olivia spits her champagne out. Well, we almost made it through the night without her embarrassing me. "Are you serious?"

"Yes."

"Woo hoo! Great job, kiddo. How much of that do you get to keep?"

"None of it Liv, it's for charity." I remind her.

"Oh... right."

Professor Hagan is practically jumping up and down when she says, "Apparently, there was a bidding war between two overly enthusiastic gentlemen."

Olivia's eyebrows shoot up and she downs her champagne.

"Oh no." I whisper to myself. "Let me guess. One was named Nash and one was named Stan."

Olivia smiles. "Yeah, and I can bet which one won."

"I wouldn't be so sure. Nash wouldn't have wanted to lose, but he's not one to throw money around. This may have been the opportunity Stan was looking for." I take a swig myself feeling horrible that the guy still thinks there is a chance. I panic as I start to glance around trying to find him. I've barely said two words to him all night.

"Don't worry." Olivia says, "I sent him off with Melinda and Colt."

"Oh, thank God." I turn back to Professor Hagan. "So, who had the winning bid?"

"Oh, I'm sorry, we don't release that information."

Olivia and I say "What?" in unison.

"No, our clients remain confidential."

Olivia rolls her eyes. "That's a stupid rule."

"Olivia!" I snap, even though I agree with her.

Professor Hagan shrugs. "I'm sorry, it's our policy."

I down the rest of my champagne, shifting my weight from foot to foot. I'm ready to get out of these heels. I'll find out from one of them tomorrow what happened. "It's fine. I'm just glad that something of mine sold to benefit the hospital."

I watch as two workers from the gallery approach the first picture I took of Sammy and Chief. I continue to stare as they look behind the picture and slowly remove it from the wall. I'm so happy it didn't sell. I didn't want to part with it. Even though I have the original, I don't know how long it will take me to afford to mount it professionally. Professor Hagan told me that I might be able to keep some of the pieces that don't sell, and I don't want anyone to have that piece. That picture changed my life.

"They're going to clean up tonight?" I ask.

Professor Hagan turns to see what I'm looking at. "Tim, you're not taking those down tonight, are you?"

Tim and the other worker gently lean the picture against the wall after removing it from where it hung. "Just the ones that sold."

"Wait, that picture sold?" Realizing I said that rather loud, I try to act a little more nonchalant.

"Yes. The buyer demanded it be delivered first thing tomorrow morning, so we're prepping it."

Professor Hagan asks, "On a Sunday?"

"Yes, the buyer stated they need it tomorrow for something."

I then look behind me to make sure the cliff picture is still on the wall, but it's not. It's also been taken down and leaning against the wall where it hung. I point to it and ask, "Did that one also sell?"

Tim looks where I'm pointing at and nods his head before going back to what he was doing. I now realize I need to work on prints that I'm not so emotionally invested in. I didn't want to share that picture with the world. It was something that I felt should stay between Nash and me, and now it will hang in some stranger's house. A stranger who will never appreciate it as we have. I feel my face start to flush, and before I can stop it, a single tear falls down my cheek. I feel Olivia wrap her arm around my shoulders and tell Professor Hagan goodbye. I expect Professor Hagan to stop us, but she doesn't.

I mutter a profanity under my breath as Olivia hauls me down the stairs. "You've had a big day, kiddo. It's time to go home and get out of those heels."

I look at her and wipe another tear from my face, so thankful I have her to lean on yet again. "What would I do without you?"

She smiles and squeezes my shoulders and hails a cab.

"Am I mistaken, or did we arrive in a limo?"

"Yes, Cinderella, but I sent it home with your family and friends an hour ago."

We both slide in and I lay my head on her shoulder. "Thank you...for flying in, for the limo, for...everything. I couldn't ask for a better friend."

CHAPTER 61

I walk through the door and see Olivia sprawled out on the couch reading my latest romance novel. "Hey, how'd he take it?"

"He cried." Olivia tries to stifle her laugh, but she fails, miserably. I sigh. "Liv..."

"Sorry, but come on. He didn't even get to second base, and he's crying over losing you?"

"Nash and I haven't gotten to second base, and I cried over losing him."

She stops laughing. "That's different and you know it. Plus, you never lost him, you pushed him away."

I sigh. "I'm aware."

She puts the book down and turns to give me her full attention. "So, what's the plan?" The first step was easy. I was keeping Stan around for lots of reasons, none of them the right ones. I've also been keeping Nash at bay for lots of reasons; none of those being right either. "Tell me you have a plan."

As many hours as I've spent thinking about this and analyzing it, I still don't know how to move forward.

"What did Stan say about the picture?"

"He told me to talk to Nash."

"Which confirms Nash bought it."

"I assume so, yes."

"Are you going to talk to him about it?"

I nod my head, take a deep breath, and drag my phone out of my pocket. I pull up his name and think about what I'm going to say. My hands shake and I realize I'm too nervous to call him, so I type a text instead:

Thank you for coming last night...and for helping me find my footing. I'm not sure I would have walked in without you there.

I set the phone down and wait. A few moments pass, and I look up at Olivia. A few more moments pass, and I begin wondering if maybe he's working. And then the screen of my phone lights up and dings.

There was nowhere else I would have rather been. I enjoyed the exhibit. But you would have taken that next step, Jen. I was just there to give you a little nudge.

"What'd he say?" I show the text to Olivia and then stare at it myself. I debate on whether to casually talk about the night or get straight to the point. I've never been a patient person, so I move on to the picture.

I hear you may have purchased something last night?

I set the phone back down like it's a hot coal and wait, again. Why am I so nervous? As I lean down to pick it up again, it rings. I stand up and move around the room not knowing what to do.

"Answer it, Parker." Olivia pats me on the back, walks into my bedroom, and shuts the door.

"Hey." I barely recognize my own voice.

"Hey, beautiful. I thought we could talk instead of texting if that's okay."

"Yeah, sure."

Awkward silence surrounds us, and I close my eyes wondering when this became so difficult between us. Luckily, he resumes the conversation.

"So, it looks as though things went well last night?"

"I think so. I didn't know what to expect, but my professor was pleased."

"Good."

A few more moments of silence pass. "So, um, I hear you may have a story to tell me?"

"Is that right?"

"Yes, I heard something about a bidding war taking place over one of my pictures. You wouldn't know anything about that, would you?"

"Perhaps."

"Well?"

"Well, what?"

"Aren't you going to tell me what happened?"

"I thought Stan might have already told you."

"No, we barely spoke last night, and when I went to break things off with him this morning, he told me I should talk to you." I wait for him to respond, but all I get is silence. "Nash?"

"You broke things off?"

"I did." Telling Nash makes it all the more real, and confirms it was the right thing to do.

"Why?"

Continuing to try and find my way back to us, where things may never have been easy but at least they were always real, I show my vulnerability and let him in, just a little. "I think we both already know the answer to that." I wanted to say because I love you, but I'm just not that brave yet. Too much has passed between us these past few months. I think I know where he stands, especially after him showing up last night, but I'm not fully ready to take the leap.

"I bid on the picture. I'm not sure if Stan was nearby or saw what was going on, but before I knew it, he was outbidding me. One thing led to another, and we both acted like two Neanderthals fighting over the same club."

"And I'm sure you came out as the winner?"

"Uh, yeah! He was doing it for the wrong reasons, and I wasn't about to let him win."

"And you were doing it for the right reasons?"

"Yes. Regina and Sammy deserve to have that picture."

I was about to argue with him when it finally registered what he said. "What? You didn't buy that picture for me?"

At first, I hear silence and then a big exhale. "Shit Jen, no, I'm sorry. Is that what you thought?"

"Well, yeah. I thought you were both fighting over buying it for me because you knew what it meant to me. Without Sammy and that picture, I wouldn't be here." And that means the only two pictures I cared about are both gone.

"I'm sorry, Jen. I bought it for Regina and Sammy." I realize I'm acting stupidly and that gift to them is greater than anything he could have given to me. "Jen, say something, please. I'm sorry, I really am."

"Nash, stop. That makes me so happy!"

I hear him sigh and I can hear him smile through the phone "Good. I have something that's going to make you even happier, then."

"Oh yeah, what's that?"

I hear rustling through the phone and keys jingling. "Get ready, I'm coming to get you in five minutes."

"Why?"

"You'll see."

"But you don't know where I live."

"Sure I do. I've known for weeks."

"But…"

"You asked me to keep my distance, so I did."

"But you kept texting me."

"Of course. I told you I wasn't going to give up. Put on long sleeves and jeans, I'm bringing S.J." He doesn't give me a chance to respond. But we both know I didn't need to. I'm already running to my bedroom, excitement coursing through my veins.

I run in and see Olivia sprawled out on my bed, still reading. "Went well, I take it?" She glances over her book with the biggest shit eating grin she's ever given me.

"I'm a shitty friend and I don't deserve you."

She goes back to reading her book and then smiles. "I know." She then looks up and winks at me.

CHAPTER 62

J hear the hum of the bike before I see him. When he comes into view, I want to throw up. I feel giddy, like an eighteen-year-old being picked up for her senior prom. There has been so much distance between us, distance I put there. I'm not quite sure what to do or say, but I'm so damn happy to see him that I try to let those feelings go.

And I do as soon as he removes his helmet and smiles. "Hey, beautiful. Time to go for a ride."

I snatch the other helmet from his hand and jump on without a word. I grasp him and in that moment, when no words cross between us, I know that I'll never let him go again.

He pulls away and drives faster than the last time we rode. Lost in him, I don't realize where we're going until we're there. We pull up outside Regina and Sammy's house, and I see a large box truck parked outside of their house. The side of the truck reads: Tyler's Art Gallery.

I dismount, and he does the same. He turns back to me and removes my helmet. He then pushes a stray hair behind my ear, and I reach up to grab his hand. The world around us melts. I see the love I've always seen. I was just too afraid to admit it to myself. There is no pity, no anger, no disappointment. Just pure love. He caresses my hand and says, "Come on, I want you to see this."

We leave the men unloading the picture and run up the porch. I yell at Chief in the backyard as we do, laughing like two giddy teenagers. Nash rings the doorbell, and Regina comes to the door.

She pulls her robe around tighter. "Hey, you two. I wasn't expecting anyone. Sorry, I look a mess."

Nash asks, "Can we come in?"

"Of course, of course. I'm sorry, where are my manners."

"Well, I'm sorry we showed up unannounced. But we both want to give you and Sammy something." I hear the excitement in Nash's voice and feel the energy coursing through him as he holds my hand. "Is he here?"

Regina glances at our clasped hands and smiles. "Yeah, he's upstairs. Let me go get him." She starts to walk up the stairs and yells, "Sammy."

Nash looks at me, smiles, and laces his fingers through mine. I squeeze back. We then hear Sammy thundering down the stairs. "Hey guys, what are you doing here? Did you come to play catch?" He abruptly stops halfway down the stairs. "Wait, let me go get my mitt." He turns to dash back up the stairs, missing a stair and barely catching himself before he goes tumbling backward.

"No Sammy, wait," Nash yells out. "We're not here to play catch." Sammy whips around, disappointed. "We have a present for you and your mom."

His face lights back up. "A present? What is it?" He comes barreling back down the steps and bounces up and down in front of us.

"Sammy, calm down. Goodness." Regina makes her way to him and places her hands on his shoulders so he stops bouncing.

We then hear a knock on the door. Nash lets go of my hand to let them in.

"I have a delivery for Nash Wilson."

"That's me."

Sammy runs up behind him to see what it is. "Why did you have something delivered to our house?"

"Because it's for you and your mom." Nash signs the delivery receipt and then moves out of the way, latching back on to my hand.

"Mom look, it's huge." Sammy starts to jump up and down again, following the men in the house. "What is it, what is it?"

"Sammy, calm down." Regina places her hands on her son's shoulders again.

The two men get halfway through the family room and then stop. "Where would you like it, Mr. Wilson?"

Nash turns to Regina. "Where would you like it?"

Confusion covers her face. "My goodness, what is it?"

"Gentleman, can you take the paper off so she can see it?"

It takes them a few moments, but as the paper starts to fall away, her face goes red and tears spring to her eyes.

"Look Mom, it's me and Chief."

Through hushed tears she says, "It's beautiful." Nash and I watch her, and his hand squeezes mine. "Oh my gosh, this is ours?"

"It's all yours," Nash says with a smile.

Sammy asks, "To keep?"

"To keep. It's a gift, from Jensen and me. We wanted you to have it." I'm overwhelmed with pride and joy, and love how the words *Jensen and me* sound coming out of his mouth.

"We'll hang it for you, ma'am, you just need to tell us where."

"Oh my, I...I don't know, it's so big. Where do you think it should go, Sammy?"

"Here." He jumps up and points to the wall over the fireplace.

"I think that's a great place. I can't thank the two of you enough. This is such a wonderful gift."

I realize I haven't said anything the whole time we've been here, but Nash speaks for both of us. "You're welcome. We hope you enjoy it for a long time."

We spend a few more minutes talking, and then Nash tells Sammy he'll see him next week. We walk back to the bike and I realize I'm shaking.

He rubs his hands up my arms. "Hey, you okay?"

I look back at the house. "Did you see their faces?"

"Yes, I did. You did that, Jen." My eyes move back to his. "Don't give me that look, *you* did that."

I walk right into his arms and he holds me. He whispers again, "You did that. You brought them that joy."

I pull back and see how proud he is of me. I whisper in wonder, "You're right...I did." He laughs and twirls me around as I try to wiggle out of his embrace, but he won't let me. Silently, I pray he never will.

"Did you see what that did for them? You changed their lives, Jen, with a simple photograph. A photograph filled with love between a boy and his best friend. I can see your passion for photography in that one picture. That's an amazing gift."

I want to downplay it, be humble and tell him he's wrong, but I know he isn't. So I let my heart do the talking. I slowly lean in and watch as fear shadows his face. As I get closer, the fear fades away when he realizes what I'm doing, and this time I hope he sees through me like he always has.

I'm finally ready to surrender to the doubt and the fear. I'm ready to surrender to him and allow myself to feel once again. I see his eyes close at the last minute and our lips gently touch. And when they do, I'm expecting rainbows and ponies and firecrackers. But the truth is, it's so much better than that. It's knowing for the first time in a long time that I'm home. It's brief, but strong, and feels so right that the guilt and shame I'm been carrying around for almost two years washes away the second we both pull back.

I look into his eyes. "I love you, Nash. I'm sorry it took me so long to come back to you."

He places a finger over my lips. "You never left me. You walked away, but you've had my heart this whole time, and I've had yours."

He's right. Fear, guilt and shame kept me at arm's length. But I no longer want to be at arm's length. I just want to be in his arms. I lean in to capture his lips once more and the kiss becomes stronger, more urgent. We melt into each other completely that you can't tell where one begins and the other ends. The world falls away around us until we hear whistles in the distance. We pull back and the men from Tyler's Art Gallery are walking down the porch, and Regina and Sammy are staring at us. We turn back to each other and start laughing. Regina says something to Sammy, he waves, and she smiles, gives us a little wave and closes the door behind her.

With a smile plastered across my face, I reach for my helmet. "Let's go home."

He hesitantly says, "Okay..."

"Your place. Liv's at mine."

CHAPTER 63

e pull into his driveway and I dismount. He does the same. I wait for him to close the garage door, and he takes my hands in his. "I have something to show you." He backs down his hallway, his eyes never leaving mine.

I see the anticipation in his eyes and love how he looks like a bemused teenager. He pulls me through the house toward his bedroom and then stops.

He mutters, "Shit." And his eyes find mine. "Okay, so this isn't what it looks like. I mean, what I want to show you is back here, but it's not—oh God. I'm blowing this."

I jiggle his hand and smile, "Nash, stop. I didn't think that. Now, what do you want to show me?"

Watching my eyes, he lifts our joined hands and kisses the palm of mine. He then leads me down the hallway, and as we turn into his bedroom I have to catch my breath. Hanging above his bed is the picture of our cliff. I slowly release his hand and move closer to the end of the bed to stare directly at the photo. A tear trickles down my face. Nash's arms steal around my waist, and his chin leans lightly on my shoulder. I spin and face him.

"You bought this one, too?"

"I had to after you said it was your favorite. Plus, I couldn't stand the thought of someone else having it. That's why I bought the other one for Regina. No one can appreciate them as much as the people who are moved by them."

"You were moved by them?"

"Are you kidding me? All of your pictures moved me. Jen, I could see your heart and your passion spilling through every single one of them." He turns me to face the picture again, "But this one…this one made me breathe again." He then steps in front of me, and I'm nearly overwhelmed by his honesty. "I've avoided anything that has made me feel since Mark died…since that night, until you. You came along and ripped my soul open again. And to see that view through your eyes, and then to hear you call it our cliff. I couldn't let anyone else have it, because it's just as important to me as it is to you. I knew that day on our first hike that there was something between us. I saw, in that moment of you looking out over the edge, how strong you were even though you felt weak. How you smiled even though you were in pain. And I know a part of that pain will always be with you. But I believe in our love, and I know you. And I love you, Jen. Broken and strong, all at the same time."

"Like you?"

He smiles and then wraps me in his arms. "Like me."

Unafraid, my heart opens as I lean back and gaze into his eyes. "I love you too, Nash. More than you can ever imagine."

"I know you do, Jen." He winks at me before turning me back around as we both get lost in the picture. "I was going to give it to you when you were ready, but in the meantime, I wanted it close to me."

"How did you get it hung so fast?"

"I paid extra for them to deliver it this morning."

"This morning?"

"They were at my house when I called you. How'd you think I got them to Regina's so fast?"

I don't think I've ever doubted anything that Nash has ever told me. Yet we always had to walk this tightrope of holding our feelings back for one another because I wasn't ready. I turn around and lean in to taste his lips. Before, our kisses were slow and loving. These kisses are hungry and passionate. He responds by bringing up his hands and running them through my hair. He finally pulls back for air. "Jen..."

I whisper, "Don't stop." I feel him hesitate for a moment and then his head drops, and my eyes close. His exploration is tender and slow at first. But then we ease into it. He thrusts his hand into my hair and my hands move to his waist. We continue to kiss with such passion running through us that I don't know how we're ever going to stop. I grab the hem of his shirt and pull back from him so that I can lift it over his head. The sudden movement has left me cold, and I shiver back into his arms, back into his warmth.

"Jen, wait." I look into his eyes and see concern. "Let's just..." I see him struggling. He doesn't want to stop any more than I do. I don't give him time to think. I crawl back into his arms and crash my lips to his. He has to forcibly push me back. "Jen, please. This is not why I brought you back here." Astounded, I watch his face and work to get myself under control.

He takes a few steps back, and his chest moves up and down. God, Olivia was right. How did I not see it all this time? He's beautiful. But his heart is even more beautiful. He's waiting for me, and I no longer want to wait.

I walk toward him. I keep my distance but lace both of my hands through his.

"Nash." He's looking at the floor, trying to find the strength to stop this. "Nash, look at me." His eyes find mine. "Just like the first time you brought me to our cliff...I had the urge to move toward it, where it was scary and I could fall, but it was so breathtaking all at the same time. That day I walked to the edge because it was worth the risk, and then you pulled me back, where I felt safe for the first time in a long time. But these past few months without you in my life has shown me that I would rather live on the edge *with you* than to not have you at all.

"There are a lot of things I've been confused by and unsure of, but this is not one of them. This is the first thing that has felt right in a long time. I want you to make love to me."

We stare into each other's souls, and his hand unwinds from me. He moves it to my chin. His rough, calloused hand cups my face as he pulls me toward him, where I feel the loss between us drifting away just as Nash said it would.

CHAPTER 64

"*C*all me when you land."

Olivia looks over my shoulder and smiles. She releases me and walks up to Nash and hugs him.

"She's my family, so take good care of her, you hear me?"

Fire burns in his eyes as he looks at me. "She's my everything, so you know I will." I melt when he says things like that.

"I know, but I want to make sure we get each other. If you don't, be prepared to lose a very important part of your body." She says it with absolutely no humor in her voice, and Nash's eyes go wide and then he shifts between his feet and adjusts himself. "That's what I thought."

Laughing, I wrap both arms around his waist. Resting his arm on my shoulder, he gives me a squeeze.

"Damn, you two look good together."

I look up at him as he looks down at me and we both smile. He then gently leans down and kisses me. I pull back breathless. Olivia has already walked away. She raises a hand without looking back, waves, and disappears in the sea of people.

We stand for a few more moments with Nash stroking my hair. "Ready to go?"

"Yeah." I say feeling sad as I always do when she leaves.

"She'll be back." We turn to walk back to the car, me still tucked underneath his arm. "Or we could go see her?"

I look up at him. "Really?"

"Sure! Shirley Jr. can make that drive." He winks at me, and I feel excited about us taking a road trip together.

We ease back into the silent comfort that's always been between us. As we climb into the car, he asks, "How about a hike?"

Nash and I haven't hiked together in months. I've done it by myself, but it's not quite the same. I've missed it probably more than anything else. Smiling as I gaze into his eyes, I say, "I would love to."

CHAPTER 65

I walk into the garage and yell, "Nash?" I don't see him, so I continue to walk and then I see him fiddling with something in the back of his truck. "Hey, what are you doing?"

"Nothing. Just getting a few things ready before we go."

"Speaking of, we need to get moving if we're going to make it up and back before dusk."

"Give me a few more minutes." I walk over to him and distract him with a kiss. "Get away from me or we won't make it out there." We smile at each other, and I walk back into the house.

Before I reach the door, he yells, "Hey, would you grab me ten bottles of water?"

"Ten?"

"Yeah."

That seems like overkill, but I don't question him. "Okay."

An hour later, we're finally pulling out. "Do you think we're going to make it before it gets dark?" I ask.

He reaches over the console of the truck and grabs my hand, and then looks up and out the front window. "I think we'll be okay."

We pull into the parking lot and we both hop out. Thankful I brought a sweatshirt, I wrap it around my waist and walk back to the bed of the truck. I see two larger packs than what we usually carry. "What are those?"

"Just some new packs I bought."

"What for?"

"Just in case."

"In case of what?"

"I don't know…here, turn around."

He places the pack on my back and I almost fall over. "Are you serious?" I turn back to him.

"What?"

"What's in this?"

"Just some stuff."

"What kind of stuff? I'll never make it up there with this much weight on my back!"

"Sure you will." He heaves a similar pack onto his back, and I can see his is heavier than mine.

"Nash, what's going on?"

"You ask a lot of questions." He smiles and then sighs, "It was supposed to be a surprise…"

"What was?"

He walks up to me and tries to bring me into his arms. We both laugh at not being able to get that close to one another with our gear on. "I thought we could spend the night under the stars."

My bottom lip quivers upward. "Aw."

"Yeah, yeah, I'm a pushover when it comes to you." He goes to walk away, but I pull him back in.

"I don't know about that. You want to know what I do know?"

"What's that?"

"That you love me."

He pushes a strand of hair behind my ear. "Always will."

I smile.

"So, since the surprise is ruined, can I look through this pack and see what the necessities are?"

He laughs and turns me around to remove my pack. Ten minutes later and about ten pounds lighter, we're on our way.

We get to the top just as the sun is starting to set, and we both stop to admire it. He takes a swig of water and then hands it to me. As I'm taking a drink, he removes my pack and sits it down next to me. I hear him rustle around behind me, but I continue to stare and wish to God I had brought my camera. The next thing I see is my camera. It takes a brief second for my eyes to adjust from far to near.

I reach for it and smile at him. "You brought my camera?"

"Yeah, it was in my pack. Sorry, I couldn't bring the tripod without ruining that surprise too."

I take the camera from his hands and sit it down on top of my pack. I then grab a fistful of his shirt and pull him toward me. Our lips meet and my stomach flips. He eventually pulls back. "Okay, okay, we keep this up and you're going to miss it."

I graze my lips over his ear and whisper, "There's also a sunrise." He smiles as I lean into him to kiss him again.

"Oh, I'm counting on it. But we have all night for this. Take your picture."

I run my finger down his face. "I don't need a picture to remember it."

He captures my hands and squeezes once before gently letting them go. "I'm going to get out some snacks while you do your thing."

I spend twenty minutes taking pictures and then the sun is down. I turn back and see Nash has set up a nice campsite. Fires aren't allowed, but he's spread out a blanket with two sleeping bags nearby. There is a bottle of wine, cheese and crackers, and other goodies. There are two lanterns giving enough light for us to see while creating a romantic setting.

I walk toward him while removing the camera strap from my neck. I set it down on the blanket and unwrap my sweatshirt from my waist.

He looks at me. "Cold?"

"A little."

"Then get over here, woman, and snuggle." I smile and walk toward the blanket. I kick off my shoes and land in his lap. We both sigh and hold each other. "You going to be able to sleep out here?"

I pull back and look him in the eyes. "Sleep? Who said anything about sleeping?" He smiles and kisses me. He then rolls us over and hovers over me. He looks down at me and runs his finger over my cheek. "I love you, Jensen."

"I love you, Nash."

EPILOGUE

a cool autumn breeze swirls down the hill as I watch Jen lean down to pick up twigs and leaves that are lying on Jeff and the baby's headstones. She glances up to check on our three-year-old daughter, who is running around the cemetery without a care.

"Mackenzie, no running," she yells.

Mackenzie stops and pouts. She's just like her mother, can't stand to be told what to do. She looks at me and whines, "*Daddy.*"

Jen looks over her shoulder at me and shakes her head. I smile at her as she goes back to cleaning the stone. She finally stops and looks down. I can only guess what she's thinking. When we finally got together, we both had things to work on. I wondered if she wished she was with Jeff and not me. She struggled with the what-ifs, all of the bad things that *could* happen, especially when Mackenzie was born. Jensen was right, it's not the fairy tale. Sometimes both of us hold back because we still don't feel like we deserve to be happy. I'm not convinced I deserve it, but the truth of the matter is, I am happy. We both are.

Mackenzie looks down at the ground with her arms crossed and her bottom lip sticking out. Jen makes that same face, and every time she does, I give in, no matter what it is. I can't imagine where Mackenzie learned that. I watch Jen tickle her until Mackenzie gives in. They both roll to the ground laughing.

They get up and begin to walk toward me. Mackenzie begins to run again, completely forgetting she just got in trouble for it. Jen smiles and shakes her head. Mackenzie throws herself into my arms. "Daddy, let's go see Uncle Mark."

I tousle her hair and say, "Okay, kiddo." I set her down, and she starts to take off running again, but before she can, Jen leans down and grabs her hand.

"Hold on, you're going to hold mommy's hand." Mackenzie's small chest makes itself bigger and then she lets out a rush of air. Jen looks at me. "I can't imagine where she gets that."

"Don't look at me!"

Jen smiles and grabs my hand with her free hand, and we start to walk toward Mark's grave. Mackenzie starts to sing, screaming some song that we've listened to a thousand times today, and Jen looks at me and smiles. I smile back.

I see her get stronger every day and she still amazes me. Jensen is the best wife and mother I could have ever hoped for. She was on the edge of letting her loss consume her, but she pulled herself up, fought her demons and took another step. Because in the end, that's really all any of us can do.

SNEAK PEAK OF NEXT BOOK

For a sneak peak of my next book, Futile Love, please join my newsletter at www.brookemcbride.com.

CONNECT WITH BROOKE

Newsletter: Join for a free preview of my next novel
www.brookemcbride.com

Facebook:
www.facebook.com/brookemcbridebooks

Facebook Reader Group (Brooke's Nook)
www.facebook.com/groups/brookesnook/

Amazon:
www.amazon.com/author/brookemcbride

Goodreads:
www.goodreads.com/author/show/18499045.brooke_mcbride

BookBub:
www.bookbub.com/profile/brooke-mcbride

Instagram:
www.instagram.com/brookemcbridebooks/

Twitter:
www.twitter.com/BMcBrideBooks

Pinterest:
http://www.pinterest.com/brookemcbridebooks/

Website: www.brookemcbride.com

ACKNOWLEDGMENTS

My thanks must start with God for the gifts He's given me, the people He has put in my life to support me and a life that has allowed me to pursue my dreams. I pray that every reader is blessed with a memorable experience when reading this book.

There are several people I need to thank for getting this book into the hands of readers. To my mom, for agreeing to sit down and read one of my earliest versions that needed a lot of work. But you suffered through it and told me to keep going. Thank you. To my mother-in-law for being one of my very first beta readers and for supporting me and encouraging me along the way. You never let me quit and gave me the confidence I needed to seriously pursue my dream. To my dad, for supporting me on the business side of this journey. To my best friend Emily. Thank you for being by my side since second-grade and for a lot of the inspiration in the scenes with Jen and Oliva. And for taking the time to read it and support me.

To my husband, we made it! And I say we because I couldn't have done this with you. All the moments we spent at writing conferences together and the long drives home with me analyzing every little detail of what my next move would be. For supporting me financially and emotionally and being my biggest cheerleader. For taking care of our son when I was holed up in my office. And for never letting me quit! To my son, you're too young for me to thank you for much except for just being you. You've taught me more than you'll ever know.

To my dog and writing partner Dori. I miss you on my lap snuggled keeping me warm as I type. I miss you forcing me to get up, stretch my legs and mind so that we could go outside for fresh air. I miss you glancing up at me as I read dialogue out loud and wondering if I was talking to you. Thank you for being one of my greatest gifts. You were a part of this journey for every step of this book except the publishing and I miss your companionship.

To the owners and staff at the local McAlisters, Panera, Pronto Café, and Starbucks, as well as the Rolling Hills Saint Joseph Library: thank you for giving me an office away from home. Thank you for giving me a space where I could seriously pursue my dreams. And thank you for providing the sustenance and resources I needed to keep going. So many of you asked about my work and complimented me during moments when I needed it the most.

To Lauren Watson Perry, your work is amazing. Thank you for tolerating an anxious debut author who didn't know what she was doing. But I knew enough to hire you and you didn't disappoint.

To Sommer Stein with Perfect Pear Creative. Thank you for walking me through the steps of what a cover needs and providing me with guidance every step of the way.

To Ines Johnson who helped me with so many different aspects of getting this book into reader's hands. Thank you for your sense of humor, your professionalism, patience and wisdom.

To my readers. I write for you. Well, that's not entirely true. I write for me because I have to. I have things in my head and my heart that demand to be heard. But I toil over the words, the details, the characters so that you can experience an escape from the everyday stressors of your life and jump into another world. A world with people you become invested in and hopefully an experience that stays with you long after turning the last page. Thank you for taking a chance on a new author and for your support. I pray I didn't disappoint!

ABOUT THE AUTHOR

Brooke is a recovering anxiety-laden mom who overcame severe depression when she took her husband's advice and decided to write a book. She found a way to escape her own anxiety and depression by creating characters who were going through more than she was and found a way to give them their happily ever after's. A romantic at heart, Brooke also loves to dive into other character worlds by reading two to three novels a week. Brooke graduated from Northwest Missouri State University with a degree in Business Management and a master's degree from the University of Missouri in higher education administration. She values her faith, loves iced coffees and loves dogs typically more than people. Her favorite season is fall and she lives for college football. She resides in Saint Joseph, MO with her husband, her son and her 4-lb dog Dori.

FOL

NOV 0 7 2023